A Perfect Madness

A Perfect Madness

Frank H. Marsh

❀ *Brandylane*

Printed in the United States.

ISBN: 978-0-9838264-3-9
LCCN: 2011945354

Brandylane

BRANDYLANE PUBLISHERS, INC.
brandylanepublishers.com

For my dear deceased friend,
Dr. David L. Dungan

"There is a divinity that shapes our ends,
Rough hew them how we will."
(Hamlet, V, ii, 10)

<u>ONE</u>

Prague, 1992

It wasn't Anna's idea to take Julia's ashes back to her beloved Prague. She would have sprinkled them up and down the banks of the Merrimack River running the rear property line on their small farm outside Franklin, New Hampshire. It was a God-given place to Julia for sure, as still and reverent as any cemetery except for the flowing sounds of the passing waters, which she loved. To have done so, though, meant betraying the only real promise she had ever made to her mother, a promise crammed full with the final chapters of a long odyssey her mother began years back, in 1939, when Prague found itself standing naked with all of Europe in a gathering storm of madness. So Julia's ashes would be buried soon where they should be, next to Rabbi Loew's grave in the Old Jewish Cemetery, even though no new soul had been allowed to rest there in over two hundred years.

The promise, strange as it was to become, came from Anna the year before Julia died. Following the Velvet Revolution, Prague had quickly beckoned all that was good to come home again to the old city. So they went there together, Anna and Julia—Anna out of curiosity, or better, perhaps, from the metaphysical tugging of ancient kin long dead and buried there, Julia to find the lost innocence of her youth buried along with her heart somewhere beneath a rubble of trampled dreams fifty-two years earlier. The dreams would still be there waiting, she would tell Anna during one of her many stories, scattered along the cobbled brick streets in the old Jewish quarters. But she was dying now at seventy-four. A doctor herself,

1

Julia knew the end was near, so the promise given by Anna was all she really had left.

When their plane began circling the great city that day, waiting to land, the special moment came. At first Julia sat silent, looking down on the vast carpet of red-tiled roofs covering the city, wondering if distant memories of magical places and golden dreams would betray her. Stories she had told Anna many times were there waiting. It was then that the strange promise was pulled from Anna's lips by Julia. When death came to her, wherever it might be, Anna was to somehow smuggle her remains into the Old Jewish Cemetery. There she was to dig a small, shallow hole alongside the great Maharal Rabbi Loew's grave, where God stayed close, and bury her ashes. For Julia it was the necessary place, the place where many of her childhood dreams had played out. She would go there to talk with Rabbi Loew and his gentle golem, called Josef, about the struggles of her people and the madness in her own life. No one else would be there except those that danced and played in her imaginary world, and that was good enough for her. Rabbi Loew and his golem were legends then—and her friends. Sooner or later, she believed, they would come to her, stepping out of the misty stillness covering the graves, and listen to her cries.

One afternoon late, she decided to try and make another golem, one she could see and touch and of the female gender. Following the instructions in her father's tomes on Jewish mysticism, she set out to complete the task. Carrying buckets of wet clay dug from the banks of the Vltava River to the cemetery, she fashioned the form of a woman alongside the rabbi's grave, three cubits long, lying on her back, and then shaped a face and arms and legs. Then she walked around her golem six times, the days God took to create the world, reciting loudly various combinations of words she had pulled from the Book of Genesis. But the mud-shaped golem stayed still and quiet, like Josef. After chanting new combinations of words and walking around her golem many more times with no result, Julia decided that the secret to life was where it should be, with Rabbi Loew. And she was glad, because he was her friend.

After they had landed and were departing from the airport, Julia cried, "We must hurry to the cemetery now before the luggage is unpacked. The ringing of hand bells will start soon, telling everyone to leave."

The skies over Prague had turned to a gray dusk by the time Anna and Julia arrived at the historical gate that separates one's existence from eternity, a place where, for a brief moment, the ends of time come together and become one.

"Hurry," Julia urged.

Anna stood still, though, trapped in a timeless zone, gazing through the open gate at the crowded graves squeezed together in the small plot, their headstones looking like so many crooked and jagged teeth. There were no clear rows before her, only confusion. Over 100,000 souls layered twelve deep in their graves, all yielding in turn their identity to the top tier of buried bodies. Yet the totality of each grave clung silently persistent to its own tiny share of a thousand years of the Jew in Prague.

"Which one is Rabbi Loew's grave?" Anna asked, unable to distinguish any clearly marked headstone.

"Look closely, there towards the middle," Julia responded excitedly.

Anna had missed it at first, but then she saw a blackened and weathered headstone with coins and pebbles strewn out before it, some resting on bits of folded paper.

"Rabbi Judah Loew ben Balazel. 1520-1609."

"Yes! Yes!" Julia shouted, making her way slowly through an army of tall headstones circling the good rabbi's grave like concrete sentinels.

"Why the rocks and paper?" Anna asked, reaching down to pick up a small yellow note faded by time.

"No, don't! They are private prayers to Rabbi Loew asking for help or advice. It would be like listening in on someone's confession."

"I suppose some were answered?" Anna said, trying hard to share this special moment with her mother.

Julia knelt down and gently traced her fingers across the rabbi's headstone.

"Maybe, but mine weren't."

"You left messages too?"

"Oh yes, many. The last two on the day before my brother Hiram and I left for England. The Nazis had begun closing all roads to the city then. I asked that Papa and Mama would soon follow. But they didn't," Julia murmured, her voice trailing off to a whisper.

"And the other note?"

"To my precious Erich, about whom I have told you many stories. I was sure we would meet again someday when the world came to its senses, and be married. It was very romantic."

"Did Erich believe in the golem?

"I don't know. I think maybe he believed because I did. I told him, if Rabbi Loew made the golem, then he had to have a direct line to God. That's why so many people left their prayers and wishes with the good rabbi, and still do. He was seen as a Jewish savior by many. But Papa always got too intellectual when I talked about the golem, said he was like the good fairy. I know Erich agreed with him, because he said many Germans saw their ancient warriors as still alive, but he wouldn't say he did."

Anna looked tenderly at Julia and the tears forming in her eyes as she continued talking about Erich. How old she looked at seventy-four, stooped and wrinkled all over. Time had not been gentle to her. She often referred to herself as a lonely woman—she would call it that loneliness that is so hard on the young, but so sweet to the old—and in a sense that was true. Only an occasional twinkle in her eyes gave hint to the joy she once held for simply being alive. No one had danced through life to so many different tunes as she had. She gave so much, it seemed like all of nature borrowed life from her. Blessed with an insatiable curiosity about the way the world worked, she would spend her Sundays around Old Town, simply watching life happen. So intimate and passionate was her love of life, she seemed a part of every living thing. There wasn't one thing about living she didn't like, because it was a one-time affair. She knew that when it was over, it was over. But now she had become obsessed with death and the journey her soul would take when it came.

"How often would you come here?" Anna asked, still mystified by the rabbi's grave.

"Once a week, maybe. I tried to come every day, though, after the Sudetenland was annexed by Germany. It was one of the few places where Jews were not spit on."

"With Erich?"

"Oh yes, with Erich. Many times we were here together. Especially when darkness came and the city was quiet."

"You made love in a cemetery?" Anna asked, grinning, amazed at such a revelation from her mother.

"Certainly. It was funny, though, that when we first would come here and lay together, he was very shy, thinking for a long time we were being watched. But I told him the golem was asexual and cared little about what we were doing. What was important to him was that we were in love," Julia said, laughing loudly before continuing.

"We came unashamedly at first, then secretly until I left and he was to return to Dresden. When the final hour came for separation, there were no more words to say. I left my prayer with the rabbi and walked home alone. We both vowed, though, that our love would stay here with Rabbi Loew's grave until we were together again."

"We should go to Dresden while we're this close; perhaps he is still alive and living there. What a surprise that would be," Anna said teasingly.

Julia frowned and turned away, yet Anna's words had quickened her dying heart. She had left him here, standing alone by the gate after their last moments together. Now, fifty-two years later, all she could recall about him was the warmth of his body. Nothing more. Not even the outlines of his face.

Before she could respond to Anna's jesting words, the caretaker began walking among the headstones ringing a hand bell like a town crier of old.

"You know now what you must do when I die, and where," Julia said, quickly pointing once more to Rabbi Loew's grave. "Now we must hurry into the Pinkas Synagogue before they close the doors. Papa and Mama will be there."

Julia and Anna walked a few paces from the cemetery gate to a small courtyard fenced around a side entrance to the synagogue and stepped inside the door. Neither one was prepared for what followed. With each step they took, silent voices from thousands of faceless victims reached out to them from behind the countless rows of names spread across every inch of the synagogue's stone walls. All that they were and ever would be was there, squeezed into each letter of their names. This was all any of us would ever know about them, Julia knew. Yet each name knew the others. They had all walked the same road to their deaths. Looking around, Julia believed there was no place on earth large enough to contain so much sorrow staring back at her from the eighty thousand names spread across the walls.

Turning to her right, she walked slowly along the side wall of the nave, occasionally touching a name or two as if she knew them. Suddenly, as if lifted from within the host of names by some mysterious force, two names she had long pretended would not be here were hurled into Julia's searching eyes. Jiri Kaufmann and Anka Kaufmann, names she had not seen written in fifty-two years. Julia could not bring herself to touch her mother and father's names, though Anna did. Later, on the return trip to

America, Anna would hold Julia's hand as they discussed the strangeness of love and its force after so many years of silence.

From the moment the Nazi atrocities at Auschwitz were revealed, Julia tried to believe her mother and father had died some other way, at some other place and time. Suicide at home maybe, as some Jews in Prague did. At least it would have been their choice. But truth has a way of hanging around long enough to keep reality from becoming fiction. For Julia, though, closure of her loss was finally there before her, two small names among the thousands huddled about them, all sharing the same horrific ending.

Julia could no longer hold back a lifetime of waiting tears as she and Anna moved upstairs in the synagogue. There the drawings and brightly colored paintings of children waiting on their deaths in the gas chambers were spread across the walls like a thousand rainbows. No fear or sadness. Only a radiant hope that danced and sang endlessly through their colors. There were so many of the truly innocent before her that Julia could only wonder where God was hiding then.

Julia stopped before two paintings that had caught her eye.

"Brehova Street, Anna! I recognize the row of houses and apartment buildings," she beamed, wiping the rivers of tears from her face. Then she reached out and touched the name, Viktor Fischer, scribbled across the bottom of each painting, connecting the distant past with the present. His small round face appeared before her eyes as it was when she left Prague in 1939, frozen in the wonders and expectations that would come from a thousand tomorrows. Though several years younger than she, Julia would always stop for a few minutes to laugh and play games with him. As Julia moved along the thousands of paintings, she realized other childhood friends would be there waiting to say hello after fifty-two years of separation. She began to sob uncontrollably. The scene was something Anna could understand but neither feel nor share with her mother. She knew that such moments in history belonged only to those that were there and no one else.

Taking Julia in her arms, she said softly, "They are closing now, Mother. We will come back tomorrow if you like. But right now you must tell me more about Rabbi Loew's golem on the way back to the hotel."

"Yes, yes, the golem, my playmate. We must talk of him more."

Before leaving, Julia turned back once more to gently touch her young friend's paintings.

"I am sorry, Anna. I didn't expect this to be so heavy after all these years. It shouldn't be, I would think."

"All your life has been heavy. I'm not sure you could have existed if it weren't so," Anna smiled, reaching out to take Julia's hand.

Julia moved away from Anna and stood still for a moment looking at her.

"There were some wonderful, light years, too—my childhood and my moments with Erich. Those were good times, if one could say that, for Jews in Prague."

"You've never lost your love for him, have you?"

"I don't know, maybe. There were other times."

"Even after all you suffered—our family erased from the face of the earth?"

"He was a doctor, not a German soldier, or the Gestapo. And everything that happened was so long ago."

"But still he was your enemy."

"That was then, but I never hated him. He was my lover, you know. We would have married had things been different," Julia said softly.

Looking at her mother's tired face, Anna could still see at times the faint shadows of a loveliness and grace that once captured the hearts and minds of all those she came in contact with. It was easy to imagine her raven hair, now white, tumbling across her face as she ran to meet each day with a precious joy known only to a few. The pain that had followed her through the years was there to be seen, though she would deny it.

"Was Erich my father?" Anna asked, surprising Julia.

At first, Julia appeared stunned by the question, but then gently smiled. "I don't know. There were so many," she said, laughing before quickly turning grim again. "Perhaps we should talk no further about him, or the Holocaust. I saw what I wanted to see. Anyway, we need to return to the hotel. The evening plenary session convenes at 7:30 and I would like to rest for a little while."

Anna took Julia's arm as they began the short walk back to the hotel. She had asked the question a thousand times throughout the years about her phantom father, and always the answer, "I don't know." Perhaps Julia really didn't know. Perhaps she had experienced many men. It was an extraordinary time then, a time when ancient rules were papered over and hidden from the eyes. Not even God could be found, save on the lips of those dying in the gas chambers. Anna decided then and there that she would no longer concern herself with Erich. He was too dear to her mother.

TWO

Stepping into the lobby of the Continental Hotel, it seemed to Julia and Anna that every doctor in the world was there, squeezed tightly into one compact voice, jabbering thunderously a multitude of different languages all at the same time. What was being said didn't make any sense, but no one really cared. It was being there and living such a moment that mattered. All had come to inhale until they were giddy the fresh air of freedom in Prague, and to sip like fine wine the reawakening of the city's rich culture, so long trampled into silence by the Nazis and then by the Communist Party.

Julia eagerly sought out among the mingling throng the one familiar face that had lured her back to Prague after so many years of a self-imposed exile. Would she recognize her cousin Abram? During the war years, he had been transported first to Treblinka and then to Auschwitz by the Nazis, along with her mother and father and everyone else in their family living in Prague. He was twenty-eight then, healthy and strong bodied, ready to be exploited in heavy labor by the Germans for three years. With the Russian army nearing the death camp, many guards began murdering the remaining Jews as they prepared to abandon the camp. To escape the slaughter, Abram crawled beneath a decaying pile of dead bodies, laying face down to shield his nose from the rotting stench, and waited until the last truckload of guards had left. In time, Abram's mind would heal from the atrocities he had witnessed, but not his soul. Like the few Jews who had survived, there was nothing waiting for him after returning to Prague but memories. All his family had vanished like pollen in the wind, never to be seen again. Still, until the Velvet Revolution finally set him free, he was destined to endure a second lifetime of brutal treatment, this time under the Communist regime. Now bearing only a faint image of the man he once was, broken in spirit and health with lungs ravaged by tuberculosis, finding Julia in America restored a wondrous hope he had once harbored a long time ago.

Abram's surprising phone call had left Julia dazed and gasping for air. Fifty-two years had passed since she left her father standing alone at Hlavni station, their eyes drenched in sadness, each looking to the other one last time as the train pulled slowly away, carrying Hiram and her and scores of young Czech children to Rotterdam. All were dead in her family, Julia had been told at the war's end. Even aunts, uncles, and cousins had perished in the death camps. No one was left. That Abram was alive was a gift that only a loving God could give her now, she believed.

Julia finally spotted Abram resting with his back against a long wall near the elevators.

"Abram, Abram, here!" she cried hoarsely, trying to make her voice heard above the rising shouts of the happy throng reverberating around the lobby.

Her voice reached Abram. Turning to his left, he saw Julia trying to push her way through the jungle-like mass of jousting bodies blocking her path to where he was standing. Waving to her, Abram slowly limped towards her with support of a wooden cane.

"Abram, my sweet cousin," Julia screamed, before rushing to him and collapsing in his arms, crying with joy.

Minutes passed before either one would let the other go, and then only because of the attention they were receiving from the curious crowd of strangers pushing and moving around them. At times they could hardly stand with the weight of the growing crowd shoving against them in the small hotel lobby.

Wiping her eyes, Julia found her voice again.

"How long has it been, Abram?"

"I count fifty-two—you left in 1939," Abram replied, bracing himself once more against the wall. "Walls and chairs are my good friends now; it is difficult for me to stand long."

"Yes, fifty-two years, almost a lifetime."

Abram turned to Anna, who was standing slightly behind Julia, saying nothing, but smiling at her mother and Abram.

"You are Anna, I know. You look like your grandmother Anka. She was as soft and gentle as God's hands, you know," Abram said, taking hold of Anna's arm first, then embracing her. "She was my favorite aunt. We will talk some more later so that I may know you better, but now I'm afraid I must be rude. There is much I need to talk with your mother about in private. You understand, don't you?"

Anna nodded. No explanation was needed. Looking at her mother and Abram, it was easy to sense the crushing emptiness of the moment that overshadowed their joyous reunion. There were but a few tomorrows left for both of them. Like so many families swept cruelly aside by history, nothing was left of theirs now except the two of them, with each knowing they probably would never see the other again. In her letters, Julia had pleaded with Abram after his return to Prague from Russia to quickly come to America, but his answer was always the same: "God kept me alive through the dark valley of death, so that I might die in Prague, as history intended it to be for my family. There is no other place for me."

Julia never questioned his reasoning. He had endured the horrors of the Nazi death camps for three years, and then forty-seven more years of hard labor in the terrible gulags in Russia, when he should have been a free man. He simply disappeared from the streets in Prague one day, not to be seen again for all those years. His political fights against the Communist Party in Prague before the war had not been forgotten by the party after it seized power under the Russian umbrella. Now death, like the dropping sands in an hourglass, was nothing more than a passing moment to him. His broken and aged body held little hope for life much longer; so he would wait here, in his beloved Prague, for that which was sure to come and find him. Nothing mattered now except his dear Julia's existence and presence before him, and that he would share with no one, not even Anna.

After a short period of silence, Abram spoke directly to Julia. "We must go someplace to talk, where our voices can be heard. There is a small coffee house across the square. Not too exciting like the University Café in the old days, but there is some intimacy to be gained there."

"Not now, Abram," Julia said. "I need to rest a while. I will meet you for dinner there at seven."

Saying nothing, Abram nodded, turned and shuffled back into the crowd towards a side exit door from the lobby. Anna found the whole scene unnerving. Two people, long dead to the other, feeling the strange rush of family love again. Yet she knew Abram and her mother shared a common history she was not a part of, at least for the moment. Her time of sharing would come in the days ahead, listening to her mother's final stories before she closed her eyes for the last time.

Later, as Julia prepared to leave their hotel room to meet Abram, she took Anna in her arms, holding her tightly. "There's so much to talk about with Abram. It will take time. He was with Papa and Mama at Auschwitz. I have never known the moment they died nor how they went—he will tell me."

"I'll wait up for you. The stories will be there for you to tell during the long journey home," Anna said, gently wiping away the small tears forming in her mother's eyes.

"You must go to the Charles Bridge while I am gone. I never tired of doing so. Especially when the night was very dark with only the stars to keep you company. I could feel the winds of a thousand years of history spinning across my face," Julia whispered to Anna as she shut the door behind her.

Anna did go, but while the evening was still light. Picking her way through the labyrinth of streets between the Old Town square and the river, she moved in awe across the magnificent ancient bridge. Before her lay thirty religious statues, fifteen along each side of the bridge, that through the ages had watched over the transit of millions. Anna knew nothing about the Christian saints given a statue there, except one, St. John of Nepomuk, and then only from the wonderful stories Julia had told her when she was a child. It was magical for those who rubbed his face, which she had done a thousand times and more. And the good St. John, Julia would sing out with a thespian flair while Anna clapped her hands with anticipation, was thrown, bound and gagged but very much alive, from the bridge by a jealous King Wenceslas because he refused to tell all the queen had revealed to him in confession. At that very moment, Julia would shout gleefully, dancing and flipping the lights on and off in the room and sweeping her arms upward, a cluster of bright shinning stars suddenly appeared over the spot where he was drowned, lighting the way for him to heaven. That is why he is magical.

Anna gently touched and caressed the burnished statue several times with both hands, trying to feel her mother's fantasies when she had stood before St. John as a child, and then again as an adult swept up in the rapture of her love for Erich. They would both come to the bridge together to listen to the voices of the river below and then to touch the shiny brass face of Nepomuk and make sacred wishes as they did at Rabbi Loew's grave.

God would never distinguish between a Jew and a Christian where love was involved, they knew. But as the cry against the Jews grew louder in Prague with the approaching insanity, they stopped coming for fear of being watched by the authorities.

With evening shadows falling, and not wishing to navigate the winding streets leading to the hotel in the dark, Anna started back across the bridge. Nearing the end, she stopped for a brief moment in front of a statue of the Crucifixion. She knew little about the Christian religion, and even less about her own. She had not been to the synagogue in Franklin in over two years, though the rabbi would drop by to visit. Julia had stopped going altogether until she received the surprising letter from Abram.

As Anna stood in front of the Crucifixion studying the agony in Jesus's face, she felt the presence of someone standing near her and moved away instinctively.

"I'm sorry if I startled you. But I was watching how gently you touched St. John's face, and for a minute I thought you were someone I knew, but I am mistaken."

Anna looked at the voice's author.

"It is beautiful, isn't it—the art?" he said, looking carefully at Anna's face.

"Not really. I find it sad."

"That is a strange thing to say. Most people, I think, would find it a magnificent work of art. It dates back to 1648, you know."

"The sadness is in his death, not the art."

"That is even stranger. Christians would say there is a glory in his death," the stranger said, puzzled by Anna's words.

"I wouldn't know since I'm not a Christian, and a glorious death doesn't interest me. What does, though, is the crazy idea that someone would take it upon himself to die for all the bad things I'm responsible for. That makes no sense at all," Anna replied and started to turn away, not wishing to talk further with the man.

"You are an atheist then?"

Anna studied the man's face a second before responding, wondering how she stumbled into such an insane dialogue five thousand miles from home.

"No, I am a Jew—an agnostic Jew, if there is such a thing," she said, turning her back to him and walking away.

"Are there many Jews like you?" were the last words Anna heard as she quickened her pace, leaving the stranger alone by the Crucifixion.

When she reached the end of the bridge, Anna looked back and saw the man still standing beside the statue looking at her. How she would describe the strange man to Julia was her only conscious thought as she quickly started up Karlova towards the Old Town square. There was nothing about him that merited remembering except his eyes. Not his eyes, actually, but the sockets where they should be. It was as if they had been hollowed out and brushed over with a dull grayness that one only sees in death. He wasn't blind but he might as well have been. And she was haunted by those eyes.

Back in the safety of her hotel room, Anna sat down on the edge of the bed to gather her thoughts. More angry than upset that she would stumble into such an unguarded conversation with a total stranger, Anna took pen and paper from her briefcase and wrote down, sentence by sentence, what had been said. Sin and forgiveness were inseparable emotions private to the soul. This much was true, she knew, whether you were a Jew or a Christian. But having someone pick up the tab for the mess you've made, made life too easy. It was like letting the neighbors pile all their dirty dishes in your sink, if you're the chosen one to wash them. However, dying to get them clean made no sense at all. And maybe, just maybe, your dirty dishes shouldn't be washed at all, but handed back to you.

Anna put down the pen, crumbled up the paper and threw it in the wastebasket next to her bed. The episode was too brief and silly to let it bother her as it had. She was a cardiologist, not a theologian, and trying to heal a sick heart was all she knew and cared about. Healing the soul belonged to God, and He'd had thousands of years to get it done right, if He existed at all. Tired and exhausted from the long trip to Prague, Anna lay back on the bed, drifting off for what she had imagined would be a short nap before taking a late supper. Five hours later she awoke, startled by Julia knocking over a chair while trying to undress in the dark.

"Mother?"

"Sorry, thought I could make it without awakening you."

"I need to get up anyway. I haven't had dinner, and I am really quite hungry."

"Supper? You're way into the early morning. It's after one."

Anna looked at her mother, puzzled by her long absence.

"You're too old to be a night owl, especially with your cousin. Where have you been?"

"Warped in time, I think, walking with Abram everywhere our youth had taken us. There wasn't much left to see, though. Mostly our imagination of what had passed," Julia said, her voice pitched in obvious sadness.

Anna summoned her mother to sit by her on the bed and began to gently massage her neck.

"A stroll in one's memory is sometimes better than the real thing. It shuts out the ugly," she said.

"I suppose. But the passion is missed. There were distant feelings, though, and anger."

"Anger?"

"Yes, at what once was and could have been, had things been different. Even fifty years is not enough to heal a broken heart, Anna."

"Did Abram speak of Erich?"

"Not really. I listened for hours to his stories about Auschwitz and the Russian prisons he was lost in for years. He should write a book," Julia replied, getting up from Anna's bed to check the safety latch on the hotel door.

"He told stories that I didn't want to hear anymore, that was all," she said, walking back to her bed instead of Anna's.

"About Grandpapa?"

"Yes, and more. We will talk again in the morning, but now you must go to bed hungry," Julia said teasingly, as if she were punishing Anna for missing dinner.

Then, turning the small bed lamp off, she added in a hushed tone, "We should go home tomorrow, not Friday, I am very tired. Abram will never leave Prague, even after he dies, so we said our last goodbyes, just as we did fifty-two years ago. We can make arrangements in the morning." These were the last words Anna heard before Julia closed her eyes to sleep.

Shared stories would fill their time on the long trip back to America, but the sudden cancellation of an exciting trip and medical conference bothered Anna and made no sense. She had traveled five thousand miles to see a graveyard where her mother's ashes were to be surreptitiously buried, meandered halfway across the legendary Charles Bridge, only to engage in a disquieting conversation with a total stranger over the crucifixion of Jesus, and now she was to go home. Perhaps tomorrow there will be answers, not stories, Anna mused as she found her own precious sleep.

Morning came too soon for Anna and Julia. Each would have been content to let the morning pass by unnoticed. However, Julia's abrupt altering of her long-awaited return to Prague was fixed in stone the minute Anna suggested giving the day to the old city and then taking an early morning flight home the following day.

"There is nothing more for me here, nothing," Julia said in an unusually sad voice, one that Anna had seldom heard from her mother.

Julia tossed her small luggage piece on the bed, which had remained unpacked, and began putting her toiletries in a small case she had used for thirty years. Stopping, she turned to Anna, who was still lying in bed. "You will have mountains of time to take in Prague when you return with my ashes, but we must hurry now. There is a train leaving for Rotterdam in less than an hour."

"A train to Rotterdam? I don't understand. Our return flight doesn't leave until six in the evening," Anna said, clearly puzzled by what was taking place.

"This train crosses Germany over the same route that carried my brother and me and five hundred young children to safety only a few days before Hitler occupied Prague. That should be reason enough," Julia responded, showing impatience with Anna's questions.

"You are trying to reach back over fifty years, Mother, and—"

"Stop! You have no right to judge me, not now, or ever. Only those who were there at that moment can judge me, and they never will."

With this outburst from Julia, Anna quickly got out of bed, standing for a brief second looking at her mother, stunned by the stinging discipline in her voice. She had suddenly become a stranger to her.

Finishing packing, Julia said nothing, and moved quickly to the door, looking at Anna as if she wanted to apologize for her sudden outburst. All she could offer was a forced smile, which to Anna was worse than no apology.

"Coffee and pastries are waiting for you in the lobby," she mumbled, stepping into the hallway, leaving Anna alone to her thoughts about what had taken place.

Fifteen minutes later, they were on their way to the train station, riding in polite silence like two strangers forced to share the same taxicab. Once there, Anna's offer to carry her mother's small luggage piece was quietly ignored as they boarded the train and found their compartment. Even though Julia still seemed angry, her stories would begin again in time, Anna knew. They always did when traveling.

Julia leaned back against the cushioned seat just as the train's movements began to accelerate, realizing she was leaving behind for the second time her beloved Prague. One's remembrance of suffering can invade the mind with tiny flashes of fantasy, uncertain in their truths, yet bold and absolute in their pronouncements. Some opt to pass through unnoticed or ignored except by a few still-frightened souls. For Julia in leaving Prague the first time, having the frightened soul of a young woman was never an option, only the anguish of realizing she probably would never see her family again. Like the present moment, the train had pulled out slowly and then rapidly accelerated away from the conquered city, carrying five hundred children and young adults across Nazi Germany into another world they had never known—but one that would let them live. From the moment she and Hiram boarded the train, they were pushed into service as caretakers for scores of hysterical children doubly frightened by separation from family and the scowling brown-shirted Nazi guards standing at both ends of the car. Patience and compassion for crying and unruly children, an ancient virtue of the German family, was absent. These were Jews, though, which required no excuses from the guards. Twelve hours later, Julia and Hiram and the trainload of children refugees from Prague crossed into the Netherlands and safety.

Julia closed her eyes for a second, listening to the monotonous clicking of the train's wheels passing over the connecting rails, keeping time like the rhythmical ticking of her father's treasured metronome. Though she was only five at the time, Julia remembered now, faintly, her father's madness one day over her inability to keep time with even the simplest of musical beats. Every day thereafter, except on the Sabbath, she was required to sit alone in the parlor facing the ticking metronome for one hour, nothing less, counting and tapping her feet in time with it. For two months the torture ran unchecked until the instrument somehow miraculously disappeared, never to be found again, at least by her father. Julia believed the good Rabbi Loew had sent his golem to steal it away when everyone was sleeping, having visited his grave every day for a week with silent prayers for deliverance. But her mother knew differently, and would only smile at Julia's golem stories. When the day came for Julia to leave Prague, she had carefully wrapped the metronome, placing it in the small suitcase Julia would be taking to England. Two days later, as

Julia settled into her temporary quarters outside London with the other refugees, the sudden discovery of her childhood metronome brought loud shrieks of tearful joy that would overshadow her sadness for days to come. Later Julia would find the note from her mother hidden beneath a pink sweater she had secretly knitted for her coming birthday. It was then that Julia believed they would all be together again soon—a belief that quickly shattered into a thousand pieces five months later when German troops stormed into Poland. World War II had begun, spinning the many roads Julia would travel. The metronome would follow her wherever she went and, in the end, come to rest on the mantle in her home in America, there to teach Anna, as it had her, how to keep time in a crazy world.

Julia opened her eyes and looked out at the passing scenery as the train began slowing down for Chemnitz, Germany, the first stop since leaving Prague. Nothing was familiar, nothing to help her capture the same moment fifty-two years back. There were no green-clad German soldiers crowding the passenger platforms this time, gawking arrogantly at the packed railcars of terrified Jewish children, only small groups of casually dressed people, summer tourists mostly, waiting to move on. Each station, and the land in between, seemed the same to Julia. It was as if she had never passed this way before.

"This is a terrible mistake," she said, glancing at Anna sitting across the compartment from her.

"A mistake?"

"Yes, a damn foolish one, riding this train trying to live in the past as if it were here in front of me."

"And it's not?" Anna asked gently, sensing the disappointment in her mother's voice.

"No, and it never will be. Your mind may tease you some, letting you feel a distant warmth or horror for a moment, but never the completeness of the experience itself."

"You must be right, Mother, because the world's full of middle-aged people emulating and dressing and running around like twenty-year-olds and asking their therapists if that's alright," Anna said, laughing, trying to lighten the moment for Julia, who immediately began laughing with her.

Happy that the coolness between them had warmed, Anna began reading the *International Herald Tribune* again, which she had picked up before leaving the hotel. Folding over the front page, she stopped suddenly, focusing her eyes first on a small photograph at the bottom of the page before reading the few lines next to it.

"What a strange thing," she blurted out. "A grotesque naked body of an old man was found late last night sprawled across Rabbi Loew's grave in the Old Jewish Cemetery. And—"

"What are you saying?"

"The story says the man lying across Rabbi Loew's grave was naked and wrinkled with age as an old rhino, his eyes staring at nothing, much like the piles of dead waiting for the furnaces at Auschwitz. In one hand was a small crumpled pink name tag, the kind babies used to wear in a hospital."

"How did he die, does it say?"

"No, but the indications are it was suicide," Anna said, handing the paper to Julia and pointing to the picture of the dead man.

"He looks so much like the man I talked with briefly on Charles Bridge."

"What man? You're not making any sense."

Anna then told Julia about her encounter with the strange man on the bridge by the Crucifixion and the insaneness of their dialogue. It was as if their meeting was a prelude to what was to come later. That is, if he was the same man. She couldn't be sure, Anna told Julia, but the lifeless eyes were the same.

"That is a good story, much better than the ones I've told you lately. We must talk about it some more after I have rested," Julia said, leaning back against the cushion again and closing her eyes.

It was a good story, but it bothered Anna that the dead man might very well be the stranger on the bridge. She really couldn't tell for sure, but the closer she looked at his face the more certain she became. The article said little about him, though, not even how he died or who he was. If he was the stranger, it would be foolish for her to think their brief conversation earlier on Charles Bridge was connected in some way to his death. Yet, if suicide was the cause of the man's death, her sharp words criticizing the atonement could have pushed him over the edge. It doesn't take much, when someone is looking for an excuse to die.

Looking at Julia sleeping, Anna believed one year, maybe two, was all that was left of her mother's incredible journey in this world. Maybe it will continue in the next one, if there is one. It would be a shame to deprive God of such an experience. Feeling drowsy herself, Anna stretched out on the long compartment seat. The one story she had expected to hear from

Julia this morning remained untold: last night's visit with Abram. Why she had been purposely excluded by Abram still puzzled her. The deaths of her grandfather and grandmother in the gas chambers meant nothing to her, other than the sadness Julia might still feel about their loss, or the way they died. She didn't know them, or any of the other six million Jews that were murdered. They were Jews and she was, too, and that was the closest she would ever be to them. Julia had told her beautiful stories about her mother and father, and Anna knew she would have loved them dearly had she known them. And she would have loved Erich, too—more so, in fact, if he were her father. When the stories began again on the long flight home, which they would, she would ask Julia about Abram and Erich, but mostly about Erich.

THREE

Prague, 1938

It was during the second year of his medical studies at the German University in Prague that Erich fell in love with Julia. Madly in love, is the better term, with a Czech student in her medical studies also, who just happened to be a Jew. "Not just a Jew," he would say to other German students who questioned him about such a precarious relationship, but a brilliant, beautiful woman, aspiring to be a doctor like he was soon to become. Yet, it was the worst of times for lovers such as they. With the *Anschluss* in Austria now complete, Hitler was looking eastward to the Sudetenland and Prague itself. What was happening to the Jews in Germany only compounded the fears of those living in Czechoslovakia. Still, whether it was plain foolishness, or plain passion, Erich and Julia seemed to believe the times didn't matter. Their love was real, and they thought themselves different from all that was around them. However, their world would matter to his father, Erich knew, and for now, he could say nothing to him of Julia and his love for her.

Julia had entered his heart and life one autumn morning coming through the forward door of the large classroom, quite late to a special lecture on Husserl's phenomenology. Hesitating for a second, surveying the crowded six-tiered rows of students, she spotted the empty seat next to Erich and immediately moved to it, dropping her books loudly on the table.

"Good morning, Erich Schmidt, I am Julia Kaufmann," she proclaimed boldly, glancing his way before turning quickly to face the large blackboard on which Professor Edelstein was busily scribbling a series of Socratic questions for the class to consider.

Though they had been in the class together for one week, Erich had paid little attention to Julia until this morning, as he watched her move rapidly with an unusual grace to the vacant seat beside him. A grace on grace, he would later call it. She was short and petite, with long, flowing raven hair and deep-set eyes full of laughter, the kind you like seeing life through, and skin so femininely delicate one would shy to touch for fear of harming it. She was beautiful, was all Erich could think, just beautiful. What would eventually capture Erich's heart, though, was that which few could see until they knew her: an irrepressible liberation and beauty of the soul that could exist in the worst of times.

For the next several sessions, Erich sat behind Julia, or in front of her, but always near her. Before class and after, furtive glances would be exchanged between them—sometimes a nod, but nothing more, as if saying the game would go no further. Finally, perhaps emboldened by the intense morning discussion on the ancient Greek virtue of courage, Erich walked straight to Julia at the end of class, and in the firmest voice he could muster announced his interest in her.

"I am going to the Old Town Café for morning coffee and would like very much for you to join me."

Julia waited several seconds before responding to the invitation she had secretly hoped would soon come from him.

"Are you sure that is what you want?"

"Certainly. Why do you ask?"

"I am Jewish and you are, well, German. The days are becoming extraordinarily difficult for the Jews there."

"I know, but this is Prague, not Germany."

"Prague may not be different either. Hate has its own legs, and has a way of moving on. There is much angry propaganda here now against the Jews—the Nazis are good at that."

"Things will settle down, I'm sure. Anyway, we're just two small people in all that is happening. So, will you have coffee with me?"

"Yes, but first I must talk with my father; he will want to meet you. Then perhaps tomorrow we can share a table together," Julia said, smiling as she turned from Erich and walked away.

Meeting Julia's father and asking his permission to take her to a café for coffee seemed so formal and wasn't what Erich had expected from her. His whole life had been formal, regimented by a father that followed only one path in life: tradition. As a father, he was undemonstrative and could neither share his feelings with his family nor deal with the feelings they had for him. He had never uttered the words "I love you" to Erich, or to anyone else in the family, and Erich often wondered how he and his mother ever got to the marrying stage. Any sex between them had to be an expected formality of marriage, nothing more. From the day he first could remember being in time, every waking moment seemed regimented. It was only in the dark shadows of the night that his imagination became free to think of things that might be. And as he neared manhood, it seemed to Erich, in looking back on his life, that all of his childhood had been collapsed into a single afternoon. And even then he pretended love was always there, or something like it, until the day it came to him with Julia. Nothing he had experienced growing up in his family had prepared him for the emotions he felt the moment Julia first touched his hand, nor the warmth afterwards. From then on, he believed that love could grow many different blossoms because the seed was the same in everyone, planted in us at birth by God. Dried up long ago by the arid formalities of his own father and mother, he had simply failed to nourish it, and it had died. He liked to believe it was still there in his father, too, perhaps, thirsting for the wellspring of human touch.

Yet doctoring came easy to Erich, though not by choice. It was a necessity for his salvation if he wanted to remain a Schmidt, because it was a tradition. Both his father and grandfather had studied with the great bacteriologist Koch at his institute in Berlin, eagerly embracing the new science and the miraculous revolution it was bringing to medicine. Though doctoring was in Erich's blood, his mind fancied other intellectual disciplines much more than medicine, especially the fields of philosophy and theology. In 1926 this fancy was confirmed. At age seventeen, he reluctantly accompanied his father to attend a conference being held at the renowned eugenics research institution in Cold Springs Harbor, New York. There the exciting new world of eugenics swirled around Erich and his father like the newness of early spring winds, though he quickly developed a distaste for its radical preaching. Led by an American doctor, Charles Davenport, and the renowned German physician-geneticist, Fritz Lenz, social Darwinism moved to center stage carried on the arms of a science already showing the first signs of a madness that was yet to come, one that would hark back to the ancient Greeks when wholeness was the norm, and anything less was unworthy of life. If all that we have built as an advanced civilization is to be preserved, cleansing the gene pools by sterilizing the unfit must become the scientific standard, Davenport and Lenz and many of the other leading scientists attending the conference loudly proclaimed.

With Erich fidgeting by his side, Dr. Schmidt listened in awe to the major scientific papers underscoring the sweeping eugenics passion in the United States for sterilizing criminals and mental patients and prohibiting marriage between people of different races. Some went even further in their rush to embrace the glorious movement, like Foster Kennedy, whose pronouncements quickly caught the ears of Dr. Lenz and his fellow Germans, especially when he openly suggested the whispered word, "euthanasia."

"Why not, with Christian compassion, euthanize the mentally disturbed, the physically unfit who threaten mankind's very existence," he would say and write.

"Compassionate euthanasia," the coined phrase being tossed about so casually by many at the conference, troubled Erich greatly. He had been thinking about existence lately and the miracle of life, and it seemed to him to be the most remarkable thing that one could ever imagine, coming into this world as we do, as nothing more than a piece of protein. Everything we have been and everything we will become is tied up in that small world, a microscopic glob of molecules that somehow stays connected to our ancient history. So each day, until his father admonished him for doing so, he would ask the same question to those who would listen: "How could we even begin to think of ending another person's existence when that was all he would ever have?"

Politically, though, Theodore Roosevelt himself had years earlier endorsed the eugenics effort to save humanity (which did impress Erich considerably), while on the social scene, the idea became quite fashionable with F. Scott Fitzgerald's snappy song "Love or Eugenics" floating melodiously across nightclub dance floors all over America. Even the revered Supreme Court muscled its way into the act in a sickening case involving a state's request to sterilize a young mentally disabled woman. On a dismally cold and cloudy day when the sun refused to shine, perhaps as an omen of terrible deeds to come, the great Justice Holmes strode to the bench and, uttering the words "Three generations of imbeciles are enough," unhooked the moral reins holding science and medicine back. Shortly thereafter the shameful sterilization of 40,000 mentally disabled women rolled across America like a giant tsunami.

What puzzled and bothered Erich more than what the scientists were advocating, though, was the large number of theologians and ministers, and even rabbis, who had lined up behind Charles Davenport and his colleagues in science, when what they were advocating was clearly wrong, at least in his young mind. Perhaps America was not the stately and righteous guardian of human rights the rest of the world believed it to be.

"What is there to keep us from crossing the line, from becoming far less than what God intends us to be?" he asked his father boldly one afternoon, as they were standing amid a crowd of American doctors.

Quickly silenced by his father's cold stare, he wandered outside the conference hall and looked eastward across the harbor and ocean to where he imagined Europe might be. Everything is changing, he mused. What we are today, we may not be tomorrow. For a moment he thought of Nathaniel Hawthorne's sorrowful story of the fanatical scientist who becomes obsessed with his beautiful wife's single flaw, a crimson birthmark on her otherwise flawless cheek. Determined to rid her of this sinful imperfection, he creates a powerful potion to make the mark disappear, which it does, but his wife also dies. Hawthorne and Emerson were the only two American writers Erich found any enjoyment in reading, because they seemed to embrace Nietzsche's criticism of the paramount ideal of human perfection being so eagerly embraced by science and society. He wasn't ready for this new world of medicine like his father was.

"What a glorious day for all of humanity," Dr. Schmidt shouted out, while standing on the deck of their ship, to a flight of sea gulls swooping low over the tops of the breaking waves, searching for their morning meal. "Darwin's survival of the fittest can now be manipulated by science, and we, the scientists, the keepers of the faith, will set the moral bar for all of civilization to follow."

Erich hardly knew his father at times, and never before had he seen him so joyously arrogant as he was at this moment. What seemed to impress his father most, though, was the rapid enactment of laws throughout America providing for compulsory sterilization of the criminally insane and other people considered genetically inferior.

"America, that bulwark of liberty, is leading the world in preserving the human race, and Germany must seize the lead in cleansing the Aryan race," he would repeat over and over to Erich, like a broken record, as they left the conference for home. What was to follow would bring Erich to Prague and to Julia.

The second morning at sea Dr. Schmidt suddenly began humming Fitzgerald's popular song. "We must find and buy a copy of that song," he said, stopping the incessant humming for a second.

"It is only a catchy song, nothing more," Erich replied, disgusted and embarrassed by his father's childish actions.

"No, it sings out loud what the American people are really thinking. They're afraid that the advanced races of mankind are skating backwards, sliding down a slippery slope to be swallowed up one day by ignorance. We must sing the same song to those who will listen."

Erich shook his head. Never before had such unbridled giddiness pushed out from his father's strict bearing. He seemed almost human. It was as if he had been suddenly swept up in the "rapture."

"We too must become part of this sacred mission," his father continued babbling.

"What are you talking about? What mission?"

"To save the great Aryan race from extinction. What else? We will embrace the National Socialist movement like Lenz, who is committed to such a mission."

Erich rose from his deck chair and walked to the railing, joining several other passengers looking at the angry ocean surrounding them. The beckoning waters had been there an eternity, he knew, churning and rolling and giving birth to all life. They would still be there long after Germany and the Aryan race had been erased by God and returned to dust.

Looking back at his father, Erich saw nothing, only the tradition he hated. He had no desire to follow in the footsteps of his father. Healing and touching sick bodies was distasteful to him. Instead, it was the sick mind that roiled and captured his interest. The growing field of psychiatry would bring him the fame he had long imagined, and possibly a distinguished professorship in a few years alongside the great German psychiatrists at Berlin University and Munich, or even the German University in Prague, where the great intellectual movement in Prague had first reached out to him. Kafka and the other great writers of the Prague Circle were there alongside the city's artists and men of letters. Philosophy and the metaphysical presence of being were open for the world to see and study. What he had to do was leave his studies at Berlin University to go there.

Having looked at the rising and falling horizon too long, Erich felt nauseated and returned to the chair next to his father to rest.

"You have turned green," his father said, amused. "A bouncing horizon is not something to favor too long."

"Let me rest my head a few minutes and we will talk some more."

After a few minutes, Erich turned to his father and picked up the disturbing conversation again.

"Father, you cannot join the National Socialist movement. It is political; you are a doctor, a physician, a defender of the Hippocratic Oath—not a politician."

"You are so pitifully young and wrong, Erich. Hereditary health is before us now, tugging at us. It's not something we must wait for. You saw with your own eyes what is taking place in America. They are leading the way, but soon they will follow Germany."

"And do what?"

"Sterilize all of the unfit, not just a few, and even develop a racial policy. The black man has no standing there."

"And Germany?"

"My boy, listen: biological laws are the laws of life and National Socialism is nothing more than applied biology. We must purify the Aryan race if Germany's health is to survive, and that will be the physician's task, yours and mine—don't forget that."

"That is nonsense and evil, Father. I've never heard you speak like this before."

"Why? Treating the hereditarily sick by sterilization should be seen as a God-given blessing. Think of all of the mentally disabling illnesses that will be eliminated. What a utopia to live in."

"What about the Jews? Will we sterilize them, too?

"No, I would think not, though they do intermarry at times with other races, which they shouldn't do. Perhaps prohibiting them from doing so would be enough. They are doing that now in America between the Negro and the white person."

Erich stood up, leaning against a cabin wall for support. Not only was he deathly seasick, he was sick of his father's ramblings. Finally he said in a faint voice, challenging his father, "I will not be a part of this nonsense. Prague is where I will be in the fall to study philosophy and psychology and finish my medical training, not Germany. They don't speak of such trash there, only of the liberation of the mind."

So Erich did go to Prague to finish his preliminary medical studies for the coming years of clinical training. There the great writings of Husserl and Freud and Jung saturated his daily thoughts, leaving little time to think of home and Germany. Never had his mind and soul been so free. His father, now alienated from him, had joined the National Socialist party, marching in lockstep with its racial ideology of cleansing the Aryan race. But Erich had no time for such madness. He would go home to Dresden only twice during his years away, then only to see his mother whom he cared deeply for. And it was when he returned from home the second time that he would seek Julia's companionship.

After asking Julia to have coffee with him, Erich was indeed summoned, as he later would laughingly refer to it, to her home for a formal introduction to her father, Dr. Jiri Kaufmann, a distinguished professor of psychiatry at Charles University. The confidence Erich initially felt as he set out for the encounter quickly abandoned him the moment he crossed the Old Town square and entered Josefov, the ancient Jewish quarters. Though many Jewish families lived outside the quarters, Dr. Kaufmann resided in the same small house on Kaprova Street that his father had, and his grandfather before him, only a stone's throw from Maisel Synagogue, where his family had worshipped the Hebrew God for over 150 years. He had met and married Julia's mother there, a good and gentle woman by everyone's account. Together they represented ten generations of Jewish blood in Prague.

Erich stood in front of the small stone house looking up and down Kaprova, which seemed empty of all life except for an ugly stray dog on the corner, barking loudly at him. He wondered how many secret eyes had been watching from behind the drawn curtains as he walked past the row of houses leading to Julia's. Tomorrow, Mrs. Kaufmann would spend the day explaining his evening presence in their neighborhood.

Julia opened the front door as he started through the walkway gate.

"I was afraid you might not come. But believe me, to Father some traditions are still worth holding on to, even though it is 1938."

"It's a stretch for just a cup of coffee," Erich said, laughing as he followed Julia into a small study where Dr. Kaufmann stood alone in front of dark wooden shelving stacked with medical texts and journals.

"Father, this is Erich Schmidt, one of my classmates at the university."

Erich stepped forward with his hand extended but was met with a disarming silence by Dr. Kaufmann. Unnerved by the awkward moment, Erich glanced nervously around the study, then at Julia. This wasn't what he had expected. Dr. Kaufmann's rudeness would be the easiest way to dismiss him from Julia's life, Erich thought, just as Dr. Kaufmann turned to face him.

"Please forgive my manners, Erich. My mind has been running back and forth between German and Czech, trying to find the appropriate words. While I prefer Czech, it seems everyone is speaking German these days in Prague, which perhaps is trying to tell us something," Dr. Kaufmann said, leading Erich by the arm into the living room, where Mrs. Kaufmann was busily filling magnificent gold-rimmed cups with freshly brewed coffee.

"Please sit down, Erich. We will speak German."

Erich sat down on a small settee facing Dr. Kaufmann and Julia, who was sitting next to her father. He still couldn't fathom the formality of what was happening. Everything seemed so weirdly strange to him. It was as if he should now ask for Julia's hand in marriage. In his twenty-eight years of living, being here visiting in Julia's home was only the second time for him to be in a Jewish home. Few Jewish families had lived near his home in Dresden, and those that did, kept mostly to themselves. He knew only a few of the neighbors by name, and one Jewish boy who lived several streets away. It was in his house that he sat the one time drinking a cool glass of water on a very hot afternoon. One day during summer recess with his father away, he had journeyed through the neighborhood, wandering several streets away from home. Benjamin Keiler was tossing through the air a small airplane made of balsa, when he came upon him. Watching the futile efforts of Benjamin to make the plane sail farther then a few feet before plunging to the ground, Erich asked if he might try, which he did. But he had even less success with his flying skills and felt ashamed he had asked to try. In a while, Benjamin's mother called him to come inside for a cool drink, and he took Erich with him. They had become friends for the afternoon, that was all, and Erich never saw Benjamin again, nor his family. When he returned to his own house that day, he said nothing to his mother about where he had been. Not that she would have minded, but that she would tell his father, who cared even then nothing for Jews, even those holding prestigious professorships at Berlin University. Erich thought more about Benjamin's house that night in bed than he did about trying to fly the plane. While there he had been intrigued with a lone candle burning in the living room where they sat drinking the cool water, and believed it must be some kind of witchcraft, but was afraid to ask. The Lutherans burned candles, too, he knew—in church, though, where it made some sense to do so, not in the home. Sensing Erich's uneasiness,

Julia smiled and leaned forward to offer him a bagel that her mother had baked earlier in the morning.

"You'll find these much better than the ones served in the coffee houses."

"Yes, I will try one. Thank you," Erich said, deciding to play along with the proper game of manners being displayed by his hosts. Out of the corner of his eye, he caught a lone candle burning on a small table in the foyer, very similar to the one he remembered burning in Benjamin Keiler's home, and turned to look at it.

"The candle is in memory of my father," Dr. Kaufmann said quickly, noticing Erich's interest. "It is a Jewish tradition to light a candle on the anniversary of a loved one's death. Do you not do the same?"

"No, I might visit a grave with my parents, that is all," Erich responded, beginning to feel uneasy by the direction of the question. He knew nothing about Jewish customs, and really didn't care to know. Their religious beliefs had always been sort of mystical to him, with weird intonations from a rabbi that seemed to make little sense.

"Julia has asked permission to visit with you away from the university," Dr. Kaufmann said, smiling for the first time. "You may think it strange that she must request permission at her age, but things may start to unravel here soon as they already have in your country."

"I would hope not. Czechoslovakia is a sovereign country," Erich replied, glancing again at the burning candle, which he now enjoyed, knowing its meaning.

"Have you noticed the increasing number of refugees coming into Prague from Germany—mostly Jews, I'm afraid, and some gypsies?"

"No sir, I haven't," Erich replied, trying hard to look straight at Dr. Kaufmann. "Actually, I have little interest in politics. Becoming a doctor is all I want to do."

From the frown on Dr. Kaufmann's face, Erich knew immediately his detached response to the question was not what Dr. Kaufmann wanted to hear from him.

"You are aware of the Nürnberg Laws that prohibit German citizens from associating with Jews?" Dr. Kaufmann asked in a more unwelcoming tone of voice.

"Yes. But I really don't care. We are in Prague, not Germany. Julia could be a Bedouin Arab and I would still want to have coffee with her."

"Are you a Christian, Erich?" Dr. Kaufmann asked, carefully measuring Erich's mannerisms now as if he were a patient.

"Would it make any difference if I weren't?" Erich replied in a sharp tone, turning the strange questioning back on Dr. Kaufmann, who seemed surprised by his hostile reaction.

"No, no, it would perhaps help me understand you better, if I knew more about how a Christian looks at what is happening to the Jews here in our small corner of the world. Please forgive me if I've offended you."

Julia suddenly stood up, her eyes bristling with frustration.

"Father, forgive me, but this questioning is all nonsense. We are talking about going to a coffee house where other students gather, not a formal engagement."

"You are right, Julia, the coffee house is fine; there will be nothing further though, nothing serious. You do understand, Erich?" Dr. Kaufmann said, leaving the room, taking his coffee cup with him.

Yet the chemistry between Erich and Julia deepened, as each knew it would and desperately wanted. Visits to the coffee houses after classes became treasured moments that were soon followed by weekly dinners at Julia's home, an insistence at first by her father as a way of gauging Erich's true feelings and intentions towards Julia, being ever mindful of the insane babblings of Hitler now filling the airways in Prague and the rest of the Republic. In time, it would become unsafe for them to be seen together, he knew. But as the weeks passed, Dr. Kaufmann's fears and those of Mrs. Kaufmann gave way to a growing respect and friendship with Erich. Long discussions in Dr. Kaufmann's study would follow the dinners, on subjects of every genre. And in time, Erich became more certain than ever that psychiatry was his future. Understanding the complex intricacies of the mind could eventually uncover the soul itself, he believed and stated to Dr. Kaufmann. And then, the demons that haunt so many people could be dispelled forever. He also began to acquire an elementary knowledge of the Jewish faith, which had been largely absent throughout his studies in the Lutheran schools he attended as a child.

One evening, for no particular reason, he posed a question that puzzled not only Dr. Kaufmann but Julia as well, because of its isolated detachment from their conversation on Jungian thought.

"Jews sometimes seem to think they have a monopoly on suffering, don't they, Dr. Kaufmann?"

But Dr. Kaufmann was quick to answer.

"Yes, but only where there is no reason for it except being a Jew."

And with that the evening dialogues were over. Later, walking back to his apartment, Erich stopped at the edge of the Old Town square and sat down on the steps in front of St. Nicholas Church, looking at Kafka's house next to it, to think on his question about suffering. The Lutherans in Germany, and most of the Catholics with them, seemed to care little about what was happening to the Jews there. Yet, to think on their long suffering in Europe would make a stone weep. There had to be something deeper to cause Germany and the rest of Europe to want Jews to suffer. It made no sense otherwise, he thought. He had no answer though, and thought perhaps Julia would bring the truth to him, as she always seemed to do.

In December, during the holidays, Dr. Kaufmann was overly anxious to begin the evening discussion, but in a more somber mood. As he lifted a journal from his study desk, Erich and Julia and her brother Hiram, who sometimes joined in their discussions, hurriedly gathered around him like little children might do in anticipation of hearing a wonderful magical story. Dr. Kaufmann opened the journal, *The Archive of Racial and Social Biology*, and began to read from an article authored jointly by Dr. Ernst Rudin, a Swiss-born psychiatrist of international renown, and Dr. Viktor Schmidt, Erich's father. The article was titled "Steps Toward Making Racial Hygiene a Fact Among the German People." From his prestigious position as director of the Research Institution for Psychiatry of the Kaiser Wilhelm Society in Munich, Rudin had enlisted Erich's father and others working at the institute to become Nazis. The surprising article concluded by praising the Nürnberg Laws for preventing the further penetration of the German gene pool by Jewish blood. Stunned and ashamed, Erich bowed his head between his hands, saying nothing. His father had finally crossed the line, was all he could think. But what Dr. Kaufmann did not read to Erich and Julia was his father's solemn exhortation that the individual physician must become a genetics doctor, a guardian of the Nordic race. Dr. Kaufmann knew the emotional pain that passage would cause Erich.

Dr. Kaufmann gave the article to him. "I'm sorry to spring such shameful words on you this way, Erich. You may have the journal and do with it what you like; but you should never disavow your father, only his words and what he stands for."

Erich looked at both Julia and her father. How far his emotions had traveled to love, as he did, these two good and gentle people: Dr.

Kaufmann, who had become his mentor, and his dear Julia, whom he had fallen so deeply in love with. He had disavowed the Nürnberg Laws when they were enacted, and in doing so, spread denial in his mind to the horrific probability that was sure to follow—the extermination of the German Jew. What he must do, he vowed to himself like a young warrior called to a sacred mission, was to hurry to finish his studies at the university and quickly return to Germany, where he could speak as a doctor against the genetic madness sweeping through the medical profession. He had been away too long. But now Erich wanted only to cling to the goodness surrounding Julia and her family like the encircling arms of Mother Mary.

Erich rose from his chair and laid the article on Dr. Kaufmann's desk. Before he could speak, Julia touched his hand, then held it tightly.

"There is a sadness in our hearts for the terrible pain you must feel," she said, kissing him softly on his cheek.

"Several years back my father spoke of this craziness when we visited the eugenics institution in America. Nothing was said of the Jews, only the misfits, the insane and physically disabled. I am ashamed. No doctor should take comfort in such foolishness."

Dr. Kaufmann stood behind his study desk for a second more, looking at Julia and Erich holding hands.

"These days are not the best of times for a Jewish girl and a German boy to be in love," he said, trying to smile. "Evil always seems to find a way of emptying the heart of everything that is good."

After he had left the room, Julia embraced Erich, clinging to him as they walked to the front door.

"Surely nothing will come of this, will it?"

Erich did not respond, but peered into the cold, dark night waiting on him for the long walk home. Snow mixed with ice was beginning to fall, harkening the advent of the terrible Prague winters. Perhaps another omen, he thought, pulling his jacket tightly around his neck.

"You must think seriously about leaving Prague, you and your family. Go to England or America," he shouted back to Julia as he disappeared into the swirling blackness before him.

FOUR

B ack in his small, two-room apartment, three streets past the German university, Erich pulled off his wet clothes, tossed them in a corner, lit up a cigarette, and sat down naked behind a makeshift desk stacked with medical textbooks. He was clearly shattered by the article coauthored by his father, essentially condemning the Jews to death. Politically, the Jewish race might be thought to be expendable by the virulent voices within the Nazi party, but surely not from physicians, Hippocrates's heirs. Compassionate euthanasia might be seen as ethical to some, he believed, but not when it's based on race. Erich tried to shut his eyes to the truth that was clearly spread out before him in the article. His father had always been a paragon of the compassionate German physician, but that was before he had become totally obsessed with the eugenics movement. All sense of the sacred line carefully drawn over two thousand years ago between a duty to treat the sick and helpless and duty to the state had been cast aside by him like so much rubbish.

"I will never forgive him for shaming me this way. God can forgive him—that's His job, isn't it?" Erich yelled out, a slamming his fist against the wall, breaking the plaster.

After his trip to America, he had carefully avoided another confrontation with his father and had dismissed the entire field of eugenics as a medical fairyland, not what doctors should be about. He would become, instead, a compassionate psychiatrist and heal the crippled minds of the world. In doing so, he would purposely shut out the frightening nightmares spawning across all of Germany by Hitler's National Socialist Party and its calling for the eradication of the Jewish race. This veil of ignorance had served him well, keeping his feet dry from the bloody flood of terror now washing away the last pockets of resistance offered by reason and goodness. Only a few faint voices in medicine and the churches remained to denounce the spreading evil, and they, too, would become silent. Where had his father been in all of this? Erich kept asking himself. Sleep would come hard to him tonight, as it would for the rest of his life.

The next morning as he entered the long hall leading to the pathology lab, a group of student members of the volatile German Sudeten party were gathered around the door leading into the lab, leaving only a narrow entrance and exit aisle. After he stepped into the large room, the students began chanting loudly, "Germany Forever! Germany Forever! Throw out the Jews! Throw out the Jews!"

Erich turned around in time to see Julia with two other Jewish medical students struggling to make their way through the aroused students, who had now linked their arms together, completely blocking the doorway. Stunned by the students' hostility, he froze for a brief second before moving to Julia's aid. Placing his hands on the shoulders of two male students nearest the doorway, he said in a loud voice coated with a threatening authority inherited from his father, "What are you imbeciles doing?"

"They are Jews, they no longer belong here," a tall, blond student shouted back at Erich.

"They may be Jews but they are Czechs just like many of you. Now let them pass." His voice boomed louder as he pushed the two students away from the doorway, opening a path for Julia and her friends.

Once inside, Julia followed Erich to their lab station, which they had purposely chosen so they could work together. She immediately began trying to calm her friends, presenting a steeliness Erich had never seen before in her. It seemed so antithetical to her gentle nature and grace that it rattled him for a short moment. She showed no tears, no fright. Only the grim fierceness of a cornered animal prepared to fight for its existence glistened in her eyes.

"I should thank you, and I do, but they are nothing but bully-cowards. Nothing more. And yet we had been friends, all of us," Julia said, turning away from Erich for a moment to stare down the tall, blond student now standing alone by the door, glaring at her.

Erich knew this day had long been coming. The large German minority in the Sudetenland had been seething with undiminished hate against the

Czechs and Jews and everyone else, from the very moment they were literally given to Czechoslovakia by the Versailles Treaty at the end of World
War I. Hitler had promised they would soon be free, and they believed
him.

"We must be vigilant, Erich. They have begun to hate their Jewish
friends now, and anyone who stands with them," Julia said.

"I know, Julia, and it's hard for me to accept, since I'm German, too."

"Father says that it's the beginning of the end of all that is good in
Prague and the rest of the nation."

Before Erich could respond, Dr. Neumann, a distinguished professor
of anatomy and a Jew, entered the lab. The class chatter stilled, but not
completely. Stomping of feet began softly at the rear of the classroom, then
grew bolder, causing the glass vials and beakers on the lab tables to shake
violently, some tipping over. Horrified at the scene unfolding before him,
Dr. Neumann raised his hand for silence, only to be met with an outburst
of derisive jeers.

"Out with the dirty Jews!" one yelled, then another.

His face red with embarrassment and rage, Dr. Neumann retreated
from the room as single voices quickly became a taunting chorus chanting,
"No more Jews! No more Jews!"

As if on a signal, the chanting stopped as quickly as it began. The tall,
blond student had moved to the door, where he turned and raised his hand
to silence the rebellious students in one motion. Then, looking straight at
Julia and her fellow students, he screamed, "You Jewish vermin, you pol-
lute the air we breathe. Leave and crawl back in your holes. This is your
only warning."

Erich could restrain himself no longer and rushed towards the sneering
student. Before he could reach him, several students grabbed and wrestled
Erich to the floor while others pummeled him with their fists and books.
As Erich lay on the floor unable to protect himself, the students began
kicking him, but stopped immediately as several shrill whistles sounded
from a cadre of Czech uniformed police running down the hall to the
classroom, followed by Dr. Mann, the rector of the university. With order
quickly restored, Julia rushed to Erich's side and began wiping the blood
oozing from his mouth and nose with a lab towel. She had never felt closer
to him than now, nor surer of her love for him.

As the police escorted the tall, blond student along with several of his
colleagues from the laboratory room, he looked back at Erich and Julia

shouting, "You Jewish lover, you have betrayed your homeland. The authorities will hear of it because I will tell them."

Erich said nothing and turned away to join the few remaining students in the room who were huddled around Dr. Mann answering his questions about the incident. Erich was the only German in the crowd and Dr. Mann took note of that fact. The rest were either Jews or Czechs, or both, all citizens of Czechoslovakia. What became shockingly clear to everyone was the unexpected volume of gathered hate showered in the room by a rather small group of Sudeten German students. It was clearly not what the other students wanted to face, nor the university. In time this hate would become a monster frightening everyone in sight and closing down the university. For now the university would continue its mission of liberal education. All the students that participated in the assault on Erich were summarily dismissed from the university, and the cold Prague winter became spring.

Spring and young love have always been equals. When one, they soar apart from the world as the poets have long written. And so it was with Erich and Julia. Their days and evenings together became more intense, each grasping for the last seconds of the day entwined in the arms of the other. However, any thoughts of marriage between a German and a Jew at that moment in history were mired in the hidden terror of uncertainties about what the future could become for both of them. This terrible fact became more apparent to them than ever during the traditional convocation at the university.

Dr. Arthur Guett, a prominent physician and high-ranking Nazi health officer, delivered the prestigious lecture to the graduating seniors. Striding to the podium as if carrying a new commandment tablet from God for the young graduating doctors eagerly looking on, he began in a strong voice. "Listen carefully to my words today for I am giving you two new maxims that all German physicians must follow. One, the ill-conceived love of neighbor that you harbor must disappear forever. This is an absolute if you are to understand the second one, that it is the supreme duty of the state, and no one else's, to grant life and livelihood only to the healthy. The life of the individual has meaning only in the light of that ultimate aim."

Erich glanced quickly around the crowded auditorium; no one stirred. The silence was deafening. Then Dr. Guett added a stern admonition for all to hear, one that seemed to bother no one but Erich and Julia.

"As physicians, it is not your job, and never will be, to determine whether something is true, but rather, whether it is in the spirit of the National Socialist revolution."

With the word "revolution," as if on cue, the tall, blond student who had been expelled from the university jumped to his feet wildly applauding and shouting his support. Immediately, row after row of other German Sudeten students mixed with Czechs leaped to their feet to join the growing cheers. At first, Dr. Guett did nothing but smile, secretly satisfied with the outburst of support for his radical remarks. After a few minutes, he raised his hand and the demonstration and shouting grew silent. Continuing for the next forty minutes, he meticulously demonstrated the staggering growth in the ranks of the mentally insane and disabled and those suffering from incurable diseases in all of Europe and the threat this carried to every country's wellbeing, not just Germany's.

Dr. Guett stopped talking then and, inhaling the drama of the moment, looked slowly around the crowded room, taking on the aura of a great thespian preparing to deliver the most compelling lines of the play. "My fellow physicians, at this very moment in history we must embark together on a journey that will bring a spiritual reawakening of our sacred profession. To accomplish this, every doctor, when put to the test, is expected to embrace the ice-cold logic of the necessary—nothing less will do. It is the health of the country we should be concerned with, more so than individual disease."

Then he paused, clasped his hands together in front of his chest and looked upwards towards the ceiling as if awaiting the final divine words from God before shattering the silence with his concluding remarks. "Fellow physicians, we must prevent the bastardization of the population through the propagation of the unworthy racial alien elements. We, you and I, are the sacred guardians in keeping our blood pure."

Dr. Guett had barely finished his closing words, when the tall, blond student rose to his feet again, and in mob-like fashion led the resounding cheers of the growing number leaping to their feet. The restless crowd now included many of the German professors at the university. Dr. Guett's words had sounded the ancient trumpet of the Goths calling to arms all who would listen, and the students and young doctors were thrilled. A holy cause now beckoned them that gave greater meaning to the word doctor. The medical profession was to be recast in the service of a larger healing— the "protector" of the future life of the German people.

As the years passed, Erich would be haunted by the demons revealed that April day. But for now he could only grasp a small piece of the emotional rollercoaster Julia and her father were hanging onto. He glanced quickly at the row of distinguished Jewish professors sitting to his right. No one was speaking. None had risen to challenge Dr. Guett's remarks. Their eyes fixed on some unknown distant object. It was as if the sun had suddenly disappeared from the sky and they were hiding deep in the cold darkness of a great cave, waiting for the beast to come and devour them.

Erich suddenly reached over and took Julia's hand, lifted it to his mouth and kissed it, hoping the tall, blond student and everyone standing with him would see it. Kissing Julia's hand in public was the strongest protest he could make against the filth that had spewed forth from Dr. Guett's mouth. And it didn't go unnoticed by several of the German students and professors, nor by Julia's father, who smiled and nodded to Erich. Later, as they stood to leave, Dr. Kaufmann placed his hand gently on Erich's back and whispered to him, "Please walk Julia home and stay for dinner. We have much to talk about."

Then he turned and walked over to the Jewish professors who were still sitting in their muted state and sat down among them.

Walking with Julia was always a special time for Erich, but today he had no stomach for dinner or any serious dialogue with Dr. Kaufmann, who had come home early from the university. Instead, he left Julia standing alone on the front porch, greatly puzzled by his sudden silence and distance. He was disturbed by the dichotomous emotions playing out in his head between Dr. Guett's message of hate and the mystifying logic of necessity that lay behind the message. He no longer dwelled on hate because it was everywhere, saturating the air like seawater, until it dripped from the trees, drowning the few remaining blossoms of reason. It was the logic of the necessary so deftly concealed and emboldened by the sacred white coat of medicine that Dr. Guett's malevolent words hid behind that bothered him. He had used a medical metaphor to blend with the biomedical ideology of the Nazis, the cleansing of the race. A sick Germany can become healthier by sterilization of misfits with hereditary disorders. That is, if it stopped there. Would medical killing be next, disguised under the name of compassionate euthanasia? Yet physicians had always been the protectors of the health of a nation deeply obligated to the promotion and perfection of the health of the people. Nothing more should be expected of them by the state. No, Erich concluded, pushing logic aside, Dr. Guett's words were ill suited for young physicians and dangerous to the mind. He would think no further about them; yet he would stay troubled by the words, recalling them many times later.

Returning to Julia's home, though it was quite late, Erich knocked on the front door. After a few minutes, Dr. Kaufmann turned on the porch light and opened the door just enough until he could recognize Erich as the late night caller.

"Why are you here so late Erich? Everyone is in bed."

"I must see Julia."

"She is asleep. Please come back tomorrow."

"I am here, Father," Julia whispered, standing in the hallway behind him.

Without waiting for her father's approval, Erich took Julia's hand and led her out on the porch.

"I love you, Julia," was all he said, before turning and walking away into the darkness.

He had spoken these words many times before during their moments of lovemaking, but this time they carried beyond the simple utterances of young lovers in passion. They sprang from his soul. He had uttered them the first time they lay together in their secret Eden along the banks of the Vlatava. Inexperienced and clumsy as he was, she had simply held him tightly to her body, ignoring her own sexual awakening, for which he was thankful, and whispered softly, "I love you, Erich. I always will. Forever."

Julia watched Erich disappear into the night, and then felt her father's comforting arm around her shoulders.

"He is a troubled young man Julia, troubled and haunted."

"Haunted?"

"Yes, haunted, I'm afraid, by what he sees as the truth now."

"Truth should haunt no one unless it becomes mixed up with evil," Julia said, puzzled by her father's observation of Erich.

"I know, but Dr. Guett's lecture shredded Erich's innocence into a thousand pieces. It's difficult to see one's reality shattered before your eyes as Erich has."

"His reality?"

"Yes, his reality, not the reality you and I know and live in. I believe he understands now, for the first time, the futility of the Jews trying to stay alive in Germany, and perhaps even here in Prague. That is what Dr. Guett was telling all of the German students today."

"Oh Papa, how horrible," Julia cried, using the pet name she used to call her father as a young girl.

"We must be patient with Erich. Truth can become so fragile when one's existence depends on it. Now go to bed. We will talk some more tomorrow when the sun is shining and the day is bright."

Julia went to bed, but would not sleep. The terrible dream that she might lose Erich was there, waiting somewhere in the room for her eyes to close, and she would not let that happen.

FIVE

W e are all equal at our beginnings. But only for a moment. Then we become what history has long promised we must be. A few do escape, though, grabbed at birth by other gods promising a different destiny. The rest remain to struggle with what awaits them. Such was Julia and her family's promises given by history. The ancient Hebrew blood of her ancestors flowed through every vein in Julia's body, leaving no other course but that which was about to come.

Standing next to Julia, Erich's eyes focused on the official announcement recently posted by the university barring all Jewish students henceforth from the university, including the medical school. Before Julia could finish reading the devastating news herself, derisive cheers began to break out from the Sudeten students when they saw her with Erich.

"Get out, go, Jew, back to your filthy hole where you belong."

Erich quickly took Julia's hand, leading her outside into a small courtyard and then away from the campus. The German university's decision to dismiss all Jewish students was not unexpected. During the hot summer months, he had huddled almost nightly with Julia and her family around their radio, listening to the growing thunder of the Third Reich, now no longer distant, demanding autonomy for the Sudetenland. Nothing changed, though, until the following spring, when the Austrian *Anschluss* fell from the darkening clouds gathering over Prague like a thunderbolt hurled by Ares, the Greek god of war. No one spoke. There was nothing to discuss. But Julia glanced hurriedly at Erich to capture his face, as if it would be the last time they would be together.

At first, Erich refused to return to the university without Julia, insisting that were he to do so, it would be tantamount to accepting the newly adopted anti-Semitic policies. Instead, Dr. Kaufmann urged, he must become a voice of reason within the university, crying out at every opportunity against the rising sea of hatred now threatening to engulf all of Prague as it had Germany. He would do so, Erich promised Dr. Kaufmann, and do it well.

Monday morning at the university came slowly to Erich and the other students, as if history had decided to sit down and rest, perhaps to catch its breath and look around one last time before stepping into the smoldering fire waiting patiently for it. Sitting down in the main lecture hall, Erich glanced quickly around the room before realizing that he was alone in his row of twelve seats. No one sought his company, nor would they in the weeks ahead. The Jewish students were gone as well, and most of the non-German Czech students. The ones remaining now professed their own carefully rehearsed allegiance to Germany. Later Erich would say to Julia and her father, "The bugs are sneaking out of their holes."

Two weeks passed before Erich felt comfortable with the drastically changed student body. Everyone knew of his continuing relationship with Julia, but said nothing to him, as if waiting for a signal to do so. Then it happened. The wild shouts of the Sudeten German students rang out across the campus, their stamping feet echoing down every hall as they emptied the university buildings. Screaming on the airwaves, Hitler had promised that the liberation of the "oppressed" Sudeten Germans was near and that the Sudeten National Socialist Party would lead the way. Having left the empty classroom, Erich walked across the street and sat down on a curbside bench and looked back at the campus walkways filling with shouting students gathering throughout the university. The sound and fury unfolding across the campus became deafening, much like what he had witnessed years back with his father at Berlin University. It was then that the mind of reason began to weep as great bonfires began devouring a thousand books of knowledge, sending their ashes high into the night sky, never to be read again. The sight before Erich was little different than what he imagined the ancient German tribal warriors looked like as they danced in a frenzied madness around their fires at night. Even his father seemed moved by the burning of such knowledge. Years later, though, when asked by Erich about the dark night and the burning of the books, he could hardly recall it.

Before the students could move across the different streets ringing the campus to demonstrate their joy by smashing the store windows of all known Jews, the Prague police arrived and cordoned off the campus until a controlled calmness took hold of the students. One by one, the rowdiest were forced to line up in a long row and wait on the police captain to take down their names before hauling them off to the central office. As the captain, a lean and timid-looking man wearing tiny spectacles, started down the line of students, he stopped abruptly in front of the tall, blond Sudeten German student. "Name?" the captain asked meekly, noticing the National Socialist Party armband on the student.

"Franz Kremer."

"Age?"

"Twenty-seven."

"Are you a student at the university?"

"No, but I will be again when the Führer comes to Prague," Franz answered in a voice loud enough for Erich, who was sitting directly across the street from him, to hear clearly the threatening words.

At the sound of Franz's voice shouts of approval rolled down the line of students like the rumbling of distant thunder. Fixing a freezing stare on the captain, Franz continued, "Now is the time for you and your men to take a stand. You are either with us or against us. And rest assured, we will remember you when the given day comes."

Looking across the street at Erich, he screamed, "You piece of dog dung. You lover of Jewish devils. Hell will not be big enough to hold the Jews when we're through with them."

Erich tried to smile at Franz's words, but couldn't. He knew such words were no longer empty boasts, but would soon be filled with the gaseous insanity of intolerance already sweeping into Czechoslovakia and the rest of the Eastern European states. Later he would come to believe it had always been there, hidden from ages past by brittle bits of reason, waiting for the right moment to show its face again. Erich turned away, leaving the police captain to wrestle with his own courage in the face of Franz's warning.

After a twenty-minute walk that carried him through the Old Town square and across the Charles Bridge to Mala Strana, he entered a small coffeehouse sitting at the edge of the Vltava River and made his way to an empty table. The coffeehouse was number two on the list of his and Julia's favorite places, because at nighttime they could stroll unseen to a host of hidden places along the banks of the great river to talk and make love. Many times they would simply lie for hours entwined in each other's arms listening to the gurgling waters passing nearby, or to the soft voices of other young lovers seeking their own Eden among the heavy shrubs and foliage growing at the edge of the river. Other times they would talk, always pretending, about their future life together, children and doctoring and maybe leaving Prague, but never about what they knew was sure to come.

Erich sipped the strong black coffee and wished he had a cigarette to help calm the angst squeezing his body and mind with its paralyzing fingers. Surely as he stood there looking at the police captain and Franz, he knew Franz was right. The Sudeten Germans would be yanked free from the Czechs at Munich in a matter of days, and Prague would soon follow in a few months.

Erich sighed audibly. It seemed no one, not himself, nor even the great powers, had the stomach to defend anymore what was good. Duty to the state had become paramount to truth, when it should be the other way around. He was witnessing the wrenching birth of a monster that would kill its mother. Prague would soon be dead.

Erich studied his empty coffee cup like a seer reading tea leaves, hoping to find an answer to the promise that history had in store for him. For the first time in his life he felt frightened over his very own existence, not just Julia's and her family's. He decided that he must go to Julia and persuade her to leave with him now, as they had talked about, and if not with him, with her father and family. They could travel south with other Jewish refugees making their way to Palestine, or to Lisbon, or the Netherlands.

But he had nothing, only the meager allowance his father was still willing to provide each month, even though they had not spoken from the day his father's terrifying position on treatment of the Jews became known. Erich sighed again, only louder, causing patrons at a nearby table to glance his way. He knew the Health Ministry would soon begin calling in all the young German doctors for service, too, and his name would be on the list when he graduated. For now, there really was no clear way open for him to escape what history had promised him.

Fifteen minutes after leaving the café, Erich knocked on Julia's front door. As soon as she opened the door, he could tell she had been crying, because crying to her was a constant distant thing, never to be expected from the way she grabbed and took hold of life every conscious second of the day. There wasn't a moment of living that she regretted. "They were given moments," she would say, "and that makes them holy." So Erich was puzzled by the watery sadness in her eyes. Hearing his familiar knock, Julia had rushed to wipe away the outpouring of tears brought on by the humiliation her father had faced earlier in the afternoon while seeking the company of his colleagues at the University café.

Dr. Kaufmann was sitting alone in his study, facing the small front window, watching the last light of the day grow gray. It was always a special time of day to inhale what God has given us, he would tell Julia and her brother Hiram. And together the three would watch the evening shadows grow bold with descending shades of darkness and shapes until there was only blackness. For Julia and Hiram, though, it was not the glory of God that filled their eyes with wonder, but the tugging on the imagination as they eagerly sought out the faces and monsters of the world hidden among the moving shadows. Not every day, but some, Julia would find the stoic face of Rabbi Loew's golem staring back at her before quickly fading into another strange form. But now she saw nothing, the face of the golem having vanished along with her childhood dreams.

Dr. Kaufmann did not turn around when Erich and Julia entered the study. He was lost now in the past, wandering somewhere with his ancient fathers who, so many times, had been cast from Prague like lepers of old. He had taken Julia with him for a late afternoon lunch and coffee with a mixed group of Czech writers and medical colleagues, all old friends, at the University café. Entering the café, Dr. Kaufmann took Julia by the arm and walked towards a large table around which sat four men and a woman. There were no empty chairs awaiting him and Julia. Dr. Kaufmann also noticed the absence of his two Jewish friends who usually dined with them. No one looked at them as they neared the silent group. Before he could speak, Dr. Polacek, a professor of anatomy at Charles University, looked up at Dr. Kaufmann and Julia, and in a cold rehearsed tone said, "Do not sit down with us. You are no longer welcome here."

"I don't understand. We are Czechs and old friends, not Germans," Dr. Kaufmann stammered, clearly stunned by Professor Polacek's words. All the people seated before him, though, stared at their plates, none daring to look at him and Julia. He had become a leper.

Without looking up, Professor Polacek repeated his admonishment to Dr. Kaufmann. "Once, yes, but not now. You must leave us alone. Go away."

Before Dr. Kaufmann could respond, Julia tugged on her father's arm, turning him away from the table to face her.

"Come with me, Father," she said, taking him by the hand. "Believe me, no one here is worthy of breaking bread with you."

Then Julia looked at her father's old friends, all sorely shamed by their disavowal of his presence with them. She knew them all well, had played with their children and dined in their homes and sat in their university classes when she grew to womanhood; yet a lifetime of friendship had wilted and died this day because the sun had disappeared from the broad skies over Prague.

"Cowards! All of you," she said in a loud voice, causing those around to look at her, and then at the table of professors whose faces were paled with fright, none daring to watch their friend leave.

Dr. Kaufmann meekly followed Julia to the door, saying nothing. Nor did he speak again during their long walk home from the coffeehouse. After entering the house, he went straight to the study, turned his chair around to face the window and sat down. Three hours later, when Erich arrived, Julia brought him into the study, hoping to break through the spell that had captured her father, who still had not spoken or moved. Urged on by Julia, Erich tried to initiate a dialogue about nothing with Dr. Kaufmann to have him question the silliness of his thoughts as he always did. But nothing came. Nothing in the silence that followed. And soon Erich quit trying. The professor, now suddenly grown old from hurt, continued sitting in silence long after Erich left, no longer looking at the close of day and the sights he loved, but staring blindly into an emptiness that covered his window with a terror heretofore unknown to him and his family.

Mrs. Kaufmann brought a sandwich and a glass of milk for her husband and set them down quietly on his desk. Reaching to him, she gently touched his neck, then left the room, leaving Julia alone with her father.

Julia continued trying to break into her father's mind, speaking to him softly every few minutes at first, then yelling in frustration, something she had never done, not even as a child. Still he remained away from her world, staying as silent as a fieldstone. Refusing to leave him alone, Julia curled up in the soft cushioned chair facing his desk and drifted off to sleep. Falling asleep in the huge chair was a loving ritual for her that had begun when she could barely climb into it. It was there, in the years that followed, that she would listen for hours until she grew sleepy to intense eclectic discussions by her father and his colleagues on matters of the mind and body. Their strange, long words meant little to her, and it was her father's face and eyes that she would always watch. They spoke his passion for the subject and for life itself, in a way that words could never capture. All this was missing now in her father. The great winds of life that had filled his sails for so long had stilled. He seemed as nothing.

Hours later Mrs. Kaufmann stroked Julia's cheek to awaken her, as she would do when Julia was a child. Looking around, Julia saw the empty chair where her father had been sitting, still facing the window. Before she could say anything, her mother said, "Father left for the university to meet with the rector."

"Alone? The Munich Dictate is to be signed today freeing Sudeten from the Republic. There will be trouble, I'm sure," Julia said frantically, jumping up from the chair.

"Your brother is with him. They will be fine. Your father is an honored professor there."

Julia rushed to the kitchen, doused her face in cold water and, ignoring the wrinkled clothes she had slept in, hurriedly left to walk the short distance to Charles University, hoping to find her father and Hiram.

But Dr. Kaufmann had turned away at the last minute from his intended mission at the university to hurry to the American and British Embassies to request visas. Though many Jewish friends had already done so, and many had left Prague, he had never given thought to his family leaving Prague—it would have meant surrendering all he believed in. Yet he had wrestled with it from the moment the cruel insults were hurled at him in front of Julia in the café. Keeping it bottled up inside for the unspoken hours that followed, the decision to do so escaped him until he recalled, as he walked with Hiram towards the university, the rotund flushed face of Ladislav Simek, his dearest friend, who had been sitting at the table, too ashamed to look at him or Julia. Boyhood mates, they had sat side by side throughout their school years, even through medical school, separating at the end only in their chosen specialties. If Ladislav wouldn't raise his voice to defend him, then who would?

"Can't we wait to see what will happen, Father?" Hiram asked, unsure about his father's sudden decision.

"No, Hiram, there will be no more springtime for us in Prague."

SIX

Prague, 1939

E rich sat quietly by himself in the lecture hall, the events of the pre-
vious evening still clouding his mind. Within minutes after the
Munich Dictate was signed, ripping the Sudetenland for good from the
Czechoslovakian borders, hundreds from the National Socialist Party,
including many German Sudeten students, had taken to the streets across
the so-called "liberated" lands wildly smashing and destroying everything
Jewish in their path. Nothing was left untouched. To Erich, it was as if the
ancient gods of old had risen from their stone graves and, rubbing the dust
of a thousand years from their eyes, set forth again to destroy all that was
good and decent. Where does this German thunder come from? he had
repeatedly questioned himself throughout the night. Even the holiest of
the Germans, Martin Luther, had slaughtered thousands of Jews and non-
Jews. Perhaps the odor of intolerance is wedded with violence and has its
own special gene, Erich finally concluded, because reason has no room
for its smell. To see it this way, intolerance must be a wide pathway for
evolution, clearing the way for dumping the unfit that stand in its way. But
such crazy thinking was his father's along with a growing army of other
German doctors and scientists, not his. So why would he even consider
such a ridiculous connection?

Erich was shaken from his thoughts by the entrance of Rector Mann
onto the stage followed by a high Nazi medical officer in full uniform, who
had been kept hidden from the students until now.

"Students and future doctors of the Third Reich, be seated," Mann ordered in a military tone. "Those of you who will not become German doctors are excused, unless you too wish to hear the good news being offered today by Dr. Weber from the Health Ministry."

Extending his hand, Mann brought Weber to the large lectern positioned boldly in the front-center of the large hall, emblazoned with the ancient university crest. Erich watched the short, squash-like medical officer move to the podium, wearing tiny rimless spectacles that only emphasized his rotund bald head. Though he was from the Health Ministry, he wore the officer's green ensemble of the German army, complete with a side arm and Nazi insignia. Observing the man, Erich wondered if his own father too had relinquished the sacred white coat for the Nazi uniform when he succumbed to the call of the Nazi temptress, so cleverly disguised behind the mask of eugenics. Years had passed since he walked away from Berlin and his father in disgust at the growing voices calling for the cleansing of the Aryan race. His father's voice had been one of the loudest and most influential in the medical profession in supporting the virtues of sterilization. What Erich did not know now was the full extent of his father's involvement in the Nazis' medical ethos, the Nazification of the medical profession. Nazi policies with regard to sterilizing or killing people considered unfit for a society of the strong had been subtly combined with a vigorous enthusiasm for extending various forms of medical care to the entire German population. In this way, his father and the other doctors could continue to view themselves as authentic physicians, regardless of whatever evil smell the Nazis showered on their profession. Later, Erich would come to realize that a society of the strong did not include the "pitiful" Jew.

"Good morning, future healers and saviors of the glorious Third Reich," were the most understandable words Erich heard from Dr. Weber's high, shrill voice, as he began what would become to some, including Erich, a very troublesome speech to follow. For thirty minutes he talked of Germany's awaited day in the sun, praising its righteous might that all nations near and far trembled from. Then in an awkward gesture, he flung his short arms open wide, which caused him to look even more ridiculous to Erich, and made the pronouncement that the students must be the new medical and biological warriors for the state. Erich heard little else, his mind fixed on the words "biological warriors," until Dr. Weber spoke of a new shortened curriculum for the medical school, one that would focus on military medicine and population politics and racial biology, not that which would ordinarily be expected of a well-trained German doctor. His mind raced ahead to what this man was speaking in truth about, that the students were to become involved in a holy synthesis of marching boots and books. They were to engage in paramilitary training as students with a commitment of their bodies and minds to an all-out war against alleged enemies of Germany.

Then they came, as Erich knew they would—the only words that would give any rational meaning to what Dr. Weber was saying. They had always been there, unhidden for many years. But no one heard them as doctors except the likes of his father, who saw only what the greatness of science could do when combined with an ideology calling for racial purity.

Pausing before he spoke, Dr. Weber looked slowly around the room, staring at times at different students until they became uncomfortable with the coldness in his eyes.

"The Jews are our misfortune, a grave misfortune to a greater health for Germany. But let me say, that problem will be dealt with in time, medically, I promise you."

The silence invoked by these words was deadening, as if no one had heard them. Or perhaps they weren't even uttered, in of all places, a medical school. For Erich and some other students, it was like preaching a sermon to a full congregation on why believing in the Trinity was such a terrible mistake and needed to be dealt with. Erich, though, looked down at his textbooks, away from the source of the vitriolic rhetoric steaming up the lecture hall. His father's day had come, and in time he knew he would have to go home to face him.

Dismayed from the continuing blackened words spewing forth from the doctor, Erich started to walk out in protest, but thought better about doing so. Such a defiant act alone would be silly and laughed at and would accomplish nothing. Besides, something the man had said earlier before the ranting against the Jews began had stirred his interest. All medical studies would be shortened, which would allow hundreds of students to join Hitler's great crusade immediately.

Erich wasn't about to join Hitler's legions, but a pretension of doing so, he realized, would turn him loose much earlier from the clutches of the university. He could graduate in the coming spring, a matter of months, two years ahead of time. How qualified as a doctor he and the other students would be, absent the extra years of clinical work, was not his problem. He would be a psychiatrist, anyway, far removed from all the blood and guts pouring and leaking out of wounded soldiers, treating only their broken minds, might they have one. It seemed the ancient Nordic gods were smiling on him again, and would soon do so for Julia and her family, something the Hebrew God seemed reluctant to do at the moment, he thought. Surely now, a medical degree, albeit a woefully shabby one, would carry Julia and him far away on the happy wings of sanity to a safe new homeland.

When Dr. Weber finished, Erich stood up, applauding wildly in pretended joy with the other students at what he had said. Spotting Franz Kremer, the tall, blond Sudeten student whom he detested, Erich waved to him with a forced smile, then walked over to where he was standing.

"A wonderful message, don't you think, Franz?"

Franz studied Erich's sudden change of character, for their dislike of each other went far beyond mere opinions, striking at the heart of anti-Semitism. He hated Jews with a passion, while Erich slept with them. It was that simple. The persona Erich projected now was strange, and probably a sham, Franz quickly concluded, yet the door was always open to converts. Whether from fear or a belief in the cause didn't matter, so long as they became Nazis. In fact, to Franz, a conversion out of fear was far more reliable than belief. Fear makes demands on the most basic of our instincts—surviving; nothing else matters. One's soul can easily be bargained for then, because one has become nothing more than a terrified blob of human cells, each fighting for survival regardless of the cost.

"Yes, a great message of hope for us," Franz said finally, responding to Erich. "I am surprised, though, by your remarks. They seem strange coming from you. The little Jewish whore is no longer important to you?"

"Julia? No, she is history, a mistaken experience. Forget her. I have been studying the words of Professor Franz Hamburger of Vienna, a true medical believer in a real renaissance of medical science on Nazi foundations. You have heard of him, I suppose?" Erich said, inwardly delighted in the sophistication of his lies to Franz.

"Yes." Franz replied, though he hadn't. "Do you agree with him?"

"In every way. He is a very influential thinker."

Erich was unsure whether he could carry the façade any longer without laughing in Franz's face and turned to leave. Pausing at the door, he looked back at Franz and the Nazi armband he was wearing.

"Tell me, where can I get such an armband?"

"You must join the party first, like your father, Dr. Schmidt. He would be proud," Franz said, half smirking.

Stunned by the mention of his father, Erich struggled to keep his composure. To hear his father's name tossed so casually into their conversation by Franz brought threatening new questions to Erich, not the least of which was how important was Franz to Berlin now.

"My father? Do you know him?"

"Not personally, but the Gestapo does. He is a highly respected doctor whom the party will look on with great favor when the Jewish question boils over."

"What does the Gestapo have to do with my father?" Erich asked meekly, regretting terribly his rash decision to talk and josh with Franz.

"Not so much your father, but you."

Franz's words came at Erich with the fury of a winter storm. Laced with an icy demonic fear he had never felt before, they coursed through his body like a winter river, numbing his mind momentarily and blocking out the face of reason. Ice climbing with his student friends in the Austrian Alps always produced an exhilarating thrill laced with fear, too, but it was of a kind without which such a dangerous undertaking would be meaningless; yet the hidden meaning there was that you might die. Later, looking back on this brief episode with Franz, he concluded that the power of this emotion when turned loose and allowed to roam unbridled was far greater than anything the human mind could handle. Rather, it was totally alive and animalistic, like a herd of cattle stampeding wildly and uncontrollably, frightened by the jagged bolts of lightning and booming thunder of a storm. Without an understanding, the mind becomes blank, empty of reason, and we know nothing of what we might do to stay alive. There are no boundaries, except for the strongest.

Franz noticed Erich's sudden pale, stupor-like appearance and took hold of his arm.

"Are you ill, or did I frighten you?"

"A little of both perhaps. I suppose the idea of the Gestapo here secretly in Prague would frighten anyone. But tell me, if you know, why their interest in me? Is it because of my father?"

"You are not my friend yet, Erich, nor my enemy. However, we need not choose now which it will be; that time will come soon enough. I will tell you this, though: your relationship with Dr. Kaufmann and his family has not gone unnoticed."

"They are nothing more than friends."

"They are dirty Jews. Nothing more needs to be said."

Erich stared at Franz, trying to fathom the disease of hate festering in this man's body, oozing out now from every pore like sickened yellow puss. Where does such hate come from? Erich could only shake his head at the wonder of Franz's ignorance, and even that of his own. He knew very little about him except that his father was a very wealthy manufacturer in the Sudeten and was a main financial source for the National Socialist Party there. From the first day Franz entered the university, he would boast constantly about his father's direct line to the Chancellery in Berlin, and the important party members who would gather around his father at state dinners as if he were Hitler himself. Through such boasting, he immediately became an important leader of the Sudeten students, very dangerous, and never afraid to challenge the university over who should control the minds of the students. Quickly reinstated from his suspension by the university after the Sudetenland became Germany's, Franz ruled the student body, and he knew it. At the moment, though, he was tiring of the game being played out with Erich, and looked at him with mounting anger in his eyes.

"I will tell you this also. Hitler will come to Prague soon and the Jews will be arrested. The important ones first, like your Dr. Kaufmann and his friends, and then the rest."

"Franz, we are to become doctors, you and I, not soldiers. Politics and the Jews are not our concern," Erich said foolishly, trying to insert reason into the terrible discussion and help dispel his own fears.

"Ha! You fool. Didn't Dr. Weber's words just yell out to us to arise as doctors in defense of the Third Reich? There is much to be done with glory for everyone."

Erich noticed for the first time the large gathering of students beginning to crowd around him and Franz, eagerly anticipating some sort of physical confrontation. They were there for Franz should he need them. Erich knew what they wanted, but said nothing more, and began pushing his way through the circling crowd. Then he stopped and looked back across the open circle at Franz.

"You are right, Franz," Erich said, smiling. "Glory does await us. What kind I can only guess, but I do know we will be doctors, and that should make us different from all the rest." Then he saluted mockingly and walked from the lecture hall. He would go to Julia and her family to find the warmth he so desperately needed now, but he would wait until evening when the shadows were longer and he would less likely be seen.

Standing alone, hidden in the spreading fingers of darkness cast by the Old Town Hall, Erich waited patiently for the astronomical clock to strike eight before starting across the Old Town square to Julia's home. Paranoia is the first triumph of fear, and it was beginning to smother him. All else comes easy, he kept telling himself, once reason sinks in the rising waters of paranoia. And it is then, when reason drowns and dies, that monsters appear and everything becomes false, including who you are.

At the first strike of eight from the massive clock, Erich walked rapidly around the corner of the Old Town square, stopping briefly in front of St. Nicholas Church to listen for any light taps of following footsteps before disappearing into the winding streets of the old Jewish quarters. Julia's street seemed darker than usual to him this night; few lights shown in the houses and apartment buildings along the street as he made his way to her place. Turning into her walkway, Erich saw two menacing shadows moving slowly towards him from the right and braced himself for what he believed was about to happen. The shadows moved closer but abruptly stopped when a ray of light from Dr. Kaufmann's study suddenly split the night with its brightness. No longer able to conceal their identities, the bolder of the two stepped forward to confront Erich.

"We have been waiting on you."

Recognizing both men as classmates, Erich heaved a sigh of relief.

"Karl, Rudy, what are you two doing here? I nearly pissed in my pants from fright."

"Good," Karl said. "You should be afraid. Perhaps you will come to your senses now and leave Julia to her Jewish friends. Next time someone who is not your friend could be standing here."

Erich looked closely at the faces of his two friends and saw only despair, no longer the carefree happiness they had shared through their early years of schooling back in Germany. Every winter break, the Austrian Alps awaited their frolicking in the deep snow and their fearless skiing on the steep slopes, each racing the other two regardless of the danger. Summer found them eager and daring to try to scale the highest of the rocky trails. But when they came to Prague together, they tolerated Julia's gradual intrusion into the threesome only because of their close friendship with Erich. A greater loyalty, though, had fractured their tight circle now: duty to the state. And like the changing shapes of drifting clouds, all else would disappear, never to be the same again. What one might feel and believe today would be gone when tomorrow came.

Rudy, the youngest of the three, spoke next. "We have joined the National Socialist Party, Erich, and you must join, too. It is right that you do."

"Nothing is right anymore, Rudy. Everything is strange, even friendships."

"We are still your friends. Why else would we be here? We came to warn you," Rudy said, with some hidden pride in his voice.

"And Julia?"

"She has never been our friend, only yours," Karl spouted loudly.

How distant these dear friends had become in a matter of minutes, Erich mused. He no longer really mattered to them, nor they to him. One's future carries little meaning when undressed by fear, only that which you are afraid of, and what tomorrow might bring. But Erich knew they were as afraid as he was in a world that no longer made any sense.

"You should leave before the wrong parties find you here," he said, placing his hands on his friends' shoulders as if it were a final goodbye to another time. Then he turned away from them, hurt and angry at their callous dismissal of Julia's friendship from their life. As he had, they too had broken bread in her home.

As he stepped onto the front porch, Julia opened the door quickly before he could knock.

"I watched you from father's study talking with Karl and Rudy. Are there problems?"

"Where is your father?" Erich asked, ignoring Julia's question.

"Waiting for you in the kitchen. We can have coffee and some dessert there."

"The kitchen. I have arrived at last," Erich said, laughing nervously.

"No. It is warmer there. The night seems strangely colder for some reason," Julia said, turning away from him.

Entering the small kitchen where Dr. Kaufmann and Hiram were, Erich glanced hurriedly around the sparsely but brightly decorated room. How strangely different it was from his own in Dresden. There, uniformity in design and purpose set the décor. While unspeakably clean, nothing was alive. No warmth or love leaped from the walls to grab you as it did here. Four seemly ancient wooden chairs of questionable reliability and a table leveled by a carefully measured stack of wooden chips under two legs occupied the center of the room. On one wall were two odd paintings of bearded old men, whom Erich believed must be religious because they meant nothing to him. Everywhere, in the windows and along the counter-tops, brightly colored flowers sat in an odd array of containers, bringing their own special joy to the soul's eye. But it was the pleasant mixture of lingering aromas that stirred the senses of all who entered.

Seated, Dr. Kaufmann rose when Erich entered the room.

"Please come sit down," he said, extending his hand to Erich. "Mrs. Kaufmann has brewed a pot of fresh coffee and baked my favorite apple strudel for a late dessert."

Erich sensed a hidden embarrassment in Dr. Kaufmann's politeness and looked to Julia for some kind of explanation, but she continued to avoid his eyes. Hiram, though sitting directly across the table from him, would not look at him either. It was as if he had intruded on some holy day, though they had not meant it to be so. When Mrs. Kaufmann set the apple strudel dish in front of Dr. Kaufmann, the faintest of tears could be seen glistening in the corners of her eyes before she turned and left the room. Dr. Kaufmann started to slice the warm dessert but stopped and laid the cutting knife back down on the table. He was clearly sick at heart with what he knew he must say to Erich, but before he could begin, Mrs. Kaufmann returned to the kitchen leading by hand a young woman, trailed by two small children. Their clothes were soiled with filth from days and nights of hiding from police and rampaging mobs roaming the streets in every Sudeten town searching for Jews and gentile anti-Nazis.

Erich needed no introduction to the frightened woman, nor did he especially want one. Her kind had not gone unnoticed. A steady stream of weary and frightened refugees were pouring into Prague, first from Germany and Austria, but now from the Sudetenland, their horror stories numbing the civilized minds of those who would listen. It didn't take a bold imagination to grasp what life would be like for Jews when Hitler came to Prague. History's mistakes are forever repeated because the world will always sit smugly apart in its false innocence asking the same question: how did all of this come to be? Erich looked at the scared and crippled humanity huddled in the corner of the kitchen and knew then there was no more time left. After the woman told her story of watching her mother and father and other Jews chased naked through the streets in Karlovy Vary before being murdered, no one could bargain another tomorrow from God. One could only wonder years later where He had gone.

"Erich," Dr. Kaufmann began again, his voice more unsure than before, "we will break bread together this last time, then you must go."

Stunned by Dr. Kaufmann's abrupt words of dismissal from their life, Erich searched Julia's face for an answer, but she quickly turned her back to him, sobbing softly.

"You do understand the danger we face each time you visit Julia. The Czech authorities were here today, your German friends tonight."

"The authorities here in Prague?"

"Yes, inquiring about our religion and race, even what language was spoken at home. They wanted to see my library and the books and journals I read."

"They know you are Jews?"

"Of course. That was their only reason to be here. It is happening to all the Jews in Prague," Dr. Kaufmann responded, surprised at Erich's naïveté.

Before continuing, Dr. Kaufmann took a long, deliberate sip of coffee, set the cup down and looked longingly at Mrs. Kaufmann, pulling from her the needed strength and understanding she kept stored for him. At the same time, Julia moved around the table and stood close to Erich, their arms touching at first, then took his hand, gently pressing it to her side as her father continued.

"I am afraid when Hitler takes Prague, the end will begin for many of us—Jews and anti-Nazi Czechs, maybe gypsies. They will have the names, just like they did in the Sudeten."

"I will not come here anymore. Perhaps they will leave you alone then," Erich said without hesitation.

"As a man, your innocence continues to amaze me, Erich. No, we could be wrapped in the arms of your Jesus for protection, and they would still come because of who we are," Dr. Kaufmann said, smiling faintly at Erich before continuing. "Now you must leave, please, there is much for my family to discuss."

Erich could hardly breathe. It was as if a giant bell jar had suddenly dropped over him from the ceiling, trapping him in its vacuum and sucking the last bit of air from his lungs. If Dr. Kaufmann's words were true, Julia's fate would be no different than that which awaited her family.

Ignoring Dr. Kaufmann's request that he leave, Erich inhaled deeply twice before insisting that all the Kaufmann family must leave Prague immediately, and that he would go with them. Hearing Erich's boldness,

Julia released his hand and began to sob softly again as she waited for her father's words, which she knew would crush Erich, as they already had her.

"You wear your honor well, Erich, thank you. But arrangements are in place for Julia and Hiram to leave by train to Rotterdam and England as soon as their visas are issued. Mrs. Kaufmann and I will follow when we can."

Erich became silent, thoroughly whipped and unable to speak, his throat dry and hot. Julia would not look at him. Covering her face with a hand towel, she began to cry uncontrollably. Instinctively, he moved to Julia, taking her in his arms. In a few seconds, though, her spine stiffened and she backed away from him, no longer crying.

"Erich can come with us, Papa," Julia sang out, like she always did as a little girl when the sun finally broke through on a cold gray day in winter, filling everyone and everything with its healing warmth.

Dr. Kaufmann's heart ached unmercifully as he looked at Julia and heard her happy words. He had talked with her one day, not too long ago, about such a moment as this and what they could expect. Nothing is ever promised by God, he had told her, not even love. We receive what we deserve by our own goodness maybe a few seconds in our life, but it ends there, nothing more. All the rest comes to us by grace, if it comes at all. Julia's happiness was Erich's and would change in time, he knew, because happiness is made up of a million tiny moments, each one different, each one waiting to be lived. They are there waiting in the darkness where there is no light, but we must always believe so, or there would be no hope.

"I am afraid not, Julia. Your and Hiram's visas will be conditional on traveling with hundreds of young children as chaperones. You must attend to those in your assigned car."

"But Papa—"

"Our conversation is over, and so is Erich's visit," Dr. Kaufmann said, interrupting Julia. "You understand, Erich, what may be at stake here—my daughter's and son's lives," he continued, turning to face Erich. "Perhaps you can find some way to follow, but not with a trainload of Jewish children."

Erich remained silent, staring at the floor, mired in a despair he had never experienced nor understood. Many months later, while reading Kierkegaard's *A Sickness Unto Death*, he began to understand the magnitude of his depression and the sickness that had seized his mind after Julia left for England.

"I must be going, I suppose," were the only words Erich could muster, looking across the room to where Julia stood crying next to her mother. Then he went to her and whispered so no one could hear, "I will wait for you tonight in our sacred place. It will be the last time, and then I will stay away."

Julia said nothing, nor looked at him as he walked to the front door with her father. There Dr. Kaufmann unashamedly embraced Erich for several seconds before watching him step into the night, gradually fading from sight and their life. As he went, the last words Erich would ever hear from Dr. Kaufmann rang continuously in his ears: "You have been a dear friend, Erich. Some day we will be together again, I'm sure. Goodbye and God bless you."

SEVEN

Germany, 1991

Julia gazed fondly on Anna trying to sleep stretched out across the compartment seat, her body rolling slightly back and forth with each twist and turn of the fast-moving train. One generation was all that separated her from the fiery horrors of the war that had painted the passing countryside blood red fifty years ago. Now, looking through the dusty train window at the wide autobahn running alongside the tracks, every lane as far as she could see was filled with hurrying motorists speeding back and forth to their own individual destinies. It was a scene Julia would have eagerly exchanged for all that she saw on her first train trip across Germany to Rotterdam. Then massive iron tanks and long cannons and marching green-clad men were everywhere, loading her young eyes with terror as she held two frightened children in her arms. How strange. A distant moment and a present moment separated by a space of time, yet inseparable as the future.

Anna's generation and those that followed might care about history and the boundless magnitude of the human slaughter that took place along the passing countryside and elsewhere, but they would never feel its sorrow, Julia believed. And it is a feeling that becomes more silent each day, as the last days of the last warriors grow near. So it is with those whom fate let live in the death camps of Germany, like her cousin Abram. They will always feel it during some passing moment because they were there.

England, 1939

Anna was there, too, though she didn't know it, nor did Julia: a seed in Julia's womb coming alive the evening before she boarded the train for Rotterdam. Rushing to secretly meet Erich at Rabbi Loew's grave, they lay together with muted emotions in the dark and stillness of the cemetery, each giving their love to the other for the last time. But Julia was never certain that the treasured moment was Anna's time to enter history. Within two weeks after she left Prague and arrived in England, the British were rushing to mobilize what forces they could gather to wrestle with the German monster when the time came, which everyone knew would be soon. In the outskirts of London, all the streets around the temporary refugee camp where Julia boarded were cluttered with army trucks loaded with thousands of British soldiers, readying to depart for France. The exhilarating madness that always accompanies the rush to war before the killing and dying begins covered the city like a spreading plague. Julia provided no exception. Swept along by the mounting excitement, she would leave every night after bedding the young refugee children under her care and rush hurriedly to a nearby pub. There, struggling with her poor English, she would keep company with small groups of unnamed soldiers, listening the best she could to their history, laughing with them, but most of all reminding them of all that was still good in the world.

In time's passing, many emotional and conscious human acts are blended with a mixture of good and evil. In one moment, all the goodness of humanity may flicker brightly then quickly dim when doused by its own polluted waters. So it was with Julia one terrible night when her own sense of right and wrong would be scarred. Leaving the pub late for the dark walk home alone, she reached the narrow path leading to her dormitory. Running alongside a wide green where children laughed and played unafraid each passing day, the winding path took her through a magical tunnel fashioned by rows of young common oak trees on each side, their long, fingered branches entwined like thousands of loving hands clinging to each other. The gang rape came swift and brutal from the shadows lurching forward from behind the trees. Torn and bleeding and violated, Julia lay face down naked in the dewy grass, hidden from every passing eye except God's. Her rape by a drunken group of Her Majesty's soldiers came not because of who she was, but because she happened to be there—an existential moment when a wrong seemed the right thing to do.

Hours later the cold wetness of a passing shower gradually revived Julia's senses, and she made her way back to the dormitory, collapsing on the tiny cot in her room. Too hurt to cry, she stared blindly into the darkness hiding everything around her, including the terrible shame she felt. In the morning she would tell only Eva Stransky, her new friend, about the night's horrors.

From Bratislava, Eva had little in common with Julia except that they were both Jews; but they had become quick friends on the refugee train, sharing many stories about families and lovers during the long hours crossing Germany to Rotterdam. When Julia's story of Erich and her deep love for him was told, Eva said nothing but only smiled and nodded. No judgments would ever pass between the two, even after Julia gave birth to Anna some nine months later. When the time came to complete Anna's birth certificate, it was Eva who insisted to the government authorities that Anna's father was a Jew hiding somewhere from the Germans in Prague now that the war had started. His name was Eli Kahn, Eva continued with her resolute lie, a young silversmith from Brno. Julia had sat silent, not with embarrassment at the flow of fanciful tales from Eva, but rather in awe at such boldness in protecting Anna's honor. On paper at least, she would not be born a bastard, open to society's silent judgments and hidden smirks. And so, Julia became the fictitious Mrs. Kahn, married by a fictitious Rabbi Thien, with Eva as a fictitious witness the day before she left Prague behind, much too late to have her visa corrected.

Months later Julia sat looking wishfully through one of the two windows in the small family quarters assigned to her after Anna's birth. A cold, icy rain rattled the window with loud drum like rat-a-tats each time the gusting storm winds blew against it. Julia held Anna a little more tightly in her arms, as if the gods that had changed her life now wanted Anna as a sacrifice. With each wild rush of wind against the window, she would stir in her sleep before the gentle voice of Julia's soft lullaby reassured her that all was well. Julia wondered silently if her father and mother too were searching now through such a similar storm, trying to find the same god to curse for what had befallen them. Two months after her arrival in England, she had received a one-page letter from her father. At first, she left the letter unopened on her drop-leaf table, as if it were some ancient scroll that would crumble into a thousand tiny pieces should she touch it. But Julia's fears were its contents. Hitler's goose-stepping green men had been in Prague since mid March, unfurling their swastika banners from every open balcony across the great city. Even Hitler himself came to Prague then, racing ahead of his advancing army to Hradcany Castle, where he posed triumphantly, as Caesar might have done in Rome centuries before, from a high alcove window, looking down at a defeated people.

What else could there be for her dear father to write? Julia thought. The day of the Jew in Prague would soon be over. Putting Anna in her crib, Julia returned to the table and picked up the letter. Gently caressing it, she brought the envelope to her nose, catching the faint aroma of jasmine, which her mother always dabbed across the top of her letters, and began to cry. Not openly, but in a whimper, like a lost child. Even with Anna by her side, she felt more alone than she ever remembered.

Dearest Julia,
We wait each day for the mailman to bring a letter from you but nothing comes. There is little we are allowed to say to you. I would like to hear from you—that, for me, would be the best thing. Sadness fills our empty house with you and Hiram gone. If only dear God would bring peace so we could be together again before it is too late. This month was Grandpapa's yahrzeit. We lit the candle and you should too. You will remember to let it burn for twenty-four hours. If you have no picture of Grandpapa to put by the candle, pretend one is there and tell it everything you can remember about him, as we have.
Don't forget us, or your precious homeland, and God will protect you.
Papa

There would be no more letters from home. "Don't forget us," is what dear Papa had said. "What could be more certain," Julia cried aloud, startling Anna, who began to cry with her. Before Julia could think further about her father's letter, Eva burst into the room, frantically waving in her right hand several papers rolled up like a scroll. Her enthusiasm quickly dampened when she saw Julia's tears.

"You've been crying."

"Yes, my first letter from home."

Handing Anna to Eva, Julia carefully folded her father's letter, placed it on the table, and looked through the window again at the heavy cold rain forming large puddles of water in the small playground area next to the dormitory. If only Anna were older, Julia wished. They would play together in the small muddy oceans, having great sea battles with great armadas made of paper, as she and Hiram did a thousand times over when the heavy rains came to Prague. Like Ares, the Greek god of war, their father would watch over the titanic sea wars from high above on the back porch. There he would build more paper ships for whichever side had less so that no one could claim victory when the day came to an end. Those were the golden times of childhood, when nothing else mattered except the closeness of family, the kind old people think of as their mind slowly withers away.

Refusing to cry again, Julia turned back to Eva, who was walking back and forth holding Anna, singing softly to her an ancient Slavic lullaby.

"There will be no more, Eva, letters from home."

"Maybe. Some may have come through before the war began."

"Yes, we can hope that happened," Julia said wishfully. "Now tell me, what is the news? It must be monumental, the way you rushed in here yelling."

"It is!" Eva cried, bursting with joy again. "Colonel Moravec is forming different groups from the Czechs now in England to return to Czechoslovakia and join the resistance there."

"Colonel Moravec?"

"Yes, Frantisek Moravec, the Czechoslovak military intelligence chief who escaped to England the day before Hitler arrived. He is a hero to everyone back home."

Eva put Anna in her crib, gently tucking her in, then turned to face Julia.

"We must go, join together, and go back to fight," she said deliberately, trying to rein in her excitement.

"What of Anna?"

"Do you think Anna is any different from the thousands of children left behind in wartime?" Eva asked, surprised by Julia's question and hesitation.

"No, but she is such a little baby."

"My sweet Julia, there are 10,000 mothers waiting with open arms to care for your Anna," Eva said, taking Julia in her arms.

Julia broke away from Eva and walked over to the tiny makeshift crib she had fashioned using one of the dresser drawers and looked at her sleeping child for several moments.

"Anna is a Jew. Have you forgotten? What if they can't find any Jewish family to take her and she's placed with a Protestant—or even worse, a Catholic?"

"Do you think God gives a shit who clothes and feeds and loves little children, so long as they do it?" asked Eva, amused at Julia's surprising innocence.

Stunned by Eva's brashness, Julia turned away momentarily to gather her thoughts. She had never heard Eva use such a vulgar word before, but each day brought a new dimension to their growing friendship, whether she wanted it or not.

"I care, Eva. I care whether God does or not."

"You should, but the caring ends there. Wars have a habit of mixing up all sorts of faiths and then telling you yours doesn't count anymore if you try and go solo."

"What if the foster mother is an atheist? Anna would be an atheist if I shouldn't come back. I couldn't stand that," Julia pressed, fighting to hold back new tears forming in her eyes.

"There are no atheists in war. Some like to brag they are, but they're as scared as you and I will be, once the fighting starts," Eva said. Putting her hands on Julia's shoulders, she added, "We will fight together and come home to Anna together, I promise you."

"We will see," was all Julia could think to say.

Every time Julia looked at Eva, she envied without shame her beauty and richness for life. She had felt that way about life, too, until the terrible night of her rape. Something was stolen from her, swept away and lost in the changing winds of fate. Fearless, Eva would fight Beowulf's monsters barehanded should she have to. Yet she was draped with a simple peasant grace few people would ever know. Their deepening friendship began at the crossing of their lives the moment the refugee train chugged away from Prague headed for Rotterdam. Entering the car where Julia and Hiram were desperately trying to calm the mounting fears of twenty or so crying children, she immediately took over the scene. Gay lilts burst forth from her husky voice, unending for over an hour. With calmness restored, she walked back and forth in the aisle, laughing and making funny faces at the younger children and pouting and winking at the older ones. There was no end to her energy. Later she sat down next to Julia who was holding a sleeping child and simply announced, "My name is Eva. You and I will be good friends."

Now, as Julia looked at her friend, whom she trusted greatly, she found herself being asked to go to Colonel Moravec's headquarters and give him her life.

"Two Czech women who want to be heroes, is what we will tell him," Eva said, laughing loudly.

"Perhaps by chance we will find Erich in Prague and he can join us. He would, you know."

Eva stopped laughing, looking in amazement at Julia.

"Erich is our enemy, a German, until the war is over. We shouldn't forget that."

"No, he is different. You will see when we are together after the war."

"Perhaps, but we must get to Prague first. We will go to Colonel Moravec tomorrow early, to begin our journey."

EIGHT

Prague, 1939

S tanding on Charles Bridge, Erich listened for the soft gurgling voices of the Vltava River passing beneath him but could hear nothing. It was as if it too had been silenced in sadness this day, like all of Prague, by the loud rumbling of German tanks moving slowly across the bridge above its flowing waters. It was a good day to be alive, if you were a Nazi.

Finally, Erich caught the faint noise of water rushing against and past the ancient stone pillars supporting the bridge. It was a sound, though louder, that for no particular reason thrilled Julia each time they came to the bridge together. It was always as if she had never experienced such a sound before as the river went by. "A river has so much to say, so many stories to tell, if we will listen," she would say. "The voices from the bottom are deeper and different from the voices in the shadows on top." At first he was amused at the display of such playful wonder from her; yet in time, the ritual of listening to the river's voices became a separate moment in time for both of them, a moment when nothing else mattered except the joyous innocence of being in love. He was alone now with Julia gone, and the river had grown quiet, its eerie darkness now haunting him. Only the silence of an uncommon sadness could be heard rising from the waters. Prague had fallen.

Earlier in the day, Erich had journeyed to the Hradcany Castle hoping to catch a glimpse of Hitler, whom he had never seen. Standing behind a row of steel-helmeted soldiers, he watched, more in fear than awe, as Hitler exited his touring car and walked alone towards the massive open doors of the great castle. Shouts of "Sieg Heil" immediately rose from the Sudeten Germans like hosannas on high as he passed their frantic faces. At the door, Hitler stopped and turned, focusing his eyes on Erich's face for a second, as if he knew him. But no smile came from him. Gods don't smile, and at that moment Hitler had become one—a very modern god, but still of the ilk the ancient Germanic gods were in arousing the frantic passions of all who would look upon him. Erich felt it, too, but later he dismissed it as a moment of weakness, a moment when reason can be temporarily pushed aside by some unexplained emotion.

Darkness now covered Erich as he left Charles Bridge, walking slowly back to his apartment near the university. He had stayed too long thinking about Julia and where she might be. Approaching the Old Town square, waves of cheers from a huge throng massed around the statue of Jan Hus, the Protestant martyr, rang through the crisp night air. Standing at the edge of the square, Erich recognized several Sudeten German medical students and turned quickly up a side street away from the square towards the Carolinum of Charles University. The crowd was growing restless and nasty. Small groups began to tear away from the outer edges, racing madly around, smashing store windows and doors of several small Jewish shops facing the wide square. As the frenzy intensified, Erich wondered where the German soldiers were that had poured into the city all afternoon. Even now the distant strains of moving trucks and tanks could still be heard, and would be throughout the long night. Tomorrow would find a German soldier on every corner, but tonight belonged to a quickening madness.

Erich stopped when he heard the rapidly moving steps behind him and turned to face a group of hostile students and men shouting obscenities, rushing towards him thinking he might be a Jew. As they neared, one medical student recognized Erich and quickly silenced the virulent jeers of the angry mob now encircling him.

"He is a German, a medical student like I am, not a Jew. Look at his face," he shouted above the howling men. "He soon will be a soldier for the Fatherland."

Like hungry predators deprived of a kill, the mob growled and raced quickly on, hunting for another prey.

"We must follow them," the student said, taking Erich by the arm, "lest they turn on you as an enemy of Germany."

"I am a German citizen. How could I not be for my country?" Erich responded, looking incredulously at the student.

"You are seen by many students as a friend of the Jews—that is reason enough. Come with us, if you value your life tonight."

Erich said nothing more and began walking with the student towards the chanting mob, which had gathered next to the Estates Theatre. Someone began singing "Watch on the Rhine," and soon everyone joined in the rousing national anthem, including Erich. Singing for God and country cleanses the soul, his father had told him one Sunday morning many years back. Standing with his father and mother in Dresden's St. John's Lutheran Church, together they sang out Luther's "A Mighty Fortress is Our God" at a level that would have deafened the angels, and it thrilled him. His soul had been cleansed. He was singing for God. The same thrill surged through Erich as the crowd broke into harmony during the second stanza, and his lungs exploded with great gusto singing the patriotic words.

"Dear Fatherland, no fear be thine. Firm and true stand the watch on the Rhine," rolled from his lips with such intensity that even God might tremble at its force. Then he stopped singing. An elderly Jewish man and woman were closing their small leather shop across the street from the theatre when several men broke from the crowd and raced towards them.

"Jews!" they cried. "Stop them!"

The crowd quickly followed, blocking the door to the store and forming two circles of screaming voices around the old man and woman. Erich was the last to cross the street and stood away from the outer circle but close enough to seem a part of it to others who might be watching him. At first, only venomous tongues shouting obscenities threatened the man and woman. Then, as if it were playtime in kindergarten, unnamed hands began to shove the helpless two Jews back and forth across the circle, slow at first, then faster until they collided with each other, falling to the pavement. Two men quickly yanked the man and woman to their feet to start the game again, but this time the man and woman fell apart from each other from exhaustion and lay very still. For a second no one moved as the circle grew smaller around them. One man, maybe forty in age, handsomely dressed in suit and tie, seeming very much like a doctor or lawyer, walked over to the old man and woman now sprawled out on their backs. Looking down on them, he paused for a moment, then spit twice on the man, striking him in the face. Others quickly followed, until the faces of the old man and woman were covered over with gobs and mounds of dripping spit and phlegm and smelly tobacco juice. The last of the crowd tried to urinate on the two old Jews but couldn't as everyone roared in laughter. Frustrated, the man lashed out with his foot, kicking the old man in his side, then his head. Others joined then, kicking the man and the old woman, too, even stomping on their stomachs and then their faces. Only the old woman cried out at first, but grew quiet like her husband when the toe of a shoe shattered her temple and eye socket, flinging the eyeball to the pavement beside her. Laughing, the guilty man calmly picked up the eyeball and placed it on the sealed mouth of the now dead woman. Silenced by their own violence, the rabble began to disperse, each feeling giddy with the murder of the old man and woman.

Erich remained standing alone for a few minutes in the dark shadows of the street until the mob was gone, ashamed at what he had witnessed and not done. He had made no effort to interfere with the killing of the old man and woman, nor had he wanted to. An unrelenting fear had seized him earlier, when he faced the crowd mistakenly shouting the same obscenities at him as they had the old man and woman. Kneeling down in the blood still draining from the two mangled bodies, filling the cracks in the sidewalk beside him, Erich lifted the arm of the old woman and then the man, searching for a pulse, but found none. Julia's face flashed before his eyes, and then the faces of her parents. At the right moment on a given day, they could have been the shattered bodies lying dead before him.

It had come to this, as Julia's father knew it would, though perhaps sooner than expected. God would be beseeched tonight by a thousand angry voices and more, asking where He was in all of this. Perhaps the old man and woman did, too, Erich thought, standing and wiping the blood from his hands on his trousers.

He had been too occupied to hear the small police KdF-Wagen pull up beside him in the street but turned immediately when the car door slammed shut. Still clad in a Prague police uniform, the officer nodded to Erich and walked slowly over to where he was standing, looking first at Erich's bloody pants and then the two lifeless bodies.

"Pretty bad sight, huh?" Erich said nervously to the officer in German.

"You did this?"

"No, no, some wild men did who ran away. I was trying to see if they might still be alive, that's all."

"What is your name?" the officer asked brusquely.

"Erich Schmidt, and—"

"From Prague?"

"No, Dresden. I am a medical student at the German university here."

"Dresden, you say?" the officer asked, noticeably changing the rough tone of his voice to a more pleasant manner.

"Yes, my father is Dr. Schmidt at Berlin University."

"You have papers, I assume?"

"At my apartment. We can go there—"

"That won't be necessary," said the officer, returning the small notebook to his breast pocket. Then, after slowly circling the bodies, he stopped and squatted down, looking intently at the old woman's face and the eyeball resting on her lips.

"You don't see that kind of mess every day, do you," he said, pointing to the poor woman's bloody, caved-in face.

"I guess not, but we see a lot of bad things over at the hospital," Erich responded, feeling more at ease now with the change in the officer's demeanor.

"Do you know who they are, anything about them?"

"No, nothing."

"Jews, would be my guess," the officer said, abruptly turning away from Erich and walking back to his car. "We've seen a lot of this today."

"Are you just going to leave them here?"

"Why not? Let the German patrols deal with the old man and woman. They're running the show now."

"German patrols?"

"Yes, curfew checks. The Gestapo put them in this afternoon. They'll run from ten at night to seven in the morning. I'd forget about the dead Jews and get home," were the last words Erich heard as the officer sped away.

Staring for a second more at the mangled bodies, Erich wondered if they might be kin to Julia. They would be gone in the morning, taken to the morgue for claiming. But what if they had no kin, no one to wish them well into the next world? He was disturbed at the thought. A pauper's grave, or a cadaver for the medical students to fish out of a tank to carve on—this was all that was left for them. No one, except maybe God, would ever know they were here, or even existed. They had become a statistic for future historians to fool with, that's all.

Before leaving, Erich stood looking at the deserted streets facing him. Faint sounds of mechanized vehicles moving somewhere over distant roads could still be heard, but that was all. Quickening his pace, he crossed an empty roadway through downtown Prague and turned up the street leading to his small apartment at the end of a side alley. Once inside, he lit up a half-smoked cigarette, sat down on his bed and cried, much like when frightened as a child. But no one was there to hold him as his mother would do. Shaken by the horrors of the evening and the unrelenting fear he felt, he lay back on the bed, staring at the ceiling, trying to work through all that had happened. Even though he was only a German student in Prague, his relationship with Julia had been too open for the world to see. Besides, he had been warned. At this time in history, a Jew and a German were like opposite poles of a magnet, never to embrace. But he had tried to, and that was his sin before the authorities. With the Nazis in control of Prague, the Nürnberg laws would soon hang heavy over the city, turning many of its people against all Jews and those that befriended them. Erich sighed. Returning to his studies at the medical school here in Prague was no longer an option. Instead, he would assume the much-copied role of the prodigal son of old and go to his father in Berlin to seek reconciliation with him. There the prestigious wings of his father would carry him far in finishing the final semesters of his medical studies at the great Berlin University. Then, in time, he would find a way to escape Germany as others had, and go to Julia in England where his world would be right again.

NINE

Berlin, 1939

Traveling to Berlin from Prague became an eternity for Erich. No sooner had the train left the station than it was brought to a standstill, the first forced stop of many, as long columns of Germany's huge army crowded the roads and railroad crossings ahead. Moving slowly alongside the endless winding of marching men and trucks and cannons and tanks, all moving eastward towards Poland, Erich believed that war was near. Hitler would not be satisfied just with Prague and Austria; Poland was too inviting, and perhaps even the vast Ukrainian fields of Russia. When the train stopped at a point where the rail tracks and the road ran parallel across the Elbe River, Erich could see clearly the face of each passing soldier, seemingly all blue-eyed and blond to him, though they weren't. As the train started its own journey across the Elbe, he wondered how many of these young warriors would be sacrificed to slake the thirst of the few in power. What if he were with them? Would he be as afraid of dying as he was now? Watching the cold-blooded murder of the old Jewish couple without protesting had stained him like Cain when he slew Abel, leaving his badge of courage on the sidewalk covered with their blood.

Long into the day, Erich's train joined another row of tracks, and then another, as it moved slowly into a wide rail yard leading to Berlin's central station. Freight cars loaded with war material filled all but two tracks. Erich wondered if war might come while he was in Berlin, as he watched hundreds of loaded transport trucks exiting the rail yard, each carrying their share of deadly weapons to the awaiting German army gathering on the Polish border.

Away in Prague for seven years with his medical studies, he had seen little of Germany, twice by his count. Had he tried, he couldn't have imagined the greatness of the beautiful city that lay spread out before him. The scene was exhilarating. Wide boulevards lined with massive trees and glistening marbled buildings had replaced quaint streets once rowed with small stores and houses, many Jewish. Nazi swastikas flapping wildly with each burst of wind from passing traffic, mostly military, hung from the street corner lamps like Christmas banners, reminding everyone of Germany's might. Having taken Austria and Prague as it did, an air of invincibility covered the streets like the deadly gases in the Great War. But it was to the broad skies over the city that Erich looked. This time, when war came, the enemy would come from faraway lands across the oceans like invading aliens from distant worlds, filling the skies with vast armadas to destroy the land and people. The Great War had not touched the homeland, stopping at its borders. There had been little to rebuild when the armistice came; but this time, Erich believed, the skies would be filled with a fire unseen since the dawn of man, destroying all who stood in its way without mercy.

Erich's determination to see his father and finish his studies at Berlin University seemed to weaken with each step he took. He no longer knew the city and was forced to seek directions to the university from two approaching elderly women. After giving him the directions he sought, the younger of the two abruptly asked him, "Why aren't you in uniform like the rest of our young men, ready to defend the homeland?"

Taken aback by the woman's sharp rebuke, Erich offered no answer and moved quickly past her. Such a question would be asked again, he was sure, and he began rehearsing different responses to find the most believable as he walked on towards the university.

The towering university had not changed, but a huge swastika now fluttered from the tall flagpole at the entrance, where the flag of the fallen republic once unfurled. Entering the building, "Heil Hitler" filled his ears from a small group of uniform-clad students standing near the hallway leading to the administrative offices. Not knowing whether their greetings were for him, or for each other, Erich chose silence and quietly entered the rector's office, leaving the students wondering who he might be. Finding no one there, he returned to the hallway and walked straight to the students still grouped nearby.

"Please, tell me where I might find Herr Dr. Schmidt."

"Yes, he is in the auditorium speaking to a large audience of visiting professors and doctors. Do you know him?" responded several students, stirred by the mention of Dr. Schmidt's name.

"He is my father. Thank you," Erich said, turning to leave, causing the students to immediately straighten their backs and pay greater notice to someone they believed of importance.

The long and painful journey back to his father was ready to end. They had neither spoken nor seen each other during the last seven years of his absence from Germany. More angry than hurt at his son's refusal to accept the new science of eugenics and the great promise it carried for cleansing the Aryan race, Dr. Schmidt welcomed Erich's self-imposed exile to Prague. Even then, though, he could not turn him loose into the streets penniless—he was a Schmidt. Writing a short note to him, he offered only the allowance, nothing about reconciliation. No other letters would come from his father, only brief, sweet words every now and then from his mother in Dresden, always urging him to return home.

How his father would accept him was all that occupied Erich's mind. Nothing else mattered. Without his father's blessing there would be no tomorrows to finish his medical studies, no opportunities to escape Germany and find Julia. He would be conscripted by the Third Reich to fight whatever wars Hitler was preparing to start. Then he would be no different from the thousands of blond and blue-eyed soldiers who marched past his train. He would be nameless except to those that would mourn his death should it come.

Pushing open one of the wide doors leading into the auditorium, Erich moved quickly to an empty seat. No one turned to look at him. Looking around, Erich saw an odd mixture of people: professors properly attired with suit and tie, physicians in white coats, and rows of military officers in their finest uniforms. A group sitting several rows to the right and near the front caught Erich's attention. There, backs straight with shoulders squared, as if ready to stand and salute if called upon, sat many SS officers, an intimidating presence for any lecturer. Erich looked upward at the stage, which rose five or more meters above the level of the auditorium. Centered on the stage was a carefully crafted mahogany lectern with the university's coat of arms emblazoned on the front. Behind the lectern, speaking in a steady but tiresome tone, stood his father. Erich tried to focus on his words but was too fascinated by the makeup of the audience. Glancing again at the SS personnel occupying the front row, he looked no further. Heinrich Himmler's profile captured his eyes. Nothing else mattered now. Watching the intensity of Himmler's interest in his father's words excited Erich, but only until he caught the medical necessities being uttered by his father to promote and protect the health of the Third Reich. He was using his intellectual authority to justify and carry out medicalized killing.

"Our collective existence is a medical matter," he had said, raising his voice loudly for the first time and banging on the lectern with a fist. "Illness is a disgrace that can only be removed from the world by extermination of the miserable! We doctors, then, must be the true saviors of mankind and defenders of the Fatherland."

Loud cheers erupted throughout the auditorium. Leading the demonstration was Himmler himself, who had jumped to his feet before anyone else, clapping wildly. White-coated students followed, adding the voice of youth to the increasing cheers. Next came the stoic professors, rising as one from their seats as if commanded, clapping loudly but offering few cheers. Lastly, the physicians stood, some still amazed and stunned by Dr. Schmidt's carefully chosen words in support of active euthanasia. Erich stood, too, and applauded, though not out of praise for his father's words, rather that he had said them at all while showing some human emotion.

Erich waited for a few minutes for the auditorium to empty before approaching his father, who was standing in a guarded circle away from the stage talking with Himmler and another man. At first Dr. Schmidt's eyes passed over his face. Then he stopped talking and looked straight at him, his color paling as he recognized who stood before him.

"Are you ill, Dr. Schmidt?" someone asked.

"No, not at all. My son has surprised me, returning from Prague, which I find quite wonderful," he replied, reaching for Erich's hand.

Puzzled by his father's unexpected warmth, Erich forced a nervous smile as he was introduced to Himmler and two men he didn't recognize, Karl Brandt and Philipp Bouhler.

"Prague?" Brandt questioned.

"Yes."

"You were there then, when the Führer arrived?"

"Yes, I was standing near the castle's great doors. The crowd was huge," Erich said, relaxing some.

"Wonderful! Wonderful! You were a very lucky young man to witness such marvelous history. You must tell me more someday," Brandt said, shaking Erich's hand . "We will leave now and let you and your father visit."

Standing silently, Dr. Schmidt waited a few minutes for the stage to clear before turning to Erich.

"My prodigal son has returned, I see. But tell me why?"

Disarmed by his father's distancing again, Erich said nothing.

"Tell me. Is it money? Surely, there is a reason to bring you back to Berlin."

Erich looked at his father closely. Nothing had changed. He was everything he imagined his father would be after seven years. A little more stooped in the shoulders, perhaps. More gray than color in his hair. Clean shaven as always. But the same tentative eyes, displaying some unknown weakness, remained. His eyes had always belied a falsity to the power he so desperately tried to project. It was his brilliance, though, corrupted with a willingness to push beyond the moral boundaries of doctoring, that kept him in good stead with the Nazi hierarchy. Like the great mass of German doctors, he viewed Jewish patients as a group apart from true Germans and was prepared to treat them as such. A spoken sympathy for "euthanasia" along with a radical approach to eugenics had rapidly elevated his standing in the Health Ministry. In time, he would be called upon by Himmler himself to assist in *Lebensborn*, the "Spring of Life" institution for breeding the SS into a biological elite. When it became known to him that biologically valuable children were being kidnapped to be placed in the breeding program, he said nothing, but only intensified his research on the hereditarily gifted.

"I really intend to take the German blood from wherever it is to be found in the world, to rob it and steal it wherever I can," Himmler had wildly proclaimed on one occasion to Dr. Schmidt and others as they lined up, one by one, to give their souls to him for a cause of science that had no boundaries.

How much truth to reveal, and how many lies to tell his father, became the question for Erich. "It's not money. I came back because I need your help."

"What kind of help?"

Clearing his throat, Erich tried to look at his father before answering, but couldn't, and lowered his eyes quickly from his iron stare.

"I want to finish my medical studies here at Berlin University. That is my reason."

Dr. Schmidt looked closely at his son. He was not the same angry young man who had stormed off so long ago to take his place among Prague's intelligentsia. The look of despair on his face revealed that truth. But there was more he knew that remained hidden—finishing his studies in Berlin was no reason.

"Are you in trouble?" his father asked in a softer voice.

Relieved by the inviting tone of his father, but unsure of its sincerity, Erich revealed the troubling nature of his last few months in Prague. Included in his story was the disturbing murder of the elderly man and woman. Nothing was said of his love for Julia and her family.

"They were Jews?" his father asked, as if they were supposed to be.

"Yes, I suppose so. Why else would they have been attacked?"

"Being Jews was enough. But you were not involved?"

"No, but my sympathies were well known, and I—"

"That is the past, over," Dr. Schmidt said sharply, interrupting Erich. "You will speak no more of this matter here or anyplace else in Germany, if I am to help you."

"They were old people, Father, barely able to walk."

"What would you have done, if you could have helped them?"

"I don't know really. I was terrified."

"A Jew is just a Jew. That is all, nothing more. You must not forget that. You may stay with me until you find your own quarters."

With that remark, Dr. Schmidt turned and walked to his office, leaving Erich to follow him, which he did, meekly and shamed and more beholden than ever to his father.

Later that night, waiting for sleep to come, Erich's thoughts turned again to Julia. Darkness always brought her face to him. How difficult it is to keep love silent to the self, when everything about it is alive and screaming at you. Why love at all if the world hears nothing of it? Appearing silently back in the shadows of his mind, Julia's presence seemed more distant and puzzling to Erich. Fading in and out like faraway radio signals, he caught only passing glimpses of her beautiful existence before there was nothing. Fast asleep, a dream that would haunt him for months to come made its first appearance in the theatre of his soul. Standing alone, he was looking down at the shattered humanity of the old Jewish man and woman lying on the sidewalk, their faces turned to the pavement, twisted in death. Rolling the man and woman over, he looked no more than a second before sitting up in bed choking on his own vomit. The old man and woman's faces were gone, their flesh torn away by thousands of hungry, tiny maggots now eating into their brains. Later in the morning, when his father questioned the traces of vomit showing on the bed covers, Erich said nothing of his dream, blaming instead a sudden nausea from spoiled wienerwurst eaten on the train.

The same excuse would not carry the next time, which came three days later from a similar dream. His father said only, "You must be heavily troubled," then walked away not asking why. He had done this all his life, leaving the troubles of his family to Erich's mother. It was she who encouraged him to become an artist, or a great German philosopher, anything other than following in the giant footsteps of his august father. And Erich loved her for doing so, and she loved him, he believed. Still, it was his father's love he coveted most, for it would have given him respect.

The third night of dreams left Erich exhausted and beginning to question his sanity. His presence in the scenes played out before his sleeping eyes was becoming too real for his fragile mind. This time, though, the old man and woman were gone, their bodies replaced by much younger ones. Erich knew the faces before turning their heads to look at them. No hungry maggots this time, no rotting flesh, only Julia and Hiram, unmolested and staring at the stars as if they could see them. There was no vomiting by him, only a soft sobbing that comes when something precious is lost.

In time, Erich came to believe that the troubling nightmares were a clear omen of the Jews' fate should war come to Europe. None would escape it, not even his Julia and her family. The death of the old man and woman was simply God's way of telling you the truth.

As the weeks passed, Erich realized that his sudden arrival at the medical school had immediately altered the favored status of senior students among the professors. His father's immense prestige placed him above all the rest and he knew it, and he hated that it did so because of what was expected of him during the clinical rounding with patients. Stressed from the horrific series of nightmares, he would often find a small measure of rest by drifting into sleep during the morning reports. As a result, he knew very little about the patients' histories and what to expect when questioned by the instructing physician. Each time, when called upon to discuss the prognosis and treatment plan for a particular patient, he would struggle unmercifully, to the delight of the other students gathered about, none of whom cared for him. But it mattered little to Erich how anyone felt about him. After the tragic episode in Prague with the old man and woman, he had come to the conclusion that no one possessed a soul anymore, not even his father; and without a soul to question you, everything that is done and felt becomes a deception so cunningly hidden that the truth can only be recognized with great difficulty. It is then that one begins to dress in the many different clothes of pretending. None of this would change, not even when the welcoming news came later in the day that the dreaded medical thesis would no longer be required. The Health Ministry had drastically reduced the medical studies in order to provide more doctors for the state. Incompetence was of little consequence to the Ministry—all would be conscripted and ground into the war machine being assembled by the Reich.

At the close of an unusually long day, Erich was summoned to his father's office, which had not happened since his arrival. To be called to a professor's office was of no small concern to any student, but to Erich it was doubly worrisome when the professor was your father. Dr. Schmidt was sitting behind his desk when he arrived. Sitting next to him, busily leafing through what appeared to be a stack of official papers, was a man Erich had not yet met.

"Erich, my son, come in, come in," Dr. Schmidt said with a blustering, authoritarian voice, a false tone that Erich despised, a tone his father had reverted to many times in front of him when impressions were to be made. So Erich knew the importance of the stranger in the room. "Erich, this is Herr Professor Werner Catel, head of Leipzig Clinic. You have heard of his important work with children, I'm sure."

Erich knew nothing of the man, nor his work, but nodded, acting as if he did to please his father.

"A new young Dr. Schmidt, perhaps to replace the old one," Dr. Catel said laughing, turning to Erich's father, who laughed with him, though quite displeased by Dr. Catel's clumsy attempt to be funny.

"No, not yet, I'm afraid, but another semester should do it," Erich said.

"A mere formality, my boy, that can easily be taken care of, should you come with me to Leipzig. You will do well there."

Stunned by what he was hearing, yet unsure of what it meant, Erich turned to his father for an explanation.

"You must listen to what Dr. Catel has to say," was all he had to offer him.

"I am to be a psychiatrist, not a baby doctor, Dr. Catel. Why would you want me?"

"I could tell you because you are Dr. Schmidt's son, and that would be enough. But that is not an answer that will likely satisfy you. Rather, let me just say you should know that a child's mind is not always free from sickness," Dr. Catel answered, beginning to show a mild displeasure with Erich's reluctance to simply accept without questioning the opportunity being offered to him.

"But my training is with adults," Erich insisted.

"Good, children become adults."

Not used to being isolated from such a conversation, Erich's father stepped forward to the side of Dr. Catel as an obvious gesture of support for him. "Erich, your class will go straight into the military the very moment they graduate. They have no choice, nor do you, unless the Health Ministry approves a special assignment, as it has now for you," he said sternly.

It was his father's words that Erich listened to now, not Dr. Catel's. Only his father could keep him out of the military, a place where there would be little chance of finding a way to follow Julia to England. Should he try and be caught, he would be shot and his father disgraced. The one possible door he might find open could be in an unguarded hospital such as that at Leipzig. So Erich listened intently to every word Dr. Catel uttered about the new pediatrics project at Leipzig and asked only questions that pleased his father. Strangely, but not to his liking, he found himself professing considerable interest in the idea that he would be an important part of a clinic that was expected by the Health Ministry to become exceptional in its degree of specialization. There all the children would receive the blessings of medical science. None would go untreated, which pleased him greatly.

Later, dining with his father at the faculty club, Erich felt a closeness to his father that had been years in the making. Their talk was of home and family and Dresden, nothing about the war, which both knew was just over the horizon. Before parting for the evening, Dr. Schmidt looked wistfully at his only son for a second.

"These are extraordinary times, Erich, and to survive we must be extraordinary, too," he said, expressing unusual concern in his voice.

When his words were finished, in the rarest of moments, he reached across the table and touched Erich's arm. It was the best he could do, but it was enough for Erich. Then he got up and walked away, leaving Erich standing alone in the silence of the night, still wrapped in the warmth of his father's touch and words, all of which was new to him.

TEN

Scotland and England, 1940

M rs. McFarland, a stout and stoic Presbyterian with gentle manners, opened the front door to her small cottage the moment the
three women turned from the road onto the stone pathway leading to the
cottage. Rising early to tidy the rooms and prepare a makeshift nursery
for Anna, she had sat reading and knitting by the living room window for
hours, anxiously awaiting her arrival. Childless and a widow of World War
I, Mrs. McFarland's life consisted mostly of small farming and the church
and gossiping, which was not a sin in her eyes. It was a Christian way of
knowing your neighbor's hurts and needs, she would say, even though
they might be personal. As a Scot and Presbyterian, Mrs. McFarland
believed that man by nature was a mess, though she thought of herself as a
good woman. Attending Wednesday prayer meetings and Sunday services
and any other time the church doors were open, Mrs. McFarland tried to
make sure she wouldn't be forgotten when God's grace was passed out
among the Presbyterians in Scotland. Besides, the saintly John Knox had
preached twice in the small stone church she attended. What could be a
better reference for getting into heaven than that?

When the call went forth from the government for Scottish homes to
house children from cities in southern England targeted by Germany's
deadly bombers, Mrs. McFarland's doors swung open wide and never
shut until the war ended. But Anna would be her only child, and from
the moment she lifted Anna from Julia's arms she loved her. Watching
from her front window, she saw Eva and a Red Cross worker, followed by

Julia carrying Anna, come into view as they topped the long, winding road up from the small village below. At Julia's insistence, all three stopped to inhale the beauty of the surrounding green hills and glens below sprinkled with grazing sheep and tiny brooks that looked like moving ribbons of silk. "Mt. Sinai couldn't be any closer to God than this," Julia whispered to Eva as they moved on to Mrs. McFarland's cottage.

Neither Julia nor Eva could speak much English then, but words weren't needed when Mrs. McFarland reached out with her strong arms to embrace Julia. Seconds would pass before either one would release the other. Later, riding back on the train to London, Julia would recall the strangeness of Mrs. McFarland's embrace, telling Eva it was as she imagined God's would be, should He have real arms to hold her. Placing Anna in Mrs. McFarland's arms became a gift then, a moment wrapped in a burst of joy she couldn't explain. Eva only smiled and nodded and felt good too because Julia did, but she knew the pain of separation would not be far behind.

Later in the evening, back in London, Julia began to cry the minute she opened the door to her apartment and saw Anna's empty crib.

"What have I done, Eva? God will never forgive me."

"For what?"

"The sin of bringing Anna into this world out of wedlock and then giving her away."

"You're talking crazy now."

"No, no, it's as if Anna was a sacrifice to God that shouldn't have been made. I'm not sure He will trust me anymore."

"It will pass," Eva said, deciding to humor Julia.

"God hasn't always been gentle with Jewish people. You know that, Eva," Julia said, sobbing quietly.

"Yes, but she'll be living with a Protestant, that should soften Him up some. Just think, a Presbyterian and a Jew under the same roof."

Julia frowned at Eva's words, her eyes widening as if expecting God to strike them both down at any moment.

"Luther was a Protestant, too, and he burned ten thousand Jews," she protested.

"Luther wasn't a Presbyterian, he was a German," Eva responded, trying hard to keep from laughing at her friend's silly chatter, but her resolve quickly gave way to loud guffaws that shook the room.

Julia laughed, too, and felt clean again. Anna would be fine with Mrs. McFarland. They both had the same God, didn't they?

Later in the evening, after Eva had left, Julia pulled Anna's crib next to her, and began singing softly to the emptiness before her.

All love is of one thing, a singularity, Erich had told her one night while they lay together among the graves in the Old Jewish Cemetery. "You can't separate it into two parts, any more than you can divide the basic matter of the universe," he had said. Such heady chattering was always too much for Julia, especially when wanting to make love to him. The idea of love was simple and shouldn't be cluttered up with the heavy baggage of philosophical conjectures. Yet listening to his distant voice now gave hope to Julia that such idle talk might be true. Mrs. McFarland could be singing to Anna this very moment, gently rocking her, too, covering her with the same love they both possessed. Sleep came easy then to Julia, a deep and welcoming sleep that left her rested in mind and body for all that was to come tomorrow and the tomorrows after.

Disappointment damned Julia and Eva when they first offered their services to Colonel Moravec, the Czechoslovak intelligence chief who had escaped Prague. Their expected early return to Prague was quickly squashed by their total ignorance of the English language and Eva's somewhat dismal German. Nonetheless, they were happily welcomed and initially assigned to a unit of the Czech government in exile that had begun working closely with British Intelligence. For twelve weeks, beginning every day at dawn till dinner, they were unmercifully subjected to a pounding of English into their tired brains, branding the mind as if hot cattle irons had been used so nothing would be forgotten. Sunday was the day of rest, not Saturday, their Sabbath. But Eva, who had long figured that God, at this particular moment in history, didn't give a rat's ass, jokingly convinced Julia that Moses certainly didn't stop looking for food on the Sabbath when he had all those hungry Jews bitching at him for being lost in the wilderness. So Sunday became a day of rest. For Julia, Sundayswas also when she had the joy of writing short nursery rhymes in Czech to Anna, singing along as she did, as if Anna were there with her. Whether Mrs. McFarland could pronounce the rhymes properly, brogue and all, was of no matter to Julia. It was the love that she would bring to Anna's young soul that emboldened her heart. In time, though, the rhymes turned into broken English, then a wholeness as Mrs. McFarland sang them to little Anna with a sweetness and joy in her voice that any mother would envy.

At first, Julia would not write a letter to Mrs. McFarland until it was proper and correct, believing she might think her ignorant and poor as a mother. Only short notes penned by the Red Cross worker asking Mrs. McFarland to recite the rhymes the best she could went to her. On the day Julia chose to write the first of many letters to come, one hour would pass before she accepted the first page of what she had so meticulously put down. By comparison, Mrs. McFarland's letters, which arrived regularly on Wednesdays, were always short sentenced and folksy simple, filling Julia's mind with bright, colorful images of what Anna must look like.

Twelve weeks into Julia's absence from Anna, a letter arrived from Mrs. McFarland inviting Julia to spend the approaching Easter holidays with her. She need not concern herself with the Christian festivities of the weekend, and would have two glorious spring days to be with Anna, Mrs. McFarland wrote. So Julia went, choosing to leave on Friday afternoon. Arriving alone late in the evening this time, and trudging up the long, sparsely graveled road to Mrs. McFarland's cottage, she stopped to rest. Looking across the rolling hills and deep valleys, made mysterious by the night, Julia felt for the first time a lightness of being, the insignificance of her own existence. How can we live in so many distant and disconnected worlds, she sang out loud to no one. Erich's, Anna's, her family's—all separate from hers. It's in these moments that wonder comes along, she believed, when we must live beyond time, where all that we are arises with our thoughts.

A distant dog's barking startled Julia, shaking her from the moment she was in, and she moved on quickly towards Mrs. McFarland's cottage. Within seconds, a light marking the cottage appeared at the rise of the road, breaking through the thick blackness surrounding her like a lonely harbor light. An eerie quietness returned as she reached the stone path leading from the road to the cottage. Standing on the door stoop, cradling a restless Anna in her arms, Mrs. McFarland fired the chilly spring night with her radiant smile as Julia approached.

"I thought maybe, my dear, you would like to put Anna down tonight yourself. She's been waiting up a long, long time to see you, you know."

Taking Anna into her arms and kissing her, Julia burst into tears, crying openly. "I know, and I thank you for that."

Later that night, with Anna fast asleep, Julia listened for hours to the first of many stories she would one day tell Anna, stories about her infant years and a kind and gentle woman named McFarland who loved her and raised her and who just happened to be a Presbyterian and not a Jew. For each visit, Mrs. McFarland carefully wrote the stories on sheets of faded stationery, giving them to Julia to put with the ones that would someday come from Julia about Anna.

As the evening passed, neither one seemed willing to end the day, passing back and forth their own life stories until each felt they had known the other a lifetime. Julia had come to wonder how such a small house, empty of family, could hold so much love. Her own had been greatly different, full of family voices whose echoes would long be heard in the silence after they were gone. Perhaps it was so with Mrs. McFarland. Three years of marriage can become a lifetime of love, when that's all you are given. Entering the Great War at nineteen years of age, Robert McFarland died somewhere on the fields of Flanders face down in a rain-soaked crater with the back of his head blown off. Mrs. McFarland never married again, nor cared to be in the company of single men. "Surely if I did," she would say when asked why, "there'd come another war or two and take him from me. And I want no more of that kind of sadness." So the love she kept within for Robert burst forth like a nightingale's song the moment she first took Anna in her arms. Julia knew then that when the day came for her to take Anna back, Mrs. McFarland would die once more inside.

Morning brought more unexpected surprises to Julia, though not altogether pleasant. Sitting down to a late breakfast, Mrs. McFarland placed before her a small, warm bowl of haggis, smiling as she did.

"A good breakfast is that you need, dearie, if you are to walk the hills with me this day," was all she said.

"Would I be rude to ask what it is?"

"Not at all, most people do. A full meal is what it is—oatmeal, onions and sheep mixed together and cooked. That is all you need to know."

Later during their walk to the nearest neighbor and beyond, Julia asked again what it was she had tried to eat but couldn't. When the truth came, Julia smiled.

"I can understand now why the Scots fought as much among themselves as they did against the English, eating such a meal."

Then realizing she might have offended Mrs. McFarland, Julia stopped smiling and quickly apologized for her rude remark.

"Nae, you needn't say you're sorry. They would've fought the same without the haggis, just to be fighting. Battling flowed through their veins, not blood," Mrs. McFarland said, putting her arm around Julia, laughing.

But then she grew silent for a moment, watching a young spring lamb trying to steady itself and suckle from its mother. Julia noticed the beautiful moment, too, but also the small tears in Mrs. McFarland's eyes.

"I am afraid the hills will be full of widows again," she said. "Most of the young men, and those fit to fight among the older ones, have already gone. But you know that, with your Erich gone."

Julia felt ashamed. She had not told Mrs. McFarland the full truth about Erich, or Anna's birth out of wedlock, or the terrible night of her rape. No one knew outside of Eva and never would.

"Will you be leaving tomorrow for London?"

"Yes, but after you have gone to church to celebrate your Easter."

"Come with me then, you and Anna. We will sit together."

"Have you forgotten, I am Jewish?"

"Aye, today is your Sabbath and tomorrow is mine, and I'm sure the good Lord doesn't care which is which."

"Your neighbors might. No, I will sit with Anna and talk of God to her and wait for you. Besides, I know nothing of your service and would feel foolish," Julia said, yet fascinated with Mrs. McFarland's suggestion. What a wonderful story, though, it would be to tell her good father and mother someday. Sitting and singing and praying on Easter Day in a Christian church, and a Presbyterian one at that.

"You need not feel foolish, dearie. The preaching you can ignore. It's the reading of the Old Book and the singing that would be for you."

Most of the congregation was already seated when Julia arrived and took her seat next to Mrs. McFarland, who was holding Anna. Many of the women were dressed no better than she, with scarves of poor color covering their heads. Others, wearing the brightest of their Sunday best, sat proudly with their families, all the while looking around at Julia. But the pride was Angie McFarland's this day, sitting next to Julia—a distant young warrior from Prague who would be fighting alongside their own Scottish lads against the Germans. Nevertheless, for the rest of the congregation, seeing a Jew sitting in a Presbyterian church this far north in Scotland, where even a Catholic might still fear to be, was a rare treat for the tongues of those who cared. And Julia felt it, even though their tongues kept silent. The final amen would not come too soon for her.

Riding back to London on the late afternoon train, the wonders of the weekend played on Julia's mind like the soft chords of a Brahms's lullaby. The sweetness of Mrs. McFarland was everywhere. She had boxed a small dinner of raw vegetables, with buttered raisin bread and oatmeal cookies, none store bought, for Julia to eat on the long ride home. Looking back at the day, getting through Easter services wasn't too bad, Julia thought. Everybody was polite, some more than others, and smiled. It was the preaching that was miserable. An hour and a half of condemning sin and about everything else rotten in the world didn't leave much room for talking up what was good. That is, unless there was a lot of explaining to do among the church folks. Praying was special, though, because the good Lord was asked to protect all those souls soon going to war enough times to include her and Eva, Julia believed. Then everyone recited the 23rd Psalm, her father's favorite, which sent cold shivers down her spine with the "valley of death" waiting in Prague for her.

Julia felt good now. In all her life, with churches circled around her, she had never once sat through a Protestant or Catholic service, not that she didn't want to, or was prohibited by her father. Julia knew she wasn't welcome unless she was ready to become a Christian, which she would never do. Mrs. McFarland was different, though. Being a Jew was who Julia was, and being a Presbyterian was who she was. Nothing else mattered and Julia loved her for it. As Julia was leaving, Mrs. McFarland had taken her hand and said, "We are family now, you and me. So you must not call me Mrs. McFarland anymore. Angie is my name, you know, and I love you dearly." What wonderful stories she would keep to tell Anna someday.

Julia watched the early evening shadows racing along beside the train and over the open green fields and hills, where every now and then a gathering of sheep stood together watching the train pass by. As the shadows darkened to night, lights began to appear among the sprinkling of cottages on the hillsides near the tracks. Easter day was over for these good people, Julia thought; and her own Passover, too, she guessed, unsure when the Jewish festival celebration of freedom was to begin and end. A nostalgic sadness smothered Julia, pulling the air from her lungs. Longing for home is a terrible thing; only now did she know and understand this.

ELEVEN

Eva and Hiram came into Julia's view the moment the train rolled to a stop alongside the passenger platform in King's Cross station. Stepping down hurriedly from the car, she rushed to embrace both of them. Why Eva and Hiram were together was a story Julia wanted to hear, but it would come later when she and Eva were alone. Right now, her brother's face was all she wanted to see. Months had passed since they had been together and talked. Julia looked at her brother, older by two years than she, now proudly dressed in a Royal Air Force uniform. After months of studying English, as Julia did, he enlisted in the RAF, along with a group of other Czech men. Hiram's intellect and advanced schooling moved him quickly into the pilot training program for the new four-engine Avro Lancaster bombers arriving weekly at Mildenhall.

"I will be flying out of the Mildenhall air base, forty or so miles from here," he said, beaming with that wide grin that set him apart from most other men.

"You are so easy to look at, and my brother, too," Julia laughed, throwing her arms around Hiram's neck and kissing him. Hiram was handsome, in a distinguished way. "A fine Jewish-looking man," their father used to say teasingly, as if there were such a thing.

Like his father, Hiram was overly proud of his Jewish blood, perhaps more so than Julia. Together, they had initially frowned on Julia's close relationship with Erich, but each gave way as the goodness in Erich became apparent. Hiram had hoped his sister would come to see the rapidly increasing walls of hate rising everywhere throughout Europe against the Jews, and the terrible ending that was sure to come from her relationship with Erich. But the day Julia told him she loved Erich—"every inch of his German skin," she had said, bursting with rapturous joy, he embraced Erich as he would a brother. They became even closer the day the Sudetenland was annexed by Germany and the trashing and beating and killing of Jews began. Fearful for Julia's safety and his mother's, he rushed home to find Erich standing on the front porch, a steel bar in hand, ready to face alone what might come. Through the passing of the night they sat together on the steps, talking endlessly at first, then resting, but all the while listening to distant angry sounds in the night, of marauding youths looking for someone to hurt. When the given grace of dawn came, he eagerly embraced Erich before he left, as he would his father, or anyone else he loved. From that day on, no one would speak ill of Erich in front of Hiram.

After greeting Hiram, Julia glanced at Eva, who was waiting patiently to be hugged, too. Three days of separation in alien lands can seem like a year, where the feeling of belonging still eludes you. Julia and Eva were embraced by their small group of Czech comrades, but still looked on with great suspicion by many others as intruders in their kingdom. Ever mindful of this fact, Julia and Eva never left each other's side, always appearing humble and grateful wherever they went in public. Even Hiram felt the silent glances at first, too, but as casualties among the airmen rose, the glances were replaced with smiles. Little would change for Julia and Eva, though, until the Nazi blitzkrieg that crushed France and England stood alone—a time which was soon to come.

"Did Hiram keep you company while I was in Scotland with Anna?" Julia asked, fishing for a reason Eva and Hiram were together.

"Yes, quite nicely, I might say," Eva replied teasingly, causing Julia to step back with a puzzled look at her friend and then at Hiram.

"We went to a small synagogue together Saturday, hardly a place to get in trouble. It was Passover week, you know, or had you forgotten?" Hiram said.

Julia had never thought of Eva and Hiram being together. "A sophisticated intellect" was the best way to describe Hiram, though he always kept his feet firmly planted on the ground with his head just beneath the clouds. Eva kept her head nowhere near the clouds, and her feet deep in the rich soil of her farm home along the winding Danube River, edging Bratislava. Coarse in language and manners and poorly educated, she was everything Hiram wasn't or likely to become. A peasant of the land, Eva inhaled the staleness of life others avoided as easily as the fresh air around her, never complaining, never afraid of what the next storm might bring to her life. Unreligious all her life, she believed that all God requires of anyone is that they live and die the best they can. Eva was as beautiful as Julia, yet in a different way. Long sought as a prize by the young and old men working the endless vineyards and fields around her, no one could reach her heart. Strangely though, it was Julia who filled her soul with love.

Walking between the two as they left the train station, Julia took hold of Hiram's and Eva's hands, eagerly entwining her fingers with theirs to capture for a few moments longer the warm happiness of being together. After but a few steps, Hiram stopped and turned to Julia, discarding the mask of gladness he was wearing when she arrived.

"Denmark and Norway have surrendered to Germany. The Netherlands and Belgium will be next. When that happens, they will crush the French army and take Paris," Hiram said.

"France—how can that be?" she asked, stunned by the unexpected news.

"Stupidity mostly, ignoring a festering sore until it became cancerous. That's what Europe did, thinking it would get well by itself. The German cancer will spread here, too, when it is ready."

"It will be more difficult for them to move their army across the channel. The British will not quit so easily," Julia said defiantly.

"Perhaps. But Hitler will come after England as sure as he marched into Prague," Hiram said, walking away from Eva and Julia back towards the station.

Hiram's reference to Prague brought tears to Julia's eyes. Germany was there and would be for years to come, if not forever, it seemed to her. And they will be here, too, maybe. Then nothing would be left of hope and all of the tomorrows she wished for Anna.

"There is no promise, not even from God, that children will have a world to live in, that things will always be the same," her father had whispered to her the evening before she left Prague with Hiram. "Even God was not that foolish to think this might be. But we must smile and hope, as if it were so."

Then they walked onto the front porch and sat down on the steps together for the last time, looking at the stars and the passing moon and all else they had seen a million times before. After long moments of silence, he took Julia's hand and held it tightly, whispering again to her, "You must remember that a time of happiness has no separate existence of its own, no separate breath apart from the moment we experience it. When that moment passes, what we lived withers in the darkness and is gone. It takes courage to love life, Julia, and for that it takes a gift for life. You have that gift, my precious daughter, more than anyone in the family." Then, standing, he started to return indoors but stopped and looked back at Julia for a long minute, knowing without thought that the future would take her from him.

"You remember Goethe's words, don't you, Julia?" he asked, with tears now covering his face.

"What words, Papa? I don't remember."

"His words from the game we used to play when you were ten, reading the great philosophers and trying to figure out what they were trying to tell us. Goethe was one of your favorites."

"I still don't remember, Papa, there were so many," Julia said, trying desperately to find the words her father sought from a distant time.

"'There is nothing more valuable than this day.' I'm surprised you have forgotten such beautiful words. You shouldn't, they will carry you in the days ahead."

"I won't, Papa," Julia said, but her father had already gone inside, leaving her to cry alone.

Later, she knew the words spoken by her father were true. The great joy she had experienced with Anna and Angie McFarland the last two days was gone, as if it had never been.

Hiram stopped at the main exit door and took Julia in his arms, holding her close for several seconds.

"I must stay here at the station and wait. The train to Mildenhall should leave in less than an hour."

"We will wait with you," Julia said quickly, refusing to let go of Hiram's hand and starting back into the station with him.

"No, go. You have your own schedule to worry about, and it's late. We will be together again soon, I promise you."

With that, Julia embraced Hiram, sobbing at first, then unleashing a sea of tears unabashedly, causing a few in the station to look her way.

"We'll all be together soon, won't we, Hiram? Papa and Mama and you and me—our family."

"Yes, in time. Who knows, England may sue for peace, if France falls," Hiram half jested, signaling to Eva with his eyes to leave quickly with Julia, which she did.

As they turned a corner away from the station to begin the long trek to their billets, Eva released her hard grip on Julia's hand, then gently took hold of it again as they walked along in silence.

"It seems we are always saying goodbye in this world," Julia said after a few minutes, wiping the tears from her eyes. "I wonder if we'll ever stop doing so."

"I don't know. Goodbye is too harsh a word, so I never say it," Eva replied.

"That doesn't seem right."

"Well it is. You never leave a person as long as they can remember who you are and were. If they can't, it doesn't make any difference what you say, or if you're gone, or standing there with them."

"Well, it still doesn't seem right not to say good-bye, to wish them well."

"When I left home to come to Prague, my grandmother didn't say one word of goodbye, 'cause she didn't know who I might be. In fact, she thought I was one of those Hungarian whores who slip now and then into Bratislava when business is slow in Budapest, and she said she certainly wasn't going to say goodbye to some whore she didn't know," Eva said, trying hard to keep a straight face, even though what she had said was true.

Julia stretched her eyes wide at Eva's words for a second, then burst out laughing. The depth of Eva's homegrown intelligence and wit continually amazed her. With little formal schooling, what she could come up with at a moment's notice to untangle a sticky conversation could challenge the gods. To Julia, Eva could give light to the darkest of nights when the moon and stars stayed hidden and to the days when there was no sunrise. Her learning came from a wisdom deep in the soil around her, a thousand years of listening to all who came before her, and who had worked the land as she did. But in her training with Czech intelligence, Eva would always defer to Julia because she could reach inside the nuts and bolts being put before them haphazardly and find the solution they wanted to hear.

Thirty minutes after leaving the station, they neared the dense row of trees near the billets where she had been attacked. Julia stopped and looked and listened, not for any human shadows that might be waiting along the dark pathway before them, but for the sounds of the night. Even now, wherever she went, they always seemed to be around her.

"God's guardian angels," her mother had told her one night, as they listened to the rustling sounds together. "They are moving about, here and there as fast as they can, watching over all of us when we sleep."

When she told Hiram about the angels, he laughed and teased her for days about such foolishness, making her cry each time. Then late one night when she was listening to the sounds in her bed, he tiptoed in and said, "The sounds you are hearing are the souls of bad people rushing around, trying to find a place to sleep, maybe even with you," causing her to cry even louder, much to his delight. Julia didn't believe in angels anymore, but she still loved the sounds moving through the trees at night, as she did the voices of the river, because they told her she was alive.

"Are you alright?" Eva asked, puzzled by Julia's sudden behavior.

"Oh yes, I'm fine. Wait—you can hear them, can't you?"

"Hear what, for god's sake?"

"Those sounds—the wind and the leaves and the—"

"You are tired, Julia. Your head is too fuzzy-full of joy and sadness, when there is room for only one or the other, not both at the same time."

"I know. But they'll still be there tomorrow night and all the nights afterwards, and I'll keep on hearing and loving them. They are part of my existence. Do you understand?"

"Yes, but I don't know why," Eva answered, clearly frustrated with everything being said. Sounds were not what they should be talking about. It was the letter in her pocket from her own brother in Bratislava telling her what was beginning to happen to all of the Jews in Czechoslovakia. But Eva knew it was his way of letting her go, just as Hiram had Julia, but for a tragically different reason. She would wait until tomorrow, or maybe never, to tell Julia about the letter.

Later, when they arrived at their quarters, Eva reminded Julia of their expected move tomorrow to Chichley Hall in Buckinghamshire. There they were to begin a long and vigorous training as Czech agents through the British intelligence program labeled M16. If all went well, it was then they would return to Prague. Julia only nodded to Eva, offering a faint smile as she closed the door behind her. Tomorrow meant nothing now, only sleep with a few dreams thrown in, perhaps, of Anna and Erich.

TWELVE

Erich, Leipzig, 1940

Erich and Leipzig were never strangers. He had traveled there many times alone and with his family from their home in Dresden, to attend the great music festivals held in the city throughout the spring and summer months. How could he not like Leipzig? Art, his first love, called to him from every corner, and the musical notes of the old German masters filled the air wherever he walked. St. Thomaskirche's magnificent baroque organ, played by Bach and Mendelssohn, was there, still to be listened to by those who continued to nurture their soul with an ethereal passion for life. He would be comfortable there, working in the pediatric clinic, waiting for the right moment to leave Germany. Perhaps through neutral Switzerland he could find safe passage to England where Julia had gone. Time seemed on his side now, he believed, and the dark nightmares of the two murdered Jews in Prague would grow distant and no longer haunt him.

Professor Werner Catel, a distinguished psychiatrist in his own right, reluctantly welcomed Erich to the Leipzig Pediatrics Clinic for no other reason than his father's prestige and standing in Hitler's Chancellery. Introductions to the medical staff, and anyone else who might be important, were always prefaced with "He is Herr Dr. Vicktor Schmidt's son." In time, his father's name became a suit of impenetrable armor, protecting Erich's pseudo-prestige wherever he went in the clinic. He had become politically important at the age of twenty-nine, and no one would try to cross him. But Erich cared little for those around him, and carefully avoided offering the slightest hint of friendship when working with them. Maintaining such a detached persona would keep him free of obligations and serve him well in the trying days to come. What he really wanted was experience, nothing more, before he tried to leave.

Three months into his work at the clinic, Erich received an urgent note from Dr. Catel requesting that he accompany him to the Görden Institution in Brandenburg in the afternoon. Nothing more was said, leaving Erich puzzled at the sudden development, yet thrilled over the opportunity to visit Görden. Everyone in medicine was aware of the extensive research being conducted in this important hospital, especially in exciting new treatment protocols for the mentally ill. Psychiatry was at its best there, Erich knew.

At two o'clock he was in Dr. Catel's office, anxiously waiting to start their visit to Görden, a visit that never came. Instead, Dr. Catel had gone alone to Görden, leaving word for him to be in his office the first thing in the morning. When morning came, he went to Dr. Catel's office, still quite angry at being left behind.

"It is official now, Herr Doctor. We are to have our own Special Psychiatric Youth Department here at the University of Leipzig," Dr. Catel said, smiling broadly as Erich entered the office. "We are to play a leading role in developing the most advanced therapeutic possibilities for treating mentally ill children."

Unimpressed, Erich asked curtly, "Why was I left behind? You should have a good reason."

"Your tone is insolent, Dr. Schmidt, but I will overlook it because of your father. Now come with me, I want your opinion on a special case brought to the clinic early this morning."

Dr. Catel strode from the office and down the main hall with Erich following and took the emergency exit steps to the second floor, where two other doctors were waiting for them. Both ignored Erich, who was not their favorite person. Turning to their right, the group walked down a short hall to a small, isolated ward in which there was only one patient, an infant boy named Knauer, born blind, with one leg and part of one arm missing. "Apparently an idiot" had been written in red on his bedside chart by the attending physician, who was not with them. What immediately seemed unusually strange to Erich and the others was that the infant had been admitted to the hospital by his father and not by a physician.

Looking at the pitifully disfigured child lying before him, Erich knew why the boy was here but refused to believe it.

"Dr. Schmidt," Dr. Catel began, staring hard into his soul. "Would you agree there is no known way medically to heal the mind of an idiot?"

Erich nodded hesitantly.

"What then would be the most humane treatment we could offer this poor child to cure his miserable existence?"

Erich worked feverishly to clear his mind from what he was hearing. Dr. Catel had purposely trapped him. The bastard had cast out a line baited with compassion and he had grabbed it like a starving pond fish.

"It would seem to help him die peacefully, but that's not a matter for doctors to decide. He is still a human being—a person, though a woeful one," Erich said, finally finding his voice.

"Yes, perhaps. But he came here for treatment and we have none to offer that will change his horrible existence, other than relieving him of it."

Puzzled by Dr. Catel's words, Erich and the other doctors looked to each other for an answer.

"Are you suggesting we should euthanize this child?" Dr. Mauer, the senior doctor in the group, finally asked.

"I've said nothing of the kind, but it is on the table. The baby's father has requested we do so."

"It is plain and simple murder, and I'll have no part of it," Dr. Mauer said.

"It is not murder, if it is an accepted medical procedure authorized by the Health Ministry. Would you not agree?" Dr. Catel asked, turning back to Erich.

For a quick second, Erich thought back to his voyage to America with his father, and to Cold Springs Harbor's genetics center, where the earliest thoughts of eugenics began, even killing the unfit. His father believed medicine would someday come to this, to a carefully planned way of cleansing the gene pool of all the miserable souls. For Erich, though, nothing had changed.

"But it isn't," he responded emphatically. "And if it were, it would be the worst kind of wrong, one clearly beyond anyone's imagination."

"Your father would not agree."

"I know, but he has his own soul to contend with, not mine."

An uneasy silence followed Erich's words, their meaning clear to everyone in the group, including Dr. Catel. No one said anything, or wanted to, because the idea of euthanasia as a necessary medical procedure to protect the health of the citizenry was too theoretical and too controversial, even to Erich. No Christian doctor in his right mind, he believed, would ever consider taking this final step to reality, even though many would agree with the ultimate end being sought. Would we not safeguard the health of the country by eliminating the diseased few? had been the argument thrown at medicine by the Chancellery. And it was even more compelling, Erich knew, in a national crisis such as war, and Germany was at war. After several more moments of an awkward silence, Dr. Catel searched the faces of the other doctors, hoping for some sort of response, but none came. Meeting the request of the father to mercifully kill his child would be impossible now without involving the Chancellery in Berlin.

"We will talk more about this matter tomorrow," Dr. Catel said, turning and abruptly leaving Erich and his colleagues in the child's room.

Seconds later the two doctors left, leaving Erich alone by the child's bedside. In the years of his medical training, he had never examined, nor worked with, nor tried to treat such a child. Leaning over the bedside, he suddenly clapped his hands loudly, causing the child to stir, trying desperately to see through eyes that saw only darkness. Taking the tiny fingers on the child's only hand, Erich gently squeezed them but felt no response. Only a crippled animal lay before him that would never be more than it was now.

"Tell me, young Knauer, what is it like to be a blind idiot?" Erich said out loud to the child. "Can you even hear me? Smile or do something, or they will kill you."

There was no answer, nor would there ever be. To imagine existing within such a life was beyond the limits of human thought. Yet there it was, sprawled our hideously before him, a person only by definition systemically. Before turning to leave, Erich looked at the child once more and sighed. Nothing in his life, not even the church, had prepared him for the present moment.

Walking to the elevator, his mind slipped back to a faraway day in a treasured philosophy class in Prague, to an ongoing debate over one's existence, always with Julia in attendance. Painting an example of an unwanted life similar to the pitiful Knauer child, the professor posed a question to the class, "Would it not have been better for the child to have died at birth, never taken its first breath of life?"

Julia was the first to raise her hand. "John Stuart Mill would argue no," she proudly proclaimed. "It would be better to have lived even for one second, taken one breath, than never at all. Life is that precious."

"Why?" the professor responded. "Where is any value in such a life? Where would it come from? Certainly not from such an existence we are talking about."

Julia had no answer and sat embarrassed, not looking at Erich.

"You give up too easily, Miss Kaufmann," the professor said. "Think for a moment. Could you not argue that life itself has an intrinsic value, a worth in itself simply because it is life?"

Again, no one would take the bait, except Julia.

"Then no life would be without value. All would be equal," she replied proudly.

"Yes, but that idea would be very difficult to accept, I daresay, by many. Would it not be then that the dregs in our society, the outcasts, would be of relative worth to those of us sitting here today in this classroom?" the professor said, smiling at Julia, as the rest of the class laughed, even Erich at first.

Refusing to concede her argument to the professor and the class, Julia waited a second before answering, to be sure her voice would speak her convictions clearly.

"No, that is not so, Professor Wise."

There was no laughter this time, only surprised gasps at the boldness of Julia's reply, challenging a professor so blatantly.

"Where is your reason, Miss Kaufmann, since you have questioned my conclusion?"

Julia did not look at Erich this time for support, nor hesitate to respond.

"You are mixing apples and oranges, Professor Wise, intrinsic worth with systemic—that which we are born with at our first breath with that which society decides we are worth."

"And?"

"It is the systemic worth that gives way to evil at times. We care not for the intrinsic worth, only what we believe someone is worth."

Nothing more was said in the hush that followed Julia's remarks. But the joy in Professor Wise's face over her ramblings could not be mistaken. Erich would later learn that Professor Wise was one of the first Jewish professors to disappear from the university and Prague, never to be heard from again.

Though he disagreed with Julia's arguments, he had sat quietly, not wishing to challenge her. A life's true worth is in its potential, he would have argued, not in merely existing. And when that potential is missing, life has no value. This would allow matters of greater worth to take priority by society. Do we not say this when we hang a murderer who has wasted his potential, he would have insisted. But he worshipped Julia and would do nothing to possibly embarrass her in front of a class of angry young German students. Later, they would discuss each other's position with her father, whom he deeply respected.

After leaving the child's room, Erich quickly left the hospital and wandered aimlessly among the artisan shops in Leipzig, many still open. His favorite shop, a menagerie of old maps and great literary books of knowledge, was closed, however. The front windows had been smashed in one rainy night by rampaging members of the Nationalist Socialist Party, most of whom were university students, leaving the priceless tomes to be trampled in the mud and water along the streets, where they lay for weeks, rotting. Only a few ragged glass pieces of the Star of David, marking the store as Jewish owned, remained on the front door as a reminder of the violence. Little was left of the owner's devotion to knowledge.

Erich walked into an open beer garden and sat down at one of the many empty tables. Most of the young men who gathered here every day before going home were missing, now soldiers for the Third Reich, the joy of their melodious voices silent like the city. Everything was changing with the war. One could sit here for a day, watching in unmoving time, and yet, nothing would be the same tomorrow, Erich felt. If he was going to try to leave Germany, he must do so soon.

"Herr Dr. Schmidt, may I talk with you a moment please?" said a small man, dressed much like a peasant of the fields. Though he didn't know him, Erich easily imagined who the man might be.

"I am Rudolph Knauer, father of the child you saw today with Dr. Catel in the hospital."

"Did Dr. Catel send you to speak with me?" Erich asked, irritated with the unwanted intrusion.

"Please, no. I was sitting in an empty room next to my child's, and could hear you and the other doctors talking."

"Then you must know that I strongly disagree with Dr. Catel's recommendation that we kill your son. That is what we would be doing, killing him."

"I know. But let me tell you, please. I am the one who petitioned the Chancellery for the mercy killing of my son. The decision to do so did not come easy to me, yet, you have seen how pitiful my son is."

Rudolph Knauer's mention of the Chancellery in Berlin surprised Erich and bothered him. Whatever the final decision was regarding euthanizing the young child would come from Hitler's personal office. Since Dr. Catel had involved him, along with the other doctors, his name would now be on the lips of those handling the case in the Chancellery. A dubious honor at best, and certainly a frightful place to find one's name, whichever way the decision might go. More importantly though, Erich knew that every word he uttered now to Mr. Knauer, or to anyone else about the case, would easily find its way back to Berlin.

Suddenly drenched in paranoia showered on him by this man who had appeared from nowhere to talk about killing his son, Erich listened carefully to the man's story. It was Dr. Catel and Dr. Brandt who sought the petition from Mr. Knauer to have his son euthanized because of his horrible disabilities, and then carried it to the Chancellery. Hitler, they happily promised to a weary father, would look with great favor on such a request. Mr. Knauer's story ended then on a second promise that Dr. Brandt would come to Leipzig soon to examine the child.

Erich decided to end the conversation. He knew little of Dr. Brandt, other than that he came from a distinguished medical family in Alsace and was a young, gifted surgeon. Being Hitler's personal physician was enough to know the importance of the man and what he would bring to the Knauer case.

"He is not a man to be taken lightly," were the only words his father had used to portray Dr. Brandt after Erich called to talk with him later in the evening. But it was what his father voluntarily revealed to him that kept Erich awake during a long night of fitful nightmares, screaming to a world that had no ears to hear. The old Jewish man and woman had come back to haunt him once again. Both looking together at him through the old woman's dislodged eyeball, they smiled and cried, then smiled again. As a member of the Reich Committee for Hereditary Health Matters, which he had never heard of, it was his father who had passed onto the Chancellery

Mr. Knauer's petition to have his child killed. Now, with Hitler's orders in hand, Dr. Brandt was coming to Leipzig to see that it was done.

Erich stood at the doorway of the child's room, not wishing to enter. The gentle air currents moving through the long hallway would be better there and help keep him awake. Standing near the window was Karl Brandt. Tall and impressive and young, he seemed to fill up the whole room. Erich could not help but be impressed by the man's aura of elegance. If one were to need a goodwill ambassador for killing innocent babies, Dr. Brandt would be his candidate. Though he was talking directly to Mr. Knauer, who was standing next to his child's bed, to Erich it seemed the words were meant for every doctor in the Third Reich.

After explaining to the crying father that the Führer had personally sent him because he was very interested in the welfare of his son, Brandt stopped for a second, gently stroking the child's hair before continuing.

"Your child has no future. His life is worthless."

Then, as if granting a wish from the good princess in a Grimm fairy tale, Brandt said with great pride, "You and your family will not have to suffer from this terrible misfortune any longer because the Führer has granted you the mercy killing of your son."

Nothing more needed to be said, and Mr. Knauer continued to thank Dr. Brandt between loud sobs of crying until escorted from the room by a nurse. But the ears in Erich's mind would hear the distraught father's pitiful sobbing long after he had left the hospital. When evening came, he went back to the room to watch Dr. Catel administer an overdose of morphine to the child, killing him in seconds. For a moment, Erich wondered how it feels to kill someone, especially a helpless child. But it was the dying and being dead that he thought most about. There's no prettifying death, leaving all that you know and stepping into a strange new dimension that you had never seen before where all you knew and were is no more. To Erich, unless the soul has eyes to see and ears to hear and a mouth to speak, it seemed dying and being dead would be the most frightening thing in the world.

Later still, he sat alone in the same beer garden where he had talked earlier with Mr. Knauer. Sitting several tables away from him were the two doctors who also witnessed the child's death, as he did. They sat silent, swirling their warm beer, acknowledging no one, not even each other. What had happened was so sudden and unexpected, especially in a children's hospital. Like Erich, they knew an ancient prohibitive line of medicine had been crossed. A cure for sickness of the mind and body had been discovered: the eradication of life unworthy of life. Soon, both doctors left the table, going separate ways without speaking to each other, or to Erich.

Alone with his thoughts now, Erich wished only that his father was with him now to explain his role in the grim killing of the child. After all, it was he, with Brandt, who had carried the petition requesting to do so, to Hitler. It would be difficult for any son to see his father as a failure, Erich believed, but that was how he now looked upon his father. The true prestige his father had so earnestly sought at first in the world of science, to have his name etched alongside that of Koch and other great German doctors, had eluded him. All that his father would ever achieve would be that which the Chancellery might give him in exchange for his intellect. How could his father ever have agreed to such a poor exchange, Erich wondered, when he had preached to him so many times that the integrity of the mind was the only thing sacred in the world. It must be defended above all else, he would insist, or man's idea of God would die, and then nothing else would matter. Erich believed his father then, and still did, but could do so only by pretending.

THIRTEEN

I t is the wind blowing through the Black Forest pines that sounds like the howling voices of fairy tale monsters and witches and dragons and little children lost. And Erich heard them all again, as he had at ten, hiking with his father through the dark woods. He would stay close to him then, holding his hand until the voices stopped and only the birds could be heard singing to each other. The voices, he knew, were make-believe, but he wasn't sure. They were there too often not to be. Poets and dreamers lived there, too, sometimes. And when they did, Erich went with them, hiding in secret runaway places that the real world knew nothing of. It was so now, the voices. But they were not the poets and the dreamers, or the fairy tale monsters, he knew. Children's voices, thousands and thousands, all as one, it seemed, filling the forest with their sounds. Heard loudest among them was the silent voice of the child who could not speak, whose hand he had gently squeezed the day he went to sleep forever.

Erich had come to the forest late the night before, staying at a small inn near the edge of a wide wildflower field where a trail begins, leading into the forest. The woods and the streams nurtured him, and he was never happier than when he wandered aimlessly among them. Before he could leave Leipzig, Dr. Catel had requested that he and Dr. Schneider, the assistant chief of psychiatry, and one other doctor that Erich didn't know, accompany him to the Knauer child's room to observe while he killed the infant. Then they were to sign the record as witnesses to what was still essentially a crime. There was nothing unpleasant about the boy's death. But death is never unpleasant—it's the dying that's so hard to watch. When the child stopped breathing, and the vile smell of his loosened bowels covered the air, Erich fled the room. Now alone in the innocence of the ancient forest, he realized it was not the sickening stench of the dead child that had made him run away to hide, it was himself covered with his own shit. Dr. Catel had purposely involved him as a witness in the killing of the child, making him an accessory of record. As it was with the old Jewish man and woman, he had just let matters be, saying nothing, offering no protest against a terrible wrong. That he would be a coward to the end, and die a thousand deaths for being so, was all he was able to feel now.

Before leaving the hospital grounds, Erich had sprawled out on a grassy knoll in back of the hospital watching a small riverboat trying to navigate the rain-swollen Weisse Elster River below. The spring rains had come and everything was green and fresh, and he imagined for a quiet minute sailing on the river straight back to Czechoslovakia where its life began. But Dr. Schneider, who had been looking for him, came and sat down next to him, waiting a few minutes before speaking.

"I don't blame you for leaving, Erich. It wasn't a pleasant sight to watch, though in the end it did bring peace to the father."

"I'm not so sure," Erich answered, sitting up and turning to Dr. Schneider. "His guilt is much greater than ours; not before God perhaps, but in his mind. Could you kill your own child, as he did?"

"I don't know. Maybe if he were suffering horribly. That would change everything."

"The suffering, yes, but not the killing. It would still be there, hanging before your eyes every day and night. You and I murdered that baby just as sure as if we pushed the morphine syringe with our own thumbs. We watched and said nothing."

"I know, and that's why I'm here. We're to be transferred to the Görden Institute in Brandenburg to help establish a new psychiatric department for children under a Dr. Heinze. The man has the credentials, I hear."

Puzzled by the sudden news, Erich struggled to make sense of what he was hearing from Dr. Schneider. The reason for Dr. Catel's trip to Görden was apparent now.

"Will you go? You have a choice, I think?" Erich said.

"No, not unless ordered to by the Health Ministry. From what is rumored, there will be more children like the Knauer child there, all waiting to be treated in some way, or to be killed."

"We could both go there and protest, if what you say is true."

"No, thank you—our deaths would be the next ones. No, I'd rather die defending my country. It would be a hell of lot quicker and certainly more honorable," Dr. Schneider said with some pride in his voice.

"Perhaps that's what they want from both of us, to defend the Reich by killing the unfit. It's perhaps the only way to stay alive until the war is over," Erich said sarcastically.

Erich studied Dr. Schneider's face. He had found him to be a man of some charm and character. Like Dr. Brandt, he too came from a distinguished medical family in Alsace, which mattered little to Erich. What did, though, was that he was the only physician to welcome him warmly when he first arrived at Leipzig and show him some respect. The curse of his father's prestige had silenced the rest. When the proposed killing of the Knauer child first arose, Dr. Schneider's voice was the loudest heard in protest, though he grew silent when the deed was done. Asked later about this, he had no answer except that he was afraid, like all the rest of the doctors. But when Erich confessed to him his own silence in Prague as the old man and woman were murdered, he seemed surprised by Erich's guilt, and said only, "But they were Jews. Knauer was a German."

Stunned by Dr. Schneider's blunt response, Erich said nothing further to him and walked away. Later, driving down to the Black Forest, he realized the absurdity of the entire conversation with Dr. Schneider, but knew the truth was there to be seen. Compassion seems to carry its own good reason for killing one's own but need not be found for the Jew.

Erich was glad he had not told Dr. Schneider about Julia and his plan to leave Germany, which he might have done had the conversation continued further. He had been alone with his thoughts too long and needed to share his thinking with someone, as he always had done with Julia. But there were only empty faces around him, their conscience now tightly harnessed to the Nazi movement itself. Erich figured some had done so from cold fear, the greatest of all human motivators. Others were after money, or the fictitious shades of prestige, like his father. What would he come to barter for when the time came? he wondered.

Erich sat down to rest on the forest floor by a small bed of wild bluebells, doing their own thing, struggling to survive in the sunless solitude surrounding them. They had blossomed where their seeds fell by chance, dropped by distant birds from faraway places, perhaps, or carried there by the warming winds of spring. It seems none of us end up on the road from which we started. But the end is there for us, as sure as it was at the beginning. The world is just a barrel organ, Julia's father had said one evening during a long, intense discussion, which God himself turns. This way, we all dance to the tune that is on the drum. We may not think it so, but we do. It's there playing over and over, the same tune for all of us. For now, he had argued, we are dancing to the discordant sounds of Hitler's Third Reich. The night's discussion ended then rather sadly, Erich remembered. But he recalled that Julia had said, "Whether we are to survive is how we dance, not the tune, and you and I must always dance together, Erich." There was small comfort in her words, though. The child's death had joined the dance too.

Opening the knapsack he always carried in any season, Erich took out a small metal flask half filled with warm dark lager. Julia had given it to him one early fall day driving from Prague to the nearby Biskid mountains, where they had hiked many times together.

"Warm beer and nature's solitude are a tough combination to beat when totaling up God's gifts to us," she had said that day, laughing.

Laughter to Julia, though, was the greatest gift from God, because it quiets our hurts and disappointments, and even death, should it come near. But laughter also can hide us from who we are, Erich believed, allowing us to seem what we're not. He had observed this phenomenon too many times in his friends and strangers, all trying to be more than they were. And he wondered how different his and Julia's laughter would sound when they were together again, each having so much to hide from the other. He would not be the same, nor she. Nor anything else. Nothing ever is after there's been a lot of killing in the world. Where would their love be in all this mess? The longing he felt for Julia swept over him in great waves of despair. And he cried out to her, as if she would suddenly step forth from behind a tree and come to him through the shadows of the forest, laughing.

Drinking the last of the beer, Erich tucked away his emotions the best he could. The outburst of self-pity felt good, though he detested it in others. Placebo therapy, Julia's father called it, excuses that never erase the weakness you are hiding. It helps us to survive, to be something when all else fails. And for Erich, the task ahead was to survive with his soul somehow intact.

Used by the Romans two thousand years back, the ancient trail he had chosen to hike on led to Switzerland, but he was ill prepared to flee Germany without first returning to Leipzig. As he started to turn back on the trail leading out of the forest, a loud shrill voice called out, startling him.

"You there, halt!"

Not sure from which direction the voice came, Erich froze when he heard a loud rustling movement through the leaves and underbrush to his right, much like a charging wild boar would make. Two Wehrmacht soldiers, each carrying a light 9-millimeter machine gun, stepped from the woods and cautiously approached him.

"Do not move," the closest soldier said, pointing his gun at Erich.

"Your knapsack—quick, empty it on the ground," the other said scruffily.

Erich did so, trying all the while to control the churning fear that was beginning to numb his whole body, making it difficult for him to move. The metal flask fell harmlessly to the ground, along with a half-eaten piece of sauerbraten and hard bread wrapped in butcher's paper.

"Your pockets, empty them, too."

Erich pulled his pants pockets inside out, showing nothing but two keys, a handkerchief, and a folding wallet holding his identification papers.

"Stand over there," the first soldier said, waving the gun at Erich and pointing to his right.

Erich stood still trembling, unable to move. He was to die right here and no one would ever know.

"What are you waiting for?" the other soldier screamed, shoving Erich hard, causing him to stumble and fall against a small tree stump by the edge of the trail.

Then the soldier picked up Erich's wallet from the ground where it had fallen and glanced hurriedly through his identification papers.

"You are from Leipzig?"

"Yes, the hospital. I am a doctor there," Erich said in a whispery voice, literally having to force the words from his mouth.

"A doctor? Leipzig is miles away. Why are you here?"

"To rest, I suppose. The work has been heavy lately," Erich responded, becoming more frightened with each question.

"Where were you headed?" the second soldier asked, moving closer to Erich to compare his face with the ID photograph.

"Nowhere in particular. Just hiking. I came here when I was young with my father and walked this particular trail."

"It is being used now by many deserters to try and escape to Switzerland. Two were killed here yesterday," the second soldier said, returning Erich's wallet and papers to him.

"It's strange that you are not in the army," the first soldier said, still wary of Erich.

"To you, perhaps, but not to the Health Ministry. Someone must stay behind to heal the wounds of our soldiers when they return from battle," Erich slowly responded, regaining some composure.

Both soldiers seemed pleased with his answer, and one gathered the backpack and the contents from the ground and handed them to him.

"You may go, but do not use this trail again. You are lucky we didn't shoot you," he said.

"Thank you," Erich said weakly, before starting back to the trailhead where his car was parked. After a few steps, he stopped and looked back at the two soldiers, who were still watching him, and waved to them, then quickly increased his pace, adding distance.

Darkness would cover his way soon. He couldn't hear the waterfalls near Triberg yet, and knew many miles remained before he would be safely out of the forest. No forest is safe from one's imagination at night. What is real before you is not what you see. And the voices of the night that speak to you are different from those of the day. Sometimes they don't belong to this world. But to Erich, darkness had always been a glorious time for the mind to try to picture the infinite. His love for psychiatry began with the nights. One could be quite insane, he believed, and yet find sanity at night because there were no truths in the dark. Fears of the day are hidden then, in the shadows of the night, just as one's sins are secreted away in the murky gray recesses of the mind. He had never been afraid of the dark. Long before his days in college, when night came, he would wander the streets and tree-lined parks of Dresden guessing what the shadows of distant objects might be. He became odd then to his father, and a worry to his mother, mostly because his father swore by the inviolability of science as a believer would the Holy Bible, not the hodgepodge of Freudian and Jungian psychology. If a woman was crazy, her genes were, too. It was that simple to him. No such woman should be allowed to pass on such crazy genes to the next generation. For him eugenics had become the new covenant for mankind's salvation, as the New Testament was to the early Christians.

But the silent, twisted face of fear stayed close to Erich this night, seemingly darting back and forth in front of him from the surrounding blackness of the forest as he slowly made his way along the trail. Then it stopped for a moment and began walking along beside him, looking very much human, saying nothing but smiling all the while at his troubled and trembling soul. Later it would talk with him, not aloud, but deep down within him where no one else could hear. It was that real. And it frightened Erich. Later he would come to believe that something else has to exist alongside the reality in his life. It gives one's life more thickness to imagine a clandestine side to things one knows are real. So the terrible fear he felt of dying had become just that, a being he could not see but knew was there where the real and the imaginary world could no longer be separated.

The encounter with the military patrol had left Erich shaken and more confused than ever as to what the future now held for him. He knew no one close in Leipzig to talk to who might feel as he did about the murdered child. Dr. Schneider, who had initially shared his concerns about euthanasia, was silent now as to what he might do should such a case arise again. Where anyone stood on the question of loyalty to Hitler's Third Reich was a question he couldn't ask, nor would anyone answer had he done so. This was so because Hitler himself had penned the authorization to kill the Knauer infant on his personal stationary from the Chancellery, quickly dispatching Karl Brandt to deliver the message and see that it was done. To everyone involved, the letter became a strange god-like tablet that sanctified the killing.

Erich's years away from Dresden had dismissed old ties and weakened others, changing serious thoughts once shared with friends to idle chatter. Perhaps that is what happens in time to old and distant friendships, as matters of one's soul become less important to them. This is particularly true for those we love, where just existing is their only passion. His mother was of this kind. A beautiful Nordic woman from Hamburg, she had never moved far beyond the shadow of his father. Poorly read, she rarely spoke, and when she did it seemed of nothing. Respect though, came to her easily through marriage to his father, whose academic credentials, even then, were towering. But respect also came to her through her own father's death, dying as he did in the terrible battles along the Argonne forest during the Great War. With most of his company lying dead in the water-filled trenches around him, manning a machine gun he single-handedly stopped advancing French units until the few left of his company could escape.

Then, in a matter of minutes, he was blown to pieces by two well-placed mortar shots and a hero's tale began. Months later she stood, holding her mother's hand as Field Marshal Hindenburg presented the Iron Cross to her, recounting her father's great heroic deeds. Others received the coveted Iron Cross that day, too, including a small man standing next to her with a silly-looking mustache that made her laugh, Corporal Adolf Hitler.

Erich saw the night lights of Triberg as he crossed over a slight rise leading down to the small town. History carpeted his mind as he paused for a second to look at the distant lights dancing and flickering through the forest like a thousand small candles. Cuckoo clock merchants of old, carrying their priceless wares, must have crossed this same rise in the trail centuries before, marveling with disbelief, as he was now, at the same sights. But such moments are really for poets. We see them for what they are for only a passing second in time, and then let them go their way. A poet's eyes see them for an eternity because he sees them from his soul.

Erich took one last look at the lights before him and then started down the trail, which widened considerably as he drew close to the outer limits of the village where his car was parked. A parting gift from his father, he initially shied away from using the small Audi roadster when he first arrived at Leipzig. Resentment among the staff over his favored position with Dr. Catel was more than enough without flaunting such a luxury in wartime in front of their eyes. But having such reliable transportation available continued to anchor the illusion harbored by him that somehow it was his only means of escaping Germany.

He would go first to Dresden to visit his mother for a day, then return to Leipzig before undertaking the questionable move to Görden. It would be after midnight when he arrived to awaken her with a scare.

As simple as his mother was, she was clean from all that was going on around her, Erich believed. She had not been dirtied by the outcry against the Jews and everybody else in the world. Though she had often worried that silence about a wrong was greater than the act itself, she believed God would understand and forgive her. To her, no sin of man was beyond forgiveness so long as you believed in being saved, which she did every day of her life. For Erich, though, it was she to whom he would go for forgiveness, not God. He had done this all his life, as he would now. She would listen and never judge, and when she spoke, it was always, "I understand." The feeling of forgiveness, of being clean, could not be greater if it had come from God.

Erich talked for hours into the night with his mother. Emptying the trash from his soul took that long. He talked of Julia and the deep love that owned his heart, and of exchanging their sacred vows witnessed only by Rabbi Loew, though he lay buried in the ground next to them with his golem. All was said with a tenderness his mother had never seen in him. Then he spoke of the old Jewish man and woman and the murdered baby and his desire to flee Germany. All the while he talked, his mother listened and said nothing, studying his face from time to time, as if trying to find the innocence her son once carried. At the end, Erich spoke of his father, which she knew he would. He always talked of his father last, and then with great reservation, as if he were standing in the room hovering over them. There was no warmth in Erich's words, only timid inquiries about the man he loved but couldn't reach. The world is so different when we open the door to it, his mother thought, looking at him. It is those we lived with and loved and should know that elude us in the end.

Leaving, Erich embraced his mother, clinging to her as he had as a child, not wanting to let go. Finally he said, "I will be moving to Görden next week, a new assignment, a new psychiatric treatment program for children."

"I know, your father has told me of it and your position there. He believes you will rise high in the eyes of the Reich Committee there."

Before continuing, his mother brushed a heavy strand of Erich's long blond hair away from his face and placed his hands in hers.

"My sweet Erich, you have been running away so long. Maybe when the war is over you can become the painter of great pictures you dreamed of doing. But now you must find your duty, whatever it's to be."

"My duty?" Erich thought it odd she would use such a word.

"Yes, whatever you find it to be. Otherwise, you'll keep bouncing around like a puppet dangling aimlessly on a string. Life imposes strange duties on all of us, but those in war are even stranger."

Erich left then, still puzzled by his mother's odd soliloquy. He had never heard such serious words from her before, nor to such length. Perhaps she was only repeating his father's admonitions from a time they talked about him. Even though it was doubtful, it pleased him to think that his father had done so.

FOURTEEN

Julia, Tempsford, England, 1942

The RAF Lysander, carrying Julia and Eva and two other Czech agents, ascended smoothly from Tempsford's grassy runway into the cold blackness of the winter night. Freezing in the same blackness hundreds of miles away, Prague awaited them. They were going home at last. Not as they wished, though, to live, but to fight and perhaps to die. Julia cared and worried about the dying because of Anna and Erich, but Eva didn't. To her, death was as essential to living as the air she breathed. All the days ahead are hidden from us and always will be, she would say to those who would listen. And whether it's living or dying that's there waiting for us, what was to come would come, as sure as the morning light first floods the skies each waking day.

It was what both of them had wished for so long and trained for so hard, to jump one moonless night into the dark skies above their homeland and descend in silent fear to its sacred soil. There they were to join with another resistance group with plans to sabotage the gas works in Prague, and then, hopefully, reestablish radio contact with British intelligence for navigating bombers to the Skoda iron works in Pilsen. The final part of their orders shattered any illusion that Julia held, that somehow they might survive the barbwires of danger that lay before them. If they should become separated during the jump, they were to try to join up with a third group of agents already in Prague preparing to assassinate Reinhard Heydrich, the blond beast, Protectorate of Moravia and Bohemia and slayer of Jews. Julia knew escaping the clutches of the Gestapo would be hopeless once the assassination has been carried out. Operations Anthropoid, the plan had been surreptitiously tagged, as a Halifax lifted off carrying seven brave Czech soldiers to their ultimate fate. Their appointed time to drop close to Prague was December 28, two months before Julia and Eva would follow the same route, knowing that finding them would be as daunting a task as killing Heydrich.

Once in the air, Julia leaned back against the small pack she was carrying, in addition to the parachute strapped in front. Looking across the aisle at Eva, she began to laugh, imagining she looked the same way, like an overly stuffed scarecrow. Underneath their jump suits, each wore two wool sweaters, a shirt, bra, military shorts instead of panties, long pants and two pairs of socks. Wrapped around their waist was a money belt stuffed with thousands of Reich marks, which added a voluminous stomach on both of them. Eva began laughing, too, because she knew what Julia was thinking. But scarecrows can't be afraid and Julia was. The fear of bailing out into the unknown had haunted her when she thought of it, hanging in her throat and teeth like sour vomit. Only through laughter could she kill the taste.

After a few minutes of nervous laughter and chatter with Eva, each having to shout to the other over the loud roar of the plane, Julia closed her eyes to rest for the three-hour trip. There would be no more prayers to God, which Eva thought Julia was doing. They had been said many times before by her, until the casualty lists came out showing all the boys dying everywhere there was some fighting. She figured then that God wouldn't listen to one person, and a woman at that, when so many were dropping dead in foreign lands who had probably prayed to live just like she had done. Staying alive in war, she had come to believe, was no different from playing Russian roulette, except there were a million guns pointed at your head instead of a six-shot revolver.

Shutting out what lay ahead for her and Eva, Julia's mind became crowded with bundles of thoughts of times that had passed. Much had changed since she arrived in England, a lifetime ago, so it seemed. Hitler's great boast of bringing England to her knees had vanished in the summer winds blowing across the English Channel. Even the terrible bombing of London that began then in late summer appeared less. Still, Hitler now ruled all of Europe, including the Balkan countries, and had launched a massive invasion of Russia. But England no longer stood alone, as America had entered the war. Soon, England would be invaded by thousands of fresh, young faces from America, none too eager to fight and die like their fathers had in the Great War, but there only because they were told to be. From the beginning, it was not their war to die in, but that would change as everything else did.

It was mostly the thoughts of Anna that hummed in her mind, keeping company with the monotonous droning of the plane's motors. Anna was two and a few months now, healthy and strong as the new spring lambs dancing around in Angie McFarland's fresh green fields. Nothing put before her on the dining table went untouched, even the morning breakfast bowls filled with haggis. Carrots and greens and shepherd's pie were her favorites, though, and had made her a Scottish tot with fat, rosy cheeks kept raw and chafed by the cold winds blowing and swirling across the hills where she played. Anna loved Angie McFarland, whom she saw as her mother, though Angie talked of Julia throughout each day. She would read every letter to her from Julia, some two and three times, when days passed without a new one. Even then, she would change the wording to keep a fresh and exciting picture of her mother in front of Anna's young eyes.

At night, she would read and tell a story to Anna from the Old Testament and teach her a Hebrew prayer and song, as she promised Julia she would do. In time, the Hebrew prayers became her own, though she would always add "In Christ's name" before the amen. One sunny November day, Angie took Anna with her to the public library in Edinburgh, not too many miles away from her own village, where she found a book explaining Jewish holidays and their dates. Then, with Christmas coming, she would celebrate Hanukkah with Anna, too. It was not something Angie promised Julia she would do, or Julia even expected from her. "It just seemed right," she would tell those in the church that questioned her about a Christian celebrating such a holiday.

Later she would add, when Passover came and the questions grew louder, "Would you want a Jewish mother to raise your child as a Jew, tell me now, with you being Presbyterian and all?"

The questions stopped then, though some still thought Angie strange, that perhaps she had a troubled soul.

The brief visits by Julia were the hardest. And though happiness and laughter abounded, no one escaped the sadness that hid its face beneath the smiles. When goodbyes were said, each seemed to be a rehearsal for the day the final one would come, as if it might lessen the pain. When the time did come, Angie sensed it the moment she looked at Julia's face and eyes, but said nothing, hoping she was wrong. A distant face at another time, in a different war, had looked the same when his leaving time finally came. Her own Robert had looked no different when it came his turn to go and fight and die in the Great War. It is the eyes, always the eyes that betray us. Nothing in the soul can be hidden from them, she remembered whispering to him as they lay together for the last time. In two weeks she became widow McFarland.

"We will go to your church tomorrow, the three of us," Julia said, surprising Angie. "And then I will leave. It's better that I say the words now then pretend until the moment arrives for me to go."

"I know, my child," were the only words Angie could say before embracing Julia, holding her forever, it seemed.

Later, with Anna asleep for the night, Julia and Angie sat huddled together in front of the fireplace, grateful for what warmth the small fire was willing to give. Winter was at its worst now, with the sun gone for another day and the night winds beginning to blow. They had talked earlier about the freezing days and the snow-covered hills and anything else but what was on their minds.

"It is a cold, cold night, indeed. Perhaps we should turn in. Our beds will be much warmer," Angie said, shuddering and pulling the edges of her wool robe tightly about her large body.

"No, please, not yet. There is another promise that I must ask of you. Waiting until tomorrow will only make it more difficult," Julia said.

Angie sat back down, taking Julia's hand in hers and waited, watching the tears form slowly and start their run down her cheeks. Julia looked away for a moment to find her voice, and inhaled deeply before trying to speak.

"We have become a family, you and me, not all Jewish or Presbyterian, but a good family," she said, laughing through the streams of tears now flowing unheeded down every part of her face.

"Yes, yes, very much so, I would say," Angie said, very close to crying herself.

"I want your promise that should I, or my brother Hiram, not return from the war, you will let no one take Anna from you—no one. You are as much her mother as I am, if not more so."

Angie had wondered how it would be when this moment came, as she knew it surely must, knowing Julia's great love for Anna. She had tried, but couldn't feel the terrible anguish of a mother parting from her child, perhaps for the last time. Only those standing at the edge of such a loss could speak of it, she realized. And now the precious gift was before her.

"Aye, and raise her I will. How could it not be—she's got my heart and is a part of me, just as you are." Angie said, smiling through her own tears. "But shame be on you. You will be standing here banging on the door the day the war is over."

Angie never knew if what she said was right by Julia, but they sat holding each other for hours more in a pleasing silence, the kind where one's mind becomes that of the soul. Tomorrow would bring more tears but that was of little matter now.

Only the hymns were different for her final Sunday service. The preaching and the looks from the congregation, though, were the two things Julia knew would always be the same. Luther's great "A Mighty Fortress is Our God" did send cold shivers down her spine, and she and Angie sang it with such gusto that those standing close quit their own singing to listen. By the third stanza, most of the congregation had stopped as the two voices, harmonizing when they could, filled the cold church to the rafters with a melodious warmth seldom heard there. Looking back days later, and times after, the same joy would sweep Julia's heart as if it had its own existence and would stay with her forever. Her father would have been pleased, too, even though it was a Christian hymn, because he knew her singing was always to God, and that's all that mattered.

After the service, when the time came for Julia to make the long walk back down to the village to go home, she lifted Anna in her arms one last time and kissed her lightly. Then she simply smiled at Angie.

"I will go now," she said, and walked away, not turning back to look.

Julia opened her eyes as the plane began a slow descent over what was supposed to be their drop zone. Everything she had learned the past two years was now to be tested. Julia looked at Eva, and for the first time saw a tiny shade of fear in her eyes. It is good, though, the fear, Eva had said many times when they had discussed the strongest of human emotions. All animals live by fear, and they will either kill or run to live another day. And in war, we become the worst of animals, seldom running, but always killing. The idea to Julia that she might have to kill someone was the impetus for many sleepless nights in Arisaig, Scotland during her difficult training in commando tactics. There she learned a hundred ways to kill a person, so it seemed at the time. But at the end, she was still unsure what she might do when such a moment came, though she told no one.

The name, make and purpose of every military weapon and mechanized vehicle, British and German, was pounded into her head much like words had been in the English class, without mercy. And soon, she became so skilled at breaking down weapons and identifying them when blindfolded that many in her class sought her company, if only to learn from her.

One evening, while walking alone around the training grounds, Julia thought about Erich and where he might be and whether he, perhaps, had killed someone in the war. It would be a terrible thing for him to do so, she knew. Maybe it was because the winter sky was so full of stars that the time came to her when they were lying together on the soft grass in the Old Jewish Cemetery looking at the same dark sky with the same bright stars above them. With thousands of tombstones as their audience, they discussed and argued in whispered voices how it might be to kill someone who was as innocent as you, even in war. It was then that Erich had expressed a concern quite like hers over his own ability to kill a stranger he didn't know, and probably never would, should he be cast into Germany's wars. It was distance that made war so palatable and easy to accept, they finally decided, both for the old men that send the young to die and, in the end, for those who do the killing. Distance hides the humanity of who we kill, lessening one's concern over their death, he had argued. If we don't see them fall and die or blown into a thousand pieces, we stay disconnected from the killing. It is only when we see the eyes of those we are killing that we cry out inside. Even then, some never see them, the eyes, though they are there before them. What would Erich do now, if he were here to jump with her? Would they run away and hide together, as they talked of doing, and let the world handle its own problems? Julia wondered.

When the red light began flashing, indicating jump time was two minutes, Julia and Eva looked at each other for one brief second, then stood quickly, tightened each other's backpacks, and connected the parachute's cord line to the static line. The jump time only seconds away, Julia braced herself in the open door, waiting for the final signal. The snow-covered earth was a scant eight hundred feet below and she was glad. The heavy blanket of snow would soften the impact, though she would be more visible to those that might be watching.

"Stay with me, God, the night will be cold and long," she whispered, leaping into the waiting darkness.

FIFTEEN

Czechoslovakia

As she hit the cold night air, Julia caught a glimpse of the big plane going away before her chute opened and she began floating down. To her left, a hundred or so yards, she saw the outline of Eva's chute as it opened and billowed out into the endless darkness above her. The pilot had flown very low to drop them, leaving Julia only seconds to look down at the ground rushing up to meet her and to guide her landing away from a row of trees lining the open field. This time there would be no sheep dump to greet her. A heavy winter snow had fallen for two days, covering the ground with its white softness to cushion her landing, as if it knew she would be coming home soon.

It was Eva's time, though, to provide the comedic relief needed for such a tense situation. Caught at the last moment of landing by a sudden gust of wind, she was pushed into the trees, crashing and breaking limbs and twigs and ending suspended upside down several feet from the ground. Had there been ears to hear that night, the steamy words flowing from her cursing lips would have shamed the saltiest of all swearers. Holding her tightly in their twisted arms, the limbs and twigs could not stop laughing, so it seemed to Eva, over her topsy-turvy predicament. But the laughter came from Julia, who had emerged from the surrounding darkness to find Eva's embarrassing position. She had followed the faint sounds of her cursing voice, muted by the deep snow covering the fields and the heavy winter air. Sights such as this become engraved on the mind so that forgetting is impossible, and she would be reminded of it many times by Julia.

Still laughing, Julia made her way slowly to where Eva was hanging, pushing aside the limbs and twigs surrounding her like a captive army. Before she could say anything, Eva looked at her and said calmly, "This fucking night stays between you and me. Now cut me down before I pass out."

Julia nodded, but her face still reddened from hearing such words, and did so this time as Eva spoke. Using her commando knife, she began cutting the parachute cords wrapped around Eva's feet and the tree limbs, freeing her to fall the remaining few feet to the ground. As she did, the deep snow quickly wrapped around her like a white blanket, leaving only parts of her face showing.

"I should leave you here, but they would find you, I'm afraid," Julia said, still laughing and reaching down to help Eva up.

Julia pushed Eva away, hurried to her feet and stood listening. Distant cries of an aroused dog could be faintly heard.

"There is a farm somewhere nearby. We need to locate the radio and supplies and hide them until we find out where we are," she said, helping Eva to her feet.

"Near Pilsen, I would hope," Eva said, brushing off the remaining snow from her arms and legs and starting back towards the place where Julia landed.

Julia stopped her for a second.

"We need to hide your parachute before we go. A German patrol may come by."

"There's no need to. We've made enough tracks to make any patrol think an army has landed. They can follow us to the ends of the earth until this snow melts," Eva said, making a new path across the open field.

Julia was slow to follow, stopping every few feet to inhale the beautiful white world spread out around her. The snows in Prague were just as beautiful, she believed, perhaps even more so because they were alive, having a thousand happy children to play with the very first moment the flakes begin their long fall from the heavens. The snow around her was quiet, though she was sure it had much to tell since the war began. It had been their friend at first, muting the sounds and softening their landing. But when the morning light came it would become their enemy, following them wherever they went until it disappeared beneath the warming rays of the sun.

Ahead, Eva spotted the cylindrical metal box resting in the snow with its parachute spread out on the ground. By the time Julia arrived, Eva had pried open the box, laying out its contents on the parachute to run through a quick inventory in her mind—a wireless two-way radio, two British Stens with extra ammunition, two small lightweight Webley revolvers, three medium explosive devices, and K-rations. Nothing else was there that might help them survive.

"Until we know where we are, hiding out in the woods to wait for the morning light is our only choice. German patrols will come then," Eva said.

Julia nodded and took out a small detailed map, which had been purposely folded to the sheet showing their drop-off spot. Focusing a small flashlight on the brown-colored map, she quickly traced across the markings to a large X.

"This is where we should be, no more than two miles east of Pilsen," she said, making a quick calculation from the mileage scale put to her memory a hundred times in training. "And here is where we can expect to join the others," she continued, pointing to a small residential area on the southern outskirts of Pilsen.

Julia and Eva, though, were nowhere near the large X on the map. They had mistakenly been dropped by the pilot many miles south of where they should be, a fact they would discover only after the cold, dark night grudgingly gave way to a frozen dawn. After moving the radio and supplies quickly into heavy brush at the edge of the woods, they huddled together through the long night, buried deep beneath a huge snow pile mercifully built by the strong winter winds blowing through the woods. Afraid to sleep, and almost to breathe, they endured the passing hours trying to interpret the strange forest sounds coming to their ears. Even then, Julia imagined, where they were would be a wondrous thing for poets to write about, a moment, it seemed, suspended in time from all things human.

Three years filled with a thousand days and nights had passed since she last felt the warmth of Erich's arms. And she ached for him now. So many roads we could have taken, had we had time to choose. He would be a doctor now in Germany, healing the wounded minds of battle-weary soldiers, she knew. Or perhaps he would be still in Prague, a thought that excited her because of their nearness to each other in body. If he were there, he would keep her parents safe someway, a thought that warmed her heart even more, pushing away the coldness surrounding her. She would find him after the war, and they would be together again, that much she was sure of. Julia's silent musings were suddenly shattered by the cracking noise of a large limb, laden with ice, breaking loose from a nearby tree and falling with a cushioned thud in the deep snow. Above their snow bed, two large limbs seemed equally as fragile, bending precariously low towards them with their thick coats of ice and snow. We should move, Julia thought, starting to nudge Eva until she heard the muffled chugging of motorcycles nearby, followed first by silence and then by a cursing voice.

"They must be our contacts," Eva whispered, stirring from the snow bed. But Julia quickly held her back.

"No, listen. They are German soldiers, two, maybe three. One is complaining about the choke on his motorcycle not working," she whispered.

"A night patrol?"

"Yes, I imagine. They must be on a main road leading to Pilsen."

The cursing stopped and loud laughter came from the soldiers.

"One is trying to relieve himself, but can't. Says his manhood has shriveled up like a dried prune from the cold and all he can do is dribble on himself," Julia said with a giggle.

Julia and Eva both smiled at the irony of such a comical moment in such a terrible time. They, too, desperately needed to attend to their own needs, but refused to disturb the growing warmth of their hiding place. Instead, they would wait until the first glint of light found its way into the woods and they were sure to be alone.

Soon the cranking of the motorcycles could be heard, along with a slow chugging of the cold engines, hitting and missing until they finally started. No more words were heard from the soldiers, only loud idling, then a piercing roar as they raced away, leaving the freezing silence of the winter night to return. Julia and Eva sighed in relief, each listening to the frightened sounds of their own heart. What their ears had witnessed, both knew, was the opening act of an odyssey to come that would defy a thousand imaginations.

The awaited light of dawn finally broke through the woods and across the snowy fields and hills, unchanging, as it had done for a thousand centuries. New snow had fallen throughout the night, but not enough to cover Julia and Eva's zigzagging footprints through the field where they landed. Eva stood looking back across the field, tracing the tracks until they disappeared over a rise leading down to the woods where her chute had taken her.

"A two-year-old child could find us from those tracks," she said.

"Yes, but we will be gone," Julia said, trudging through the deep snow towards the place from where the voices came during the night.

After only sixty paces, a wide ice-covered road spread out before them running parallel to the woods where they had hid. The closeness surprised and frightened Julia for a moment. But something else quickly caught her attention. Kneeling down, she dug away with her hand loose snow by the edge of the road and felt the hard pavement.

"Concrete, for god's sake, concrete," she said.

"What do you mean concrete?" Eva asked, puzzled by Julia's comment.

"Just that, rotting concrete—this is a main thoroughfare," Julia responded, anxiously pulling the map from her pocket.

A quick glance told her what she feared. Somehow, they had been dropped by mistake over fifteen miles southeast from the rendezvous point instead of three. Julia was sure that the road she was standing on led from Prague to Nürnberg, completely bypassing Pilsen, their destination. She had been this way before with Erich and Hiram during a summer break, when the days were long and hot. Traveling on the worst of country buses, they had left Prague for the rising hills and deep forest along Germany's border. There they would scour the forest floor for hours, hoping to find ancient relics from the wars between the Goths and Rome. Later, with Hiram napping, she and Erich would wander deeper into the woods to find another Eden, where nothing mattered except the love they would give to each other. If she and Eva traveled far enough along the road, they would find the deep woods, too.

"What are you saying?" Eva asked.

"That we are not where we should be. The pilot made a horrible mistake. This road goes straight south to Nürnberg and straight north to Prague. We are in the middle of—"

"Shit."

"Yes, that's a good word to use for where we are," Julia said wryly, at her friend's expression.

"That explains the patrol last night. This road is a major supply route for the German army. We'll look funny as hell walking down the road carrying a radio and submachine guns strapped across our breasts," Eva said.

"We won't. A little town called Klatovy should be near to the east, a few miles maybe."

"What are you suggesting?"

"Try and radio headquarters for instructions first, if we can. If it's a no go, find Klatovy and hide out until the weather breaks."

"Pilsen's out? Our contacts are there, you know," Eva said, showing some frustration with the mess the pilot's mistake had left them in.

"I know. We'll get there, but I want to be alive when we do," Julia said, trying to reassure Eva.

Even before Julia had finished her words, Eva had started walking back into the woods to where they endured the night's freezing cold. Saying nothing, she carried the radio to the edge of the road and clicked the on switch, preparing to call in their code names. But the radio remained silent, attesting to the arctic coldness numbing everything around them—its sixteen-volt batteries were frozen solid, too. Eva looked at Julia for a second in disgust, then carried the radio back into the woods and hid it among the deep brush, adding as cover at the last moment two heavy limbs that had fallen nearby. At the same time, keeping only three rations and the two pistols, Julia covered the rest of the supplies and the Sten guns under nearby brush and snow, then marked a nearby tree with her knife. Nothing could be done with the tracks they had made in the heavy snow, so they decided to make hundreds more by walking in tens of circles in the fields nearby and cutting new paths through the woods to the road.

"At least it will give the Germans something to think about should they find them," Eva said.

"Yes, but I would rather have a good God melt them as soon as we leave," Julia said in a prayerful tone, as if such a thing might very well happen.

Without looking back, both moved to the edge of the road, standing without voice for a minute, each knowing what lay before them, how the odds of their surviving had changed. Though this was their homeland, with the war on they would come as strangers to the small villagers and peasants, draped in suspicion. Some would welcome and feed and clothe them, they knew, but many would avoid them. Others would betray them to the Germans for a small handful of extra rations, or gladly kill them should they be known to be Jews. Then they would proudly show the Germans what they had done, not for a small handful of extra rations, but from pure hate.

Julia stepped forward gingerly on the frozen highway, testing her footing, but could take only a few slow steps without risking a fall. Eva fared no better, having fallen to her knees twice trying to navigate on the slippery surface. Julia quickly pointed to the dense thicket of trees that seemed to be running for miles ahead along the side of the road.

"The road is too icy. We will make better time hiking through the woods," she said, knowing they would probably freeze to death before the Germans found them.

SIXTEEN

Erich, Brandenburg, 1941

When Erich arrived at Görden Hospital, the maddening rush of activity he had expected to see in such a large, prestigious state institution seemed strangely absent to him. Empty patient rooms lined the long, dimly lit halls, and the flurry of nurses and orderlies scurrying about was missing. Everything was dirty, not spotless as one would hope to find in a hospital. Nothing was as it should be, and that greatly bothered him. Walking to the nearest ward station where a lone nurse stood busily arranging and rearranging a small stack of medical files on an otherwise empty desk, Erich introduced himself.

"I am Herr Dr. Erich Schmidt. Where is the administration office, please?"

"Yes, Herr Doctor, we were expecting you yesterday. The office is at the end of the hall, to the right. I believe some of the staff are meeting there now."

Erich nodded and turned to leave, but stopped after a few steps and looked back at the nurse and the small number of file folders on her desk.

"Where are your patients? You have so many empty beds?" he asked.

"I don't know, Herr Doctor, we do have a few, some new ones will be admitted tomorrow. That's all I have been told."

Erich nodded again to the nurse and walked down a narrow hall to his right, counting as he went the number of empty beds and those with patients. Twelve and two, he mumbled, opening the office door. A secretary, sharply dressed in a newly pressed brown uniform blouse and skirt and wearing the Nazi arm band, stood up stiffly when he entered.

"I am Dr. Schmidt, and—"

"You were to report yesterday, doctor," the secretary said brusquely, interrupting Erich.

"I know, that's the second time I've been told that. Is there a search party out looking for me?" Erich said teasingly. The woman was not amused and remained silent for a moment, looking at him with disgust.

"You are to go in Dr. Heinze's office now. There is a staff meeting."

"Dr. Heinze?"

"Yes, Hans Heinze. He has been appointed to direct our new special psychiatric youth department," the woman said proudly before walking to her desk, indicating their conversation was over.

The name Heinze meant nothing to Erich, but Karl Brandt's did, who was the first person he recognized among the large group of men gathered in the office. The second was his father, who was sitting to the left of Brandt. To his right sat Dr. Catel and then Dr. Schneider, who had witnessed the killing of the Knauer child with him in Leipzig. None of the other men were known to him, other than they were probably doctors newly assigned to Görden. Counting himself, Erich guessed twelve men crowded the room, as he moved to one of two empty chairs near where his father sat. Twelve, an unlikely biblical number for an unlikely purpose, he would later recall, thinking back on all that took place at the meeting.

No one acknowledged his presence, not even his father. Everyone sat staring straight ahead, their eyes focused on a strange-looking man sitting alone away from the group, Philipp Bouhler, the Reich Head of Hitler's Chancellery. Erich quickly became fascinated by the uncommon strength in the man's face. From the beginning, Bouhler intimidated him and everyone else in the room, except Karl Brandt, who was Hitler's personal physician, a unique position that seemed to give Brandt carte blanche wherever he went among doctors. Without saying a word, Bouhler circulated among the group in dramatic fashion, the original authorization for euthanizing the Knauer baby, which was written on Hitler's personal stationery and signed by him. In doing so, he was essentially placing Hitler in the room with them, directing all that was to come in the weeks and months ahead. No one escaped his mystical presence, including Erich, who was mesmerized for a minute by seeing Hitler's writing and signature. He remembered Hitler's hypnotic eyes searching his own the day they stood facing each other at the doors of Prague's great castle. He was disturbed then, but only for a short moment, by the ancient Germanic aura Hitler could project by simply standing still and silent and looking nowhere else but straight at you. There was no silence in his signature, though. Its metaphysical power was there for all to see and feel, as Erich did.

What followed afterwards from Bouhler's lips only verified and reinforced the uneasiness Erich felt for even being here among such leaders in Hitler's Chancellery. Everything that was to be done in Görden Hospital, beginning in one week, was to be kept secret from the public. How was that to be possible, Erich wondered, when so many bold announcements had been made with great fanfare that Görden was to be the leader, the crown jewel among hospitals treating children suffering from hereditary diseases? It was here at Görden where these lucky children would be treated with the most advanced scientific therapy in the world. Knowledge of such miraculous therapy, if there were to be any, should be spread gloriously by Germany before the entire medical world, not kept in secret. The idea of secrecy tore away the curtains that had been protecting the reason he had so treasured. The medical protocol outlining the advanced therapy to be administered at Görden was to come from the Chancellery. It would be an extension of Hitler's original directive authorizing the killing of the Knauer baby, and was to be followed without exception by the doctors and the hospital. No one in the audience listening to Bouhler misunderstood what the ultimate end of the advanced therapy was to be. Erich was to say hours later that Bouhler's shocking recitation was like a page torn from Dante's *Inferno*, much to the displeasure of his father who was dining with him.

Out of respect for his father's presence, Erich sat quiet during the tense meeting, seeking no answers from Bouhler regarding the final therapy, though they were there to be explored. Later, while the others mingled and fawned over Bouhler and Brandt, trying to show their unwavering loyalty to the Chancellery, he remained seated, isolated in thought over the startling disclosures that had been carefully laid out before him, and which he and the other doctors were expected to follow. He quickly concluded that the only saving grace for him as a doctor would be found in the way the medical decision to treat or not treat a child was to be reached. No longer would it originate and come from within the ancient sanctified boundaries of the inviolable physician-patient relationship, even though it was he who was to be in the sacred relationship. Instead, the final decision to treat or not treat a child in a given case would come from a special committee separated by distance from the ultimate outcome. He would be much like a pilot disconnected from all beneath him as he soars away high in the sky, seeing nothing of those lying dead from the bombs he has dropped. His only duty then, he believed, was to care for a patient according to the orders of the committee, nothing more. Yet he knew, from what few shreds remained of his conscience, that the final therapy to be given to a sick child would come from his own hands, destroying, as it did, any pretense that somehow he was not a part of the end solution.

When Bouhler first mentioned the committee's decision-making authority over each patient's case, it was the bold presence of his father's name on the committee that both stunned and heartened Erich at first. There would be a back door opened on every case, if his father would listen to him. Bouhler had said that a unanimous decision would be required by the committee in each case before a plus mark indicating "no available therapy" could be placed on a child's file. A simple dissent from his father, nothing more, could be the grace he sought. What Erich didn't hear, though, were the brief disturbing words being exchanged between Bouhler and his father, as he was leaving.

"Your son Erich concerns me, Dr. Schmidt. We don't want any trouble from him," Bouhler said.

"I assure you, he will follow orders and perform his duty. He was involved with the Knauer child, you know," Dr. Schmidt responded meekly.

"I do know, Doctor, and he and Dr. Schneider voiced an objection."

"As I said—"

"It is only because of you that he's not fighting now on the Eastern front, or worse, given to the Gestapo. Talk with him and report back to me at once, if he will become a problem," Bouhler said harshly.

"I understand," was all Dr. Schmidt could say before Bouhler turned his back to him and began talking privately with Dr. Heinze.

Later in the evening, Erich sat with his father at a small sidewalk café close to the hospital. He had selected the café because most of the patrons chose to dine outside in the cool night air, hungrily smoking their cigarettes like they were a part of each dinner course, leaving the inside area mostly empty. Privacy was available at the very back tables, where lovers could go and dine in secret. Their greeting at the meeting in Dr. Heinze's office had been cordial, but not warm. Even now, both sat in silence waiting for the other to speak. It was as if they had just been introduced to each other for the first time and were struggling for words that might impress the other. After a glass of wine, Dr. Schmidt stared hard at his son's troubled face.

"Philipp Bouhler is concerned about your political philosophy," he uttered in a low voice, unsure whether the Gestapo might be secreted unseen somewhere in the empty café.

"I would think so, Father. It's difficult to change what you are and have always been. You should know that as a psychiatrist."

"It's not whether you want to change, Erich—you must, or you will be transferred to the Eastern Front to fight the Russians."

Erich grew silent for a moment, looking at the strange darkness now covering his father's face. Once it had glistened with unbounded excitement when simply looking through a microscope in his laboratory at life he had seen many times before. Before this war is over, no one will be spared such a terrible darkness, Erich believed.

"What happened to you, to us, Father?"

"What do you mean?"

"We are not monsters, we're people, human beings. And the sick children are too. You should know that."

"You are wrong, Erich. Tell me, do you think God would waste a good soul on idiots like the Knauer child? He's not that dumb," his father said loudly, becoming red in the face and thumping the table with a fist.

"Perhaps He has hopes. That's all a soul has anyway," Erich answered, surprised by his father's outburst.

"You are speaking rot now. I am talking medically, as a doctor. These children are nothing, absolutely nothing. They are already dead. A garden slug would find more delight in life then these creatures."

"Perhaps we have an inflated concept of humanity—or is it a life unworthy of life," Erich said facetiously, mocking the credo being put forth by the Health Ministry.

"I would be very careful how you use those words, if I were you. The Chancellery has ears and knows of your close affair with the Jewish woman in Prague. They are watching to see where your loyalty lies."

This time Erich had no ready answer for his father. But he felt his sharp rebuke. The same cold fear that paralyzed him in the Black Forest when confronted by the soldiers began creeping through his veins again as if he had suddenly been given a transfusion of ice water.

"You've changed, Father. It's as if we're no longer of the same blood."

"No, it is you who should return to your roots. I am a scientist first, and my passion for cleansing the German race is here before me. A sick Germany can become healthier by removing the misfits. We should embark on this great voyage together as father and son."

Moved by his father's words, Erich reached out to touch his arm but stopped short when he abruptly arose from the table.

"I must return to Berlin now, to another meeting. And then to Dresden to spend a few days with your mother," he said.

Then he came around the table and stood next to Erich, looking tenderly at his face.

"You must do your duty, you have no choice."

With those words, he turned and left the café, leaving Erich to wonder if he would ever see him again. They were more distant than ever now, it seemed. Watching his father disappear into the night was no different than what he had always done, suddenly appearing in his life from the shadows for a few minutes, then quickly disappearing like a phantom into the night. Most people travel far to find out what they are, only to find they had become what they pretended to be all along. But not his father. He had never pretended. Fact and fiction were wedded in him for as long as Erich could remember. His father was the complete package now with no ambiguities, able to carry out that which he had theorized for so long in eugenics. The passion he had nursed since childhood for biology and Darwin's survival of the fittest had become the ruling voice of German medicine. His rapid involvement in the National Socialist Party first began with a mesmerizing speech by Rudolph Hess declaring National Socialism to be nothing more than applied biology. Unknown to Erich, who was studying medicine then in Prague, his father's zeal as a missionary for eugenics had brought him quickly into the inner circle of the Health Ministry. There he became a powerful intellectual voice for euthanasia as the final therapy for the misfits in society, joining the rising chorus of Brandt and Bouhler and others. Still, in doing so, he would insist that any such program must always remain in the hands of the doctor, as it has through the ages.

How his father had come to this place in his life would stay a mystery to Erich. His father fervently embraced the Hippocratic Oath, yet felt, like most German psychiatrists, that mental patients lacked ordinary human qualities, were not persons, and should not be allowed to propagate. Sterilization was the grand solution, he would argue, as America was so busily doing, always stopping short when the idea of eliminating them as a cure was placed on the table for discussion. Why his father changed, Erich knew he would never know. Their lively discussions and debates and games of the mind, always as intellectuals, never father and son, no longer mattered to his father. They did to Erich, however. The small warmth and intimacy they brought to him was all he had ever enjoyed with his father, all that had seemed real and normal to him as his son.

Leaving the café, Erich stopped and gazed for a still moment at the night skies above him, as he often did. There were no stars, only an empty blackness with no end wherever he looked, much like the quickening turns in his life. It seemed to him that he had been chasing the wind all his life, hoping to catch it one day and ride on it far away to a bright new world. But now, the fabric of his tomorrows that he had so carefully woven was unraveling, and he didn't know why. Nothing was real anymore.

SEVENTEEN

Erich, 1941

After another sleepless night, the warm shimmering rays of the morning sun made everything seem like another world to Erich. He could only wish it were so, where he could hide forever with Julia by his side. There were no more innocent Edens left, though, for those in love to discover.

Entering the hospital again, nothing was certain in his mind other than his physical presence there. What he would do as a doctor when the time came to put a malformed child to sleep forever was as distant from him as God seemed to be now. How fragile moral conscience becomes when fear and duty come through the door to one's future at the same time. He had theorized about such a happening with Julia and her father one cold, sunless winter afternoon only a few months before Prague fell. It was as if the subject had been hiding somewhere deep within the folds of his conscience, which was struggling to understand what was happening. For Julia and her father, fear was a permanent resident living somewhere in their ancient genes because they were Jews. And like the Jews of history, even though it was there, they lived and played and sang and would die as God intended them to.

"Fear, like everything else, can be good or bad. To fear God is good. To fear dying is bad. It's as simple as that," Professor Kaufmann had said, ending the long afternoon discussion.

Later Erich expressed to Julia his disappointment in such a trite statement by her father. He had expected much more than a two-sentence explanation from such a learned man. Something, maybe, from Kant's treatises on duty, or perhaps Hume's defense on the priority of emotions in one's life. Anything would be better than what Dr. Kaufmann had passed on. Julia quickly agreed, yet she knew what her father was saying. Compromise is never an option where one is faced with doing either a good or bad thing. For Erich, though, Darwin's survival of the fittest was all about fear, and had to be a part of everyone's struggle to live. It was as much a part of fitness as strength and health. We do not survive in life without fear, he had argued to Julia and her father. Hitler and those around him knew this to be true, too, he pronounced almost arrogantly, pacing back and forth in their tiny living room that day. To defeat the goodness of one's soul, there was no weapon on earth equal to fear. And it becomes doubly powerful when a political ideology seeks its own validation through scientific means like those to be implemented at Görden and other hospitals throughout Germany. There, Erich knew, the best of doctors would quickly succumb to the combined lure of science and fear, leaving only a saintly few to resist, who would in time grow silent, too. Still, he was still not sure which road he would take when the moment finally came. A compromise by the soul that might heal some distant day would be the ideal road to take, if there were such a thing to be found. Though one's soul would have to make room for a joint owner other than God if that were to happen, Erich mumbled to himself as he walked to the East Ward where he had been assigned.

Nothing in the hospital had changed from yesterday, which he had hoped it might, as he walked through the halls before returning to the nurse's station. The darkness in the halls was still unnerving. Piles of trash and discarded bandages lay in the corners of the halls waiting to be hauled away. Only the faint muffled sounds of coughing and crying from children could be heard coming from a few rooms as he walked by. Most of the rooms were still empty, their beds unused, which puzzled Erich at first. But then he remembered that the compulsory registration, spoken of by Bouhler, of all mentally and physically disabled children under three had been in effect only a few days. Soon the children would come to Görden and the beds would be filled and he would be busy being a good doctor.

Erich sat down behind the broad marble counter that encircled the station and began to read through the first of a small stack of patient records.

"Good morning, Herr Dr. Schmidt."

Erich looked up quickly to find the nurse he briefly spoke with yesterday peering intently at him from the other side of the counter.

"I am Nurse Drossen," she continued, smiling, "and I should be sitting there and you standing here. May I help you with anything?"

"Yes, what is your full name?"

"Maria Drossen."

"May I address you as Maria?" Erich asked bluntly, surprising her by his bold dismissal of the professional decorum expected from German doctors. Though he had no good reason for doing so, the situation he found himself in seemed to call for it. His eyes had been quick to follow her outline in the crisp white uniform she was wearing, which to him seemed the only thing clean and sanitized in the hospital. Strikingly attractive, but not in a pretty way, she appeared taller than most German women, made so by her long blonde hair coiled neatly in a large bun on top of her head.

"No, now please, Herr Doctor, you should begin making morning rounds, not sitting in my station. I'll be in trouble if the head nurse finds me standing here and you sitting there," Maria said, walking around to the side opening in the counter by a metal gate, waiting for Erich to move.

Erich gathered the small stack of medical records, handed them to Maria, then moved quickly past her to the front of the counter. His only concern now was the paucity of information in all the files. Each one contained only two pages, the admitting certificate with an initial diagnosis, and one daily report page, scribbled on by Maria. There were no doctor's summaries and notes, no treatment orders for the nurse to follow, no lab reports to check, no reference to drugs prescribed, nor any other details one would expect to find in a patient's record. Nothing but two nearly blank pages comprised each patient's record.

"Is this all there is?" he asked. Clearly frustrated, he slammed the stack hard on the countertop, causing Maria to back away.

"Yes, sir. That is all Dr. Heinze wants until the new medical forms arrive from the Health Ministry."

Still angry, Erich motioned for Maria to follow him as he started down the hall to his right.

"Tell me, why do you keep the halls and rooms so dark and gloomy? It would be quite frightening to me if I were a child. Children love bright and shiny things around them."

"Dr. Heinze ordered the change. He thought it would be less threatening, keep the children calm, you know, in such a strange setting."

Erich said nothing more and entered the first room with an infant patient, clicking on the ceiling light as he did. The small child was curled up on her side in a fetal position, sucking on the stub of an arm that had no hand. Erich glanced at the admitting report, which noted nothing other than the child's name and age: Brigitte Wallenhorst, age two.

Terror swept the child's face, as he gently lifted her from the bed and cradled her in his arms, speaking softly to her for a moment, then handing her to Maria. As he did, he felt her twisted and malformed spinal column, causing the child to draw back in pain. She would never walk, nor be able to sit up by herself, he knew.

"She is soiled and should be changed," was all Erich could think to say.

"It's not time to do so, Herr Doctor. A rigid cleaning schedule for these children has been set by the Health Ministry due to rationed supplies—the war, you know," Maria responded, putting the child back in the bed.

"For God's sake, this is supposed to be a hospital. Clean the child."

Maria said nothing, nor made any move to touch the child. Instead, she backed away from Erich, standing near the door as if she were not a part of the medical rounds taking place.

"Does this child stay here alone? Where are her parents?" Erich asked, becoming more demanding and upset with what was taking place.

"They have been sent home, that's all I know. All of our children are alone."

"How could anyone let their child die alone, if that is what were to happen?" Erich asked incredulously, moving back to the child's bed.

"It is not what I would do," Maria said softly.

Erich stood by the side of Brigitte's little bed for a second, stroking her soft cheeks with his fingers, then her tiny forehead and the back of her neck. Soon she closed her eyes to sleep for a while. He knew what Maria was saying. If the child were going to die, which she would in time, it would be easier to explain her death by a simple letter to her parents than face their questions. Besides, there would be too many eyes to watch what was happening to their child and the other children being brought to the hospital by order of the Chancellery.

"Where are you from, Nurse Drossen?" Erich asked, wanting to change the subject and talk about something more pleasant.

Again surprised by his sudden personal question, Maria waited a moment before responding.

"Mainz. My family has lived there for years."

"Any children, siblings?"

"None. My husband is away, stationed somewhere in Czechoslovakia. Why are you asking these questions? They seem improper."

Erich said nothing and took Maria forcibly by her arm, leading her to the side of the infant's bed.

"Tell me, if Brigitte was your child would you let her die?"

Maria immediately pulled her arm away from his grip, moving quickly back to the doorway where she had been standing.

"I don't know, but it would no longer be my choice," she said nervously, showing some fear in her voice at Erich's strange conduct.

"If it were your choice, what would you want?" Erich demanded.

"I don't know, really. Death belongs to God, doesn't it?"

"That's too easy of an answer, Maria. To whom does killing an innocent child really belong, then?"

Uncertain of his questions and intentions, Maria remained silent. Erich covered the child's bare legs with a small cloth, then left the room. As he did he heard the sharp click of the light switch as she returned the room to darkness again. Darkness and death were inseparable, he thought, walking into the hallway. Even on the brightest of days, death brings darkness to those around us when we close our eyes for the last time. No wonder the medieval churches were able to strangle the minds of the masses in the name of God. No one, least of all the innocent, could escape the darkness unless granted by the church. Even today, for those dying, what might elude us in that mystery, frightens us.

Erich paused for a moment in the hallway, thinking about the futility of even trying to care for Brigitte, and then abruptly decided against examining the other four children at this time. Their medical records were all the same, empty, and he had no authority to go further in treating the children than what he was doing now, which was nothing.

The next week a sprinkling of children were admitted to the hospital to be treated through the compulsory registration program of "misfits," as they were now called. But none came to the East Ward where Erich waited with Maria, for which he was glad. With little to do, he spent many hours of the day, and even into the night, in the medical library reading on all that medicine knew about Down's syndrome and microcephaly and malformations of every known kind, of the limbs and head and spinal column. Even vague explanations of the term "idiocy" were studied. He would learn far more, so it seemed to him, than in all his years in medical school. He had gained a vast medical knowledge, far more than the committee of doctors who would determine the end therapy to be imposed on all the "misfits" brought to the hospital for treatment. Perhaps now, he felt, he would be in position to at least provide some hope to a few of the children. The others would be lost, as the Health Ministry intended them to be.

Late on a rainy Friday afternoon, as Erich moved along a row of shelves in the library replacing texts he had been reading, he noticed an odd assortment of medical journals and papers from past world conferences on research in eugenics and other scientific areas. Among them was a publication he had never seen before, or knew existed, titled *The New German Physician*. Erich lifted the journal from the shelf and placed it with the other papers he was taking to study in his apartment. "I will see what you have to say and what I should be when I am not so tired," he said to no one as he left the library to go home alone in the rain.

When Monday came, Erich arrived earlier than usual at the East Ward to surprise Maria, who always reported in ahead of most of the other nurses and would be waiting for him. When she arrived, he immediately summoned her to follow him on the morning round, which in the past, had been perfunctorily carried out at best. This time though, he carefully examined every inch of the children's wretchedly deformed bodies, what they looked like and felt to the hand. Nothing went unnoticed, not even the tiniest moles, or the shapes of their ears and feet. When he was through, he could recite from memory all that he had found in examining each child. All were soiled in one way or another, until he finally prevailed on Maria to ignore the rigid bathing schedule and see that the children were kept clean, should the committee decide to look at them.

In the days that followed, he would continue to see and examine each child in the morning and afternoon, looking for the slightest change in their physical condition, though nothing was being done for them other than to keep them comfortable. But it was Brigitte with whom he would spend the most time during his rounds, talking to her softly and calling her name, while he gently massaged her useless legs. When he was finished, he would stand at the nurse's station, carefully entering in each child's record the date and time and details of his examination. Brigitte's would be the most detailed, noting at length what he believed to be positive signs of improvement in her muscle tone, though there were none. At times, his antics seemed almost theatrical to Maria, as she watched his meticulous attention to the slightest movement in Brigitte's legs. Nothing had changed in the days the child had been with them in the East Ward, nor would there ever be, she knew, except in Erich's foolish mind. He had for some silent reason embarked on a useless quest to heal a child whose horrific infirmities were frozen in time the day she entered the world. What he might do when the Health Ministry committee's recommendations were placed in Brigitte's and the other children's files bothered her. She could be seen as a part of the problem, should he take issue with the committee's findings. Like her soldier husband, Martin, Maria believed herself to be a good German, placing duty to the country above all else, and now she was frightened by Erich's obsession with trying to heal Brigitte.

After his last examination of the children, Erich turned to Maria to ask a question she thought strange, coming as it did at this time when he should know the answer.

"Are there unregistered children, like we are treating on the other floors?"

"I don't know. A few, maybe. Why do you ask?"

"I assume then, the Health Ministry's committee knows nothing of our children, and will not examine them?"

"You should know that they will. Dr. Heinze was here yesterday, examining your patients, wanting to know why they had not been registered. He was not pleased with all that you had written in their records either, called it a barnyard name," Maria said, closely watching Erich's reaction to her words.

Erich turned pale for a moment, nervously flipping the edges of the files back and forth before Maria took them from him, placing them on her desk. He realized now, with the intervention of Dr. Heinze and the committee, he was walking a precarious path, surrounded on all sides by uncertainty and the possibility of personal disaster. Maria watched Erich closely, feeling little sympathy for him. He was nothing like she had imagined the son of Dr. Vicktor Schmidt would be. Indeed, he seemed to her to be the meekest of the meek when compared to the grandiose aura his father projected. She believed he was afraid of what was sure to happen in the hospital, as she was, but for a different reason. And what he would do, or not do, when the time came to act on the committee's recommendations, was of no small concern to her now.

Maria waited for some kind of response from Erich, but he said nothing. His mind was elsewhere, as if he were lost in some kind of vegetative state, hearing but unable to speak. After minutes passed staring in silence at the children's files, he took the files from Maria's desk and opened each one, carefully reading through all that he had written. He could no longer pretend as he had been.

After a long pause, he spoke quietly to her. "There really is nothing for me to do, except keep these children comfortable, is there?"

Maria only nodded.

"What are the names of the consulting doctors, Maria, the ones that will make the final treatment decision for the children?"

"I don't know. The committee is in Berlin, and is secret," Maria answered quickly.

"That isn't what I asked," Erich said, becoming impatient with Maria's evasive manner.

"The ad hoc committee here at the hospital is Dr. Brandt and Dr. Heinze and Dr. Catel from Leipzig. That's all I have been told."

His father's name was missing from the committee, which surprised Erich. Had he been on the committee, the door to some kind of redemption would have been kept ajar for a little while longer by talking with him. But now, he knew, there was nothing between himself and the infinite depth of a political ideology veneered with the science of eugenics. Yet he was not ready to shut his mouth on the truth. Not only would he enlist his father's prestige in confronting the committee, he would artfully defend each child's medical condition against any prognosis that it was hopeless. Handing the files back to Maria, he turned to leave the ward.

"I will be in the library," he said, calmly walking away, leaving Maria puzzled.

EIGHTEEN

Erich, Görden Hospital, 1941

The night was good to Erich this time, no more other worlds to hide from, no more monsters to fight and slay. Dreams as they should be came to him, dancing magically throughout the night in his sleeping thoughts. Even though his father had sternly warned him about duty and honor and the consequences of failure, he still was his father's son, and Erich knew his father would help him. With the start of his morning shift at the hospital still two hours away, an early morning walk in the cool air along the Havel River was the right place to prepare the words he would soon speak to his father. He would tell him then that performing one's duty only out of fear has no honor, no goodness attached to it, unless it is the right thing to do at the moment. And surely now, all that was being expected of him was wrong.

Erich arrived at the hospital fifteen minutes early and went straight to the East Ward, where he saw Maria laughing with two nurses leaving from the night shift. As he approached them, the two nurses quickly walked away, leaving Maria alone standing by her desk.

"Good morning, Herr Doctor. You look fresh and well."

"Thank you, I am. What time will the committee be here? Do we have time to see the children again before they arrive?" Erich asked in an excited tone.

Hesitating, Maria picked up the children's files, handing them to him.

Erich hurriedly opened the first file, which was little Brigitte's. A form that he had never seen before lay on top of the admitting sheet. But he read no further. On the left side of the form, the names of his father and Dr. Catel and Dr. Heinze were printed.

"My father was with the committee?" he asked, not believing his eyes.

"Yes. Dr. Brandt was detained in Berlin. They met here very early and left. That's all I know. Dr. Heinze will be here soon to walk the morning rounds with you."

"My father was with them?" Erich asked a second time, not listening to Maria's words.

The winds of hope that had filled his sails this morning became as still and listless as an ocean calm, where he would flounder helplessly. On the right side under the heading "Treatment" were three columns with a space available parallel to each of the three names. A bold plus mark had been penciled in the left column by each name, which included his father's. Erich's heart sank and he asked Maria to get him a drink of water. The plus mark meant only one thing: the killing of the child. It had no other meaning. There was no other way to say it. All he had hoped for was one minus sign noted in the middle column, which would have allowed the child to live. His father could have done this, but didn't.

Maria returned with a glass of water, placed it on the desk, and sat down next to Erich. The blood had drained from his face, leaving him as white as the paper he had been reading.

"You look sick. Let me get you a cold towel," Maria said, starting to stand up.

"No don't, this will pass. It's not easy to accept being betrayed by your father. He knew how I felt about this whole goddamned mess. Yet, his plus mark is bigger and bolder than the other two."

"Perhaps he meant to tell you, time has so little meaning now for all of us in this war."

"No, the bastard sat across from me at dinner several days back and said nothing, not a word about the committee. Duty with honor was the topic he had chosen for discussion—my duty and his honor," Erich said hatefully.

Erich started to open the second file but stopped and put it back with the others in the stack. There was no reason to read it, he knew. The plus marks of death would be there, too. These four children were in worse shape than little Brigitte—blind or deaf, or both, and badly deformed. Two one-year-olds with dangling microcephalic heads no bigger than an apple. Another sightless and deaf with two stubs for legs. The fourth child, deaf and an imbecile—there was no other way for Erich to describe him. All were innocent victims of some misguided step in evolution's wiring at some unexpected moment in their mother's womb. But Erich knew there would be others to come, thousands perhaps, whose only deformities were hidden in the terrors of their twisted insane minds. They were the frightening ones, scorned by a society that delighted in keeping the threshold low between that which was normal and abnormal. There was no room for the delightful eccentricities of silly people.

Maria saw Dr. Heinze approaching from the far end of the main hall before Erich did and moved to the front of the station to greet him. Erich remained seated at the desk, acknowledging Dr. Heinze's presence only after he stood before him and spoke.

"Good morning, Nurse Drossen. Good morning, Herr Dr. Schmidt."

Erich nodded but did not smile.

"I have reviewed the files again, Dr. Heinze. Perhaps we should see the children now," he said curtly, handing the files to Maria and walking towards the infant Brigitte's room without waiting for Dr. Heinze.

In her room, and the others that followed, Erich carefully described in descriptive detail, to the amazement of Dr. Heinze and Maria, each and every affliction suffered by the five children and where there might be a good possibility of therapy. No one looked closely at the children, though, nor touched them. The diagnostic pictures he painted were too vivid to doubt. When they were through, Erich looked at his watch. The medical rounds with Dr. Heinze had taken only fifteen minutes; killing them would take longer—an absurdity in itself that Erich would not soon forget.

Back at the nurse's station, Dr. Heinze told Erich to come to his office in twenty minutes to a staff meeting of all attending doctors. There the treatment of these children and those that were to come would be finalized. Erich again said nothing, only nodding that he would. He had yet to speak Dr. Heinze's name, or show him the courtesy his position demanded. Ignoring all protocol, he had walked ahead of him in the hall and to the rooms, not behind him, or even next to him—as if it were his only means of protesting the absurdity of what they were acting out—a fact that didn't go unnoticed by Dr. Heinze and Maria. But Erich knew that the few grains of sand left in the hourglass would soon fall to the bottom, freezing him forever in all that was around him as if it were a new unseen dimension in time.

Maria stood silent, watching Erich, waiting for him to acknowledge her presence, even though she was standing close to him. A healthy hue was in his face again, and his hands were calm and his walk deliberate as he moved to her desk and sat down.

"I will need a notepad to take with me to the meeting. They will talk about the final therapy procedure, I am sure," Erich said anxiously, motioning to Maria, who quickly opened a side drawer under the counter, retrieving a blue notepad for him.

"I will be here when you return, should you need to talk about what is to happen," Maria said softly, as Erich started down the hall towards Dr. Heinze's office.

Six doctors, besides Erich, took their seats in front of Dr. Heinze's desk waiting for his appearance, which usually came exactly ten minutes after everyone had assembled. It was a disarming trick he had learned from waiting on Philipp Bouhler in the Health Ministry. Important people are never punctual, nor should they be. It is our right, he believed. Then for the next two hours, continually mixing patriotic fervor with substance, Dr. Heinze spelled out to the small group the medical protocol to be followed, how they would welcome the children sent to them, and how they would kill them. Everything he was saying displayed a sophistication of thought by the Chancellery and Health Ministry in planning the program to be undertaken at Görden. It would not be a one-time event, Erich realized, but a mass undertaking that had been carefully crafted by leaders in the Ministry, which included his father.

Strangely though, of all that Dr. Heinze had said, it was the lie that the doctors would be compelled to tell the parents about their child's death that bothered Erich the most. After the death of a child, the attending doctor was to write the parents a kind and gentle letter, telling them of their child's death from unexpected complications, nothing more. There would be nothing entered in the medical records of the child other than time of death and a fictitious cause. To Erich, everyone knew there was nothing more sacred in a physician-patient relationship than the truth, and the lying and the killing they were ordering were not the same. The killing could be explained with reason, as a cold necessity like Hitler had said, but not a lie. And no mother should be lied to when it came to the death of her child, or anything else for that matter. Lying is a man's way of trying to hide from God, his mother had told him, and He won't let you do that more than once or twice before shipping you off to hell, which frightened him terribly. Lying to yourself didn't count with God, though she thought it should, because you were only fooling and hurting yourself. So, he never lied again to his mother, or himself, or to anyone else. He would pretend though, which wasn't lying, because he always knew it wasn't real, much like pretending his father really did love him.

Clearly disturbed by what he was hearing, Erich grew restless, stirring in his chair, crossing and uncrossing his legs trying to get comfortable, and somehow shut his ears to the nonsense sputtering endlessly from Dr. Heinze's mouth. Finally, swept up by the drama of the moment, Dr. Heinze rose and walked slowly from behind his desk, pausing for a moment in front of each doctor until he came to Erich, where he stood in silence, staring hard at him.

"We doctors are warriors for the Fatherland, too. Everyone here should think carefully on these words, lest we forget them," he said calmly but with a hidden agenda of terror clearly behind his voice.

Then he left the room, which had suddenly become cold with an eerie uneasiness that everyone felt. No one spoke, nor stood to leave for several minutes, each afraid of what the others might think and say behind his back.

Erich did not return to the East Ward, but walked straight to the medical library and sat down at the second of the two tables there. To him, the ancient Greek playwrights couldn't have written a greater drama. Only the chorus of chanting voices was missing. All of their virtues and struggles were carefully rolled up in a bundle of nonsensical emotions and placed before him on the table. Duty and fear and courage and all the others, even suicide, were all there laid out to be seen and wrestled with. It was not an "Either/Or" moment of truth, as long argued by Kierkegaard, whom he fancied greatly. Instead, it was a decision to survive, to stay alive one more day, and then the day after, until God finally decided to change the barrel organ tune that everyone was dancing to.

Strangely, Erich tried to imagine what Julia would say if she were here with him this very moment. The courage she would bring to the table, though, would be unfair, because he had no equal to it. His father's thoughts meant nothing either, because they had long been anchored in drifting sand, blown about by the winds of change each passing day. But his mother's decision at this moment, he knew, would be from her heart, what roads she believed in traveling, though they might be the wrong ones. Courage had no merit to her because it was a male thing; only duty counted. Whether it was right or wrong didn't matter. Goodness came to you in performing one's duty, nothing more. The duty to tell the truth, or tend to your neighbor, or fight for your country were all one and the same, Christian virtues to the core, so it seemed to her. However, neither she nor Julia were doctors. Whatever they believed in, the ancient sanctity of the physician/patient relationship was missing for them. This holy treasure, carefully wrapped through the centuries with the fabric of Hippocrates's robe, transcended all other duties. And it was this treasure the Health Ministry set about changing, making the physician/patient relationship beholden to the state.

Erich walked back to the stack of journals near the door and lifted from the bottom shelf the journal he had taken and returned unread, *The New German Physician*. Nothing original was offered in the words before him until he reached the core of the arguments being made for what a German physician should be, particularly in wartime. With so many of Germany's best and bravest facing death on the battlefields, the argument went, it was imperative on the physician "to come to terms with counter-selection in their own people." He had never heard the term "counter-selection" used in medicine, or anywhere else for that matter. It was presented coldly for the first time, as a moral choice that the new physician must consider.

What came next in the treatise surprised Erich even more by its careful reasoning. Infant mortality is a process of natural selection, with the majority of the cases affecting the constitutionally inferior. But now advances in medicine dramatically interfere with this selection. Therefore, the task of the new German physician becomes that of restoring the balance of nature to its original form through the process of counter-selection. Not to do so would be ethically unacceptable. This was it, what the physician should be about, and it bothered Erich because it made good sense and was quite seductive. Unless the incurable die, true healing of the sick and protecting the nation's health would be impossible.

Still, by itself, this summons to a new understanding of what a German physician should be about was not enough to change how he felt, though it might be for other young doctors. Yet he knew, when the physician's primary duty to alleviate suffering of the sick was combined with the idea of counter-selection, two goods could be achieved without one negating the other. But to euthanize the incurable to ease suffering was an irreversible step on the slippery slope to hell, which he was unprepared to take, at least for the moment. Even though an acceptable solution to the problem he faced was before him by simply following the orders of the Health Ministry, what was missing was the sacred commitment that makes all medicine worthwhile. Without it, everything would be a lie. He would be swallowed up by the hungers of self-deception. Erich pushed aside the journal on the table, sitting for a moment before leaving for the East Ward. It was late and much remained to be decided, but waiting to do so was no longer an option for him. Even time had become a vaunted foe of sanity, so it seemed.

Dr. Heinze was waiting on Erich when he and Maria returned to the nurse's station. Looking at Dr. Heinze as he approached the counter, Erich decided there wasn't any one thing pleasant about the man. His appearance defied description, bordering on the comical obscene, if there was such a thing. In many ways, the man looked less human then the children he had just seen. Meanness and ambition have always been great ingredients to cook up a good dose of ugliness, and he had plenty of both. That Erich disliked him was quite apparent to Heinze, and he secretly hoped Erich would falter in carrying out the final therapy for the "misfits". He could then report him to Bouhler at the Health Ministry. Not only would he rid the likes of Erich from the program, he would likely weaken the prestige his father held with Brandt and the other leaders in the Chancellery, which he envied greatly.

"You have seen the children again to begin the final therapy?" Heinze asked in his high shrill voice as Erich approached him.

"No. Should that be a problem?"

"Only if their beds aren't empty and ready for the other children who will soon be here."

"Will these children die soon enough? That is what you mean, isn't it?" Erich said with sarcastic anger. "When their time comes, you will know, but for now we should leave them alone."

Fuming and red in the face from being challenged by Erich in front of Maria and two other nurses who had joined them at the station, Heinze said nothing more and walked away. Inside, though, his turbulent anger and dislike of Erich churned in his stomach, coated with the bitterness of the digestive acids held there. He would find some way to force young Schmidt's hand and bring him down. Perhaps seeking the senior Schmidt and Karl Brandt's return to Görden would force him into a corner from which there was no escape. Once he had crossed the line, euthanizing just one child, any further resistance based on his own sense of integrity would crumble into fine sawdust like termite-infested timber. He would make the call to Dr. Brandt and Dr. Schmidt, but give Erich no reason for their sudden return to Görden from Berlin.

Erich knew that Dr. Heinze would not let the ugly confrontation pass so easily and go unanswered. His own standing with Brandt and Bouhler would be in dire jeopardy, too, if he allowed any dissent from the doctors to continue drifting and unsettled. To do so would bring into question the feasibility of the whole program to cleanse the German race of all the misfits. More importantly, the moral element, surreptitiously attached to the program by placing it in the hands of the doctors, would be gone, too.

Erich waited until Dr. Heinze disappeared from sight down the hall, then moved slowly to Maria's desk, keeping the children's files with him. No words had passed between him and Maria this day. It was not that he had chosen to ignore her, but rather, whether she should be involved at any point in the terrible things about to happen. Perhaps she shuddered in the same fear he did but had pushed aside her feelings on right and wrong, reasoning that in these times, like everything else, they simply didn't matter anymore. With her husband facing death each new day on the Eastern Front, how she felt about her duties as a nurse and whether they were right or wrong was of little consequence. Yet if Maria did believe as he did, should he expect her to jump into the same quicksand he was already sinking in? When the time came, though, he decided, Maria would swallow her own moral longings and become a part of whatever duty asked of her.

Erich rose from behind the desk and walked past Maria towards the West Ward, leaving her wondering at the coldness of his behavior. As he neared the nurse's station, two nurses began busily shuffling and reshuffling papers and files they had read ten times over.

"Is Dr. Schneider on duty today?" he asked the older of the two nurses, whom he surmised was in charge.

Before responding to him, the older woman glanced quickly at the other nurse, questioning with her look whether she should say anything.

"Dr. Schneider has been reassigned to another hospital, that is all we know," she said, looking around as if she were expecting someone.

"Reassigned? To what hospital?"

"I don't know. We haven't been told anything since two men came by the station late yesterday, and he left with them."

As Erich heard these words, his heart began to race, and the palms of his hands grew hot and sweaty. He had known Dr. Schneider only a short while, but sensed, maybe wrongly, that his beliefs about the final therapy were like his own. He had spoken out strongly against killing the Knauer child back in Leipzig, yet still participated as a witness to the dreadful act. The signals to Erich, and to everyone else involved, were as clear as the deep pools of spring water flowing in Triberg, where the bottom seemed on top. Indecision was rejection, should one tarry about carrying through to the end the new therapy program set by the Health Ministry.

"Two men—who were they? What did they look like?" Erich asked hurriedly, trying to hold on to the reins of his emotions. He was clearly frightened by what he was hearing.

"I don't remember. They said very little, and were here only a few minutes. They seemed quite serious that he go with them, though, and he did."

"Without saying a word? Perhaps when he might return?"

"What I have told you is all we know. It all happened so quickly. Dr. Heinze did say a new doctor will be here soon."

"Dr. Heinze?"

"Yes sir. He came here shortly after the two men left with Dr. Schneider."

Erich started to leave, when the nurse who had said nothing spoke up.

"The new doctor's name is Franz Kremer, should that mean anything to you."

"No, nothing," Erich said and left to return to the East Ward.

But the name Franz Kremer did mean something to him. He was the tall, blond Sudeten student who had railed against Julia and all the other Jews in the world at the medical school in Prague. Swept up in the mind-numbing slogans of the National Socialist Party, he despised the weak and timid German warrior, as he thought Erich to be. Coming to Görden as a treatment doctor to erase the "misfits" polluting the German race was more than a medical undertaking to him. He believed himself more than a mere doctor, but as one of the chosen few called to defend the health and well-being of the Third Reich. His own devotion to the cause of cleansing the race was of such a nature that he believed everyone should follow it. And those that chose not to should be eliminated. Erich always felt that Franz would rise high in the eyes of the party, faster than anyone around him, and he was doing so by his presence here at Görden. Through his eyes, as it traditionally was with so many German psychiatrists, and with those that would follow, the tender face of a malformed child was no different from that of an animal. Yet it was not that they saw them as completely animal; it was that they never saw them as human beings.

Erich knew now there was more than the decided fate awaiting the children. His own existence as well could possibly be determined by Franz's sudden appearance at the hospital. Mephistopheles had finally tired of wearing the mask of fear, and was now waiting impatiently for him to make the decision to sell his soul should he want to continue living. It was quite simple. Franz knew Julia as a student, but more so, as a Jew. He also knew of Erich's great love for her and their isolated spirited intimacy, and hated him for it. To Franz, Erich had purposely spit on the spirit of the Nürnberg laws prohibiting such relationships, and in doing so, turned his back forever on the National Socialist Party. Uncompromising revenge against the enemies of the state was an easy road to power, which Franz would gladly surrender to the likes of Dr. Heinze when the time came to do so.

Erich could think no more, his mind clouded with a gray nothingness. But depression was a better word. In a way he was glad, though, because great moments can rise to the top from the deep oceans of depression, as they had before with him, and perhaps would again. Returning to the East Ward, he walked to the end of the long, dark hall and sat down on a narrow wooden bench beneath a large window. God was turning the barrel organ too fast for him to dance now. So much was happening. His father and the Knauer child and Dr. Heinze, and now Franz Kremer, were all crowding and pushing him at the same time. He could no longer risk, or even imagine, any genuine resistance to the killing program if he wanted to stay alive. There simply were no more places for him to run and hide.

Erich stood for a second, looking down from the window at a small rose garden below full of nothing but beautiful life, and studied it for a moment. With no mind of its own, a rose will always be a rose, living out its given time in the sun and rain until it withers and dies. Yet while it lives, its simple beauty fills the passions of the eye, making lovers and poets of us all. Looking back down the long, dark hall, he saw no passion for the eye, only pity. Five young precious souls were there, all longing to be set free from their crippled minds and bodies, loved by no one, except perhaps their mother and maybe God. Even then, Erich wondered why God would allow such life to exist. Unlike the rose and its given beauty, they served no purpose. Releasing them from their prison would be God's way of correcting nature's mistake.

Erich stepped back away from the window and folded his arms across his chest in a sudden moment of great elation. Would not God and the world see the greater good for everyone with the compassionate death of these miserable souls serving medical research? At the same time, would he not be honoring his duty to Germany by serving medicine and science? He could forge a connection with a neuropathologist to obtain brains for research from genetic misfits in Germany, and the world would be better for it. All that was necessary, he knew, was to have his father request the assignment of such a specialist to Görden where he could work with him. Almost giddy, Erich walked with lighter steps back to the nurse's station where Maria was waiting for him.

"Please give me the children's files, Nurse Drossen," he asked, politely smiling.

Maria did so, puzzled by the dramatic change in Erich's whole presence. It was unlike anything she had experienced with him. Even his eyes looked strangely odd, looking past her to some distant setting.

"Now please prepare four small cups of broth with luminal tablets dissolved in them, and a single hypodermic syringe with 50 mgs of morphine."

Hearing Erich's sobering words, Maria froze, unable to move, her face became flushed and her throat dry, halting questions she wanted to ask him but couldn't. She had talked boldly of this day with the other nurses on the grounds, but now that it was here she found herself as frightened as a lost child, unable to speak.

Maria's emotional collapse surprised Erich. He had thought her cold and impervious to suffering, the ideal companion to assist him in the difficult tasks that awaited them.

"Maria, we must act now, together. If we don't, I am afraid the time will never be here for us again. Do you understand what I am saying?" Erich said, his words quick, his voice strong.

Maria nodded slightly, still not moving to carry out his request. He held out his hand to her.

"Give me the keys to the cooler where the drugs are stored and follow me."

Nothing happened. Erich moved quickly, taking hold of Maria's arm, running his hand down in the large front pocket of her uniform, searching for the keys. The sudden intimate touching caused her to break free from him and stand braced against the back wall of the station.

"What is it you want, Dr. Schmidt?" she asked, trembling.

"Your support Maria, that's all," he said softly, trying to calm her.

Maria hesitated for a second, then walked past him to the small storage room where the pharmaceutical cooler and other hospital supplies were kept. Erich counted the minutes, waiting for her to return, his own resolve weakening with each passing second. At the same time, he kept a watchful eye for Dr. Heinze's presence in the halls. "The man is all evil and will corrupt the good I am trying to bring about," he repeated to himself several times for courage. "To have him standing next to me would be unbearable."

In a few minutes Maria returned from the storage room carrying a tray with the luminal mixture and morphine syringe. Together in silence, they walked to the far end of the hall and entered the room of Wilheim, one of the two children suffering with the same maladies diagnosed in the Knauer boy.

"We will keep him asleep on the same dosage of luminal the next four to five days until he can no longer awake. You do understand?" Erich asked, nodding to Maria.

Maria looked hard at Erich with tears streaming down her face.

"Yes, but I will give him the broth only after you have given him some. Then we will be in this mess together."

Erich quickly took a cup from the tray and, holding the boy's head, hesitated for a second, then slowly fed him the broth, until the child would take no more, then left the room.

In the next room, and the two after, the same routine was followed, with Maria though, holding the children while they drank the luminal broth. With only the morphine syringe remaining, they entered Brigitte's room, where the tiny child lay awake, looking around the room as if she understood what the world was all about. Erich gently lifted Brigitte from the bed, cradling her in his arm as he had done the first day they met, and softly stroked her tiny head, soothing her with his voice.

"My little Brigitte, you simply were born in the wrong place and at the wrong time."

Maria handed him the syringe and lifted Brigitte's gown, exposing her left hip and buttock, then turned away, unable to watch. Erich slowly injected the 50 mgs of morphine into Brigitte, then waited for her to die in his arms. Before she closed her eyes, a tiny smile, which he had never seen before, broke through her lips as she watched his face, causing him to turn away in tears. This moment would become a memory that he could neither confront and absorb, nor wish away with time. He knew other children would soon follow, yet it was only Brigitte's smile that he would remember.

NINETEEN

Julia, Czechoslovakia, 1942

Martin Drossen was a simple German soldier, but a good one. He didn't believe in the National Socialist Party, but he did believe in the German people. And he had gone to fight not for the Führer, but because it was his duty to do so as a good citizen. Martin's grandfather had died early in the Great War during a withering artillery barrage on the Western Front. His father's fate came one day after the armistice was signed ending the war. After spending a short leave at home, he was killed while returning to his unit near Aachen by a stray bullet fired, ironically, by a drunken soldier celebrating peace. But he had left his seed in Martin's mother then, and the legacy of honor and duty. Reared in Mainz by his widowed mother and widowed grandmother, he grew up to be a gentle person, but with little ambition. All he required from anyone who knew him was the same respect he gave them. Loving God was unimportant though, because he felt God had given him no right answers for his father and grandfather's deaths, a fact he was reminded of every day watching his mother grow old laboring ten hours a day as a housekeeper for two wealthy Jewish families.

Maria Wolken came into his life by chance one day. Entering the farmer's market to purchase a few fresh vegetables for home, he noticed her struggling to gather together an array of late spring melons that had tumbled into the street as she attempted to sample one. Rushing to help her retrieve the melons that had rolled beneath several parked trucks and carts, brought to Martin in a few short months a treasured friend and lover and devoted wife. Though Maria was deeply religious, she cared little, and worried less, that he wasn't. He was a good and generous man, with what little he could provide, and had her own father been killed in the war, she might have left God, too, she knew. Neither one, though, was prepared for what Hitler and Germany would soon demand of them. Maria entered nursing, which would take her later to the Görden Psychiatric Hospital, and Martin enlisted in the Wehrmacht. His only hope was that the war would be quickly over and he could return to his beloved Maria. But he now found himself, three years later, patrolling the main road between Nürnberg and Prague, with his many dreams of peace still distant for all of Germany.

As he sat this day astride the idling motorcycle, adjusting his goggles, Martin thought of home and Maria and wondered if she was keeping warm in the freezing winter air that had blanketed all of Europe. No one sane would be moving about on a day such as this, he mused. And running a patrol on the treacherous and icy roads in ten degree weather was asking death to ride along with him and maybe make an early appearance. But he would go, as he always did, for no other reason but duty. He would tarry for a while in the small villages passed through on his patrol, talking with anyone who might listen to what he was about. Most kept to themselves, though, saying little to him or to any of the other patrols that passed their way. He was their enemy and they despised him; not enough, though, for there were some who despised the Jews more. Many Jews had already been betrayed in their own village where they had lived for generations, and turned over to the patrols, while others were shot on sight and their bodies dumped in the passing rivers. A perfect storm of madness had come to the land, opening up its vast dark clouds to rain monsters on all those below.

Julia and Eva had each asked the other a dozen times what they were doing tromping through woods on a day made only for dying. What little body heat they had early in the morning had long been taken down by the gripping cold. Little time remained, both knew, before they would become one with the frozen earth. They would surrender, not to the Germans, but to the precious gift of a warm sleep, when all feeling becomes suspended as frozen death comes to the mind and body.

It was Julia who saw the farm buildings first through an opening in the woods. Rising out of the snow two hundred yards distant, they looked like giant stone ogres of old sniffing the air for any human scent. Freezing, yet warm from excitement, Julia and Eva stayed in the woods out of sight for several minutes, watching for any movements about the buildings. Wisps of gray smoke broke from the chimney top on the house, wafting upwards from the snow-covered roof in a slow spiral to meet the early morning clouds. Eva had experienced the idyllic scene many times before on her farm in Bratislava, and never tired of the inward joy it brought to her long days of laboring there.

"It's beautiful, isn't it," she said, squeezing Julia's hand.

"It is for sure. Beauty is the only thing constant in this dirty old world of ours that tells us God may be still hanging around. It can always be found somewhere."

"Who told you that foolishness?"

"Erich, in one of his weaker moments I suspect, but it's true."

"He hasn't been to hell yet," Eva laughed, leaving the woods and starting across the highway towards a narrow, snow-covered road leading to the farmhouse. As she did she looked back to Julia following her.

"I will talk," she said. "I am a peasant, and whoever lives in the house will be a peasant too. Besides, you are too citified and Jewish looking."

Julia smiled and said nothing. She had always wondered as a child what a Jew should look like, and no one, not even her father knew, though he joked about it many times with Hiram. She finally decided one day that it was their good Rabbi who looked the way a Jew should be. But he was a man, which meant to her that only men could look like Jews, not women, leaving her quite disgusted. This seemed true to her even now because Eva was a Jew, yet she looked no different than all the Slavs who worked the fields and vineyards around Bratislava.

As they neared the farmhouse, Julia noticed a thin wire fence circling the building as well as the barn standing immediately next to it. The gate opened into a small courtyard separate from the rest of the grounds leading to the barn. Like the outbuildings, the farmhouse was made of heavy fieldstone, one level, and elevated several feet above the ground to accommodate the heavy snows that came in the long winters. A wide stone staircase led to the front door. Before they reached the stairs, the heavy wooden door swung open. A thin older man, spare in flesh, with ruffled grey hair and a dark complexion, greeted them with suspicion and an old German Mauser rifle used by some Hungarians in the Great War. Julia and Eva moved no closer, unsure of what they should do.

"What do you women want? I have been watching you two for some time."

"We are cold and lost, I think, and want only to warm ourselves for a little while and we will be on our way," Eva answered.

"Who are you? Only fools and bad people would be out in this weather."

"I am Eva Pitsky and my friend here is Julia Simik. We are from Pilsen," Eva said. "We were trying to get to Klatovy, when the bus slid off the road some ways back."

"Does your friend here talk?" the man said, looking strangely at Julia.

"Yes I do, and may we please come in? My feet are frozen solid," Julia said softly, smiling at the man.

Saying nothing, the man stepped back into the house. Holding the rifle steadily with both hands, he nodded to Julia and Eva to enter the room. Julia rushed to the open stone fireplace holding a thick bed of hot embers slowing burning a large, newly laid log. Removing her boots, she quickly sat down on the hearth, placing her feet within inches of the glowing embers, and sighed with delight.

Eva waited by the open door for a second before entering. Nothing about the man was reassuring, especially his eyes, which asked questions when they looked at you. Less trusting than Julia, she stepped into the large room, watching every move the man made. He seemed to be alone in the house.

There were only two small rooms opening to the right of the big central room where Julia was and an open kitchen to the left with a small table and two chairs. A dirty soup bowl and spoon rested on the table alongside an empty butter dish and a slice of crusty hard bread. The toilet, she knew, was somewhere out back. He was a poor peasant by any measure, though her father's house had little more. Like many peasants in this area, each day's task in this man's life was to make it through another day, that's all.

The man walked to the kitchen and sat down by the table with the rifle resting on his lap. He watched Eva for a few seconds, then Julia as she continued to warm her feet by the fire.

"You are not cold like your friend?" he asked, staring now at Eva.

"No, I am a peasant like you. We are used to being miserable," Eva said, forcing a smile and returning the man's stare.

Seconds passed in silence before the man rose from his chair and laid the rifle down on the table.

"I have little for you to eat—soup and bread, that is all. You may warm yourselves a little while longer, then you must leave."

"We had hoped to spend a day or two until the days warm. We will pay you for the trouble," Eva said, moving to the stove and stirring what little was left of the lentil soup.

"You have not told me who you are. There are many like you on the roads today causing trouble, especially the Jews and gypsies," the man said, still staring at Eva.

"Do we look like gypsies and Jews? Look at my face and skin," Eva said boldly, moving closer to the man and brushing the hair away from her face.

But it was not Eva the man looked at now. His eyes were fixed on Julia, who was kneeling now by the fire, warming her hands.

"You do not talk much. Where is your home?" he asked, nodding to her.

"Pilsen. My father works in the iron works there."

The man studied her face for a moment and knew she was lying, then turned away and looked to where Eva was standing.

"You have money?"

"Some. Very little, in fact, a few Reich marks. You may have them if we can stay here for a few days," Eva said.

"I have my son's old bicycle. You must buy it also if I let you stay," the man said, looking back to Julia, who was sitting pulling her boots on.

Eva started to respond but stopped, and moved quickly to the door, opened it and listened. The distant puttering of motorcycles could be heard coming from the south. Julia had heard the sounds, too, and moved to the open door followed by the man.

"That will be a military patrol. They pass by here every day many times."

"Do they stop here?" Julia asked, trying to still the rising anxiety in her voice.

"Sometimes, maybe twice, to ask if I've seen any refugees or Jews on the road. If they stop, I will tell them nothing, and they will leave. But you must buy the bicycle," the man said without hesitation.

Julia exchanged glances with Eva, then nodded to the man.

The chugging of the motorcycles grew louder as they came into view, increasing to a frightening roar as it resonated through the crisp air. Julia counted six, each with a helmeted rider wearing heavy goggles and a submachine gun strapped across the back. As they neared the narrow road leading to the farmhouse, the last two slowed, then stopped at the entrance while the others continued on. Parking their machines by the roadside, they stood for a moment talking and smoking a cigarette before starting to the house through the heavy snow. Neither one seemed to notice, or pay any attention, to the double rows of tracks left by Julia and Eva leading to the house. When they drew near, Julia could hear their words, the closer of the two happily relating that he would go home soon to see his wife in Mainz, where he hoped she would become pregnant. Having a child would make him a better soldier, he believed.

"You must stay here and hide in the rooms while I go and talk with them. They won't come in. They never do," the man said, opening the door and going to the two soldiers.

"The bastard will betray us—he knows we are Jews," Eva said, moving quickly to the edge of the window, where she could see the man talking with the two soldiers.

"Probably, but it's the reward he will get from the Germans that has him out there talking," Julia said, glancing to the kitchen where the man had left his rifle. A fool's gift, she mumbled.

Within seconds of meeting the two soldiers, the man pointed to the house. Without waiting, both soldiers started for the staircase holding the submachine guns by their side. Julia and Eva were armed and waiting, kneeling quietly in the left front corner by the kitchen holding the small handguns they had carried holstered in a special inner waistband. Hidden by the front door when opened, they could be seen only at the last minute after the soldiers stepped from the doorway into the big room.

"We have the edge," Eva whispered to Julia as the door swung open.

Martin Drossen came in first and never saw who killed him. Julia shot him dead center between the eyes the second he turned his head towards the kitchen. The second soldier fared no better, falling within a second from two rapid shots fired by Eva. Before Julia could move, Eva jumped up and walked straight to the man who had meekly followed the soldiers into the house and shot him in the head twice.

"You betrayed us, you son of a bitch," she yelled at his crumpled body beneath her feet, then spat on him.

Julia hadn't moved from where she knelt, firing the first shot of her war with the Germans. She looked closely at the bloody face of Martin Drossen, who had fallen only a few feet from her, eyes open, frozen in death, staring at her. His moment on the stage had come to this. Erich was right. It is only when you can see the face of those who have died, those whom you have killed and never knew, that war has any meaning at all. Without the face, there is nothing to remember, only a statistic. Julia leaned over Martin and gently closed his eyes, then looked at Eva.

"We have killed three men this morning Eva. I wish God would tell us which side He is on now, then we would know what to do," she said in a remorseful tone.

"My sweet, gentle friend. Do you think God is hanging around to see which side is going to win this war?"

"This man seemed to be a kind German, that's all," Julia continued, pointing to Martin.

"He was. That's why he is dead. He wasn't ready to kill us, or anyone else. Only animals fight wars."

"Are we animals now?"

"Yes, fully grown ones. Like you said, we've just killed three people," Eva said, walking to the door and looking toward the road where the two motorcycles were parked.

"Right now we need to try and stay alive ourselves. These bodies and the motorcycles have to be hidden before they are missed by other patrols."

Julia rolled the soldier Eva had shot onto his stomach, trying hard not to look at the man's lifeless face. With some effort, she pulled a small leather wallet from his pants pocket, took the few Reich marks it held, and replaced the wallet. The peasant man she would leave alone. In Eva's eyes he had betrayed them, but to Julia he was just an ignorant man trying to survive for one more day.

Martin Drossen carried a beautiful brown embroidered leather case for a wallet that held five Reich marks and one photograph of a young woman in a nurse's uniform. Written across the bottom of the picture were the words, "Together in love always, Maria." Julia looked at the photograph for several seconds, then for reasons hidden from her by the drama of the moment, she placed the photograph in the inside pocket of her jacket. Later, whenever she would look at it, doing so kept before her Martin Drossen's gentle face, reminding her always of the day she became an animal trying to survive like everyone else in a world full of hate. Perhaps, she would think, when the killing was all done, she could go and find the young nurse and tell her of Martin.

Eva burst through the front door and walked to where Julia was sitting by Martin's body, streams of sweat dripping from her face.

"We can't use the man's spring pond to hide the bodies in—frozen over solid. But I found a better place. Let's take the old man first," she said, signaling Julia to lift his legs.

"Where are we taking him?"

"Just follow me and try and step in my tracks," Eva said, backing through the door and down the staircase.

Julia saw ahead the fresh tracks made by Eva leading to the old man's outhouse, and shuddered at what they were about to do.

"You won't like it, but it's all we have. Somehow it seems we are always around shit when it's there," Eva said.

When they got to the outhouse, Julia saw that Eva had kicked the toilet loose from the wood floor it was resting on, exposing the pit full of human feces and lime below.

Eva stopped at the door and looked at Julia's questioning expression for a moment.

"We can't hide them under the snow—they'll find them when it melts," she said.

"I know. We should do it quickly and be done."

The old man was the first of the three to rest his soul in the outhouse, with Martin Drossen last. Each was pushed with some difficulty through the hole face down so their arms wouldn't catch on the floor. When it came Martin's turn, Julia tried to avert seeing his face, but couldn't, and cried a little inside. When they were through, though, thinking back on where Martin and the others were made her glad she had kept the picture of Maria—it shouldn't be rotting in such a filthy mess.

As quickly as they had disposed of the three bodies, Eva moved the toilet back over the hole, leaving it unattached because of the heavy damage she had done kicking it loose from the metal ties securing it to the floor.

She then followed Julia back to the house, leaving their tracks as they were in the snow. They looked no different than if the old man had gone to the outhouse several times. Before going into the house, both picked up large handfuls of snow to cover the gathering pools of blood left by the three men. Julia continued to bring in more snow while Eva scrubbed the floor with a short wooden floor mop she found in the kitchen. When the mop turned red with blood, Julia cleaned it the best she could in piles of snow away from the house. After fifteen minutes, only three small spots remained where the blood had stained the floor. Both then carried more snow to the fireplace, dousing the flames and then the embers. Julia quickly kicked some of the dead embers across the floor onto the remaining stains, mashing and scuffing the floor with them. The stains could still be seen, but only if you came in looking for them. When she was through, she went to the larger of the two bedrooms where Eva was trying to reduce the only bed quilt the man owned into a tighter roll.

"The damn thing is too dirty and smelly to take," she said, tossing the quilt back onto the bed, though it could help keep them warm in the nights ahead.

"Leave it. We need to get as far as we can from this horrible place before other patrols come looking for the two soldiers."

On their way out, Julia looked back at the kitchen and spotted a pint bottle of vodka sitting back in the far corner of the countertop.

"We can take that—it might be warmer than the quilt and certainly won't have any lice," she said, nodding to Eva.

Walking down to the road, they decided to deliberately make two new rows of tracks in the snow alongside those the soldiers had left coming to the house.

"The returning footprints might fool them for awhile. What we do now is just a guess," Julia said, as they both stood by the parked motorcycles, looking at the frozen landscape all about them.

"God surely is not going to let us freeze to death standing here next to these fucking German motorcycles," Eva yelled, frustrated with the indecisiveness about which direction they should go.

"We have to go south," Julia finally said, "and push the motorcycles on the road until we find a heavy stand of trees and brush that will hide them from passing eyes."

"But our radio and weapons are back the other way, toward Prague," Eva said, pointing north where the snow-covered road seemingly disappeared from the earth as it blended into the vast whiteness surrounding it.

"I know, but our best chance is to reach the great forests further south of here. The Germans will not come into the forests without a reason. There should be more farms along the way, too," Julia said, kicking up the parking arm on one motorcycle and walking it onto the road.

Twenty minutes passed before they came upon an unusually heavy grouping of trees and brush ahead on the right. Moving as fast as they could on the icy road, Julia saw a small opening through the roadside brush leading into the woods, and moved into them with her motorcycle. Eva quickly followed in Julia's tracks with the second motorcycle. Then she tore the distributor loose from each machine, walked further into the woods, and threw them into an isolated cluster of brush and leaves.

"Too bad they didn't teach us how to ride these crazy things back in England," Julia said.

"Unladylike. We would surely be 'straddling' such a big machine with our legs, you know," Eva laughed in a mocking English accent, flavored with her Slavic tongue.

Julia laughed, too, but more from relief, in gaining distance from the three men they had killed. The Gestapo were too good not to find the dead soldiers and the motorcycles, and even them, unless they were too far away to care about. By her calculations they were ten to twelve miles from Klatovy, a small town to the southeast of little importance to the Germans, except for the railroad nearby. From there it might be another eight miles to the deep forest along the German border. They would be safe there, and maybe so in Klatovy, if they could find one God-fearing person still willing to help them. She had always loved this part of Bohemia, mostly because of its raw beauty. Somehow it always stayed fixed before you, unchanging in the summer heat and winter snows. Looking up at the broad skies, Julia's spirits gladdened when she realized that what she most wanted was happening. Patches of deep blue had begun peeking through small holes in the heavy blanket of gray clouds that had kept all warmth from the earth. With each passing minute the patches of blue grew bolder until the long fingered rays of the afternoon sun broke through the shattering grayness, bringing their healing grace to earth's life again. The warming air, though, was taking its toll on the snow and ice, making the roads much more treacherous to walk on, and slowing Julia and Eva to a snail-like pace. Yet, they both knew, the slushy roads would slow the Germans, too, as they moved supplies. Other than the patrols, the roads should stay empty until late in the day, or perhaps even tomorrow, giving them a slight advantage in avoiding more confrontations.

After two hours they reached a narrow road turning southeast to Klatovy. The village, Julia knew, was no different from many of the other small towns scattered around Pilsen except that the railroad was there, which meant the Germans would be, too. Ahead a hundred yards, a rail line could be seen crossing the road, which she believed ran between Klatovy and Pilsen. Upon reaching the crossing, she paused for a moment, looking west towards Pilsen. Their contacts with Czech and British intelligence were there, unless the Gestapo had found them. There were no contacts in Klatovy. Even so, the small village would bring them nearer to the great forest where they could hide safely for weeks if necessary, until the warming spring winds arrived and the Germans tired in their hunt for them. Either way would be like testing the waters of hell once the hidden motorcycles were discovered. Looking down a long span in the rails leading towards Klatovy, Julia quickly saw that passing trains had cleared most of the snow from the tracks and shoulders. Moving quickly onto the gravel shoulder, she began walking at a much brisker pace with Eva close behind. They would be in Klatovy in less than two hours, she yelled back at Eva, as they moved deeper into the snow-covered hills rising around them like giant puffs of white clouds that had come down to rest on the earth for a while.

TWENTY

Erich, Brandenburg, 1942

In the weeks after euthanizing little Brigitte and the other four children, Erich stayed largely to himself, ignoring all social invitations from colleagues and anyone else associated with the hospital, except Maria. Together they had taken the long fatal step away from everything they knew was good and right, making each one's guilt the other's as well. Standing silently in Brigitte's room that terrible day, still holding the dead child in his arms, he had turned to Maria and simply said, "All these years, we've been educated to help the sick, to heal them—not to kill them. And look at this child. This is what you and I have done." And then both parted, saying nothing further, nor daring to look at the other.

When late hours of the night came to him that first day, his soul had no answer for what had taken the place of medicine—the killing of the five "misfits"—and was strangely quiet, as if it were no longer a part of him. Written words of lies twisted his mind, as he penned letters to the parents of the murdered children, attributing their deaths to unexpected complications. It would be so much easier to say they were killed out of compassion, an enduring Christian virtue in medicine, which everyone understood. At least then it would be seen as a good death. Yet, all virtues have their own bad moments if taken too far. How many crippled children could one kill in the name of compassion and still remain virtuous? he wondered.

For a while, his mind traced back to a long discussion he shared with Julia and her father late one evening on this very subject. What if telling the truth causes a greater harm than lying? had been the question raised by Dr. Kaufmann. He had quickly answered, with Julia agreeing, that lying would become the virtue then, not truth. But Dr. Kaufmann pressed the question further.

"Then killing someone who is innocent for a greater good, perhaps to save the lives of ten people, would become the virtue." Erich had no answer, nor did Julia.

"It is the principle that is the real virtue, not the act. Should the principle die, there would be no more innocence," Dr. Kaufmann said, closing the discussion.

Near one in the morning and still unable to sleep, Erich changed back to his street clothes and left his apartment for Maria's, which was located several blocks closer to the hospital than his. There she shared a small three-room flat situated over an empty kosher meat shop, whose Jewish owner had simply disappeared one evening with all his family. Arriving at the apartment, Erich banged on the door four times before Maria responded.

"Dr. Schmidt, what are you doing here?" she asked, opening the door slightly, greatly puzzled by Erich's sudden appearance at her door, something which had never happened before.

"I thought we should talk about this day. Do you mind?"

"Tomorrow would be better, it's so late."

"No, tomorrow won't do, not really," Erich said, pushing his way past Maria into the apartment.

Maria hesitated, then closed the door, and that of her bedroom. Erich studied Maria's face for a moment and was bothered that she displayed no anguish over what had happened earlier, the terror they had brought to the children's rooms. Instead, her emotions seemed as hard as the floor beneath his feet. Yet, he knew, neither one of them would emerge spiritually unscathed from what they had done, and would do so again in the days ahead.

"Would you like a cup of coffee, or a beer perhaps," Maria asked.

"Coffee might help, thank you. Is your roommate sleeping?" Erich questioned, looking towards the bedroom.

"She is home with her sick mother, why do you ask?"

"What happened today is only the beginning, I'm afraid. We've been ordered to keep it secret from the public. That is what the ministry wants."

"Why should we pretend it's a secret? Everyone will figure out something bad is happening to the children if no one ever sees them again."

Maria poured two cups of black coffee. She was both glad and angry that he had come to her door. He was a miserable man, that much she believed, hurting terribly as she was but for different reasons. Deeply religious to the edge of obsession, she loved all children, whether whole or not. And misfits among God's little creatures were to be loved as much, if not more so, than those that were normal. Compassion from love was Christlike, she had been taught, and gave great meaning to her calling as a nurse. Killing those you love out of compassion, as she did the children, bothered her deeply because the duty to do so had been commanded by the state, not God. Had it been God, she would own no guilt, because God is good.

Erich's supposed compassion, she had discerned, came from fear not love, and she despised him for it.

Maria took several sips of coffee waiting for Erich's answer to her question, but none came. Instead he said, "I want you to be my friend, Maria. It's difficult not having someone you can talk to, someone you can trust. I have no other friends here at Görden."

Erich's words muddled her mind. They were not what she had expected to hear from him. All she knew about him was that he was a deeply disturbed young man with important ties to the Chancellery through his powerful father, nothing more. Whether she could trust him with her own problems and stories was a question she had no answer for at this time.

"I will listen and talk with you, if that is what you want, but we will never be friends. It's very simple—I don't like you and never will," she said dismissively.

Maria's quick rejection to his offer of friendship stunned Erich, pushing him to silence for several minutes. He hadn't expected such cold words from her. He now felt she would betray him, too, spreading false rumors and reporting all words he would utter to her to Dr. Heinze and the Health Ministry.

"I am sorry, it was a terrible mistake to come here," he said, taking his empty cup to the kitchen sink, then walking to the door.

Maria followed him to the door, and for no reason she could later think of, gently rested her hand on his arm.

"There are things happening that we must accept and do, if we are to survive these terrible times. Ending any child's life bothers me deeply, as it does you, I suppose, but I know it removes suffering from the child. That fact alone is enough for me to do my duty," she said softly.

Erich stepped into the hall and looked down the unlit stairway to the street. Maria's words could have been his. Compassion and science had led him to perform his duty, too, so he believed, in bringing death to the five children, certainly not the twisted desires of the state to purify the Aryan race. Still, the cold fear of what they might have done to him had he not obeyed remained like warm vomit from a sick stomach, choking his thoughts and mind.

Starting down the steps, he stopped and looked back at Maria, who was still standing in the doorway to her apartment watching him.

"We may be on a slippery slope before this thing ends," he said.

"I know, but we'll be alright," was all Maria could think to say, before closing the door.

Erich reported in two hours late the next morning. The night's late visit to Maria's apartment had been a mistake, leaving him more unsettled than ever. His ward was empty of patients for now, for which he was thankful. He knew, though, that the beds would soon be filled as the state-mandated registration and reporting of handicapped children grew in number. They would come by the hundreds to be killed, unknowingly, to achieve a greater good no one really understood or accepted. Stopping by Dr. Heinze's office, Erich completed the death certificates of the five children, indicating the cause of death for each child as "multiple emboli to the lungs, etiology unknown." It was as good a lie as any of the others he would soon use. Before he could leave, Dr. Heinze entered the office with Erich's old nemesis, Franz Kremer, now very much a doctor, too.

"You know Herr Dr. Kremer, I believe," Dr. Heinz said smiling at Erich.

"Yes, we were classmates in Prague for a short time."

"Good, then no introduction is necessary. You must be old friends," Dr. Heinze said, still smiling oddly, Erich thought.

Neither one spoke though, nor acknowledged the other's presence. Looking at both of them eyeing each other like two circling boxers waiting for the fight to begin, it would be difficult to tell which one hated the other the most.

"Herr Dr. Kremer has been assigned here by the Health Ministry for a few months to assist us in establishing the children's new therapy program. I've already told him of your early success with the children," Dr. Heinze said in a proud tone, no longer smiling at Erich as he had been.

Slightly dazed by Franz's sudden appearance at Görden, Erich said nothing in response to the weird praise from Dr. Heinze, accolades for euthanizing children. From the moment he walked into the office with Dr. Heinze, Franz had fixed the slant of his eyes on Erich's in an unyielding war of nerves and stares to see who would blink first. Dr. Heinze watched the dynamics for several seconds, then turned to Erich, smiling oddly again as he had before.

"You will take my place and accompany Dr. Kremer to view a screening of the new film, *I Accuse*, in the auditorium. Afterwards you are to write a report on its value, if any, to the Health Ministry."

Neither one speaking, the two archenemies left the office together and started walking down the hall to the right where the hospital's small auditorium was located. Anyone nearby watching the two men could not help but feel some of the intense hatred flowing back and forth between them like electrical charges, its high voltage no longer insulated by the niceties of their profession. They were locked together in a world separate from all around them, where time itself no longer seemed to matter.

When they had walked but a few steps, Franz asked, baiting Erich, "How is your Jewish whore?"

"Julia was not a whore, she was my friend then. You had no Jewish friends, I suppose," Erich said, turning the question back on Franz, who merely shrugged his shoulders at the suggestion.

"Never there, or anywhere else. I am pure. You should know that."

"Perhaps."

Both men stopped at the auditorium door, childishly waiting for the other to open it. Neither one would until Maria and two other nurses approached. Erich stepped forward and held the door open until the three had entered, then moved quickly inside ahead of Franz.

"You should be more careful with what you say and do, Erich. You don't know who I am, and what I am about," he said as he walked past Erich and took a seat close to Maria and the two nurses. Erich sat alone.

No one had seen the movie, though rumors about the contents could be heard throughout the hospital and in the cafés and beer gardens of the city. What begins as a simple happy story of a wholesome German family quickly becomes heart wrenching when the beautiful young wife is taken ill with multiple sclerosis. In the movie's most tender moment, the husband, a physician, responding to his wife's pleas to do so, gives her a lethal injection. As she closes her eyes in death, a moment of ethereal joy spreads across the husband's face, watching her terrible suffering end. But Erich saw much more than a sad story of unconditional love being played out on the screen. And he wondered if Franz and all the other doctors watching had read the same message hidden in the tenderness of the moments before them. Because the wife had given her husband permission to kill her, ending all suffering was the most moral thing one could do. Yet, still hiding ominously behind the scene was the admonition that this same compassionate act must be available for those who are incompetent and cannot ask for such a wonderful death, like the mentally ill. Erich knew in a second that a subliminal dagger was being thrust at the heart of these sick people—because the state would take over the moral responsibility to act, allowing no one else, family or friend, to do so.

In the days to come, the hospital halls would echo limitless discussions of the morality of doctors and nurses assisting an incurably diseased patient to die in peace. It was the definition of disease, though, that bothered Erich the most, because many of the mentally ill were already thought of as diseased. The public and doctors throughout Germany could not help but be moved by the deep feelings of sympathy and love expressed in the film. Many were already there, taken in by the highly saleable idea of Christian compassion spewing forth from the Health Ministry like an awakened Mount Vesuvius. Evil wears many different clothes, and the real reason, cleansing of the race, was deftly attired in the royal colors of Christian compassion.

When the overhead lights came back on, Erich looked around at the audience. Maria had been crying and was busily sopping up her tears . She was not alone; others had been moved to tears by the gentle death of the doctor's wife.

"A beautiful death," one said.

"A righteous death," another said.

Still another: "A blessed doctor."

Franz Kremer said nothing because he knew, like Erich, the film meant nothing where goodness was concerned. Soon, "misfits" of every age would be brought to the hospitals to die. Then he hoped the Jews would follow. Franz glanced over at Erich, the man he hated worse than Jesus. To him Jesus was a monumental fraud, no better than the next Jew, and had made an unholy mess of everything in the world. In his school studies, Franz prized reading of Dostoevsky's Grand Inquisitor, who wanted to execute Jesus a second time. Had the story been true, he would tell anyone who would listen, the Jesus myth would have ended there.

Erich hated Franz, too, but for a different reason, which he felt was just. Franz could never accept that he had loved and slept with a lovely Jewish woman who possessed above all things a beautiful soul. Now with the world at war and the Nazis in command, Franz would kill Julia outright should the opportunity present itself. But Erich also believed, perhaps as the psychiatrist he was, that Franz's misguided hate of Julia came more so because she chose to fall in love with someone other than him. Earlier, before Julia looked to Erich's love, she had spurned Franz's persistent, many times drunken, overtures. This triad of hate would be there at the end, Erich knew.

Franz ignored the ebullient conversations around him and walked over to where Erich was sitting. The tension he brought was explosive.

"What was your reaction to the film, my weak friend?" he asked sarcastically.

"You should stop playing your childish games, Franz, being such a miserable ass. You and I both know what the film is about, what it is telling us will happen."

Franz's face turned red from anger at Erich's words, his hands knotted in huge, tight fists, as if he would try to pound him senseless with them at any moment. Then, for a reason Erich would never know, Franz suddenly relaxed, turning quiet for a moment before speaking again.

"I suppose you're right. We should end our silly quarrels from the past and get on with what is expected of us," he said calmly, surprising Erich.

"Good, then we will quarrel no more, though we will never be friends," Erich said loudly, turning his back on Franz and leaving the auditorium.

Later in the afternoon, he returned to the East Ward, peering into each empty room, wondering what the next child might look like who would die there. *I Accuse* had made him realize even more the reality of what was to come, and he found himself strangely at peace with it. There was no exit from all that was around him, he knew, and so he had begun to feel that to cope with what was coming would be to comply, to do that which was expected of him, his duty. He need not hide his fears any longer behind the gentle face of compassion. He could endure until the war's ending and he would find Julia then and begin again to live as a man.

The days became long for Erich and Maria and everyone else as the trickle of misfits entering the hospital steadily became a flood. It had been decided by Dr. Heinze that the children should be kept mildly sedated for several weeks to give the impression they were receiving the advanced treatment promised. Erich, with Maria and the other nurses on duty in the ward, welcomed the plan happily. In time, it fooled their minds into believing what they were doing was what they should be about as doctors and nurses, looking to their patients with compassion. But the end was always the same. A quicker death for some from morphine. Others a slower death from luminal.

Erich began to throw himself into the medical scene, working fifteen hours a day trying to grasp the whole picture, at least scientifically. Before sending the parents home, he would examine the entire family for any obvious conditions he believed might lead to their child's malformations. Then, methodically examining the child's condition daily with Maria at his side, he would map a treatment plan that would lead nowhere but to death. In time, such long hours would come to nourish his illusion of medical authenticity and help keep him sane.

When a particular child who had unusual malformations died, he would send the body to a research laboratory, rather than the crematory, where Dr. Bracht, a neurosurgeon, anxiously awaited. He had come to Görden at Erich's father's request, much to the chagrin of Dr. Heinze and Franz, and was enthralled by the great number of children's brains at his disposal. Together, he and Erich would dissect the brains, looking for physical signs or strange diseases that might somehow cause such malformations of the body or the mind. Sometimes Erich would think of Julia and Rabbi Loew's sacred golem while looking at the twisted pinkish gray tissues of a child's brain, and believed someday such a story might be true, that life would somehow spring from a test tube.

He had grown fond of Maria, too, as the months passed, not in any intimate way, but with a new respect for her own sense of duty. He kept his distance socially but felt good when she was with him in the ward. Her presence by his side became a necessary factor in his own role as doctor. Early on he turned to luminal pills as the favorite method for euthanizing the children under his care, seldom opting for a quick death from morphine. In most cases, the children would develop breathing problems, eventually succumbing to bronchitis or pneumonia. At times he would treat these ailments, carefully charting every change in a child's condition, no matter how small, as if he were trying to heal them, not kill them. A child's death seemed always like a failure to him, should it come either earlier or later than the expected time noted in the chart. Should a child linger too long, suffering, he would quickly finish them off with a lethal injection of morphine. When such a death did happen, he would meticulously review his notes looking for possible errors in luminal dosage prescribed, food and water intake, or any other factors that might have contributed to an error in his prognosis for time of death.

One afternoon while awaiting the arrival of new patients, he decided to visit several of the "good" wards, a name he had given them, that held patients who would see and walk in the sunshine again. He would talk there to other doctors about their cases to learn, always pretending as if he had similar ones in his own "special" ward to attend to. To get to the "good" wards, he had to pass through several wards like his own, including a larger one under Franz's supervision. On this particular day, Franz was serving as a guide for several teachers touring the hospital. When he saw Erich approaching, his voice rose in volume and his mouth twisted in a sneer as he glared at him. Then he suddenly pulled a terribly emaciated child from its crib and held her by the leg like he would a small dead animal he had just killed.

"These children will die as God intended them to do, naturally, not by any drugs," he said proudly.

Starving the misfits to death was a method used by many of the doctors, Erich knew. It saved time and money, and required less monitoring from the staff, though many of the nurses seemed uncomfortable with its use, compared to outright killing. But to Erich it was a terrible wrong, letting your patient die such a slow death. Giving food and water to the thirsty and hungry was the greatest of Christian virtues, and to deny them that was far different from the compassionate deaths Erich sought and now believed in.

But he said nothing as he listened to the boasting of Franz for a minute, thinking to himself how very different he was from such an evil man. For Franz, the children being killed should die because they were already essentially dead, separated from a life and world that had no room for them. Compassion had no meaning to them, and never would. There was no pretending in Franz—what he was about, the killings, was very much who he was. Erich had actually killed more children than Franz, but none died alone. Their deaths always came in the arms of Maria or his own. That factor alone, he believed, provided the moral wall separating him from Franz and other doctors like him.

When he was finished talking to the teachers, Franz casually tossed the pitiful child back into its crib as he might a dirty towel, all the while smirking at Erich, daring him to say something. Ignoring his taunting looks, Erich moved past Franz and the group of teachers, who had turned their attention to him, thinking he might be someone of importance, and walked down the hall to the good wards. Though Erich believed he was practicing medicine in treating the children to be euthanized in his ward, it was here that one's calling to the ancient guild of Asklepios was still felt in his soul. While there he would read the medical records of patients suffering from undiagnosed illnesses, pretending he had been brought in to their cases as a consultant, deciding in silence the ailment and the treatment to be given. Then he would return another time to the wards to see if he had been right. When he was, which was more often than not, he would glow with pride at his diagnostic prowess. Nothing came from any of this pretending though. All the other doctors there, mostly older, knew he was from the killing wards, and allowed his little game to play out, knowing the supposed relief it brought to him. Only by chance had they been assigned to the "good wards" and escaped his fate.

When Erich returned to the East Ward he found Maria sitting in one of the rooms holding a tiny year-old baby boy in her arms, gently rocking him. The boy was blind and had no arms below his elbows and had been left by the child's mother at the front door of the hospital. Maria looked up when he entered the room.

"A new patient for us to kill," she said without any hesitation.

Erich ignored Maria's callous remark and picked up the child for a cursory examination. "He is blind."

"I know. What better way is there to escape your fears than having no eyes to see them? You would dream of nothing then," Maria said, taking the child from Erich.

Taken back by Maria's sudden melancholic attitude, Erich asked, "Are you okay? You seem tired."

Looking first at the sleeping baby's face, then at Erich, Maria began to cry softly.

"We are doing the right thing, aren't we?"

"Maybe. In our eyes we are, but I'm not sure about God's," Erich responded, looking more closely at Maria, wondering if she had reached a breaking point from the constant smell of death around her. Some nurses had and were placed on leave.

"The churches have been silent. That is a good thing, isn't it?" she asked.

"Perhaps, but like the rest of us, they stay silent to survive."

Maria rose from her chair, kissed the sleeping boy on the forehead, then laid him gently in the bed, covering him with a light blanket as Erich had done little Brigitte on the very first day everything began. Turning back to Erich she said, "I wonder, how is it with death, to die? There must be something we feel. The change is so great."

"That's a strange question to ask, with all the dying going on around us."

"I thought maybe you knew, that's all, maybe from cases where one was said to be dead but wasn't, and then told of what it was like."

"Perhaps we change only a little, maybe not at all. No one knows, but it would be nice if we did. I think then we wouldn't fight so hard for that last mouthful of air," Erich said, taking Maria's hand and leading her back to the nurse's station.

"Your hours have been too long. I will speak to the supervisor about giving you some days away from the hospital," he said, still holding Maria's hand.

Maria abruptly stiffened, pulling her hand from his.

"No, say nothing, please. They will think I'm weak, when I should be strong, with Martin and all the boys fighting for us in the East. Martin would be ashamed should he know."

Then she began to cry again.

"I never knew there would be so many. Surely there are no more crippled children left in Germany."

"You may be right. Perhaps things will get better for everyone in a few more months," Erich said, taking the file of the new patient from Maria's desk and reading the notes quickly.

"Start him on luminal tablets in five days; three weeks is too long to wait for this child," he continued, walking towards the young blind baby's room, leaving Maria alone.

TWENTY-ONE

Erich, Görden, 1942

I t was an exciting and stimulating time for Erich. His ward stayed mostly empty with only twenty children admitted during a five-week period, all imbecilic by diagnosis. Their time to be euthanized, however, had been purposely extended over several days, providing him with the opportunity to bring in Dr. Bracht to study each child's external disabilities more thoroughly before dissecting their brains. Prior to this time, his view of these malformations had only been that of observing a dead child lying on a gurney when brought to his laboratory, which told him nothing about their movements. Both he and Erich had theorized wrongly that all imbecilic brains of blind and malformed children would produce observable lesions, or other damaged areas in the tissues of the brain.

Maria had returned to a more pleasant mood, too, though she had heard nothing from Martin in over two months. But the invasion of Russia was going well, and she believed he would be home soon. One sunny May afternoon, she left the hospital on her break to bask in the surprising warmth of the sun after such a cold winter. Going to the rose garden, she found Erich sitting there reading a tattered copy of Nietzsche's *The Gay Science*. Maria knew nothing of the man, nor of any of the other great German philosophers, and always found talk of philosophy boring. Erich loved Nietzsche, though, particularly the poems in the book, because they held special memories for him. He would read them for hours with Julia, trying to grasp the completeness of their meaning, which he knew would open a window to Nietzsche's own disturbed soul. In the end, they would always find themselves sailing together above the world on the sheer beauty of his words.

"May I sit with you for a moment?" Maria asked. "The day seems so special."

Erich nodded but continued reading. Maria had found him different when he was away from the East Ward and the hospital. She had been with him at several social gatherings of the staff, and he always seemed a different person, at least to her. It was as if there were two minds wrapped carefully together in his body, each one choosing a separate place in time to let itself be known. Franz, and those like him, were always the same, preaching the gospel of the Third Reich, which by now had become boring. To her, there was a certain strange softness about Erich that made him different from most men, but it kept him weak also, which she didn't like. Few men, she knew, would be found sitting in a rose garden reading poems.

"Read me one of the shorter poems and tell me what it means," Maria said on an impulse, startling Erich for a second.

"I would like to but I can't—there's too much history tied up in this book, which I treasure very much."

Maria measured Erich's words for a second before speaking again.

"What was she like?"

"Who?"

"The woman you read these poems to," Maria said, looking wistfully at him.

Shaken by Maria's perception, Erich closed the book and sat silent for a few moments, staring at a particular small rose that seemed to be struggling against the larger blossoms for its own place in the sun. "Your skin is softer than the petals of a rose," he had recited to Julia once from a silly poem he had written for her. But she didn't laugh at him, and he loved her even more for it.

Erich looked over at Maria, who was sitting next to him, and saw that she was serious with her question.

"She was beautiful. That's all I can say—beautiful."

"Where is she now?" Maria asked, pleased that he had finally responded.

"I don't know. We were in Prague together at the medical school before the war started."

"Was she from Germany like you?" Maria asked, taken with the romantic overtones of this sudden conversation with Erich.

Crossing his arms and looking around the garden slowly, Erich sighed aloud, as if captured by the completeness of the roses before him. It seemed a lifetime since he had talked with anyone about this remarkable woman he loved so dearly.

"Her name is Julia. She is not German but a Czech—and a Jew."

Maria's face reddened when she heard the last word and she quickly looked away from Erich. Had she been given a thousand guesses to describe Julia, none would have included the word Jew. He seemed so German to her, the kind that would have no place in his heart for a Jew. Erich felt her misplaced embarrassment and wished he had said nothing, though it felt strangely good to him to have spoken Julia's name again openly, not covering it within the silence of his mind.

"She's a good woman, I'm sure," Maria said, turning back to Erich, "but not one I could ever have imagined you would love."

"We will let this stop here. She was beautiful, that is all, and I loved her," Erich said, rising from the garden bench and starting back to the hospital, leaving Maria alone.

"Dr. Schmidt," Maria yelled to him. "I will tell no one, never, I promise."

Erich stopped and looked back at Maria, her face still bright red, but with tears in her eyes.

"Thank you, Maria. See, we have become friends after all," he said, then walked into the hospital.

When he arrived the next morning, Maria seemed rested and was busily attending to three new children who had been brought to the hospital by their parents during the night. As a group they had spent the night crying and sleeping and rocking their children, refusing to go home until they had talked with him about their children. After speaking with Maria, Erich went to them and told them they must leave.

"Your children will be fine and well cared for. I will keep you informed of their progress," he lied, looking each parent in the face, as he had others before them asking the same questions.

"We have heard that all the children brought here die," one man said, his voice quivering.

"Rumors, that is all, rumors," Erich said firmly, though slightly shaken by the man's sudden accusation. "Some have died from unexpected complications, but only a few. You must leave, your children will be well cared for. We will notify you when they are ready to go home."

One by one the parents returned to the rooms where their children lay, kissed them several times, then walked slowly back by Erich, thanking and blessing him for what they thought he would do. After they were gone, Erich decided to tell Dr. Heinze and the Chancellery about the rumors he had heard and left Maria to tend to the children. When he entered the office, he found Franz Kremer talking with Dr. Heinze and immediately turned around to leave.

"Come in and tell me quickly what you have to say. Dr. Kremer and I are busy," Dr. Heinze said gruffly, red faced as usual.

Erich sat down and told them in detail about the surprising complaints of the parents and the rumors they brought with them and asked if the Chancellery knew of them, too. After he was through, Dr. Heinze looked to Franz as if they were passing a secret between them, then looked for a moment at Erich, smiling as he did.

"The answer you want is yes. An official letter from the Chancellery is going out ordering a stop to the program. So officially, no more children are to be euthanized," Dr. Heinze said, still smiling.

Stunned by what he was hearing, Erich started to speak of his gladness at the news, when Dr. Heinze continued.

"We will continue our program, though in a clandestine way, with the children in the hospital and any that might be brought to us, until everything is calm again."

Dr. Heinze then walked over and put his hands on Franz's shoulders, his eyes full of pride as if he were his own son.

"Dr. Kremer has been elevated to a senior status and is to be rewarded by assuming an important post at Auschwitz."

"Auschwitz? What hospital is at Auschwitz?" Erich asked, puzzled by Dr. Heinze's actions.

Dr. Heinze said nothing, delighted in Erich's ignorance. Feeling uneasy with the silence that suddenly had seized the room, Erich stood up to leave. As he did, Franz half nodded to him and said sarcastically, "You still agree that we must cooperate, don't you, Erich?"

"Why do you ask? My word is as good as yours."

"Things may become heavy at Auschwitz, and you should be ready to work with me should that happen. That is all."

Erich looked once more at Franz's sickening face and left the office.

He would call his father tonight and uncover the truth about what had taken place. Franz had somehow gained the ear of someone in the

Chancellery to bring about such an important promotion at age twenty-nine. No word would come from his father, though Erich waited late into the night for the operators to try to find him. Sleep would not come to him either, until the early morning hours when he finally surrendered his mind to it while writing and rewriting imaginary love letters to Julia. His words to her, though she might never read them, calmed his fears, brightening his heart and bringing hope that the terrible things he had been doing would finally end. But later, with a new day before him, he knew that the only thing certain in his life was the will to live. Nothing else really mattered.

TWENTY-TWO

Erich, Görden

T he village people called them "the crazies," and some maybe were, but most weren't. They were just trying to figure out how to get along in a crowded world that was way too full of dos and don'ts. For the most part they were pitifully silly people who ran around shaming their family, so they were told. It didn't matter, though, whether they were just silly or insane, all of the crazies would be swept up and tossed into the Chancellery's new cleansing machines for dirty genes. Maria saw their machine first, leaving the hospital after a tiresome day doing little. Taking the short way to her apartment through the grounds of the old abandoned city prison, she came upon a crew of SS laborers working feverishly around a rear exit door. Inquisitive by nature, she stopped and questioned one worker for answers about the new construction, only to be greeted with stone silence. No one else would look at her, so she left, reminding herself to ask Erich in the morning about the strange work taking place in a building no longer in use.

Erich knew nothing about the work at the old penitentiary. For some unknown reason, the muted voices of the construction workers had bothered her throughout the evening, as if some new unexplainable event was just over the horizon. With his ward empty of children, Erich had busied himself helping Dr. Bracht dissect and study the few remaining brains of children still stored in the hospital's laboratory. They had learned nothing, but the work was exciting and reaffirmed a sense of purpose in what they were about as doctors. Someday, somewhere, someone would find the soul's portal to the brain, the link to our immortality, they believed. The pineal gland had been Descartes's secret connecting door, but he was terribly wrong, Erich knew. And since then, no one really thought about it anymore or cared. Except for a few psychiatrists, science had lost its taste for the metaphysical.

Badgered into visiting the construction site by Maria, Erich went with her to the old prison after they ate lunch together again in the rose garden. She had not exaggerated. Workers were busily cleaning the grounds and planting new grass and flowers along the walkway leading to a freshly painted exit door that was now the entrance. The prior dreary starkness of the area had been replaced by groupings of benches and chairs, each with a small religious statue standing in their midst. Even the ten-foot wall along the rear of the prison looked bright and new with its rusted iron gate removed, providing a pleasant and unguarded openness to the entire scene. Erich could not help but be impressed by the prison's renaissance. He might seek his own quiet moments there; however, he wondered what had moved the state to prettify such a dismal place.

Inside everything was surprisingly new also. The dingy and mildewed walls of the dark hall leading into the prison's quarters were colorfully coated with a mixture of shades and hues, giving a welcoming brightness to anyone entering. To the left was a large and long rectangular room with three workers busily installing telephone lines and new light fixtures. Two large tables with chairs sat at the front, with the remainder of the room empty. Two large pictures of Hitler next to a smaller one of Jesus adorned the walls.

But it was the room directly across the hall that intrigued Erich the most, where a shower room approximately nine by fifteen feet, and nine feet high with aqua tiled walls had been constructed for arriving inmates to bathe in. A pipe was fitted along the walls running to several showerheads, mounted high on the front wall. Nothing seemed strange to Erich until he noticed that the pipe was dotted with two rows of holes almost invisible to the naked eye, running the length of the pipe. He also noticed that the wall was empty of the necessary fixtures for turning on the showers. He supposed that the controls could be elsewhere, but that would be odd. Could there be a different purpose for the room, he wondered, other than as a shower room? While he didn't know the full truth behind this moment, he felt the reality of it, and shook his head in disbelief.

"Are you okay?" Maria asked.

"We should leave now," he said in a weak voice. "We probably shouldn't be here."

Following Maria from the room, Erich closed the door, which seemed unusually heavy to him. Pausing for a moment, he saw a small glass peephole for observing all that was to happen inside the room. It was a flare with the dark afterlife of an omen, Erich knew. No one would ever take a shower there.

Returning to the ward, he said nothing to Maria, who was innocently pleased at the partial renovations to the old prison. Walking home through the grounds would be much more pleasant for her now. For Erich, though, what he had seen produced a fearsome dread that numbed his body, and he would wait until these fears were confirmed before confiding in her. When night came, he would try again to reach his father, the only source of truth he knew. But even then there was always left behind the bitter taste of a lingering suspicion about what his father had revealed.

Having been successful in reaching his father this time, Erich told him what he had seen earlier and pressed him hard for an acceptable explanation. None came, though, only a promise that Dr. Heinze would in time disclose an exciting new health plan called T4 to the hospital staff and he should make no further inquiries. Then his father quickly shifted back to the shallow and empty words that had defined their relationship for so long. Still, to Erich, T4 was a strange name for a health program, and the fact that it was a code name left him more anxious than ever about what new role might be expected of him, should there be one. Pressing his father further for answers brought nothing but angry responses. "You will know when the time comes," were his father's last words before he hung up.

The next morning, and for a number of days after, nothing new came to Erich other than what his father had partially revealed. The time to learn more came a few days later, when Dr. Heinze ordered Erich and Maria to accompany him to the old prison. As they arrived, a large gray touring coach pulled to a stop by the walkway, where several SS guards were waiting. The patients disembarked, forming a line from the bus to the doorway. When several patients refused to leave the bus and stayed in their seat yelling obscenities, the guards brutally dragged them from the bus, slammed them to the ground, and forced a sedative upon them.

Erich followed Dr. Heinze into the building and to the long rectangular room that he had visited with Maria. At the far end of the room stood Franz and two other doctors, next to one of the two tables there. On the

table was an array of instruments used for perfunctory medical examinations, stethoscopes and tongue depressors and the like, nothing intri-
cate. To the far side of Franz were two nurses, one holding a heavy black
marker, the other a stamp with rotating numbers. Located further down
from them towards the doorway was a photographer, dressed in a white
coat, too, with his paraphernalia carefully arranged on a small table so that
a full-length photograph could be made of whoever stood before him.

Behind the second table sat two medical clerks with a roster of patient
names listing what mental hospital they were from. It was here the crazies
would start their short journey through the Chancellery's new health plan.

Seeing Erich, Franz motioned for him to come forward and, after
handing him a stethoscope and a handful of tongue depressors, directed
him to stand next to the two other doctors. Minutes before the deluge of
mental patients would begin to fill the room, Dr. Heinze spoke quietly to
Erich and the other doctors, reminding them of the sacred mission they
were about to undertake to save the health of the Third Reich. His final
words were, "You must be as soldiers, with your duty only to the Third
Reich and no one else."

There would be no physician/patient relationships anymore, insofar
as the crazies were concerned, only that of the physician and the state.
Erich's thoughts turned back momentarily to the movie *I Accuse,* which
had brought such a positive emotional response from all those watching
it. He had been right in seeing the real message hidden in the tender love
story: the state becomes the surrogate when a person can no longer speak
for himself. Clearly it would be the state's values, he knew, that would
determine the outcome of any given case, not the values of the patients
or their families. There would be no arguments offered of compassionate
euthanasia, as used with the young crippled children, where one could,
at least, rely on a Christian virtue to seek moral reconciliation with his
soul, as he believed he had done. What Dr. Heinze had left them with was
one specific criterion in determining whether a mental patient's life was to
end: was he capable of productive work, nothing more. Erich believed otherwise, but said nothing. To him, an economic evaluation was the boldest
of lies. There was only one single truth to be told, and it had been carefully
painted over with patriotic tones: the cleansing of the German race of all
that the state saw as weak and impure. He had gradually come to some
kind of understanding with his inner self over the killing of the malformed
babies and children because he had fashioned a moral handrail to hold

on to in the ancient virtue of compassion. Every doctor understands compassion, or should, he believed. Instead, what was before him now was a believable ideology conceived in evil, yet nurtured by science until it blossomed to full life.

The crazies waiting anxiously were a mixture of every labeled mental illness known in psychiatry, running from schizophrenics to untreatable syphilitics. Even epileptics with their momentary spasmodic attacks that often frightened people were cast into the huge melting pot they called insanity. As patients entered the room, their clothes were taken from them after their names were checked off on the roster. Those that objected were forcibly stripped. Young and old, male and female, waited naked in a line before Erich and the other doctors for their muscles to be felt and their hearts listened to and their orifices probed. Then their teeth were examined to see if they had any gold fillings. Those patients that did were marked with a large cross on their back by one of the nurses while the other nurse stamped an identifying number on their naked body. They were then pushed to a red line in front of a waiting camera to have their last living image etched in film. From there they were forced to stand bunched up against each other at the end of the room, until all the patients who arrived on the bus had completed the brief journey through the receiving line, as it was laughingly referred to by Franz and the other doctors, though not by Erich.

As they waited, some began to stir anxiously, especially the young women, uncertain as to why they were even here, having their flesh pressed and their naked bodies looked at by everyone around them. Three or four cried out for their distant mothers and were quickly injected with tranquillizers to calm them before their crying could disturb the others. There was a growing stench of urine where some had relieved themselves, urinating from the fear that gripped them. From the time of the patients' arrival, sixty minutes had elapsed, less than three minutes of medical attention for each of the twenty patients, though Erich had taken longer with his patients at first. Franz's watchful eye had made him nervous, much like in the first days of his clinical years in medical school, when every move he made was criticized by the professor. And it was so now, but for a different reason, one far removed from the wish to be a good doctor.

After the last patient had been photographed and shoved in among the crowd of other patients, Franz nodded to an SS guard. "Follow me," the guard announced. "A pleasant, hot shower is waiting for you."

As they filed out of the room, still naked, one young woman, whose only illness was epilepsy, asked, "Shouldn't we take our clothes with us?"

One by one, they entered the newly painted and tiled room, all facing the showerheads protruding from the front wall. Once inside the room they were pressed tightly together, making it difficult for many to breathe, and the airtight door shut and locked. Some tried to look around, seemingly puzzled by where they were. Others looked only at the back of the person's head in front of them, or to the side.

When the last patient left the examining room, Franz directed Erich and one of the other doctors to bring their stethoscopes and follow him. As the door was shut behind the patients, he instructed Erich and the doctor to take turns looking through the small glass peephole in the closed door. Then he nodded to the staff to turn the valve releasing carbon monoxide gas through the pipes circling the room. As Erich looked on, he grew sick and nauseated. The way the patients were dying seemed so full of suffering, he wanted to cry out at the top of his lungs to stop it. Some had fallen to the tile floor coughing and gasping for air, with a multitude of legs around them kicking and stamping on their naked bodies. The young woman who had asked about her clothes was the first to fall. Others soon followed. Some stood with their mouths open, desperately searching for a pocket of air to breathe. Some tried to claw their way up the tile walls to where the gas was steadily hissing from the pipes. Strangely though, only a few cried out, the rest silenced by their desperate struggle to exist another day. In ten minutes, all lay unconscious in a twisted heap of naked arms and legs and bodies on the floor, making it difficult for the guards to tell which arm or leg belonged where and to whom. After twenty more minutes all were quite dead. Satisfied with the results, Franz returned to the examining room with the other doctors to discuss what had taken place, to determine if there were any procedural weaknesses they could improve.

No one spoke at first. In watching the unbelievable, macabre scene unfold, the beautiful young woman who fell first quickly became Julia in Erich's eyes, and he believed with certainty, at that very moment, she had already suffered such a death. The staggering grief he felt was overwhelming and he struggled to keep from crying. The doctor watching with him had been brutally shocked, too, but maintained his composure, knowing Franz's standing with Dr. Heinze and the Chancellery.

"Perhaps more than twenty patients, maybe thirty, would fit into the room, should there be others," he said in a professional manner, very pleased with his self-control in light of what he had just witnessed.

Franz nodded approvingly, but waited still for Erich's words. It was as if he knew what Erich was thinking, and his mouth curled in a sinister smile.

"No doctor pulled the gas lever, Erich. As doctors, we did nothing more than examine the patients, as it should be. Now you must check each of the patients to verify their deaths," he said, smiling at him.

Erich heard Franz's words and he realized they made some sense to him, at least as a momentary release of the emotional web he found himself trapped in. Though there was no compassion attached to the killing of the "crazies" to relieve them from a horrible existence, as there was in euthanizing the little children, what he had done was still that of a doctor, nothing more. But Julia's face was still there in the shadows of his mind. The "new German physician" he had read about was no longer a hypothetical entity to him. Any hint of compassion in the killing of these people was rapidly being replaced by a pseudo medical standard imposed by the state: the ability to perform productive work for the Third Reich. Such standard was window dressing to many of the doctors, although, like him, they said nothing. Whether or not you could work at the required level was of no consequence, when the slightest manifestation of mental illness sent you to die.

After Erich verified the deaths of the twenty patients, three men entered the room and began tossing the lifeless bodies around like hundred-pound bags of chicken feed, looking for the cross marked earlier on some of their backs. Each time one was found, their gold teeth and fillings were quickly knocked out with a peen hammer and placed in a small holding bag to be given to Dr. Heinze at the day's end. One old man's mouth produced the biggest bounty, six gold teeth, which brought whoops from the staff, as if the mother lode had been struck. The young woman's body had been laid aside, not only for gawking purposes by the staff, but to be taken later, because she was an epileptic, to the research laboratory, where Erich's neurosurgeon friend would dissect and study her brain and body. This would become a common pattern for the future "crazies" brought in to suffer similar deaths.

When the staff was finished robbing the dead mouths of patients, the bodies were placed on a half truck and hauled to the crematory to be reduced to ashes.

Some two hours later, Erich found himself examining a second group of patients who had arrived like the first in a gray touring bus. And then, two hours more in passing, a third and final group came, ending the long day. Nothing was different and nothing changed, except that thirty terrified souls came to die this time. In all, seventy mentally afflicted patients had been permanently erased this day from the gene pool of the German race.

"A very good beginning," Franz would write in his report to Dr. Heinze and the Chancellery, saying nothing of Erich and the other doctors.

As it was with the children, Erich wrote the kin of each patient he had supposedly treated, explaining their unexpected demise. Heart attacks and anaphylactic reactions to medicine given became the favorite causes listed in the letters. It was the ending part of this task that would keep him awake for many nights to come. Along with each condolence letter, he packaged a small brass urn purportedly holding the cremated remains of the deceased patient. Whether they were was anybody's guess. At best, they were a probable mixture of several cremated bodies shoveled without care from the furnace after each grouping of patients was burned and dumped in a row of waiting urns. Blanketed in ignorance, the grieving family would ask no questions because it was the state that had cared for their loved one, who was there with them in the urn.

Cremation troubled Erich deeply, though. The idea of death and burial and rising when the given day came, was as real to him as the breaths he took. And the burying of ashes was not the same as a whole body, which God expected to see. He had come by this belief from his grandfather, who told him God didn't have time to run around trying to put together thousands of pieces of burnt bones and flesh in order to have a man ready for Judgment Day. And ever since those words, Erich believed that only a wholeness of one's body would get you into heaven. He had tried to discuss it with Julia several times but got nowhere because she always thought he was preaching to her, trying to scare and convert her. How she would look before God was as insignificant to her as a single blade of grass. So her answer to him was always the same: "Remember the closing lines of Psalm Twenty-Three, Erich. That is all I will ever need to know about dying: 'that I will dwell in the house of the Lord forever.'"

TWENTY-THREE

Julia, Czechoslovakia, 1942

"We are filthy and smell no better than the old man's outhouse," Julia said, stepping around a pile of garbage dumped recently from one of the passing trains.

"Yes, but I'll bet that old bastard and his two soldier friends smell a hell of a lot worse where they are, lying in all that crap," Eva said, laughing.

Since turning southeast towards Klatovy they had covered six miles, hiking steadily along the snow-free railroad tracks. Walking on the level railroad bed as it made its way bending and winding around and through the hills in the open country had been a blessing to them, helping to conserve what energy they had left after their violent encounter with the German soldiers. It seemed strange to them, though, that no trains had passed during the two hours they had been walking by the tracks. This concern was short-lived as they approached a long, sweeping curve in the rail line. Julia heard the striking of metal on metal first and fell prone on the gravel shoulder to make herself less visible. Eva quickly followed. The loud clanging sounds would stop and start in a repetitive rhythm, like strange code signals being telegraphed across the frozen land.

"What is happening?" Julia asked.

"They're laying new rails, for sure, that's all it could be. They're coming this way, too."

Scrambling to her feet, Julia moved quickly with Eva away from the shoulder into a narrow winding crease between two snow-covered hills, until they could no longer see the railroad. They had moved none too soon.

Within seconds a work crew and flatcar loaded with new twelve-foot steel rails appeared, moving slowly around the long curve, followed by a squad of German soldiers. Julia and Eva could hear a mixture of German and Czech voices, one shouting angrily, the others in submissive, meek tones.

"What are they saying?" Eva asked, unable to understand German as readily as Julia.

"The Germans are mad because several rails were torn loose and damaged by saboteurs, and the Czechs are working like snails to replace them. They want to get back to Klatovy, too, where it's warm," Julia whispered.

"The rails looked okay ahead of where we were walking."

"Yes, but if they come as far as where we were, they will see our tracks leading away from the railroad. They will think whoever made them tore up the rails."

"They'll not follow us far if they do. They won't leave the work crew unguarded and will wait for reinforcements," Eva said, crouching low and clearing a path as best she could ahead of Julia through the heavy snow massed in the gulley. In places it was knee deep, falling down inside her boots, adding more winter misery to her already freezing feet. After about a hundred yards, she looked back at the deep footprints trailing behind them, which the Germans would easily see and use like a roadmap to find them.

Julia saw the tracks they were making, too. Unless they moved across the windswept open fields where much of the snow had melted, the Germans would quickly catch up with them. They would leave fewer tracks to follow there. Eva had realized the same strategy, and together they moved quickly to the top of a broad rolling hill on their right, daring to be seen in the glaring sunlight now sweeping across the fields and hills like a massive searchlight, the kind one might imagine God would use to make the day, when there was no sun.

Looking from a distance like tiny field rodents outlined against the vastness of the open countryside, Julia and Eva raced rapidly from one hill to the next back towards the road to Klatovy. Distant eyes had spotted them, though, within seconds after their ascendancy to the first hilltop, following every step they were taking. As they drew near the silent observer, Julia saw a head suddenly appear and disappear quickly behind several small piles of snow. Her face lit up when she realized how the snow piles were arranged in a carefully constructed square, like the walls of a fort, and its one lone inhabitant hiding behind them was a young boy. Julia stopped and nudged Eva to stop as well.

"You have a very good hiding place. May we please come in?" she said, speaking Czech to the child.

At first the small child lay still behind the snow wall, trying hard to look as if he were a part of the frozen ground beneath him. When she took a step closer to him, his head popped up again to look at her. Then he stood facing both of them, a child who looked to be about nine, trembling with his dark eyes painted over in terror. On the front of his soiled jacket was a faded yellow star telling her, and everyone else who might see him, he was a Jew. Julia sighed aloud. Coaxing him softly, she held out her arms to him.

And when he came to her she embraced him for several seconds, holding him tightly as if he were her own Anna.

"You must live near here," Eva said, hugging the boy, too.

But the boy remained silent, refusing to look at Eva, or anywhere else, except to the motherly warmth in Julia's face. Sensing his fear, Julia wrapped her arms around him again and whispered in his ear, "My name is Julia. Now you must tell us yours—we are your friends."

The boy looked again at Julia then Eva.

"Joseph, but my grandmother calls me Josh," he said in a barely audible voice.

"May we call you Josh, too?" Julia said, holding both of his hands.

The boy smiled and nodded at his new friends.

"Is your home near here? We're tired and cold, and you must be too," Eva said, slapping and rubbing her face and hopping around in a silly way on one foot and then the other, making Josh laugh out loud.

Still laughing, Josh pointed to some fairly level fields slightly south from the direction Julia and Eva were headed. With Julia holding one of Josh's hands and Eva the other, the three began a new and unexpected journey together as they moved slowly over several hills leading to some open fields in the distance. Julia looked at the strange color of the sky overhead. The treasury of blue patches that had filled the sky earlier in the day was now fading into bundles of gray clouds tinged in red streaks from the setting sun. Darkness would surround them soon, maybe with rain or more snow. The ground snow had begun to freeze again as the temperature dropped, making walking difficult again. They had come far this day from the place where the plane had mistakenly dropped them. Shelter for the freezing night was their first priority. Julia knew, as well as Eva, without it, only God could decide if they would be alive when morning came.

As they crossed the top of the high hill leading down to the small valley where Josh's home supposedly was, a thin wisp of smoke could be seen wafting upwards from below. Josh beamed and started to run towards its source, but Julia had heard the angry shouts rising up from the valley and pulled him quickly to the ground beside her. Eva had heard the voices, too and dropped down next to them. Julia motioned to her to hold Josh and cup her hand over his mouth, should he suddenly cry out. Then she slowly inched along the ground, slithering like a large snake through the remaining snow to a point where she could look down on the terrible scene unfolding below.

Julia counted five motorcycles and an armored touring car, the kind Gestapo generally used, parked next to a stone house, much like the old man's but quite a bit larger. The German soldiers were standing in a half circle around an old woman wearing only a thin nightgown and bleeding about her face and head. Clinging to her frail legs were two small children, both younger than Josh, trying to hide their faces from the human terror crowding around them. Standing slightly to the side of the old woman was a young officer sharply clad in the black uniform of the Gestapo, shouting obscenities at her. Julia could hear every word. There was nothing she or Eva could do to stop what was coming.

"Do you want to die, old woman? I will beat you with my fists until you do, if that's what you want," he said, knocking her to the ground again and kicking her in the back and head with his heavy boots.

But the woman said nothing, getting slowly to her feet with the two children huddled close against her, their faces buried in her gown.

"Where did the saboteurs go? Where are they hiding?" he shouted again in a shrill voice that carried far over the hills to where Eva waited with Josh.

"I swear before God, no one has been here," the woman cried in pain, forcing the words through broken teeth dangling in her battered mouth.

The officer looked at the old woman for a moment, disgusted, or perhaps amazed, that she had told him nothing after suffering such a beating. Taking his Luger from the holster, he shot the old woman at close range in the head, splattering blood and brains over the two children kneeling beside her. Then without hesitation, he shot both children in the forehead. Waving to two soldiers standing near the front door, he barked a command to put the dead woman and children in the house and burn it to the ground. Nothing was to be left standing, not even the two field haystacks that Julia had spotted earlier for possible hiding places.

Within minutes the house morphed into a roaring furnace of its own, the stone walls encasing the flames within until they finally crumbled from the intense heat. Black smoke from the burning buildings darkened the skies for miles around, hiding the dying sun. What had taken place was only one small scene of the terrible retribution the Nazis would exact in human lives for what had happened. The railroad had been heavily damaged by a growing underground resistance operating out of Bratislava, long retreated to safety, leaving those living around Klatovy, like the old woman, to suffer on their own in the days ahead.

Julia had closed her eyes the second the Gestapo officer drew his pistol to execute the woman and children. She knew he would not leave and let them live. Peace has few boundaries, war even less where the innocent have no armies of their own. Later, when Josh was asleep, she would ask Eva what kind of a man would kill little children without hesitating at least for a second to think of what he was doing. He would be from another world, she would answer. Yet, those are the kind who walk among us, even as neighbors, who could kill a child as easily as they would a deer or a rabbit. The problem is, we don't always know who they are, or might be, because we are still animals, too, all of us.

With the fire fully ablaze and the Germans leaving, Julia crawled back to where Eva and the boy Josh were waiting. Both were numb from lying still so long on the frozen ground and welcomed Julia's return with chattering teeth from the cold. Eva first had spread half her body across Josh, adding warmth to the boy as well as herself. But it was not enough to hold back the cold rising from the earth beneath them. The bowels of a glacier would be warmer, Eva believed, than the ground they were lying on. After five minutes, she turned on her side and embraced Josh as lovers might do, holding his small body close to hers. When the rising smoke came into view, Eva turned her body slightly so he would be blind to what was happening, lest he cry out and struggle to free himself and run to the house.

It had seemed like an hour before Julia slowly inched her way back to the nearly frozen pair. Before she revealed to Eva the terrifying scene that had blackened her eyes with its horror, she took Josh in her arms and kissed him on both cheeks. Then, smiling through the tears drowning her heart, she rubbed and massaged his fingers and hands until a red rush of warmth returned in them. She then asked him in Czech if he understood German, which he answered "no." Speaking German, Julia offered him a candy bar, but Josh only hunched his shoulders in ignorance at her words.

Julia's eyes spoke to Eva before her words in German did describing the ghastly sight she had witnessed. Earlier Josh had told them, as they were moving across the hills towards his house, that he lived with his grandmother and two younger sisters. His mother had bled to death at home giving birth to the younger of the two sisters after his father had left for Prague to join the Czech army. When questioned about his father, he knew nothing, since he had been gone for three years. With no Jewish kin near, Josh was now Julia and Eva's problem. He would go with the two women wherever the roads took them, until he could be fostered in safe hands.

As they neared the final rise where Julia had been earlier, looking down on the nightmare taking place, her grip tightened on Josh's hand. He would want to run to the smoldering timbers and fires still burning brightly in every corner of the yard to find his grandmother and sisters. But when Josh saw the burning desolation, he stiffened and stopped. Looking neither to Julia nor Eva, only staring straight ahead, his eyes locked in a catatonic stare, not on the house, but the barn still covered in great flames. His grandmother and sisters would be fine, but not the furry pet rabbits he loved. They were there in a wire cage, somewhere, that's all he knew. What they would become later, to his surprise, was a wholesome dinner for three—badly charred rabbits with some half-cooked potatoes found in the smoldering ruins of what had been the kitchen. At first he cried when the rabbits were found lying huddled together in the smoking twisted cage and refused to hear of anything like eating his pets, but he finally settled on the meal when Julia convinced him it was their way of showing how much they wanted him to stay alive.

As night finally came to the long day, the heavens surprisingly cleared and filled with stars, all twinkling brightly from their chosen place in the universe to the earth below. It was a beautiful night by any measure, one that would not quickly be forgotten. Julia cleared a small area on the ground next to a large cone of glowing embers where the three could bed down for the night. The immediate area around the crumbled walls of the house was no longer frozen, and actually was pleasurably warm to the touch. Josh's eyes closed in sleep within minutes after Eva stretched out next to him on the ground, holding his body close to hers as she had before. She would sleep no more than two hours before Julia would take her place. They would alternate two times during the night, one sleeping, the other watching for any distant lights of returning German patrols. Eva had been right that the Germans wouldn't follow their tracks leading away from the railroad. Instead, once the tracks were discovered they quickly increased their surveillance on the only road Julia and Eva could exit on from the hills and fields they were crossing. In one of fate's strange ironies, they had become by default the saboteurs the Germans were hunting to find and kill. Julia believed that having Josh with them would help lessen suspicion from patrols and the Gestapo who might be inclined to question them. But she also believed the Gestapo would have the patrols establish checkpoints at the road's beginning and its termination in Klatovy, and perhaps other places along the way. They were good. And British intelligence had taught Julia that once the hunt began, only a precious few agents escaped. Intelligence had trained her to always anticipate the unexpected, placing her in situations few people could imagine, daring her to go unnoticed, not to be checkmated. This was done, she knew, because intelligence and the enemy's counterpart, the Gestapo, had always been a chess game played out on a board as wide as the world. And it was in the end game, when only a scattering of pieces and moves were left, that the impossible must happen. Few in her training had ever encountered an imagination as soaring and weird as Julia's. Her long childhood hours of pretending and playing with Rabbi Loew's golem had stored within her fertile brain a lifetime of all that was unreal, yet could become real if one imagined it to be. It was this same imagination that led her to the top of the class during her university years in Prague, and then at British and Czech intelligence. "A brilliance painted with two coats of common sense" was the way Erich had described it. She was smarter than he was, he believed, and everyone else around them, except maybe the professors; but even then he wasn't so sure. In analyzing a difficult case, she would jump ahead to a tailored solution that wasn't always in the books, yet would work, while everyone else continued fumbling around, trying to understand all the components involved. She had no ego in her smartness, only a burning pride in being who she was, a Jewish woman, and he loved her that much more for it.

Julia looked at her watch—it was near midnight. While Klatovy was temptingly near, five miles perhaps, they would never go there as the Germans expected. They would instead use the road for only a mile, leaving few tracks to follow. Traveling with Josh would be an added burden, she knew, but not before they turned from the road into the hills again for the long trek south to the woods and the small mountains along the southern border. Dawn would break through the darkness in six hours and the early patrols would begin their journeys back and forth on the road. None should be stirring until then. It was too cold and the roads too dangerous with snow and ice.

The night skies were clear now, with a million stars watching over them, so tomorrow's day would be beautiful, Julia whispered, gently nudging Eva awake for her turn to sit and watch the road. Before she took Eva's place next to Josh, Julia discussed with her what lay ahead and the difficulties facing them traveling with Josh. What was necessary though, they both knew, and what would blacken the days to come for him, would be their revelation to him about his grandmother and sisters' deaths. Nothing in Julia's past was there for passing such pain to a child, and she would leave the sorrowful task to Eva, who seemed willing. It seemed to go with Eva's philosophy about death, that at any time those who died were never more than a step away from living. Like next-door neighbors, Eva would say whenever she discussed it. She would tell Josh that his grandmother and sisters would always be that close, where he could almost touch them, waiting for the day when he would be with them again. It was far from what her rabbi said a good Jew should believe about death, but to Eva, it was far less complicated and soothed the living soul better. Nothing would be told about the horrors of their deaths, nor the burning of their bodies, only that they were dead. Should he press them for the truth, they would lie. So while they were there, staying the night, Julia and Eva carefully kept Josh away from the smoldering ruins where the burned bodies of his family lay looking like nothing more than three piles of simmering charcoal and ashes. Only the glasses of his grandmother could be seen, smudged and curled, resting atop the largest pile that hinted of a body beneath it.

Julia awoke at three. Eva had graced her with an extra hour of sleep before awakening her. They had planned to leave their stay at five but Eva refused to take the last turn at sleep, suggesting an earlier start because of the German dogs, something they hadn't discussed. She convinced Julia that when the patrols returned, along with the Gestapo, they would bring tracking dogs that seldom failed to find a trail. Nodding, Julia quickly gathered together the rabbit bones left from their meal and carried them back up the hill from where they had first come, dropping one or two, here and there, in their old tracks. Then she pulled down the two layers of pants she was wearing and urinated several places alongside the tracks. It was the best they could do to forge a false trail that might delay the dogs longer should they come. While she was gone, Eva awakened Josh, walked him back and forth a short distance and told him to pee. When Julia returned, she wiped Josh's face with a glove of snow, gave him the last of her chocolate bars, and stepped into the road holding his hand. With Eva in the lead to warn of black ice on the road, the three moved at a steady pace toward Klatovy.

Josh asked nothing about his grandmother and sisters, which puzzled Julia considerably as she walked along beside him. Perhaps he heard them talking when they thought he was sleeping. She decided nothing would be said until he asked about them, and then Eva would tell him. No questions would come, though, until the morning had passed and they had turned south into the hills. "Did the Germans kill my grandmother and sisters?" was his only question. And when Eva said, lying, "Probably, when they took them away," he said nothing further. Death was no stranger to him. He had watched his mother bleed to death giving birth to the younger of his sisters. And before that, he had watched his grandfather, whom he worshipped, leave life from blood poisoning. Death to him, like it was to Eva, was a natural part of living, and had always been replaced by someone's love. After his father left, his grandmother became that love; now it was Julia and Eva's turn to become his dead grandmother's proxies.

Nine hours had passed and Julia kept squinting her eyes, studying the distant horizon ahead, looking for the first faint shadows of the woods and mountains to appear. The weather was the blessing they had been waiting for. Cloudless, deep blue skies that seem to have no end ran on ahead of them for miles, no longer shielding the earth from the sun's warmth. With each passing hour there was less snow, until none lay on the hills and valleys before them. Julia was amazed at the strength in Josh's skinny legs. He seemed less tired than they were, asking only twice to stop for water and to squat away from them to relieve his bowels. They would stop and pause, though, every thirty minutes to listen for the baying of trailing dogs, should the Germans have found their tracks. But none came. The Germans did return, bringing dogs as Eva predicted, but they had followed the smell of rabbit bones and the urine left by Julia, and then the old tracks of Julia and Eva leading from the railroad. Sniffing along the road for a clear scent they could follow, they found none. Trucks and motorcycles had passed by earlier, erasing any evidence of Julia and Eva and Josh's smell. Julia's quick decision to travel another mile in the early morning darkness before leaving the roadway came from her gut this time, a feeling that distance mattered most when you were the prey and the hunter could only find you with his nose. The dogs' handlers let them sniff everything there was to smell along the roadway toward Klatovy for no more than a mile before turning back. A mile without a scent would stop any dog, Julia had figured.

By late afternoon Josh was ready to stop this strange adventure of his, and began questioning the whereabouts of his grandmother's body. What had the Germans done with it? Would they keep it for him until he returned? Julia would not answer him, nor Eva, except to say the Germans had buried her and his two sisters somewhere in Klatovy. Josh extracted from them a promise of no consequences, that when it was safe to return they would go with him to find his grandmother and his sisters' bodies. His grandmother had left without kissing him, something she had never done, and he wanted to ask her why, even though she was in her grave.

Josh's words stung Julia. She had felt the same unsettled pain when her grandfather died without saying goodbye to her. She loved him dearly, as any seven-year old would their grandfather, and he had gone without a hint of a goodbye or kiss for her. Hers was a selfish demand, Julia learned at the time from her father's wisdom, that it was she who should have said "I love you," and kissed her grandfather goodbye a hundred times and more through his dying days.

Julia put her arm around Josh as they walked along.

"Where we are going is not too far now, and we will rest and find something to eat," she said.

Finally, in the honeyed light of the late afternoon, a time just before the evening shadows unrolled to blanket the earth, Julia and Eva picked up the woods and the mountains on the horizon ahead. It was a new kind of country they were entering, the dark green of the forests and the gray of rocks that lay ahead. It would be dark, though, when they reached them. A small village was hidden somewhere in one of the deep valleys, Julia knew from her map, but whether it was east or west from where they were was impossible to know. The morning would be the time to worry. For now, they would move into the woods and find the best shelter they could away from the bitter cold the night would bring.

After making their way slowly for another twenty minutes, around thickening trees and brush in the darkening forest, bright orange flames of campfires suddenly appeared at a short distance ahead of them. Julia immediately whispered to Eva to wait with Josh while she scouted the unexpected scene. Moving closer to a small opening in the trees, she saw a group of men and women, some sitting, others squatting, in a circle around two campfires. Close to them were several children hopping back and forth playing some kind of game. They were either gypsies or Jewish refugees fleeing from the north, Julia believed. But who they might be made no difference—they were warm and would have food. Slipping back to Eva and Josh, she told them of the strange sight.

"They are gypsies. We will be welcomed, for a while at least, but we must watch them. They are not to be trusted," Eva said, cautioning Julia. Josh nodded in agreement. His grandmother had told gypsy stories too many times for it to be otherwise.

Julia knew, too, the heavy mark the gypsies carried in Prague, where they were considered the lowest of the low, even by many Jews there. But never were they considered so by her father. No man should be thought ill of without a reason. And race and religion would never rise to the level of any sort of reason in his mind. How Eva and Josh felt was of little consequence now, because an old woman gathering slivers of loose bark for tinder had noticed Julia peering through the trees at the campfires. Saying nothing, she stayed hidden until Julia moved away to return to where Eva and Josh were waiting. At that time, she walked quickly to a man standing alone away from the campfires and told him of her discovery. Together they walked to the edge of the clearing near where Julia had been and waited in the dark. In a few minutes Julia emerged from the shadows, followed by Eva and Josh. As they exited from the woods, the shimmering light from the campfires danced on their faces, creating a frightening ghostlike appearance to their sudden presence. Julia looked past the man and woman, carefully searching the scene before her for any threatening moves from the other gypsies, all standing now in a half circle facing her. Only the children, who had quickly stopped their hopping game, seemed to be smiling at her. When Eva and Josh stepped into the clearing from the woods and came to Julia's side, two women, one of whom was pregnant, approached Josh, eyeing the yellow star on his jacket.

"You are a Jew?" the pregnant woman asked.

Too terrified to answer, Josh inched closer to Julia.

"We are all Jews," Julia said, taking Josh's hand. "We have no quarrel with you. All we ask is to stay the night where it is warm and beg a little food. Then we will leave when the sun is up."

The man who was standing with the old woman by the edge of the woods walked over to Julia, studying her face and eyes. Taller and older than the rest of the men, he carried himself with the authority expected of him as an elder. An imposing man by any means, heavy muscled and square jawed, with skin darker than those around him and deep-set eyes that told you nothing. But his voice was gentle and musical, like someone singing softly to himself.

"You are running from the Germans, yes?" he asked.

"At one time we were, but they are no longer following us now," Julia answered.

"Only the morning will tell us whether that is true, yes."

"No, I am certain," Julia said, steeling her eyes on the man's, whose were fixed on her every move and expression.

"Come sit down with me by the smaller fire and tell me everything that I will know to be true or a lie," the man said, taking Julia by the arm and waving for Eva and Josh to follow.

As Julia told her story with approving nods from Eva, and answered the questions that came from him, she became fascinated with the heavy strangeness of this man. Like many Jews in Prague, throughout her entire life she had spent no more than fifteen minutes talking to a gypsy man or woman. Where she was and what was happening seemed as unreal to her now as Rabbi's Loew's golem had been in her youth. The only story kept hidden from him was that of the British and Czech intelligence, and the role she and Eva were playing, though Julia believed he knew.

When they were through talking, the only thing Julia had learned from the man was his name, Django, nothing more. He then asked that his people gather in a circle once more around the big campfire, and he would tell them about what he had learned and what they must do. Django walked slowly to the center of the circle with Julia and Eva and Josh by his side. Speaking Romany, a language neither Julia nor Eva understood, he told what he knew about them and that they should be welcomed to rest for awhile before moving on. When he came to the episode of the two dead soldiers and where they were hidden, approving smiles and laughter broke out among the group. The tale of Josh's loss of family brought a chorus of wistful sighs and looks of sorrow around the circle. Ending, he turned to Julia first and then to Eva, extending his hand in friendship as he told them all he had said to the gypsy families. Then he lifted little Josh in his massive arms and kissed him on the forehead, mumbling something to him that no one heard. Later in the night around the fire, songs were sung and stories told and new dreams made, none that Julia and Eva had heard before.

TWENTY-FOUR

Czechoslovakia, 1942

J ulia stirred at dawn after spending her first night with the gypsies hud-
dled with Eva and Josh by the fire, now only a few smoking embers.
She had made a small bed on the forest floor, using heavy straw taken from
Django's cart where he slept warmly, unconcerned about the weather.
Wrapped together like a large cocoon, with Josh squeezed tightly between
their bodies, Julia and Eva kept the cold away and slept as best they could.
As the first light from the rising sun made its way through the woods, Julia
saw the first of the many strange sights that would come to her during her
stay with the gypsies. Back in several openings in the woods, hidden by
the night when she arrived, were several small earthen mounds rising no
more than three feet above ground. Covered with pine needles and twigs
and tree limbs of all sizes and shapes, they were largely indiscernible to the
eye at first glance. Inside, still sleeping, were the families she and Eva saw
gathered around the fire, families they would come to know well and love.
She had assumed they slept like she and Eva had, huddled together with
those they loved and covered only by the heavens above them.

"You and Eva must build your own forest nest today if you are to stay
with us for a little while," Django said, coming up behind Julia, startling
her.

Turning to him, she saw a different face than that of last night.
Somehow it seemed less gentle, more rugged and weathered than she
remembered. Looking at him closely as he walked around stirring the
campfires, she realized there was nothing more astonishing than a human

face, how the slightest of shadows can create a new and different person, only to change again when the light comes and the shadows drop away. Much of life was this way, she had learned, for those who exist only among the shadows, and see nothing more than images of truth.

"You will teach us then, if we stay for a few days?" Julia asked, as he walked back to where she was standing.

"Yes, before night comes again, you and your friends will have a warm place." Saying nothing more, Django walked away from Julia, much like he would do many times in the two months she and Eva would stay with his family of gypsies.

Jews living with gypsies would have been a very odd anomaly at any time in history, but war has a habit of changing relationships and dismissing culture, when staying alive is the only topic on the table for discussion. So it was with Julia and Eva and all the gypsies they found themselves living with. Each knew little about the other, though they quickly decided their Gods were the same, which made them happy. At first Julia was puzzled because, though the gypsies were Christians and had their Jesus, He seemed very different from Angie McFarland's Jesus. He seemed more mystical, like everything around them, especially their amulets and talismans and good luck charms, which they kept with them at all times. It was Eva, though, much to the surprise of Julia, who became fascinated with their belief in the existence of bad luck, *bibaxt*, they called it. Through all the droughts her family had suffered that destroyed their grain and vineyards, she had never once thought of it as being the doings of an alien power that had its own existence instead, always accepting that's just the way life was. Now she wasn't so sure, and it bothered her deeply that she had learned such a thing as bibaxt. Neither she nor Julia took issue with their healing rituals, which came to them early the third day they were there, the day they had planned to leave the camp. Josh had awakened, coughing and unable to breathe, fighting for what air he could pull in to his small lungs in quick gasps. The chest cold that had set in the morning after their first night had seized his body and would take him away, Julia believed, and she had no way of stopping it. She had watched her little sister die from the croup when she was no older than Josh. Nothing anyone did mattered, not even praying. But Django came and took Josh from her arms, and, summoning two women to bring their amulets and talismans, placed him close to the fire. Then a healing ritual with chanting words unknown to Julia and Eva began as the women's amulets were emptied on and around Josh, while some kind of warm fluid was forced down his throat, which seemed to help him breathe better. Julia wondered if they were calling on God in their words, or to a separate power of healing, like bad luck was thought to be. Later Django would tell her that God was seldom called on, or mentioned, though he might have been there with them a few times. Yet he couldn't explain Josh's healing when pushed by her to talk about it. All he would say was that it wasn't Josh's time to quit living, as if one's existence was somehow tied to the sands of an hourglass, which Julia didn't believe. What was certain, though, was that she and Eva would have to remain with the gypsies for an uncertain time until Josh was well enough to travel.

In the days ahead, spring came and life began again. The barren brush throughout the forest turned bright green and armies of wildflowers pushed upward from beneath the thick blanket of thistles and pine needles that had kept them warm through the long winter, while young fawn danced and played nearby. For Julia and Eva, new things would be learned in an existence neither could have ever imagined.

For Julia, more than Eva, the time she would stay was like living in a theater of wondrous lore, offering something new each rising day, something that had never reached her soul before. It was like when she was a child. Her father would take her to the Vltava River and teach her how to carefully select the flattest of rocks and skip them three and four times across the dark moving waters. It seemed like magic to her then. And so it was with Django and the gypsies. Their music, more than anything, would bring her to her feet, clapping as a child would in the delight of the rhythms and sounds. All they had was an old guitar and a tamboura and a badly scarred violin, but the music that came from them filled the forest with song as if there were a thousand strings playing. Julia soon learned that anything that could create a sound became an instrument. Rubbing fingers on brass surprised her the most, creating a magical melody for Josh and the other children. One night when the dancing and singing started, the music became tribal and wild and unshackled, with several men jumping through the fire as if responding to some ancient voice within. When Julia entered the circle of dancers, she was quickly joined by Django, who held her tightly around the waist as she struggled to keep up with the rapid beat. Their bodies never touched, yet they were close enough that the scent of their sweat aroused their senses. Later, when she asked about such music,

Django would say, "It is who we are when we are free," and walk away into the darkness of the woods.

Later that night he came for Julia and took her deep into the woods where they would stay until the early morning hours, talking of things that mattered most in their lives, but nothing of war. She was fascinated that Django would care to discuss so deep a subject as death, with it always being so close to him, living as he did. Yet he spoke with the passion of a poet, choosing each word carefully, so that who he was as a man could not be misunderstood. She decided he was a good man, raw and uneducated as he was.

Although Django was a Christian, he was quite different from the ones she had known and cared about, particularly his belief in what happens to us when death does come to take us away. Coming back to earth again was very real to him, much like it was to many of the first Christians, but not as a human being. He would return as a wild animal, but never one of his own choosing, God would do that for him. When Julia asked about such a strange belief his only words were, "It's from the ancient roots of my blood that came out of India with my people."

"What animal do you hope God would choose for you?" Julia asked, watching the exuberant expressions on Django's face as he expounded on his beliefs.

"Perhaps a wolf, or a deer, like those in the Black Forest that are free to sleep and play under the stars."

"I would want to be a bird," Julia said.

"A bird—they are too puny."

"Yes, but they sing with such joy, even though their world might be ending, and they fly away from all that is bad," Julia said, as if she believed all he was telling her.

Then she told him of the Old Jewish Cemetery and Rabbi Loew and his golem and how she would like to be buried there someday when she lived again in Prague. But when she told him how the bodies were stacked on top of each other, he became upset.

"How could they go before God that way?" he asked in an uneasy tone.

"I don't know, but I'm sure at least their souls do if they have one."

"Well, I will be buried alone, standing up, so I can walk as a man before Him. I have been on my knees too long."

"That would be good," Julia said, which seemed to please Django.

Then he asked her what she thought about going before God as a Jew and not a Christian, which was not the kind of question she would have thought necessary to keep a ready answer for.

"I don't know what you're asking. The ancient Jews were afraid of Him, our book says, but I'm not," Julia said rather proudly.

In a while Django told her of his wife, who died two years back from blood poisoning, dying over three long days and nights in agony. When asked about the healing ritual for her, like that of Josh's, he had no explanation for its failure, except maybe she had done something terribly wrong in her life, or perhaps he had, though he wasn't sure what he had done that would have made God angry enough to take her from him. Perhaps God would tell him someday when his time came to go. With that, Django stood up and said they should get to their beds, that it would rain soon.

But as he was leaving he took Julia's hand and simply said through tears, "It is when the spring rains come that I weep for her because our love was born then."

Julia turned away from Django quickly, not wanting him to see her own tears, because she had left her love with Erich when the first spring rains came to Prague.

As this strange bond between them grew over the weeks, Julia would hike with Django through the mountains a day's distance to a small village, which held few folks and had no name. There they would bargain for vegetables and a pig or a goat, and sometimes for woolen yarn that had been dyed bright colors. Accessible only by a dirt road full of deep potholes and ruts and rocks, the German patrols had come but a few times to the village since the war began, taking what they wanted in food or livestock and sometimes home-brewed beer.

But the last visit they stayed longer because the Gestapo was with the patrols. Watching from the hills above the village, Julia saw their autos and knew more than Django that something serious had happened to bring them to such a remote place. Eva had come with them this day to carry a second pig back to the camp, which had grown by three more gypsy families, who wandered in unannounced as she and Julia had.

Had she and Julia been there to meet the newcomers, they would have known then who the Gestapo was looking for. Twilight would settle in before the Germans would leave and they could come down from the hills. It was then that they learned from a friendly farmer that Reinhard Heydrich had been assassinated in Prague by Czech intelligence. The countryside was crawling with soldiers and the Gestapo arresting and killing anyone they thought might be involved. Julia listened to the sadness in the man's voice, as he told them of his own loss. His two sons were visiting kinfolk in Lidice when the Germans came, and had been executed along with every man and boy in the town. When the horrific slaughter was complete, the village was burned to the ground, leaving nothing but an echoing silence for those that would later come there.

Julia and Eva glanced quickly at each other as the farmer talked. The secret operation Anthropoid connected to their own mission had been successful, and that was good, but at what price? More would die soon in the days ahead, they knew, from the Nazi's means of exacting revenge. Julia walked over to Django, who had separated from them to watch the emerging red colors of the setting sun bounce wildly across the rocky hills above the village.

"We must return to the camp tonight, Eva and I, to get Josh. We will gather what food we can here, and go immediately," Julia said.

Django seemed surprised at her words. No woman had ever told him what he must do, because he was a person of consequence, a don among the gypsies. Women had always sought his permission, rather than taking it upon themselves.

"Trying to make our way through the hills without light will be too dangerous for us. There are deep drop offs. No, when morning comes we will leave."

Django's words fell on deaf ears. Eva moved quickly to select a small pig from the farmer's sty, tied its legs together, and hoisted the squealing animal across her shoulders. Without bargaining the price as she had enjoyed doing with Django by her side, Julia paid what the farmer asked, filled her backpack with carrots and potatoes, and followed Eva, who was starting up the first of many steep inclines ahead on the mountain trail. Angered by Julia's sudden display of independence, and what he thought was a crafted insult to him, Django watched them for a few minutes as they climbed higher into the hills, disappearing from view. He would soon follow though, and learn of their deftness at navigating through the blackness that now surrounded them. They were better than he was and he didn't know why, which disturbed him even more.

Stopping only twice to rest, the three travelers ended their fourteen-mile journey as dawn came to an end, lifting the darkness from the trees. Looking ahead to where the camp should be, Julia slowed her pace, then stopped. There were no camp fires to be seen, no voices to be heard, only a stillness so soft she could hear the early morning dew dropping from the leaves to the forest floor. For a moment it was as if she were walking once again as a child through the Old Jewish Cemetery, because the smell of the dead was all around.

Julia signaled for Eva and Django to wait hidden in the trees while she entered the deserted camp alone. No sign of life could be seen. Unable to stay back any longer, Eva and Django rushed forward and joined her in the broad opening of the camp. Julia saw it then, as if she knew it would be there: Josh's woolly toy dog. Julia picked up the toy dog, lying alone on the ground next to the cold fire, and held it close to her cheek, stroking it gently while trying to get a sense of what might have happened. There was no real solution before her, other than that the camp had been vacated hurriedly by the gypsies. They had been eating, was all she knew. How else could you explain the pots and pans and plates strewn throughout the camp, some still full with roasted cabbage and pork slices.

Julia circled the camp to a smaller opening that led to several family huts. Seeing nothing to alarm her, she walked back to where Eva and Django were standing, who seemed puzzled by the empty camp.

"There is no ready answer for what happened," she said. "Unless they are scattered in the woods hiding, they have been taken by the Germans."

"The Germans will come back again, I'm sure. We should get the hell away from here," Eva said.

Julia nodded and knelt down by the pig they had brought from the village and cut the twine binding its feet, setting it free to roam the forest and root for food like its ancestors once did. Scampering away, the animal set its course towards the woods near the small opening where Julia had been. Waiting for the pig to disappear among the trees and brush, now grunting happily, Julia walked around the empty camp once more to breathe in the warm joys that had captured her heart here. What memories and stories they would make someday when she was back with Anna. Though the grunting of the pig could still be heard, now deep in the woods rooting for acorns and black walnuts along the forest floor, Julia looked no further. Picking up the backpack full of potatoes and carrots, she started back through the woods in the direction from which she emerged two months back with Eva and Josh. Had she gone farther, deeper into the woods where the pig was grunting loudly, she would have seen the bodies, all naked and dead.

They came to kill, that was all. It was their only duty as Einsatzgruppen, chosen to kill the Jews and Gypsies and anyone else Himmler and the Reich Ministry decided must die. And that is what they did, coming unexpectedly from the woods, descending on the camp like an ancient Mongol horde. Within minutes the small band of gypsies, with little Josh among them, were marched naked into the woods, lined up in a row, and shot in the back of the head. Taking the gypsies' sparkling bracelets and rings, Einsatzgruppen left singing, because it had been a good morning for the chosen.

No one would ever know what they did here. The bodies would soon be food for the animals of the forest, including the lonely pig set free by Julia. Nor would it ever be known how the chosen knew the gypsies were there. But one might suspect they knew from Django's many shopping visits to the village with no name. How else could you explain the strange man who would carry a pig strapped to his back and disappear into the forest?

At first he had refused to leave the camp, certain all of the gypsies would soon return. But it was Eva who cut through his quick denial of what had happened, pushing aside the curtains hiding his grief with her strong voice so that he might at least hear the truth. His family would not leave without him, and if the Germans took them, they were dead or soon would be. Django only nodded, as if he understood, then waved them on without him.

"You must wait for me when you are outside the forest and I will tell you my plan. But right now I want to look at the emptiness around me and listen to its silence for a few moments—some precious souls may be waiting still to say goodbye," he said, turning and walking back to his cart.

Julia hesitated for a second, then motioned for Eva to follow her as she continued on into the forest. When they emerged, Julia and Eva sat down on a large rock to wait for Django, who was following slowly, crying aloud for his family with every step taken. Looking back east across the long rolling hills and summer-brown fields, Julia felt like the world had suddenly shrunk in size a million times over. Everything and everyone seemed much closer now, leaving little room to hide in. Heydrich's death had put the Germans everywhere, in every village that lay before them.

"There is no place for us, Eva, no place. Pilsen and Prague are out," she said, openly despondent over their situation.

"Bratislava should be open. Hitler gave Slovakia its independence from Czech rule when he took Prague," Eva said, eyeing Django, who was stepping from the edge of the woods to join them.

"No, the Nazi puppet Father Tiso is there, and he is delivering Jews to the Germans as quickly as he can find them. We would be captured in no time."

"It's my home, I know the people," Eva said loudly, exasperated with Julia's indecisiveness.

"You are still a Jew and loyalty is a rare virtue in wartime, especially when one's own life is at stake."

Eva knew Julia was right and said nothing more. With a Slovakian government as Hitler's ally, they would easily be trapped by the Gestapo in Bratislava. Django had listened with interest to their words, shaking his head all the while in disagreement.

"We should go north to the tall mountains around Banska Bystrica where there will be friends and few Germans," he said, smiling proudly with the solution he had offered.

Julia had thought of the Carpathian Mountains, too. The partisans were strong there and they could reestablish contact with intelligence in London. But to travel across the open country that lay distant before them would be no different from playing Russian roulette with six bullets instead of one. Yet to stay and not try would be just as suicidal.

"How far are the mountains, Eva?" she asked.

"Depending on how far north we head from here, seventy-five miles, maybe a little more. There will be nothing to hide us. The land will be open clear up to the arms of the mountains."

Django began to shake his head again listening to Julia and Eva's words. "There is a way—an old Romani road used by my people many times when they would go and hide back in the valleys of the mountains as we wish to do now," he said, smiling sadly.

Julia looked into Django's eyes, as she had the first night sitting around the campfire. Black as round bits of coal anchored deep in the sockets of his face, they could never look at you but through you, as if you carried a shallow and empty soul. How fond she was of him. He was more a man than her Erich; he had cried unashamedly in her arms the night they sat together deep in the woods, speaking of his dead wife. But the passion she felt for Erich had wrapped itself around her soul the first night each gave their love to the other. Only time would loosen such a passion, and time no longer existed. All that had been lived, all that had happened in these years of a terrible war would be spoken of with the voices of storytellers, rich with disbelief in what had passed. There was nothing that seemed real around her now except death. Django's way would have to be their fairy tale gamble. Had she still been a child, the golem would be here to carry her away.

"Show us the road and we will follow," was all Julia said as she stood, waiting for Django to begin the long trek to the mountains.

Django smiled and beamed with pride. He was in charge again, as a man should be.

"We will go south a few miles to find the old road, then turn north for the mountains. Perhaps my family is walking on this road also," he said, motioning for Julia and Eva to follow.

TWENTY-FIVE

Erich, Brandenburg, 1943

As each week passed the gray buses came more often to Görden, bringing many patients from distant villages, crowding the examining room and courtyard at times. Long days became the standard for Erich and the rest of the medical staff. At the beginning, his examinations of the patients were far more thorough than anyone else's. He often dismissed patients from the walk down the hall to the gassing room, scribbling in their charts, "Capable of working." None escaped their fate, though. As soon as he dismissed them, they were quickly returned to the line waiting before Franz, who took no longer than one minute, often less, to pass them on to their deaths. In time, Erich saw what was happening but continued his ways in examining his patients, as a good doctor would, until fatigue finally deadened his mind. He would leave then to go and sit, and sometimes read, next to Mother Mary, one of the statues that greeted the crazies from her place in the garden.

None of the doctors, including Erich, remained in the examining room for the two hours it took to ventilate the gassing room and remove the pile of dead bodies. They would return to the hospital wards to tend to their regular patients, should there be any. Erich, though, had few to treat in the East Ward, for which he was glad, and spent his time reading and talking with Maria. They had become close friends, as he said to her one late afternoon, and they both agreed that nothing more than friendship should be expected of the other. She reminded him that she was very much married and loved Martin, though no letter had come from him in months.

A letter did come to Maria one Friday morning, but it was not from Martin. In the simplest of words, she was informed by the Chancellery that her husband was missing in action. Erich was with Maria when the news came, holding her until there were no more tears left to shed, except those in her heart. They then went to the rose garden by the hospital and sat together where he held her hand, listening to rambling shattered stories of who Martin was and all that he meant to her. When the time came for Erich to return to the examining room, she promised to wait for him, and they would talk more of Martin. Kissing her lightly on the forehead, he squeezed Maria's hand and left to face the remaining hours of the day in a room full of people whose future no longer really mattered, at least in a way they would know, because what there might have been would soon end for all of them.

When he returned to the garden hours later, the sun was resting low in the sky, lining puffs of clouds with soft, red streaks that gradually became lost in gray as evening moved closer. Erich stood in the garden for a brief moment to look at the moving scene, as he had many times as a child in Dresden. The changing colors had thrilled him then, quickening his desire to become the painter his mother hoped he would be and his father despised. "All life is brief, only a second before God," she had told him, "but art is forever." Perhaps someday, he sighed, when all was right again, he would trade the white coat for a handful of brushes and paint such a scene.

Maria had left the moment Erich disappeared from sight, returning to the East Ward to gather her things and go first to the apartment and then the church. She knew no one there, nor did she belong, but she loved its great doors that swung open wide like two giant hands welcoming all who entered. She had sat there alone for hours in the dark sanctuary, asking God's grace a hundred times to shine on her Martin's life, wherever he might be, and bring him home to her. But God's grace was nowhere near Martin, as he lay between the old man and his comrade, rotting in the filth of the outhouse, never to be found.

Finding Maria not at her apartment, Erich went to where he knew she would be, in the great Evangelical Lutheran church, whose twin spires seemed to go beyond heaven to another world. Saying nothing, he sat down quietly next to her and waited until she was ready to leave.

Later, he sat again with Maria in her apartment, holding her at times while she cried, other times listening to words that made little sense. Never before had Erich felt someone else's pain, and he doubted even now that what he was experiencing might be such an emotion. Yet he had no explanation for the moment. The closest time to now was when the grandfather he loved so much was killed in the Great War. But even then it was a selfish loss, quickly passing when others took his place. His separation from Julia was a matter of the heart, an explainable longing shared by all lovers, but there was never the searing pain he saw in Maria. It seemed to smother her from head to toe, allowing nothing to escape its crushing weight.

As the night aged, Maria fell asleep in Erich's arms, the anguish of Martin's loss still brushed across her face. He would stay the evening, sleeping fitfully next to her soft body, lest she awaken and cry out again for him to hold her. It was a new and strange experience for him. He had never finished the night with a woman by his side. Not even with Julia. Their times together were, for the most part, a precious gentle love wrapped in brief moments of ecstasy.

Maria was different, though. Away from the hospital and the starchiness of her nurse's uniform, she exuded sex in a fragile way that Julia never could, nor would he have wanted her to. Even the smell of Maria's sweat aroused the desire to take her brutally and uncaring as one animal might another. He had never experienced such a long night. Vile games came to him in his mind, the kind psychiatrists since Freud have tried to analyze and understand and sometimes called a sickness. They would stay with him until the dawn, as he tried to understand what lay beneath the terrible urge to use Maria, even though the empathy he felt for her loss and pain seemed terribly real to him. Had the night been an hour longer, he would have taken her, Erich knew, she was that vulnerable.

At first light, ignoring Erich's presence next to her, Maria slipped out of bed and went to the bathroom to bathe. Erich had already left for the hospital when she returned, deciding to shave and wash in the doctors' lounge near the East Ward. When he arrived, Franz was waiting by the nurse's station to talk with him.

"I have been ordered to Auschwitz much sooner than expected," he said, looking closely at Erich's ragged and unshaven appearance.

Erich noticed Franz's attention but said nothing.

"I must leave this afternoon," Franz continued, "and I have asked that you take over my duties here."

Surprised by Franz's gesture, Erich was both elated and fearful by what else might now be expected of him. He knew Franz was not the kind to help anyone unless there was something for him to gain in doing so. That was the way the game was played throughout the Reich, especially the Health Ministry. Even those closest to the Chancellery knew their status always depended on someone else a bit higher and closer to the catbird seat than they were.

For a moment, Franz looked past Erich at the empty nurse's station.

"Where is Nurse Drossen? We are expecting more patients than usual this afternoon, and she will be needed in the examining room."

"Her husband was reported missing in action only yesterday. She is at home or the church."

"Mourning in the church will do her no good. God hates whiners. Let her mourn among the crazies, where good will come to all of us by getting rid of them," Franz said, staring coldly at Erich for a second, then walking away towards Dr. Heinze's office.

Later, Erich returned to Maria's apartment to find her staring blankly at a letter from Martin, which had arrived earlier in the morning. It seemed odd to him there were no tears in Maria's eyes, only a frightened look of utter disbelief, the kind when nothing around you seems real. Handing the letter to him, Maria pointed to the date—it had been written months back but was only now reaching her.

"He is dead. My heart felt it last night. There is no need to pretend anymore," Maria said calmly in a soft voice.

Erich sensed Maria was probably right. Only a lucky few who were missing in action ever returned to reclaim their life.

Erich reached out to touch Maria, but she quickly brushed his hand aside and moved away from him.

"What is it you want, Erich, besides me?"

Erich could find no answer for a second to Maria's surprising words and turned to the kitchen stove as if he were inspecting it.

"Dr. Kremer knows of your loss, and in his kind way has ordered you to be on duty this afternoon in the examining room. There will be many patients to process."

"It is right they should die, but not my Martin. He was only a simple soldier trying to do his duty. They are nothing and never will be," Maria said with anger, leaving Erich standing by the stove while she went to dress.

When Maria returned, she was dressed in a newly cleaned and pressed uniform, with her face covered in powder as white as the uniform she was wearing, giving her a ghostlike appearance. Erich's stunned look made her smile, which bothered him even more.

"Don't you like it? The crazies will, I'm sure, looking at me, and maybe even laughing one more time before we kill them," she said, tracing a wide smile across her mouth with bright red lipstick. Erich quickly took the tube of lipstick away from her, placing it in his pocket, and led her to the bedroom.

"Go back to bed and end this dream you are in. Dr. Kremer is leaving for Auschwitz and I will cover for you for a few days, since I will be in charge."

Ignoring Erich's presence, Maria began disrobing. As he turned to leave she grabbed his arm, pulling him towards her.

"Come to bed with me. Be my Martin for a little while," she said, before bursting into loud sobs, the tears slowly making their way through the heavy powder on her face, carving small canyons before dripping from her chin. She looked even more hideous now, standing naked with a face twisted and smeared in a mixture of watery colored anguish.

Pushing her onto the bed and covering up her nakedness with a sheet, Erich looked down at the crumbled human mass before him and said in a commanding voice, "Stay away, Maria, until you can see the world as it is, not from that of a lost love."

As he left then, Maria's loud sobbing pierced the air as he shut the door behind him.

When afternoon came, Franz had left for Auschwitz and Erich moved tentatively to assume charge of the ongoing T4 Operation taking place in the old prison. He had never been particularly good at giving orders, and thought himself to be a poor excuse for authority, directing men to do something they might otherwise decline to do. Deciding beforehand to simply take his place alongside the other examining doctors and say nothing, he nodded to the SS staff to begin what had now come to be called "the slaughtering line," a name given to the naked patients waiting much like steers lined up in a stockyard in preparation for their sudden and violent death.

Within minutes the room was filled with the same type of patients as those before, but Erich noticed a small group of five had been segregated from the others, standing quietly to themselves while they removed their clothing. When the greater number had been examined and marked and stamped by the nurses, the other doctors stepped back, leaving Erich to examine the remaining five patients who were hurriedly shoved into a line before him. Erich turned around to look at the doctors, now smoking and talking among themselves.

"Why are you stopping? There are other patients?"

"We do not want to touch them. They are crazy Jews. They are to be separated here and everywhere else," the oldest and most distinguished of the doctors replied.

"Yes, they are for you to examine, Dr. Heinze has ordered," another one said sarcastically.

Erich knew what was happening, he had heard the rumors. Doctors everywhere were being tested to see if they were loyal to the greater good of the Reich. Those that failed would be sent away, without notice to family or anyone else. That is what had happened to Dr. Schneider months back when the crippled babies were being euthanized. Now these doctors were watching to see what he would do, one especially, who was a Gestapo informant. Any hesitation on his part could be seen as a failure.

Erich summoned the trembling group to come forward. None in the group had ever shown themselves to others, as they were doing now, standing naked before so many staring eyes. All were from the same small crossroads village south of Brandenberg, working at menial labor because of their slowness of mind, yet earning their way in life. They were standing before Erich because like the rest of the patients they had been reported to the authorities as mentally ill and registered with the Health Ministry as such. All five had been brought in a separate, smaller bus from the other patients, with the windows painted over so no one could see out or in. Strangely, though, they had been sent to Görden for observation only, not as a part of the larger group. Erich talked briefly to each about their work but did nothing else. To touch them would separate him from the other doctors carefully watching him. He knew, though, the Jews were healthy of mind from their answers to his questions, and could perform meaningful work if carefully taught to do so. His examination complete, Erich ordered them marked and stamped and to be kept separate from the rest of the waiting patients, before their short trip to the gassing room. They would be the last to enter the room and the ones he would see die, gasping for air as others in the room pushed them away. Erich could not help but watch the irony of the terrible scene playing out before his eyes. With death but moments away for all trapped in the room together, separation from Jews was still necessary for some.

Back in the examining room, Erich gave a list of those gassed to the older doctor, directing him to write the necessary letters to the families explaining their loved one's fictional death a week earlier than normal. No letters were necessary for the five Jews, he decided. It would be as if they had never come to Görden, or even existed.

Returning to the hospital, Erich went first to Dr. Heinze's office and filled out the coded report for the Health Ministry of the number of deaths processed, and then added a special addendum to the report regarding the five Jews. There he carefully noted in detail the absence of any serious mental sickness on their part and that all were fit and able to perform meaningful work. It was the only way he knew to tell the Ministry the five Jews had died for nothing. When he finished with the day's report, 125 more German citizens had been added to the growing number of those being sacrificed for the purification of the Aryan race. The eugenics movement, first begun so many years ago in America with the birthing rights of thousands of women spirited away on nothing more than the machinations of a new science and a perverted ideology, was now moving across Germany with the unbridled energy of a thousand steam engines. To some who cared, it was a joyous moment in history, the triumph of social evolution. For others, it was the beginning of the end of innocence as God intended it to be.

Maria was waiting at his apartment when Erich arrived. She looked rested, having slept the full day after he left her place, yet her eyes betrayed the terrible hurt she had suffered and was trying to reason away, relying on, the best she could, the old Christian adage that what comes to us in our lives is always God's will. From that, she had been told since childhood, we should always dismiss the terrible things we suffer as nothing more than a test of one's faith. She had believed easily in such nonsense all her life because nothing had come her way but the sunshine of each day. But even sunshine, she now knew, carried its own separate basket of tears.

For his part, Erich was glad to see Maria. She had become the only person outside of Julia to have found a corner of his soul. What he wanted now from her was absolution for what had occurred with the Jews during the afternoon. When he told her what took place in the examining room and the innocence of the five Jews, Maria said nothing. Instead, she walked around the apartment, looking in each room and closet as if searching for some phantom body, or hidden recording device, that in time might come back to haunt her with the words she would say now. In a few minutes she sat down next to Erich, who was resting on a small settee in the makeshift living room, but she offered no explanation for her strange behavior.

"What do you want me to say, Erich, that it was wrong for the Jews to die as they did?" she asked. "They were no more innocent than all the crazies we are killing."

"Perhaps, except they were not as sick. They died for who they were, which does seem different, doesn't it?"

Maria looked wishfully at Erich, her eyes becoming watery with tears.

"Why are we talking about the Jews, Erich, when my Martin is dead. So forgive me, what is right and wrong makes little sense to me at the moment."

"Why are you here then? Pity?"

"Yes, for my share of the pity I think. It's the one emotion that requires the least of anyone to give, yet it does help one feel better."

"Okay, I pity you," Erich said with a nervous smile, becoming increasingly uncomfortable with the conversation.

But Maria was not amused and turned away from him for a moment. Though she felt herself a fair person, the plight of the Jews bothered her little, growing up in Mainz as she did. None lived in her poor neighborhood, nor went to her schools. They sometimes seemed as foreign to her as the occasional French businessman in the town, especially the old ones. But to many people in the neighborhood, including her mother, it was the greedy Jewish bankers that Hitler had railed against who kept them in poverty. Even at the church, few kind words were said for them. And every Easter she was reminded that it was they who had killed her Savior. After Easter week one year, when she was twelve, she was brought to tears and chased from the playground by her classmates taunting her for acting as a Jew in the town's annual passion play. What was strange to her later when she recalled the episode was that she thought little about what it might be like to be a Jew, but more about how it would be if you were not against them.

Without thinking, Erich took Maria's hand and brought it to his lips, kissing it gently, then said, in the softest of voices, "We are alive, Maria, and we have a choice to stay alive. For that we should be glad. It's more than the crazies and Jews had."

Shocked by his actions, Maria abruptly jerked her hand away, rose from the settee, and began straightening her clothes nervously.

"You are confusing your psychology lesson, Dr. Schmidt. Pity and sex are not the same thing, and never will be," she said, opening the front door to leave.

"I meant nothing, only that I cared about your sorrow."

"Perhaps, but not likely. A hunger for sex has a way of sneaking up on you, hiding behind a lot of fake emotions. Yours is pity," Maria said, closing the door behind her.

Erich sat looking around the room at the shadowy emptiness staring back at him. Maria was right. Her hurt and weakness continued to arouse him long after she was gone, and he felt no shame for it. The fact he possessed any kind of feeling now, with all that had happened, thrilled him. It told him he was alive and still very much a man.

So he came to yet one more day in the examining room. Maria was there waiting for him, as were the three doctors who stood with him the day before when the Jews were gassed. There were no Jews to examine, only the usual four busloads of mental patients. Though she had begged off after the first day, upset by all the squirming naked flesh crowding around her, Maria wanted to return. She would heal more quickly from her own loss, knowing she was doing her duty, which would have pleased Martin.

As summer turned to autumn, the buses continued to come, sometimes in twos, with their load of patients. At times there were some Jews included, but never more than a few, for which Erich was glad. One afternoon, while waiting for the gassing room to be emptied of bodies, Erich became upset when two buses arrived carrying an unusually large number of semiconscious patients and ones who had been brutally beaten about the face. When the first patient stepped from the bus and saw Erich and the staff, he began crying and shouting "murderers" at them and tried to run away. Quickly subdued and sedated, he was carried straight to the examining room, stripped of his clothing, and tossed in a corner of the room where he lay crumpled on the floor like discarded dirty laundry. The same fate awaited the other semi-conscious patients, and when the gassing room was empty all were quickly carried in and stacked like a cord of wood near the front wall. When the other patients entered the room and saw the pile of naked bodies, they turned back and rushed to the door, which had already slammed shut behind them. Pounding on the door, they began to scream and wail unmercifully until the gas made its way into the room to still them.

Later, when one of the SS staff was questioned about the semiconscious and those beaten, he had no excuse other than to say, "Everyone in the asylums now seems to know what will happen to them when the gray buses come." When others on the staff were questioned, their answers were the same. Listening, Erich believed that the secret T4 program, so carefully guarded by the Health Ministry, had become unsheathed by the steady rise in rumors coursing through the villages and asylums. Questions began to be asked of him for which he had no answers. At first, when the killings began, the walls were silent, yielding no hints that anything other than caring medicine was going on behind them. But the rising blackened gray smoke from the crematory had become a fixture in the skies, spreading the smell of burning flesh. No questions would come from the townspeople, though, only a silent wonder after a while at how all that was happening could have come about. "Where were the churches?" some would say among themselves. "They should know. Isn't it their job to know those things that seem so evil?"

A few churches did begin to speak out, some with commanding tongues, against what they believed might be happening behind the walls of the old prison. But the mental patients continued to come at an ever-increasing pace, making it impossible for all to be examined by Erich and the staff, or carefully identified from the hospital records to confirm that they should even be there. The constant rows of human cattle waiting to be slaughtered, and the piercing stench of death that followed, was beginning to overwhelm even the sanest of the lot, except Maria. Steeling herself with constant visions of Martin lying dead somewhere in the unknown, she stood throughout each day, hollow eyed and blind to the crying faces that continually passed before her, leaving each evening unshaken by all that had happened that day. Erich grew obsessed with how those around him seemed to enjoy being a part of the killing center. He began to wonder if the time hadn't finally arrived when the rational mind would eventually accept killing when death was all around. Like mass hysteria, could it become the aegis, the mental shield for all else that was happening? He finally concluded that living in the world is nothing more than a morality play where one may easily forget his lines.

As time passed, Maria continued working in the examining room, always stoic, her mind a million miles away from the beseeching eyes of the patients watching every move she made, or every word she might say. Twice during the mornings she would go and look for a second through the glass peephole in the door to see the writhing bodies gasping for air, then collapsing. It was always a strange and puzzling sight to her, she told Erich one evening. Why did they struggle so much to stay alive, when it was hopeless? They should submit and thank God for what they'd had. For herself, she could never get over the idea of death. One moment you were here and then there was nothing. No fanfare of trumpets and clapping hands and flashing lights, just nothing. Erich recognized the silent footsteps of Maria's approaching madness with such chatter. Like a brittle dead twig, her mind was snapping. Still, each morning Maria was the first to report for work, renewed in spirit and determination to complete the day as best she could. Martin would have expected it of her, she would tell those who questioned her welfare.

With the winter months approaching, the number of mental patients going to their deaths seemed to be diminishing. By Erich's calculation, over eight thousand bodies had been carried by the stokers on metal pallets for burning in the crematory. Thousands more, he knew, had been killed elsewhere in the asylums across Germany. It was hard for him not to think of what his future in psychiatry might have been had all these people lived. In a way, he felt cheated. With all the crazies dead, he would have no patients to treat.

One day no buses came. And when none came the next day, nor the days after, the sudden unexpected release from killing played on everyone's mind, except Erich's. Secretly, Franz had prevailed upon Dr. Eduard Wirth, the chief SS physician, to transfer Erich to Auschwitz. When the transfer orders came, Erich was reading aloud Nietzsche's long aftersong, "From High Mountains," to Maria in the rose garden. They had come there together often in the recent weeks to let their day become peaceful for the night. It was good for Maria to do so, he believed. To hear the rhythmical words sing their soothing beauty held a healing grace of its own for her broken heart. They had also become closer friends than each realized. More so, too, than either one would have wanted, they would later claim. But in these passing moments in time, each seemed to hold for the other what they had lost.

Erich said nothing as he read the orders silently to himself, but the shock printed across his face was there for Maria to read. He was to report to Auschwitz in five days. While the order of transfer was clear to him, it was the second order that was puzzling and bothered him. He was to report first to Munich and there attend a trial of several university students charged with treason to the Third Reich. They had been caught distributing leaflets condemning Hitler and fostering internal dissent against the Nazi regime. Together with another psychiatrist who would come from Berlin, he was to try and develop a psychological forensic profile of the charged university students that would help the Gestapo in identifying other disgruntled students on campuses across Germany. Erich knew little about the kind of profiling being requested of him, and knew that innocent students could easily be arrested should they display any of the characteristics found in the profile he would develop. He was paranoid enough to believe his task there was another Gestapo test of his loyalty. What he didn't know, and never would, was that the special assignment to Munich was the doings of his father trying to reassure his own position with the Chancellery by involving his often-suspected son in such an important task.

When Erich handed the official orders to Maria, she grasped his hand for the first time ever and began to cry. She had lost Martin, and now it was Erich who would be leaving. And while the looming separation may have fooled her heart into believing more is there to be taken from the heart than it really ever had, she would be alone.

"Tomorrow is Saturday. We must do something special, then go to church on Sunday," she said through a flood of tears tumbling down her cheeks.

"Yes, finding a small inn by the river to stay over through Sunday would be nice, if there are any left from all the bombing. I can go from there to Munich."

Maria listened carefully to Erich's words, and knew what he was asking, what was expected of her. Any other time she would quickly have dismissed with anger what was being suggested. He was not her Martin, nor would he ever be, or anyone else, but the strange and tender bond that had developed between them tied her to him. The need to be held through the night now was too great for both of them, she knew.

"Berlin would be special for both of us and we should be there together, but we must still go to church on Sunday. It would be right to do so before you leave," Maria said, now smiling again.

TWENTY-SIX

Erich, Munich and Auschwitz, 1943

Erich knew nothing of the three university students charged with treason. Nor did he know anything about their seditious underground publication, *The White Rose*, which had boldly denounced the Nazi regime, calling for all Germans to rise up against the tyranny of their own government. Even as a psychiatrist, he was equally ignorant of how to go about developing the kind of forensic profile the Gestapo was looking for from the students, simply by observing them and listening to their words at the trial. There was no nonsense to these young people, no theatrics.

Outwardly, Erich saw nothing that would separate them from other university students except perhaps an aura of calmness in facing down the shrieking denunciations of the Nazi prosecutor and trial judge. They clearly were marching to a different gospel than everyone else, and had chosen the worst of times to proclaim it. Erich saw clearly their purpose but quickly closed his mind to it. Truth means nothing unless it is heard, and they did just that, daring to write their testament for all to read. They had refused to separate the singularity of duty and conscience, as all those fervently following Hitler had done. This fact was never more evident to Erich than when the young woman, Sophie Scholl, rose in the courtroom. Looking straight at the tyrannical judge before her, she said, "Somebody, after all, had to make a start."

Eight simple words. Everything she and the other students believed in was there for everyone to hear. One cannot do his duty when conscience is not a part of it. For Erich, though, it seemed that simply doing one's duty had its own intrinsic worth and didn't need a touch of conscience to make it right. Not to believe so would seem to shame the honor of all the thousands of German soldiers who were blown to pieces in a terribly wrong war, not for Hitler, but for duty and Germany alone. While he was unsure how to produce the kind of treasonous forensic profile the Gestapo desired, what he could offer them was a profile in courage, if only he had enough integrity himself to do so.

It was a given to Erich that the students were either mentally unstable or incredibly courageous, being saturated from head to toe in a boldness with which he was unfamiliar. When the trial was over and they were found guilty and sentenced to death, Erich knew he had witnessed the rawest sort of bravery, the kind that one can only read about in great books.

He had no stomach to witness the students' execution. It would be difficult enough to erase the events and machinations of the trial; images of their beheadings would be impossible to suppress.

On the long trip from Munich to Auschwitz where he was to report, one unanswered question still lingered in his mind: how could they choose truth over living at such a young age? If they had been old and wrinkled, it would make more sense. But the mere utterance of words that had no hope could not be worth more than staying alive when you are young. They were dead now, and others would be, too, and nothing would come from what they had said and done except the silent grief of their parents. Still, they were different, Erich knew, but he didn't know why. They had moved beyond the ordinary to a dimension in life few people would ever know. They were unafraid.

All his life he had believed he could become something more than the nothing he now felt himself to be. Art and painting had captured his early childhood dreams, but they had long since vanished, lost on another road in the wilderness of his fantasies. To be a great artist or poet, one must imagine the world as it is only with the eyes of the soul, and his were now blind. Dimmed by his experience at Görden, they could no longer see things as they truly were; they could only see that which was necessary to exist. There was not a single moment in his life now, he knew, when he could say no to doing what was expected of him.

It was the miles of lights and fires that he passed entering Auschwitz the night of his arrival that finally closed the eyes of his soul to everything but his own desire to exist. Everything seemed like a dark fairy tale to him, somewhere deep in his beloved Black Forest, only fairy tales don't smell like this one did. The smell clung to the folds in his nostrils like thick green snot frozen in the cold winter air. He knew the stench from burning bodies at Görden, but it never made him afraid to breathe as he was now. Five crematoriums were spewing their thick black smoke across the sky, but his attention was drawn to a long wide pit with colorful dancing flames licking naked burning bodies that had been doused in gasoline. Erich turned away, refusing to look anymore at all the horror before him.

When he stepped into the chief SS physician's office, Franz Kremer was there to greet him.

"Ah, my old timid friend, we are together again at last, and in the best of places."

Erich said nothing, only nodded. His hate for the man had not lessened. With his flair and posturing, Franz was a commanding figure, ranking higher in the chain of authority before anyone of his young age. Tall and Aryan looking, he had become unbearably handsome in his uniform to everyone around, even to Erich.

"Come, there will be no more trains this night and we can have drinks together at the doctors' quarters to celebrate your arrival. Tomorrow you will see Auschwitz," Franz said, signaling to his driver to have the touring car ready for them, a vehicle marked with a Red Cross symbol.

The "club," as Franz referred to it, was unusually quiet for an evening when little was expected of its doctors. Some had gone home to be with their families for the weekend, tending to neglected chores around the house and yard or celebrating birthdays with their children. Others preferred escaping reality alone in the solitude of their own quarters, where they could become drunk and pass out in peace. But all would be ready again for their long hours of duty on the selection ramp when the trains arrived, bringing the prisoners.

Looking around the rather large room filled with an assortment of wooden tables, Erich counted only four men, two sitting together, the others separate. None looked up, or cared to see who he might be, this new doctor standing with Franz. As important as Franz was, it was of little matter to them because their minds had long left this world, drowning in a flood of alcohol. Franz and Erich sat away from the four men, to talk and drink and eat snacks into the late hours of the night. Erich learned much of what would be expected of him when tomorrow came, and of the many hours and days ahead as increasing numbers of Jews arrived in the camp. How he performed his duties, whether in an unkindly or noble manner, was of his choice so long as the immediate selection policies were followed. Erich knew Franz preferred the cruelest of ways, and looked with great favor on others who did.

So the next day, he took his place alongside Franz, and for two weeks after, conducting medical selections. The bedlam in the terrifying scene played out before his eyes was beyond anything he might have imagined it could be. Where Görden had maybe thirty patients arriving at a time, here thousands of frightened prisoners scurried to leave and empty the long line of boxcars standing idle next to the ramp. SS guards with dogs shouted "Out, out! Line up, line up!" as they climbed down from the cars and formed two rows. Those that failed to move along quickly enough were shoved forward violently, or beaten about the head and shoulders by the guards. Many had little sense that a selection process of any kind was taking place. As quickly as they had climbed from the boxcars, the long rows of anxious faces moved past Franz's eyes, stopping only for a second while he looked them over for signs of physical weakness or strength. Occasionally he would ask a question of age, as if to verify his medical thinking. He then pointed his thumb either to the right or the left, much like God was expected to do on the final judgment day, for those who believed and those who didn't. Left was immediate death by gas. Right meant, perhaps, only a delayed death, one that came in the early mornings when you could no longer stand for another day of hard labor.

Observing Franz, Erich believed a good bit of medical judgment was being employed in selecting those who would live, and that was important to him. Age and physical fitness had always been an essential component of a physical examination performed by a doctor. What bothered him some, though he would say nothing, was Franz's immediate thumb to the left for pregnant women who came before him. They all seemed young and healthy, and in time would be good workers, but they were Jews and no more Jews were to be born, at least on Franz's watch.

That first night, when the trainload of prisoners lined up for selection, Erich saw they were all Jews and his mind turned for a quick moment to the five Jews that had come before him at Görden. How is it this is happening? he had asked himself then. But the question had no meaning for him this night, looking at the endless line of Jews before him. They were already dead, all of them. And what he could or could not do was of little consequence and meant nothing. The revulsion he felt then was no longer with him, and had become shaded by acceptance of what was expected of him now.

Erich had been on the ramp the first night for ten hours, being relieved for an hour of rest two times by other doctors. When there were no more trains to come and no more prisoners to see, the scene became still and quiet, swathed in a hidden silence of the horrible things that had happened there. Leaving the ramp with Franz, it was he who suggested the evening end with drinks in the officers' club.

There were several doctors socializing in the lounge when they arrived, two of whom, like Erich, were new doctors assigned to the camp. Unlike him, though, they had not been at the small killing centers where the mentally ill were being euthanized whether they were Jews or not.

"How can the things we are doing here be allowed? They surely will write about this for a hundred years," one doctor said, somewhat intoxicated.

"Yes, this is a filthy business for us," his companion said.

Erich watched Franz's reaction. Like everyone else in the room, he offered no response but continued drinking and talking. Many in the room had spoken the same words when they first came, but now they no longer talked of the terrible happenings around them. In time, except for the Nazi ideologues like Franz, the new doctors would come to believe as they did, that in the beginning it seemed impossible, and yet it would become almost routine. In time, as the days passed, Erich found this to be true. Everything happening was as one in Auschwitz. No one could escape the pervading morality in the camp that seemed to separate him and the other doctors and everything else in Auschwitz from the rest of the world. This awakening became even truer two nights later.

Working with Franz again, Erich noticed him suddenly stiffen and straighten in body, as he would do when someone of importance approached him. To his right a strange-looking man, handsome in carriage, with a brown riding crop in his right hand, walked by the waiting line of prisoners for a short distance then back again, stopping next to a mother and her young daughter. When the man pointed to an SS guard to separate them, the woman fought with the guard, biting and scratching his face. At this moment, the man with the riding crop drew his pistol and shot both the woman and child in the face. Waving the crop back and forth, he ordered all the prisoners to the gas chambers, even though some had been selected for the work force, shouting "Away with this shit" as he left.

Franz smiled, but not Erich. The scene had unnerved him.

"That was the great scientist, Herr Dr. Mengele. I'm sure he wanted the young girl for one of his research projects," Franz said.

"I know nothing of him. What kind of research is he doing?"

"All kinds, but no one really knows. He comes many times to look over the prisoners when they arrive, especially the young children and mothers. I do know he has the run of the camp in taking any prisoners for research."

"Why not take the dead?" Erich asked, utterly amazed at what he was hearing.

"No, they are always alive when they go to him. That's all any of us know."

"It was good then that he killed them."

Erich said nothing more, but waited with Franz for the last of the prisoners to be taken from the ramp and transported to the gas chambers. Then he went to the officers' club with him, got slobbering drunk, and passed out sitting in a chair, where he remained until morning came and a new day of selecting began again.

Nothing changed at Auschwitz as the seasons passed, except thousands more Jews came to die. There were not enough ovens for them and large new trenches had to be dug to burn the corpses in, some still alive when the burning began. Working through all that was happening, Erich had come to the conclusion that whether you believe something or not depends on the situation. There is no separate truth. It is in those moments that the unthinkable becomes credible for those that are a part of it. And so it was just that for Erich on a cold winter Saturday, the Sabbath day of all the Jews standing and shivering on the ramp before him.

When they came, as he knew they might someday, he was not ready. But he had known he never would be. He had hoped they would be transported to another camp when their time came, but the increasing number of Jews arriving from Czechoslovakia told him otherwise. He had thought many times of such a moment when they might appear before him, how he would act, whether he should speak to them, or whether he would recognize them? But it was they who would not let the moment pass quickly, making it easy for him.

Standing before Erich, Dr. Kaufmann with his gentle wife Anka waited for him to speak their names before walking to the waiting trucks, which would take them to the ovens. When they arrived, Dr. Kaufmann had refused to say he was a doctor, which might have kept him alive, choosing instead to stay by Anka's side until the end came for both of them. If they were to go to God now, they would be together when they met Him, he whispered to her moments before they climbed down from the boxcar to the ramp. They had come with all their family to this place to die, except for Julia and Hiram, whose lives he had never stopped thanking God for. No word had come from them in nearly five years, but in his heart he knew they were safe.

Through the time since Julia and Hiram left Prague in 1939, he had watched the houses and streets and synagogues empty and the voice of the Jew grow silent.

"After this year, the blood of our ancient fathers will be gone from Prague," he told the rabbi one Saturday, only weeks before they were to report to the authorities.

But the rabbi smiled and shook his head and said, "It may go away and hide for awhile, but it will come back as it has through the ages."

Both embraced then and he left, knowing that what the rabbi said was true. The Jew had been pushed out of Prague too many times to count over the centuries, but his soul never left. Julia and Hiram and many of the other children who had escaped would surely come home when all that drove them away had left.

Franz had joined Erich this night on the ramp, having been away on other assignments for some time, and recognized Dr. Kaufmann only moments before Erich did. He no longer looked at Dr. Kaufmann but to Erich, staring at him cruelly, relishing the strange drama playing out before him. What were the odds? Two dear friends, traveling different distant roads, meeting again as they did in such an isolated moment in history where one would select the other to die.

"It was like a Greek tragedy," he would say later to Erich, taunting him. "How did it feel sending your lover's father to his death?"

But Erich would say nothing, and would never speak of the night to anyone.

When he realized Julia's father and mother were standing before him waiting for selection, he could do nothing but stare blankly at their faces. Neither one spoke to him, both looking beyond the ramp at the trucks ahead filling up with prisoners. But, in a moment that seemed to complete the Faustian bargain Erich had long ago made with Mephistopheles to remain in the world a little longer, Dr. Kaufmann turned to him. No words were spoken. Only the unmistakable question, "Why?" was there to be read in his eyes, and then they were gone.

Watching the scene unfold, Franz clapped loudly, as if hoping Dr. Kaufmann and his wife would return to the ramp for a repeat performance. The delight he felt for Erich's agony would carry him high for days, and he would teasingly tell him so many times, just to prolong it. What he said, though, was of little consequence to Erich now, because what little piece of honor that somehow might have been left in him after all the terrible things he had done, rode with Dr. Kaufmann and his wife to the gas ovens.

When the night's selection was over, a clouded darkness swept across the empty ramp as it always did, lending an eeriness to the silent death cries that could be heard if one listened closely, from the thousands who had been there only moments before. He was alone now, and the haunting scenes in his dreams had become real. It was not that Dr. Kaufmann and Mrs. Kaufmann were any different from those who had gone before to the ovens. In the reality of things, they were Jews like the others who died. But in his mind he had separated them from all the other Jews in the world because he loved Julia. And this fact changed the equation. He had come to love and respect them more so than anyone else he had ever known. Dr. Kaufmann's imposing intellect had captivated him from the day they first met, constantly fueling the intense bonding that grew between them through the years. All Erich knew now was that he could never speak of this moment to Julia should they meet again, nor how her parents went to their deaths.

Walking back onto the ramp, he traced his fingers along the sides of several empty boxcars still smelling of the humanity they brought to the death camp. From time to time he would stop and look in one, as if expecting to find a terrified child hiding back deep in a dark corner, pretending he couldn't be seen. Looking at the almost endless chain of boxcars that delivered daily thousands to the camp and to the ovens, Erich knew he had been given a gift of time that others hadn't. He knew that the lives of those who came to be killed in Auschwitz embodied more truth than his compromised life did, and now all he had become was a man who had moved beyond forgiveness.

In the weeks ahead, until the end of Auschwitz, Erich spoke very little to anyone, nor drank and socialized in the officers' club, keeping to himself much as possible. When duty permitted, he sat alone in his quarters reading and rereading Goethe's *Faust* and Dostoevsky's *The Double*. Like

Faust, he had gone further than anyone thought he could, and pledged himself also to Mephistopheles in exchange for a few more precious days breathing in the world around him. Now his soul, he knew, would soon be carried away by the prince of demons to some distant world where the rest of the captured souls moaned in eternal agony.

For a while, he believed himself and all the doctors around him mad. No one could do what they had done unless they were. But in time, he concluded no one was really mad or crazy, not even Josef Mengele. He had learned long ago that a man didn't have to be mad to kill a tiny baby like he had little Brigitte and the other crippled children, if one found a reason for doing so, a reason to make it seem right. In time then, the unbelievable becomes believable, like what the Nazi regime was trying to accomplish here in Auschwitz. For whatever reason is used, he decided, it births another self, another personality within us that could in time adapt to killing without feeling oneself a murderer. Watching and listening to the other doctors, some spoke proudly of duty and loyalty as their reason, others of science and eugenics, but none from hatred of the Jews like Franz. Those that hated the Jews, and there were many in the camp that did, needed no reason for slaughtering them—their hatred had long ago erased any thoughts of guilt from their minds. Setting all reasons aside, Erich wondered if there wasn't a psychology of genocide, where just maybe killing was the normal thing to do and could be seen as right. After all, humans are animals, too, only dressed in the tattered clothing of a few hundred years of trying to be civilized. Surviving is what life is all about among animals, and killing other animals to stay alive is certainly a part of that. How else do you explain the thousands of wars the world has suffered?

So who was he now? Erich wondered, because he didn't know the work of fiction he had become. Perhaps he would never know; so many days of change had come his way. All he could do was to try to stay alive and go home when the war was over and start again.

TWENTY-SEVEN

Auschwitz, 1945

Himmler's order to destroy the crematories and start preparations for evacuating Auschwitz in January was not unexpected. The rumors were too pervasive throughout the death camp to be otherwise. No one really knew why, except perhaps the war was near its end, and Germany had lost, a stark truth that could no longer be hidden by the worried faces of Dr. Wirth and his medical staff of Nazi doctors. The steady flow of refugees ahead of the advancing Russian army did not pass unseen. For some, among those still waiting to die in the gas chambers, it was as if God had seen enough killing of His people to last another hundred years and had finally decided to stop it. Whatever the reason, to Erich it was an early Christmas gift that brought a warm glow to his face that had been all but extinguished the past two years.

That evening he returned to the officers' club for the first time since he passed Julia's mother and father through the selection to their deaths. It was the right time to celebrate, though it would stay silent within him. A few, like Franz, still believed in the cause, and any expression of joy over its demise would be met with swift punishment by the Gestapo.

Franz was sitting alone at a small corner table away from a mixed group of boisterous camp doctors and SS officers, all quite drunk. Since the moment the order came from Himmler, Franz had struggled throughout the day, as he was now, to understand what went wrong. Any suggestion at the war's birth of a possible defeat would have been as unbelievable to him as any idea that the earth really was flat. However, with the reality of a lost war staring him in the face, he wouldn't crawl away to hide like some mangled and beaten beast. Wirth and Mengele and the others would, he knew, for what they had done. But he would fall with the rest of the German warriors, if that is what the gods wanted his ending to be.

Seeing Franz brooding alone, Erich went to the table and sat down. Ignoring him for the moment, Franz signaled the serving orderly to bring two more steins to go with the four he had already consumed. He had aligned the empty steins upside down in a tight row across one side of the table.

"That is what's left of the great Wehrmacht, empty glasses. We are fighting the fucking Russians with glass soldiers," Franz said, gesturing with a sweeping wave of his hand and knocking over the row of steins.

Erich remained silent, looking nervously around the room for the face of any Gestapo who might be sitting unnoticed in the room. Franz's words were enough to have them both arrested.

"Things will change, I'm sure," he said in a loud reassuring voice for those in the room who might want to hear his words.

Erich knew that rampant rumors and paranoia would be on the menu every day until Auschwitz was finally closed, a classic study of where the reality of what has been done is suddenly seen for what it is, shaking everyone loose from the unreal world they had been living in. Though the terrible gas ovens were to be immediately destroyed, the lingering smell from thousands of cremated bodies had become a part of everything its tentacles touched. Mingling with the rising smoke from the bodies still smoldering in the open ditches, it covered the camp in a blanket of human memories woven together as one so they would never become unreal and forgotten.

After a long moment of silence, Franz took a last swallow of the warm beer he loved and stared glassy-eyed in a hypnotic way at Erich.

"We have no more Jews, or anyone else to kill, do we, my timid friend," he said with the familiar smirk across his twisted lips.

"Not here, but they will find others for us, I'm sure."

"Perhaps, but why wait. I am to accompany Dr. Wirth to Berlin tomorrow, and when I return, you and I can go together to fight the Russians by the waters of the Elbe. It will be a glorious ending for both of us."

Erich turned away; he was in no mood for such insane dialogue with Franz. Not at this moment, when everything was disintegrating around them. Madness and failure go hand in hand at times, and it was happening with Franz, he believed. All that Franz had planned for and worked for and killed for was crumbling before his eyes. Nothing in the darkening shadows of his tomorrows would be the same, and he knew it, and he was lost. But he was not afraid to die, and in his mind that set him apart and above all men that were, like Erich. It was a power he long believed in, that belonged to only a chosen few. For when one holds no fear of death one becomes like Nietzsche's *ubermensch*, he had argued many times with those who would listen, unloosed to be free from all reality. That is why Jesus meant nothing to him, nor what he proclaimed. He was very much afraid of dying, and turned his back on an endless glory that should have been his, had he not been.

"We should not be talking of fighting and dying, when there are many cards yet to be played," Erich said, trying to sound as dramatic as he could. Doing so always impressed Franz, because the role of evil always requires a lot of acting, and Franz was the master thespian in playing it.

Surprised by Erich's sudden theatrical flair, Franz crossed his arms for a second studying him, then leaned back, roaring with laughter, causing many in the room to look at him.

"You are right, there is more to come, and then we will face the Russians and die with great honor as we should. We must have more beer and talk of the days to come and what they will bring."

So Erich and the man he detested more than his own self drank away the last hours of a long night until neither could stand, nor cared that he couldn't. Erich had never been this drunk before, and found little enjoyment in it, especially when a swirling nausea blurred his eyes, seizing his mind and twisting his stomach into a thousand tiny knots before heaving into his throat and mouth all that he had eaten for the day. The vile vomit spewed forth from his mouth like one might expect to happen from a holy exorcism, covering Franz, who was fast asleep in his own world with its own evil spirit. In the morning, Erich could remember little of the night except that he had showered Franz with vomit and felt good in doing so.

They had been together over two years at Auschwitz, and he hated Franz every second of those days. To him, Franz came into this world corrupted; there was no other way to explain it. No one could grow into all the evil that possessed him. The problem was, as Erich saw it, the kind of diseased corruption that owned Franz was contagious in some strange way. How else could he explain his own corruption? He had been pure until the day he met Franz. His life and dreams with Julia at the time were locked in another beautiful world, clean and full of hope. Franz never had to choose between good and evil like he did to stay alive. That's the best way to explain all the terrible things that had happened. But the moments, he knew, were near now when all this would be over, everything he had done here and at Görden would pass into history. And the thought gladdened his heart and gave him hope.

On the second night after his drunken binge with Franz, the news came to Erich that Franz had been arrested by the Gestapo, then summarily tried and executed. Stunned beyond belief, Erich was afraid to ask why. He had sat and drank with him the night before when he had loudly berated the weakness of the Wehrmacht soldiers, a moment of treason. No reason for Franz's sudden downfall and death would ever be known, except through the passing whispered rumors in the camp. In the early hours of the morning, he had awakened at the table, still quite drunk and covered with Erich's vomit. Staggering into the club's kitchen to clean himself, he encountered a young Jewish girl of fifteen, quite small and emaciated, whose duties were those of a kitchen maid. Ordering her to strip off his filthy uniform and underclothes and clean them, he became aroused by her presence. Knocking her to the floor, he bared her body, too, and repeatedly beat and raped her until he was spent. When the morning shift arrived, they found him asleep, lying naked across the nude battered body of the small girl, who was semi-conscious and whimpering like a beaten dog. Without moving either one, the kitchen staff summoned the camp police who quickly marched a naked and still groggy Franz to headquarters for questioning. No excuse was there for him to plead. Being a favorite within the Health Ministry was of little help. With the war lost, those who had been important, or perceived themselves so, were scattering like straws blowing in the wind, hoping no one would find where they would come to rest.

Ending up in the hands of the Gestapo, Franz was executed not because he had beaten and raped a young girl, but because he had sexual intercourse with a Jew, an unpardonable crime. Only treason to the Führer and desertion of duty were higher crimes. The young girl did not escape either, though she was innocent. Taken to one of the open ditches, she was thrown in while still alive and burned with the other bodies already smoldering there.

For Erich, Franz's ignominious ending, if it were true, was another sign that God was changing sides. All would be over, the terrible things he was a part of, when Auschwitz closed in a few weeks. Then he could begin to nourish again the humanity that had long stayed crouched deep within him, cowering in fear. As a doctor, he would not have to stay behind when the camp was evacuated but would go with the thousands of prisoners to be moved deeper into Germany away from the advancing Russian army. He would leave one day, when they drew near to Dresden, by simply walking away. That was his plan.

No one, if they listened long enough, could fail to hear the distant rumbling sounds coming from the east. There were too many to miss, as the crisp cold days of January carried the faint booming of a thousand mortars and cannons echoing through the woods and across the wide expanse east of the camp. A phrase would soon begin that would be repeated again and again until they were actually there: "They are coming, the Russians," spread through the camp. Coming not as liberators, but to defeat the hated Germans, they would bring their own particular version of hell with them, which like the Nazi's was the stuff of fiction, being too unimaginable to be true. No female body was too young, or too old, to escape being penetrated by the conquering soldiers, who had been set loose on the towns like wild animals chasing down prey. Freeing Auschwitz's prisoners meant little to them, unless they were Russians. Saving what few Jews remained in the camp after the Germans evacuated it would be an added burden they didn't want.

As the thunder of the big guns grew louder, worry among the prisoners grew, too. Their task had become as one, to demonstrate to Erich and the other doctors they would be able to endure the long march ahead of them the day the camp was to be evacuated. No other choice was open for them to live. They would either march or be shot, or be left to die in their rotting skins for the Russians to find them.

The day before Erich was to leave Auschwitz, along with over sixty thousand prisoners, he noticed among a sickly group of Jews who would be left behind what seemed to be a familiar face. As the day progressed, the man's face haunted him, and in the late afternoon he went to find him. But the man, called Abram, hid from Erich when he saw him approaching the barracks where he slept. In time, Erich quit the search, but the man's face, especially his eyes, would not go away, following him wherever he went. He had never seen the man before, which was understandable to Erich, considering the thousands of prisoners that had come to Auschwitz during the past two years. It did seem strange to him though, that this one face he appeared to know but didn't was squeezing his mind for an answer from the past that wasn't there.

It was the worst of January's winter days when Erich boarded the army truck that would take him and others of the medical staff away from Auschwitz. A cold wind mixed with sleet blew through the camp, making it impossible to stay warm. Those that were left behind would be shot where they were found or left to freeze to death in the unheated barracks. When the Russians would arrive nine days later, large mounds of rotting bodies would be there to greet their eyes. For Erich, though, there was little he cared to remember as the camp faded from view and into a history that was yet to be written. Only the mysterious face that came before him filled his mind, crowding out all other thoughts, had he tried or cared to think of what had happened behind the closing gates. It was as if he had never been there before. Auschwitz, and the man's face when it came to him, was of another time and place. Hours later, when they were far into Germany, he would rest and sleep and know that Dresden was near and he would be home soon.

TWENTY-EIGHT

Julia, Carpathian Mountains, Slovakia, 1944

Finding Django's Romani road leading to the Carpathians took longer than expected. Hidden beneath tall grass and brush, little of the old road could be seen. Only where the ground was weathered bare by the seasons, or where families of rocks lay piled together as markers, could the tracks of gypsy carts be seen. The old road seemed to begin in the middle of nowhere, and end in the same way, too, deep in the cuts between the last of the rising hills before they curled up against the great mountains.

Julia had never seen the Carpathians, having never traveled much distance east of the Vltava River, and when they loomed before her she was taken by their odd shapes. Unlike the great Alps with their jagged peaks reaching to where heaven begins, they were more forested and rounded, with thousands of hidden folds looking in places much like a human brain. But she loved all mountains, big and small. There was something holy about them and the sounds the wind would make blowing up and down and around them. No sound was ever the same, like when it blew across open fields or through the narrow streets of Prague. It was easy to see why God first chose a mountain to look down from to tell us what was right and wrong.

But to the north, the tall mountains held more than God. Hidden among the tens of villages sprinkled throughout the deep valleys of the mountains were small numbers of Slovak partisans who maintained contact with the Czech resistance and British intelligence. So it was there Julia and Eva and Django would go to live and fight for two years, only to run once more to stay alive.

One day, when spring came early in 1944, two men came to Julia's band of partisans camped high in the mountains around the small village of Banska Bystrica and told them of Auschwitz and its horrors. Never before had the Czechs and Slovaks there heard such tales of evil as these two Jewish men offered. Both had managed a miraculous escape from the death camp, and would spend their days ahead like prophets of old, spreading the terrible stories to all who would listen. When Julia first heard them she cried unashamedly, knowing they spoke of her father and mother's fate as well. When she asked about her family, neither men knew of them, only that a small handful of those that came from Prague had escaped the ovens thus far. The words of the two men, though, added a new dimension to Eva's own silent hate of the Nazis, and in the coming months she became someone unknown to Julia, even to Django, fighting with the ferocity of a wounded beast, daring things no one else would do. The Slovaks grew to love her even though she was a Jew.

One August morning, after the summer winds had warmed the mountains, the partisans descended on Banska Bystrica, bringing with them Julia and Eva and Django. A long-planned national uprising against the Germans and Slovak puppet government had begun its ill-fated journey to disaster. Though Julia and Eva knew of the plan, little had come to them from intelligence of what their role should be. By the time the cards were turned face up for everyone to see, a quickening demise of the ill-planned uprising was taking place before them. With their fighting group quickly encircled by six German divisions, Eva and Django talked together away from Julia of the end to come and of their hope of killing ten soldiers before their own eyes became fixed in the stare of the dead, too.

Thinking of her own death was not Julia's way. It was only the silence that came with the loss of something precious that she had tried to understand. It was the only reason she had for believing a human soul existed. We go before God as a shadow, her father had told her when she was a child, and it is there we are given the light promised Moses and Abraham. But his words made little sense to her, because it is the light of living that dims and grows dark when death is around. She had seen it flicker for a while, and then go out like a candle in the wind when her grandpapa died. How to keep this candle burning a little longer was all that Julia could think of doing in the moments before her, not of dying and killing.

Thousands of partisans and rebel Slovak forces were preparing to retreat to the high mountains ahead of the advancing German troops; and Julia and Eva and Django would go with them, but then turn south, retracing the trail that first brought them here two years back.

Walking over to where Eva and Django were sitting eating bits of hard bread and cheese, Julia knelt down to tell them of what tomorrow would bring. Her words were interrupted when the first salvo of heavy German mortars crashed down upon the encampment without warning, shattering and tossing bodies in the air with every explosion. She realized the time was now, in the night's darkness, to go back into the mountains once more, not tomorrow. Screaming loudly at Eva and Django to grab what they could carry of food and water and follow her, Julia started for the narrow winding road leading deep into the first of the long valleys stretched out beneath the tallest of the mountains. The road was filling rapidly with others who knew that night was their only hope to escape the relentless shelling. Safety would not come in numbers, Julia knew, and would draw the guns once they were seen. Before she could move away from the road towards a row of low-lying hills silhouetted like moving phantoms across the night sky by the rising moon, the mortars came again, covering the road with flying shrapnel from every direction. So many fell that the earth itself trembled in fear.

When the guns turned silent, Julia looked at the carnage around her. Bodies with arms and legs missing were flopping up and down like fish pulled from the sea and left to die on land. Eva was curled up next to her, trying to stem the blood flowing from a large hole in her right thigh. Shrapnel from a nearby explosion had ripped through her clothing and skin, missing by inches the femoral artery and thighbone before lodging against her thigh muscle. Julia moved quickly to help her. Using her belt to fashion a tourniquet around Eva's blood-soaked thigh, she reduced the flow to a trickle, then doused the gaping wound with a packet of sulfur. They would try to cleanse it again later when safely in the mountains. Helping Eva to her feet, Julia turned to where Django lay unmoving several feet away, his arms twisted and bent horribly around his head and neck as if he were trying to rip it from his body. Only the left eye remained of what had been a beautiful man. All else was gone from his face. She had loved him as a friend, though he wanted more from her. And now she would leave him to rot in the fields for days until the Germans plowed him into a mass grave with people who were not his own. Julia knew no Christian words to say over his dead body, so kneeling beside him, she took his bloodied hand and hurriedly recited the Twenty-Third Psalm.

Later, when she and Eva had distanced themselves from the field of the dead, Eva said to her, "You should have screamed, 'Oh Lord, Oh Lord, why has thou forsaken me,' because He certainly was nowhere around Django and the rest of the dead lying there."

Julia looked sharply at Eva.

"Why do you say such words, you are alive. He hasn't forsaken you."

"I know. But only for awhile perhaps."

"You mustn't talk that way. Your wound will heal fine," Julia said, taking Eva's arm to steady her as they walked the narrow trail south away from Banska Bystrica.

By the third day, though, Eva's leg had grown hot and stiff with infection. When night came and they stopped to sleep, Julia rinsed clean the wound the best she could, picking off the pus-laden scabs and sprinkling on the last dust of sulfur. Two days of hard travel still lay ahead and all they would be able to do was to rinse the festering hole with cold spring water. At night she would hold Eva for hours as the fever chills shook her body, singing to her every childhood song she could remember until they both fell asleep from exhaustion. By the fifth day, when they were standing looking down through the long, shadowed valleys where Eva's home lay hidden amongst a grove of walnut trees, she had cried out during the night for her mother. She was looking down on her from somewhere, Eva later told Julia, but then her face had faded as quickly as it had come, back into the darkness.

Exhausted and unable to stand any longer, Eva sat down with Julia's help, leaning her back against a rotting tree stump for support. The gaping wound in her thigh had turned a nasty color, oozing bloody pus and bits of black rotting flesh and blood and shrapnel, soaking her pant leg a dark reddish-yellow. The smell was worse, though. And when the mountain winds stilled for a moment, the stench became unbearable. Eva knew, as Julia did, that her leg was dying and her whole body would follow soon without medical care; but the sweet scent of the rich dirt in the fields spread out before Bratislava, which they could now see in the distance, filled her nostrils and lungs, bringing music once more to her soul. From where they were in the foothills of the Carpathians, her farm home was less than four miles.

"We'll be there soon," Eva said, her hollow eyes coming alive momentarily with anticipation.

"Yes, and you'll get better. We still have much to do together," Julia said, helping Eva to stand.

Julia struggled to keep from crying as she looked at her old friend trying to steady herself so they could begin the final descent to the valley. Unable to do so, Eva quickly sat down again and looked over at Julia.

"I don't want it to end here. Let me rest a while longer, and then we can go," she said, leaning once more against the tree stump and closing her eyes.

Julia nodded and sat down next to Eva and closed her eyes to rest, too. Soon she would have to carry Eva, if they were to get to the farmhouse before dark. They had traveled a long way together, and the thought that it might end soon paralyzed her. The things they had done in the two years since leaving the gypsy camp, fighting alongside the partisans as they did, few people would dare to try. Such an odyssey would have pleased the ancient Homer well, had he been traveling with them.

Resting against the rotten stump, Eva suddenly turned to Julia and told of her mother's visit again and begged to be left here should she return.

"We will be in the valley soon, and then I will carry you home. Your mother will be waiting for you," Julia said, looking at the setting sun drifting lower by the minute. They needed to move now before darkness engulfed the mountain.

The final descent to reach the valley floor took longer than expected, but Julia was glad. It was nightfall now and they would less likely be seen by German patrols as they crossed through the vast open fields and vineyards leading to Eva's home. With Eva saddled on her back, Julia began the arduous three-mile journey, all the while watching ahead as the lights of hundreds of military vehicles raced back and forth in the distance along the road to Bratislava. Julia knew that the Slovak uprising had brought thousands of Germans to occupy Bratislava, making it impossible for her to find a doctor who would come to Eva, or even find what medicine she could to try and save her life. When they neared the small stone home, Eva suddenly loosened her grip from Julia and slipped to the ground. Leaning on Julia, she struggled to remove her heavy boots and socks, crying all the time from the piercing pain mixed with her joy in being home.

"You must help me, please. It's the soil I want to feel," she begged Julia.

Standing barefooted away from Julia, Eva moved her toes back and forth in the rich, black soil, which to her was the most wonderful feeling in the whole world. Time was ending now for her, at a point when history seemed to be going backwards, where wars were an everyday fashion, but she cared more that time was ending before the warm spring rains came that she loved so much, bringing new life to the land that was around her. The dirt beneath her feet was all she really knew and was ready to die for. Finally, she grew weary and collapsed in Julia's arms.

"You mustn't light a lamp, they will see it," she whispered to Julia. "Let me sleep here on the ground tonight, so that I can see all that is above me. Right there," she said pointing skyward, "is where the morning stars first began to sing. That's true because my grandpapa told me so when I was five."

Julia nodded and began crying softly as she stretched Eva out on the soft ground near the front door, and then lay next to her. Looking upward, it did seem that every star the heavens owned was looking down on them this night. She had never seen so many, not even as a child.

"It is beautiful," she said. "God has given us much to look at."

Eva said nothing for a few minutes, before turning her head to face Julia. "I have loved you much more than as a friend. I think you knew, yet you didn't turn away from me or make me ashamed."

Sobbing in great heaves, Julia put her arms around Eva's shoulders and held her close.

"I know. You will always be my precious friend."

Julia had never experienced a night so long, holding Eva until she stopped breathing. Death came to her gently then, without a whimper or a sigh, but as it should be, in the arms of love. Julia would wait until first light to carry Eva into the house, laying her on the floor before the fireplace. She had talked of the cold winter nights when she would lie there watching, until she fell asleep, the dancing fingers of the burning logs climb and disappear like magic up the chimney.

"It would be a wonderful way to go, drifting upward like a puff of smoke into the clouds, rather than turning to bones and dust in the cold earth," she had said to Julia one night when they talked of death.

So Julia set about readying the house for Eva's pyre, piling anything that could burn into a large heap around her that reached almost to the ceiling of the room. Then she waited until dusk to light the fire before returning to the mountains again. Free of Eva's weight, she would reach them in less than an hour. Looking back a mile away, she could see the flames leaping to the sky, carrying Eva with them as she would have wanted. The fire had spread, as Julia had hoped, to the small outbuilding, causing it to burn brighter and longer. By now the Germans were there. Such a fire was unusual and they would want to know why. It would be the morning, though, before they could uncover what had brought about the fire, and she would be hours into the mountains by then, heading north once more to where the partisans were.

Eva's face seemed everywhere Julia looked, as she hurried along the narrow mountain trail. At times the grief pushed down on her chest so hard that it was impossible to breathe, until she would stop and cry for several minutes. How could Eva have died this way, when it was she who had promised to bring her home to Anna? And she had believed her. Alone now, where she would go and what she would do to stay alive were as unknown as all the tomorrows gathered together. When Django was blown to pieces, she had refused to accept Eva's cry that God had forsaken him; but now, with Eva dead, too, perhaps she was right that God was nowhere to be found on the battlefields of war. What she had learned from the two Jewish men who escaped from Auschwitz made it seem even more so to her. All her family might have died there, too, along with the thousands that did, making it easy to believe that God was no longer interested in the mess that first began in Eden's garden.

At night, as she traveled north, Julia came down into the valleys to gather what food she could find from isolated farms backed up against the base of the mountains, always leaving behind a few Reich marks in payment. Little could be found though, this late into autumn—mostly wormy apples and rotting potatoes and a few beets kept stored in barns to feed the pigs. They were eaten though, worms and all, and the protein from them kept her moving one more day closer north to Banska Bystrica, where she hoped the partisans would still be camped. If the Germans were there, she had decided, she would try to reach the dense forest along the Polish border where many partisans had come from to join the uprising.

On the day Julia neared the hills above Banska Bystrica, she looked down on the small airfield stretched out two miles south of the village to see the Slovak flag still flying from the radio tower. It was what she saw next that brought disbelief to her eyes, causing her to cry out in the cold silence around her. Two B-17 Flying Fortress bombers had landed, bringing supplies to reinforce the partisans and rebel Slovak army still fighting the

Germans. Two hours later she walked into the command office where the American pilots were sitting drinking coffee with several OSS agents that had flown in with the supplies. She told them who she was and asked if she could fly back with them to England. That was the only question she would ask the surprised men. Forty-five minutes later, credentialed only by the stories she told of Czech intelligence gone awry and the two years of fighting with the resistance, Julia sat on one of the B-17s, glowing and smiling as a new mother might do in the company of a group of strangers. But her happiness was mostly for the sixteen Allied pilots who had been shot down over Slovakia, who would be going home to England with her. Yet they were as fascinated with her as she was with them, trying to guess who the dirty and seedy young woman was that smelled so bad, and why she was sitting on the plane with them.

Julia, though, found it almost impossible to contain the joy she felt and thought only of the happiness that awaited her. Tonight she would take warm showers and wear fresh clothes and dine with a knife and fork at a table, becoming a young woman again.

TWENTY-NINE

Julia, England, 1944

The first hours of a long night's sleep came easily to Julia. Freshly laundered white linens and the softness of the bed pulled her quickly into another world she had been convinced no longer existed. It was when she suddenly awoke in the early morning hours, unsure of where she was in the strange new darkness surrounding her, that she began to weep uncontrollably. The reality of Eva's death had finally broken through the shell of a deceptive grief that had shielded her until she was safely home in England. Eva was gone, as was Django, their songs silenced forever. And poor little Josh, too, whose song had only begun. Through her tears, Julia wondered if somehow they might all be together now: a Slovak Jew whose God labored in the fields as she did and a gypsy Christian whose God was a magical fairy tale and a little boy whose God was as real as all that he saw. Even though their faiths were different, their humanity was of the same blood. No longer trying to understand the silence that screamed at her from within, Julia wept until the wells of her eyes were as dry and empty as a desert, then fell asleep thinking of Anna and Erich.

Julia was late for the morning-long debriefing, requested of her by Czech and British intelligence. Standing before Colonel Moravec, she had no excuse, nor did he ask for one. The loss of any agent was felt deeply by everyone, but somehow Eva had seemed indestructible to all who knew her during her training because of her fearlessness.

"She will be missed," were the only words he would ever utter about her loss, though the fullness of those simple words, Julia knew, carried a deeper sense of his own grief over Eva's death.

Colonel Moravec shuffled the debriefing notes taken from Julia when she first arrived, back and forth on his desk several times before looking up to where she was standing.

"Do you know Hannah Senesh? Who she is?" he asked.

Puzzled by the strangeness of such a question at this moment, Julia waited for a few seconds before responding.

"Not personally, only bits and pieces during my training. She seems to be a remarkable woman, someone I would like to get to know when the war is over."

"Yes, Senesh is what you say and more. Several months back in March, she parachuted into Yugoslavia to reach Budapest."

"Why Budapest?"

"She is from Budapest and the Nazis had begun deportation of the Jews in Hungary to the death camps. The Allies hoped some underground aid could be established to rescue as many Jews as possible."

"Why are you telling me about Hannah Senesh, Colonel?"

"We've heard nothing from her, only rumors that she's been captured. If the Germans have Hannah, they will try to make her reveal everything about our intelligence network there. We need to know the true situation."

Colonel Moravec lit another cigarette, his third since Julia had reported to him this morning, and drew in a long breath of hot smoke, holding it in his lungs for several seconds before exhaling. Picking up three papers from his desk, one holding a photograph of Hannah Senesh, Colonel Moravec handed them to Julia.

"We want you to go to Hungary at once to find out exactly what has happened, what the Germans and Hungarians know, if possible."

Julia's mind froze in disbelief at what she was hearing and she struggled to control her emotions.

"I'm not ready for this physically, and certainly not psychologically, it's too soon," she said, her voice breaking.

"I know, but you are one of the lucky ones, Julia. The four SOE and OSS agents that flew into Banska Bystrika right before you left were captured last night by the Germans and executed."

Julia heard little else that was being said, except that she was expected to fly out tonight for Egypt, where she would meet up with Andras Janik, an agent from Budapest. Together they would parachute into Tito's domain in Yugoslavia, as Hannah Senesh had done, and from there cross into Hungary. When she asked Colonel Moravec for a short delay, so that she might see Anna and her brother Hiram, he replied quite coldly, "They will be here when you return." But he added, "We will pick you up no later than March, I promise you. The Russians should be in Budapest by then and you'll have to get out."

Colonel Moravec's final words were of little comfort to Julia. What she believed was that intelligence knew now that Senesh had been captured and her real task was not to find out about Senesh, but the Russians, and the extent of their network in Budapest. She would go, though, as if Hannah Senesh might still be free. It would give her the moral courage to do so because she cared little about what the Russians might be doing— her fight was with the Nazis. It was they that were keeping her away from Anna.

Like most of her neighbors, Angie McFarland had no telephone and relied on the radio and the church to stay connected to the world around her. Much of what she would hear in church came from BBC news. The war was going well, though their Scottish lads were still dying. Some she knew in her church would not be coming home. Like the Scottish folks before her, she had to derive the same comfort they did from the faith that the Scottish lads had died fighting. Angie believed Julia was dead, having received no mail from her in over two years, but nothing official came from anyone to tell her of Julia's death. So every night she prayed with Anna by her side that all would end well; though deep down inside where the hurt comes from, it meant she would lose Anna should Julia return from the war.

Julia's short note, scribbled hurriedly and mailed before she left for Egypt, telling Angie of her return, turned loose in Angie a roiling sea of dichotomous pangs of joy and loss. But loss is always a part of love, whether it comes early or in fifty years passing, Angie knew, and would be there for her the day Julia came for Anna. Praying may be good for the soul, but not so much for feelings that only the heart knows. Losing Anna would cut as deep as when her Robert went off to die in The Great War.

Before Julia boarded the Flying Fortress taking her to Egypt, Colonel Moravec's jeep pulled up alongside the huge plane. Taking her by the arm, he led her a short distance away where they could talk for a quick moment.

"You have lost a lot in this damn war, Julia, but so has everyone else. I give you my word, four months and you'll be home to stay."

Colonel Moravec proved true to his word, sending a plane for Julia the first week of March, bringing her home once more to England. Her war was finally over. She had been forced to flee Budapest along with several other Czech agents in January, to stay ahead of the rapidly advancing Russian forces who would soon liberate the city. Liberate was too loose a term for Julia, because the strong Communist underground in the ancient city had begun killing anyone suspected of opposing them. Already caught in the web of this ironic and twisted sense of liberation were most of the democratic and anti-Communist leaders throughout Hungary. Suspicion had become the guiding principle for being arrested, and Julia as a Czech intelligence agent would be a prize fish if caught in their sweeping net. Because of her father's well-known stand and lengthy orations against the Communist party in Prague, her name would be all over the KGB books in Moscow. Her dear, sweet cousin Abram would not escape the net, though. Breathing freedom only a few short weeks in Prague after being freed from Auschwitz, he was to disappear for forty-eight years behind the Iron Curtain descending on Eastern Europe with each mile the Russians advanced.

Leaving Budapest in the worst of all winters she had ever known, Julia made her way back to Tito's mountain fortress in Yugoslavia, where Hannah Senesh had camped for three months before crossing into Hungary. In time, she would leave for Egypt to await her final trip back to England.

But the few weeks with Tito's partisans opened Hannah Senesh's beautiful soul to Julia. Her own battles with life these past two years, even Eva's death, faded gently into a peace she had known only as a child. Sitting alone watching the rising sun spread its wings like colors of deep red across the rugged mountaintops for as far as the eye could see, she read Senesh's poems, "Blessed is the Match," and "Walking to Caesara." When she finished, she cried softy in the stillness around her for hours. Julia had learned that after leaving Tito's partisans, Senesh had crossed the border into Hungary, where she was immediately caught by the Hungarian police, who were rounding up all Jews for deportation to Germany and Austria. Enduring cruel torture by the police every day, she refused to divulge any information that might bring harm to others. Months later, no longer recognizable because of the brutal beatings by the Gestapo, she stood undaunted without a blindfold staring down executioners as she was shot by the firing squad.

Though British intelligence knew by now from other sources the terrible fate that befell Hannah, Julia still submitted her own separate report. To do so was her only way of reaching down behind the cold, black typewritten words of an official report to reveal the warmth and beauty and greatness of this woman's humanity. Where do people like Senesh and Eva come from? Julia would ask herself a hundred times for months to come. For them and their like, death held no meaning where honor and duty stood next to it.

The morning after her return to England from Egypt, she entered Colonel Moravec's office to file her separate report on Hannah Senesh, along with her report on the ruthless suppression of freedom taking place in Budapest by the Russians. Colonel Moravec could offer only a forced smile before handing her a telegram from the War Department, which Julia knew had to be about Hiram. The phrase, "presumed dead," was the best they could give her, but it was enough. The circle of dying was complete now. She alone in her family had escaped it, the finality of being that came so sudden to so many in these terrible times. Julia would not cry in front of Colonel Moravec, or anyone else, for a long time, saving her tears for the joys she was sure were yet to come in her life. Anna was waiting with Angie McFarland, and Erich was somewhere not so distant that her love couldn't reach him.

THIRTY

Hiram and Erich, Dresden, 1945

Hiram got to his aircraft about twilight, climbed into the heavy Lancaster bomber and started the massive engines to warm them up for the distant bombing run that lay ahead. Though the skies were clear, the darkening winter night would bring with it a bone-chilling arctic wind that was pushing its way south across England and northern Europe. It was the eve before Ash Wednesday, and would long be remembered for its connection to that holy day.

When the engines finally warmed, Hiram shut them down and waited in the silence of the cockpit with his copilot for the green Verey light to flash from the control tower, signaling him to move into a line with the other planes preparing to take off. After the morning briefing, he had tried to rest, even sleep for a few hours, to be at his best for the many hours of flying ahead. But the excitement of his first command of the plane overwhelmed his mind and nerves, causing his adrenal glands to pump overtime. He had flown eleven missions as copilot, and had been given the full command only hours earlier when the captain reported in ill. Hiram knew he was ready though. Months back, when a heavy burst of flak tore through the cockpit, wounding and disabling the captain during a mission over Berlin, he took command and brought the heavily damaged aircraft safely home after completing its bombing run. A small matter, he would say to those who praised him.

Lying in bed waiting for the evening mission to come, he thought of all the bright, good days yet to be lived when the war was over. He would then go home to Prague, taking little Anna with him should Julia not see the end. It was good he had promised to do so to Julia the night she first returned from entrusting Anna to Angie McFarland's loving care in Scotland. All Julia would ever say about Angie was that God must always hold in his hands a few special people for times such as these, and she had to be one of them.

Anna was five now, and he had helped celebrate her birthday with Angie, as he had each year after Julia left. Taking what presents he could find in the stores, he rode the bus to the small village below Angie's high hill where she waited for him with Anna by her side.

"Uncle Hiram," she cried, running to him when he stepped from the bus.

"Do I know you?" he said, teasing Anna.

Then, sweeping her up in his arms, Hiram held Anna high above his head as he always would do, holding her there for a moment listening to her squeals of joy. Later, the squeals would turn to wonder as Anna opened Hiram's presents, carefully saving the wrapping paper from each one like a good Scot would do, whether in war time or not. A small wooden horse he had discovered in a wayside craft shop outside of London immediately became her favorite and didn't leave her hand the rest of the evening. Even when she recited passages from the Torah, as a surprise gift to Hiram, Anna clutched the toy horse tightly for fear that it might try to run away, as she often believed her mother had done. No letters had come to her from Julia in nearly three years and she was now only a faceless shadow to her.

Anna's final performance of the evening brought tears to Hiram's eyes, as she told the story of Hanukkah and the festival of lights, which she would soon celebrate with Angie. It wouldn't be exactly right, but Angie had done her best to make it so, and to teach her, using what she'd been able to gather from the books she had read. She had bought an old metal lamp, and, with Anna eagerly helping her, decorated it with a host of paper symbols of lions and eagles, and then fashioned eight branches for candles. Together, she and Anna would light the Hanukkah lamp with its eight small candles on Christmas Eve and offer special prayers of thanksgiving to God. With no Christmas tree to be found on the barren hills around the house, Angie bundled and tied together an armful of straw gathered from the barn, which Anna quickly decorated with paper chains she had cut. Colored in bright orange and red and green, they became their joyous lights on the straw Christmas tree. "After all," Angie told Anna, "my Jesus came into this world with straw beneath his feet."

Later, when Anna climbed into her bed for the cold night, Hiram sang songs to her, ones that he and Julia had learned as children, and told her stories she had never heard about her mother. Some were true and some weren't, but all were told to make Julia more real to her than some distant face that dimmed with each passing year. No stories were told, though, about her father, and later Hiram thought it strange that Anna asked no questions as to where he was or even who he might be. All Angie would say, when Anna did ask, was that her father was off fighting in the terrible war like her mother somewhere far away, and that seemed to satisfy her. In time, the question was no longer asked of her, and he was forgotten.

When the time came for Hiram to return to the air base, he held Anna close for what seemed an eternity, not wanting to let her go. His last embrace was for Angie, whom he had grown to love as Julia had. The day he first met her, Angie was everything that Julia said she would be, as God-like as one could become while walking this earth. From the very beginning, he felt, had she been younger in years, or himself older, he would have loved her in a far different way than the gentle love he felt for her now. She was a fine, full-bodied and handsome woman, not attractive in a pretty way, but in a magnificent way that always held her grace before your eyes. It covered her like the skin she was born with from head to toe. And when he told her that God must have showered her with such grace, she turned beet red for several minutes before finding the words to answer him. "The grace of God doesn't rest easy on a person you know. The most we can hope for is to breathe it in from time to time, because we can't hang on to it."

When they parted, no one said goodbye.

"It was too harsh a word to use," Angie said.

Hiram knew she was right. The fields of our memory are unbounded, and we can never forget those we have loved and who have loved us in our lives. For him, what he would remember most was that Angie's soul sang like a bird at dawn.

The green light having flashed to go, Hiram started the engines a second time and began to taxi in between other planes moving in a row down the long runway towards the take-off point. When he reached it, Hiram turned the nose of the plane into the wind, opened the throttles full with the brake on until it seemed like the fuselage would shake apart, then suddenly released them, propelling the big aircraft down the runway like a sling shot would a rock. In seconds, he could feel the aircraft lift from Mother Earth and begin to groan as it rose higher into the night skies with its heavy load of explosives. Rising every few seconds like flights of frightened blackbirds taking wing, hundreds of bombers soon filled the sky, circling the town of Reading thousands of feet below. As the war's end seemed imminent, Hiram still could only hope this would be his and the crew's last mission. Each day when the news came, it seemed there would be no more targets left in Germany to bomb; but what was to follow no poet's words could ever describe had there been a thousand lines written.

Hours later, Hiram took the plane down to two thousand feet to start the massive bombing run with the other planes on Dresden. Looking down, he could see clearly the icy country roads and darkened woods and fields surrounding the beautiful city, appearing to the eye as if they had been painted there a thousand times or more by God himself. Ahead of him, de Havilland pathfinders had swooped in low over the city marking targets with bright flares. To Hiram, the city seemed unprotected. There was no antiaircraft fire, no dreaded searchlights that always froze a plane momentarily in the skies for enemy eyes to see and fire on. When no enemy night fighters rose to meet them, Hiram knew the city was undefended and doomed, with mercy its only escape. Ordering the bomb doors open, he watched as the thousands of incendiaries dropped by the planes ahead slowly began to build their own little pockets of hell across the city. It was as if he were watching something out of a beautiful but frightening fairy tale, as tiny dots of light would twinkle on, then suddenly burst into flames. Dresden was beginning to burn like ancient Rome did, only more horribly, and in a way that only an angry God would allow. When the second wave of bombers followed two hours later, acting like a huge vacuum pump, their fresh hail of incendiary bombs pulled the spreading fires into one gigantic firestorm.

Below, people scurried back and forth in every direction with no discernable pattern of direction, much like a disturbed nest of aimless ants running helter-skelter, seeking a hiding place that was nowhere to be found. Many reached the cellars of their homes, only to die there from asphyxiation, as the building firestorm drained the oxygen from the air to feed its hungry stomach. Like a raging tornado, the howling firestorm grasped and tugged at everything, seemingly pulling the entire city into its fiery mouth to devour. Buildings along the streets, shattered first by the bombs, collapsed in the swirling wind. Many people that could find no shelter died where they were, or were dragged bodily by the growing vacuum into the fire along with chunks of wood and metal and blazing tree limbs.

His bombing mission complete, Hiram banked the plane to climb into formation for the long journey back home. He could feel the searing heat from the lapping tongue of the raging firestorm far beneath him, which was turning all the clouds and smoke around him into a fiery red. Looking below one more time at the hell they had brought to Dresden, Hiram hoped, as he always did, the little children would be spared the horror. War is not for children, he had argued one night in a pub, it is only for adults who play games with it. Yet, had he known of the horrors in Auschwitz and the other camps across Germany and Poland, he might have thought differently. There were rumors of such truth, but everyone knew the Germans loved children, so they could only be false.

Moving into the thickening clouds closing in on the plane, a fast-moving shadow seen only for a second by Hiram smashed into the mid-section of his aircraft, slicing it in half before both aircraft burst into a ball of fire. To those who could see it, the flaming death of the two planes and their crews seemed like an old exploding star in its death throes, finally surrendering its long-held place in the universe. What it had been, its shining existence, was no more. So it was with Hiram's life, now nothing more than a thousand pieces of burning ashes floating on the firestorm's wind to no particular place. Only Julia and her cousin Abram would remain to tell those who would listen about their proud family and its long existence in Prague.

Standing in the broad meadows by the Elbe River less than two miles away from the burning city, Erich saw the huge fireball from the colliding planes briefly light up the night sky before plunging silently to the earth. He had arrived only moments before, exhausted and cold and hungry from his own distant journey from Auschwitz. When he drew near to Dresden, walking with a scattering of refugees he had joined a hundred miles back, the winter darkness before him began to redden as the sea of flames raced unchecked through the old city, engulfing everything in sight. Soon an unchecked blast of warm air spread out across the ancient river, lifting the siege of winter momentarily. The blackness that had been the night around him now glowed in such an eerie color that no artist could have captured it had he dared to try.

A deafening noise made of wailing screams and yelling came towards him from across the river. For a second Erich could see nothing. Then hundreds of human figures emerged from the shadows racing to the Elbe. Some sat down at the edge of the river, desperately inhaling between loud sobs the drafts of fresh air coming from across the river, where Erich stood watching them. Others who could scarcely see, their eyes swollen and blackened with soot, walked into the river a little ways and began dousing their face and body with the icy waters, as if they would be born again.

Erich made his way to a large rock a few feet away from the river's edge and sat down to watch the apocalyptic scene unfolding before him. With the burning city as a backdrop, only whispering shadows of the actors could now be seen. In time, calmness descended and some began walking back and forth, searching for their families. Many still stood alone, crying softly until someone came and led them away. They knew what was still happening there, of the burning bodies and the cries of the dying and the stench of the dead. Few would sleep that night, or even dare to try. The ending of the nightmare was still too distant to see.

When the first light of morning came, Erich roused himself from a grassy bed he had fashioned back in the meadows to try to capture some sleep, though all he found himself doing was shivering uncontrollably through the remaining night hours from the bitter cold, wondering what was left of the city he loved. His father was safe in Berlin, he was sure. But his mother would have suffered through the bombing alone in the cellar of her home. And it was her life he cared about.

Looking to Dresden, the thick smoke of the diminishing fires still spiraled upward, masking much of the sunlight, making the morning seem like the twilight of evening. Several German police could be seen moving among the stirring crowd, cautioning everyone to stay the day by the river until the major fires were extinguished. When they saw Erich and the doctor's insignia on his uniform, they beckoned him to come with them back to Dresden. Few doctors were alive, they told him, to treat those that might live. But strangely to Erich, they seemed in no hurry to leave, and waited until shortly before noon to do so.

As Erich and two of the police began to make their way along a back road to the city, they asked nothing of him. He was among the refugees fleeing from the advancing Russians, they supposed, and asked no questions. That he was a doctor was all that mattered at the moment. They had traveled only a short distance towards Dresden when the deafening roar of approaching bombers shook the countryside around them. It was the Americans' turn to squeeze from the dying city its last breath. Bombing in the daylight provided newer targets that had somehow escaped the fury of the two British raids, bringing death to thousands more who had emerged from their shelters into a new day, thinking all was safe again. Buildings that had survived the night and firestorm now crumbled, trapping and killing hundreds more in their wake.

Without any kind of shelter near him, Erich quickly lay flat on the ground, as everyone else was doing, hoping an errant bomb would not find its way to them. When the bombing finally stopped, one lonely plane taking photographs of the carnage appeared, circling over the city like a giant condor, its great wings casting eerie moving shadows on the dead below. As people got to their knees to stand, some whispered that Armageddon had come and they had not been chosen, and they wondered why God had passed them by. But most said nothing, drummed into a deafening silence because they knew that only desolation and death lay ahead of them in the city.

Erich's route to his home took him into the old city square past a massive water reservoir that dominated the square. Rescue crews were working feverishly ahead of him when he arrived, tossing bodies like bales of hay to the street's sides so large bulldozers could begin the greater task of clearing away debris and rubble from the crumbling building. Looking at the reservoir, Erich knew the story of Dresden's fiery death was there before his eyes. A macabre ring of charred corpses, young and old, circled its walls. Many lay across the reservoir's walls, with their arms outstretched in one last attempt to fling themselves into its cool waters. They would have died there, though, in a worse death perhaps. Hundreds had plunged into the reservoir as their last hope to survive, but soon found themselves unable to breathe in the relentless heat sweeping over the reservoir from the raging firestorm. Many, unable to swim, drowned in the ten-foot waters, dragging others down with them. During the long night, most of the water evaporated from the reservoir, causing the dead to collapse one by one into an unimaginable pile of quickly rotting flesh.

Erich turned away and would look no more. The scene was too close to that of the deep ditches filled with burning Jews and gypsies at Auschwitz. These were Germans, and that did seem different to him. No one looked at him, or cared who he might be, as he proceeded on through the smoldering devastation to his home. Along the way, bodies were being carried from almost every damaged building to add to the growing dead littering the streets. Many intersections were already filled with large stacks of the dead, some reaching ten feet high, waiting to be carted to the ancient city square by horse-drawn carts where they would be doused with gasoline and burned. Later, because there were so many bodies, flamethrowers would be used to burn them, painting a surrealistic scene that would last a lifetime for the people watching. Only those being carried from the cellars of the homes and buildings could be identified, if there was someone left to do so.

After twenty minutes making his way across town, Erich stood looking at what once had been one of the finer homes in Dresden. From the days of his great-grandfather, the Schmidts had lived in this beautiful home, envied by all those around. There was little left of it now to see. The roof and top floor had imploded from the bombing, collapsing onto the first floor before bursting into flames. It was the cellar Erich sought, though, where his mother might be and other neighbors who might have sought safety with her.

Erich walked around the side of the house to where the steps were leading to the cellar door. He stopped for a moment by a walnut tree, gnarled by time and the elements and now blackened by the fire. Memories of his childhood adventures climbing among its branches and limbs were no longer there to be seen. What he saw, though, no child could ever have imagined. Pieces of burnt flesh, in all sizes, hung from the limbs like thin strips of charred tinsel, as if someone had methodically tried to decorate the tree. A mother and child had sought shelter there beneath his child-hood tree, when a bomb exploded in the street close by, leaving what was left of their bodies hanging from the tree. In Erich's mind, the gruesome scene, perhaps, could be his mother.

Erich found the thick steel cellar door badly charred and twisted but still intact. Pushing it open, a rush of intense heat captured in the cellar swept across his face. No one, he knew, could live long through such heat.

There was no light except through the open cellar door and a small hole in the floor above, letting rays of the sunshine down like a small spotlight into the cellar. Moving slowly towards the back of the cellar, the soles of his boots became warm from the heat the concrete floor still held, adding an eerie feeling to his presence there. They were lying huddled together when he saw them, his mother and father, a mixture of ashes and bones with bits of charred flesh still attached. Nothing was there to tell him who they were except a large brass belt buckle that he had given his father many Christmases ago and his mother's wedding ring. His father loved the power the buckle expressed, not that it had been a child's gift to him. Erich picked up the buckle and ring from their ashes and left the cellar quickly to inhale fresh air again. Standing in the street, he looked one last time at the ruins before him. Strangely, he felt little loss over finding his parents dead, but it was wrong, he believed, the way his mother had died. Unlike his father, she was a God-fearing woman who would harm no soul. With the Russians only a few miles away, Dresden's war was over. So why would the enemy seek to erase it from God's eyes when they could have enjoyed its wonderful beauty as he had? Erich mused. They seemed no less the beast than Germany was.

Erich walked away then, without looking back, leaving his mother and father's ashes to become a part of the rubble when it was cleared away by the bulldozers. For his part, no one knew where he was now, having been swept along with the mass of refugees filling the roads from the advancing Russians. Though the official news from the Western Front was heavily censored, rumors weren't; and more often than not they carried enough snippets of truth that one could weave a dismal picture of what was unfolding there and on the Eastern Front. With the American army ready to cross the Rhine, hiding out in Mainz under Maria's roof would be impossible, Erich knew. So he would turn south to Triberg and his beloved Black Forest. The small village held nothing the Americans would want, except maybe to lounge unhurriedly in the warm springs. The Germans would come, though, after there was no more fighting, coming just as they did when the Great War ended, bringing their shrapnel-laced bodies and half-bodies to soak in nature's healing grace bubbling in the ancient springs around the city. They would sit where the waters flowing across their broken bodies were those that had healed the German warriors of old. Only their bodies would be healed, not their minds, and perhaps, Erich believed, he could search for his own sanity among them by tending to their mental needs.

Yet even then he might have to hide for years, because he knew the British and the Americans would want to imprison or hang many of the medical personnel who had been at Auschwitz. It bothered him some that this might happen, because he had done nothing terrible like the doctors Mengele or Wirth, who should be put to death. He had been nothing more than a camp doctor examining prisoners, doing what doctors do, and had killed no one there with his own hands. He had sentenced no one to death by his selections on the ramp. The fact that some did die was by Dr. Wirth's orders, not his. What they probably would do, Erich thought, would be to come after him for what he had done earlier to the crippled children at Görden, killing them like he did. But even there he was still being a doctor, acting from compassion, which all good doctors should do. The great virtue is in their oath, and surely they would accept that fact.

THIRTY-ONE

Anna, Prague, 1992

Anna placed the box holding her mother's ashes on the night table and stretched out on the hotel bed for a short nap before going to the Old Jewish Cemetery. The long journey from America to Prague had included two unexpected side excursions, leaving her exhausted and emotionally drained from all that had taken place. It was only through the last of her mother's stories, told shortly before she died, that the day as it was, came about.

With the war over, when Julia came to Angie McFarland's for Anna, she stayed two weeks waiting for the last of the spring lambs to be born so Anna could name them as she had done for the past three years. The days were filled with a glorious nothingness that Julia could hardly describe, the kind where only unbounded love exists. They went together as a family, one last time, to Angie's old Presbyterian church and listened to the same minister preach on forgiveness, except he never said who they were supposed to forgive. The war had been over barely two weeks and no one had started to heal, least of all those who had lost someone precious. Julia felt it strange to hear talk of forgiveness when the world hadn't had time to stop hating.

At night, with Anna asleep, Angie would place before Julia a large stack of notebook paper, penciled on every line each memorable moment in Anna's young life that Julia had missed. Angie would talk of them to Julia through stories, and Julia would come to know each moment as if it were she who had been there watching Anna, not Angie. Later, when

Anna was older in years, it would be Julia who would tell her of Angie so she would know who had cared for her, filling her with a love that had no end. "She was the purest of the pure," Julia would always say, when Anna would ask about Angie.

Years later when Angie died, which many in her church said came from a broken heart, Julia and Anna began lighting the Yahrzeit candles on the day of her death, as they did for her parents and her brother Hiram and for her sister Miriam, who died so young. After Julia moved to America with Anna and became a doctor, graduating from John Hopkins, she would plan each year to go back to Scotland to visit Angie but never did. Nor could she persuade Angie to come to America. The healing power of distance was a wee too fragile to allow her eyes to see Anna's face again, she would say. "It's best I stay in the hills of Scotland, where the memories will always be fresh."

So Anna went back this day to Angie's small Eden forty-seven years later, to fulfill the first of two new promises to her mother before making the final stop in the Old Jewish Cemetery in Prague. Carrying a small spoonful of Julia's ashes in a medicinal bottle, Anna climbed once more the long rocky road leading to Angie's home from the village below, now grown quite large. Nothing was really there that she could remember, except the small barn where the spring lambs were born. When a lamb died during birth, Angie taught her that it was the hope new life brings that she should always remember, not the dying. The ancient stone house, though, strangely held no memories for her and seemed ready to collapse at any moment. Walking to the hillside she had run down many times laughing and squealing in the spring, chasing butterflies with Angie, Anna tossed the spoonful of ashes into the warm wind rising from the valley below, watching them for several seconds as they rode the endless breeze across the green hills. No words were said. That they would come to rest, in this wonderful place of goodness, was all that was necessary for her. Anna waited several more minutes before turning to leave, fixing her eyes for the last time on the stoic beauty that surrounded her. The Scots got it right a long time ago, living here where the air was as clean and pure as new falling snow and heaven always seemed a little closer.

Of her promises to Julia, it was where Anna would go next that bothered her the most. Martin Drossen was from Mainz, and the moment Julia shot him, he left behind a young widow named Maria. They had been married but a few days before his unit left for the Eastern Front. At the time, killing Martin the way she did, shooting him in the face with his eyes frozen on her when he died, left Julia crying inside. It was not the dying that bothered her so much, but the picture she took from Martin's body, of his young bride in Mainz whom he would never see again, nor she him. Looking at the photograph, with so much love in Maria's eyes for Martin, Julia had to believe he was a good German who just happened to be on the wrong side—that is, if there were such a thing as sides when it comes to killing. But in the end, it didn't make much difference which side you were on in the war; either way you were dead and gone from this world. It was just Martin's generation's turn to become warriors and go off and fight and die alone somewhere far away from those they loved.

Julia had kept Maria's picture all these years, thinking some day she would go and find her in Mainz and tell her the full story of Martin's death. She had killed many other Germans after Martin, but it was always his face she would see. So completing Anna's promise to Julia to bury her ashes beside Rabbi Loew's grave would have to wait one more day.

Mainz was a much bigger city now than it had been in 1939 when the war began, a time when Maria and Martin were lovers. Finding a Maria Drossen was possible but not probable; yet in one quick glance in the telephone directory, there was Maria's name listed among a page full of Drossens. She would go to her, not call, in case she was mistaken, or in case Maria cared not to see her.

Maria's tiny second floor apartment had been her mother's and had been left to Maria along with the furniture and her clothes and wedding ring a year before the war ended. The poor area she lived in then was even poorer now. The shop beneath Maria's apartment had been rented on and off over the years, but stood empty now, much like most of the nearby store buildings. When Anna left the taxi, she asked the driver to wait for her; it was not the best of places to be left alone where she knew no one. She had never seen this side of Europe, believing the slums belonged only to America.

Anna knocked on the door several times, waiting anxiously, unsure of what she should say, or if she should even be there. With her knowledge of German very limited, the best she could hope for was to lift a few words from an English/German dictionary to help make sense of her mother's story of Martin Drossen's death. When the door opened, Anna faced a middle-aged woman whose appearance and facial features shocked her. It was as if she knew the woman from somewhere in the past but had no way of making the connection. Bent over and leaning heavily on a walker, the woman studied Anna for a few seconds, then spoke in broken English, "You are American tourist, yes?"

"Yes. Thank you for speaking English. I know very little German," Anna replied.

Beckoned by the woman to come in, Anna followed her as she shuffled along slowly through the living room to a small kitchen. The woman was greatly deformed. Her spine twisted and bent and gathered into a large mass to one side, all resting on legs and feet no bigger than matchsticks. When the woman reached the kitchen, she sat down in an old wheelchair pushed up against the wall, then looked up at Anna, waiting for her to speak.

"Why do you come here?" she asked, speaking haltingly.

"If you are Maria Drossen, I have an old photograph that my mother said belongs to you. There is also a story to go with it," Anna said, handing the picture to the woman.

Reaching for the picture, Anna noticed that even the fingers of the woman's hand were horribly gnarled and deformed, making it difficult for her to hold the picture steady. Looking at the picture, the woman smiled sadly.

"This is of my beautiful mother, Maria, given to my father before he went to fight."

"Your father was Martin Drossen?"

"Oh, yes. I am Elka Drossen. Now tell me, please, why you have this picture."

Anna's story suddenly came easier for her. Though eager to learn of her father's death, Elka had shared no past with him, and Anna's words seemed empty of the loss that had fashioned itself so vividly and for so long in Julia's mind through the years. When she finished her narration, Anna waited for some reaction, or release of emotion from Elka, but none came. Sensing there was nothing more to say to her, Anna stood to leave.

"There must be hundreds of war stories like your mother's," Elka said softly, nodding to Anna to sit again. "That was a terrible time and both sides did terrible things to each other, didn't they?"

Anna sat in silence, not wanting to be drawn into a discussion about the good and bad of a time and war she knew nothing about; but Elka kept talking, slowly searching for the right English words that would make better sense of what she was trying to tell Anna. What came next from her was so unexpected that it was Anna who sat spellbound, like a child listening to a beautiful fairy tale. Born at home, Elka's birth and terrible deformities were kept secret by Maria from the authorities, who would have taken her to be euthanized in the same killing wards at Görden where Maria worked next to a troubled young doctor. When he was transferred to Auschwitz, Maria returned to Mainz the next day, never to return to Görden. She had helped the young doctor kill hundreds of malformed babies and hundreds of the crazies, but something snapped inside when Elka entered the world as she did. From then on, Maria believed Elka's terrible afflictions were God's way of combining punishment for her sins with a chance for redemption. So Maria hid Elka from all eyes until the end of the war. And even then, she allowed but few of her neighbors to learn of her existence. Crippled beyond help, she had lived most of her life in the apartment, except on sunny days, when Maria would take her to the Rhine River for a joyous picnic. Later she would watch the boats moving slowly back and forth on the ancient river, loaded with tourists from America, all waving frantically to anybody who might look their way. After Maria died, three years back, Elka never left the apartment again. Instead she became even more a recluse, existing on what meals the church would bring, reading and watching an old television through the day and into the night. She would die soon, too, Elka told Anna, and death would be welcomed. God's punishment for her mother's sins had been with her too long. There was little Anna could say that would make any sense to Elka at this time, who somehow felt it was her given purpose in life to suffer for the sins of her mother, and had reluctantly accepted the role of doing so.

Anna looked at her watch. She had been here for over an hour, enthralled by Elka's unexpected life story, rather than talking about the reason for her visit, of Julia's killing of Martin Drossen, an event that seemed incidental now and of little interest to Elka. Walking quickly to the kitchen window, she saw the Mainz taxi still parked by the building, the driver fast asleep, and motioned to Elka that she was leaving. Elka pulled herself up on the walker and shuffled slowly alongside Anna towards the apartment door. As they did, Anna glanced to the right at a small end table, barren except for a framed picture. From where she stood, Anna recognized the young woman as Maria, but it was the man's face and eyes that captured her.

"This must be Martin," she said, walking over to the table and picking up the picture.

"No, that is Dr. Erich Schmidt, the doctor with whom Mother worked at Görden during the war. They were very good friends."

Anna was stunned. Was he her mother's Erich? Closing her eyes for a second, her memory brought up the face of the stranger who had spoken to her a year ago on the Charles Bridge in Prague. The stranger's face was old and wrinkled with years then, nothing like that of the young man in the photograph. But their eyes were the same. And Elka's, too, as Anna now realized for the first time, looking carefully at her faded listless eyes that once were bluer than a summer sky. Even as old as she was, the sharpness of her features produced a striking resemblance to the man, the deep-set eyes and sharp nose. Anna struggled desperately to understand and accept the truth of what was unfolding. Who Elka could be and her relationship to Erich Schmidt overwhelmed Anna, and she asked if she might have a drink of water. The only thing Anna knew for sure was that Martin Drossen was not Elka's father, though she claimed him to be.

"Are you ill?" Elka asked, taking a bottle of cold water from the Frigidaire and pouring a glass for Anna.

"No, I am tired, I suppose, from too much traveling. Tell me, do you ever hear from this Dr. Schmidt?"

"Not anymore. He used to call and ask how I was getting along and send a little money to buy groceries and medicine, but it's been over a year now without a call from him. Perhaps he is dead."

Anna could listen no further to Elka and all that was being said and walked quickly to the door. Pausing for a second to look at Elka's strained and puzzled face again, Anna thanked her for the time spent and left as quickly as she had come.

Living through the conflicting emotions of the long day had left Anna too exhausted to sleep. Sitting on the edge of the bed, she looked at the lonely box holding all that her mother had been and began to cry softly. The time was near when she would go to the Old Jewish Cemetery with her mother's ashes for burial next to Rabbi Loew's grave. In many ways, Anna's journey to fulfill the promise to Julia seemed almost as magical as that of Julia's, because she had lived through the many stories told by Julia as if they were her very own. But it was the last story Julia whispered to Anna, the afternoon she died, that gave meaning to what had happened the night they were in Prague one year earlier. Julia had said nothing to Anna then, nor wanted to, shielding her as she had always done from any unnecessary hurt that might come her way.

From Abram's last letter to Julia, she had had great difficulty containing the joy leaping out from his words that Erich was, indeed, very much alive. There was a possibility that he too would be going to the medical conference in Prague that she and Anna were planning to attend. Yet Abram's words carried a somber tone when he said there was much they should talk about before she saw Erich, suggesting they meet privately away from Anna. However, in her excitement, Julia paid little attention to such a private meeting—a lost love that had simmered in her heart for fifty years had grabbed her tired imagination, wiping out all thoughts of dying. It was not the time to do so, she stubbornly insisted to Anna, who felt reluctant to travel such a great distance with Julia so ill. But to see Erich's face and hold him close once more warmed her tired body with a gentle love long dormant in her. They would meet, she fantasized, where they said their goodbyes fifty years earlier, two old lovers in the Old Jewish Cemetery by Rabbi Loew's grave. For many years after the war, she had written letters to him, sending them to his Dresden address and the German Medical Association and any other place that might keep old records, but nothing came of them. No one knew of an Erich Schmidt. In time, she thought him dead from the war, until the letter from Abram arrived.

Julia met Abram, as he requested, at the Continental Café, where she found him sitting alone, far back in the crowded, smoke-filled dining room. He was not smiling, nor did he try to when Julia approached. There would be room only for the tears that truth often brings. Julia heard little, nor wanted to, after Abram simply stated, "Erich was a Nazi doctor at Auschwitz." Still blinded by her love for him, Julia tried at first to offer a feeble defense for such a terrible accusation, arguing that he was simply one of many swept up at no fault of their own by the extraordinary time and place they found themselves in. And it was so long ago.

"No one, not you or I, can say with certainty what we would have done had we been there, too," she said, fighting back the tears. "It's too easy to judge fifty years later."

"He was a selector, Julia, on the ramps at Auschwitz. I watched him for two years, though he never recognized me, sitting like God choosing who would live or die each passing day," Abram responded, reaching to take Julia's hand.

Putting her hands to her ears to shut out Abram's voice, Julia shook her head back and forth.

"Stop it, stop it, not my Erich, he was too gentle and compassionate, we both know that."

Abram lit up another cigarette, ignoring the finality of the harm it would bring to lungs already ravished by tuberculosis, inhaled once, then looked straight at Julia.

"I came to Auschwitz with your mother and father and was near them when they stood before Erich and were selected for death by him."

"My mother and father and Erich, together at Auschwitz?" Julia cried, as Abram's words crumbled the remaining walls of denial she had built to keep the truth away.

"Yes, they went together to be gassed, immediately after passing him."

"Did he know who they were?"

"I think so, but he said nothing to them, not even their names."

There were no tears from Julia this time. No thoughts of the terror her mother and father faced in the moments before their death. Too many had experienced the same to say one death was worse than another. It seemed so long ago that it was difficult to imagine what it was like, or if it ever really happened, by those that weren't there. But Abram was. And the smell of the burning bodies was written on his soul like the serial numbers on his arm. It was the betrayal by Erich of her parents that thickened Julia's blood now with a hatred that was as distant from who she was as the earth was from the sun. This was so because only those who know love can be betrayed. And he had been loved beyond reason by her and her mother and father. Julia slid her chair back from the table to leave. She wanted no more words from Abram about Erich.

"I must go. Anna is waiting and will be worried if I'm too late. Promise me, dear cousin, you will think long and hard about coming to live with us in America," she said, hugging Abram, perhaps for the last time, then leaving him sitting alone again.

Arriving back at the hotel, Julia immediately walked to the bulletin board for posting messages and calls, scribbled out four words, "Rabbi Loew ten tonight," on a piece of notepaper, wrote "Erich Schmidt" on the backside, and pinned it to the board. If he is here, he will come, Julia muttered to herself, leaving the room.

The time was nine-thirty. She would walk to the Old Town square and watch the vendors hawk their wares, especially those offering the brightly painted marionettes with their joints dangling like wet noodles from a host of strings. She had done so many times on Sundays as a child, enthralled as a marionette was brought to life by its owner, only to die again when he became tired with the play. Then she believed, maybe her life and everyone else's dangled from a thousand strings held in God's great hands as He looked down on the world's stage. But as she grew older, she knew it wasn't God who held the strings, but a thousand hands of people whose faces she would never see who set her course. How many times had she sat here in the Old Town square with Erich and her father, talking about this very thing. Life was much simpler then, full of an innocence and wonder few people today come to know or care to remember.

The medieval apostle's clock struck ten, and Julia watched while the hordes of tourists crowding the square rushed to see the march of the apostles across the face of the huge clock, a mechanical marvel that still seemed like magic to her after all these years. Turning away, she hurried towards the Old Jewish Cemetery, where she would be before the great clock sounded ten bongs.

Fifty years had passed, and everything seemed smaller and darker to Julia as she entered the cemetery. But his voice was the same when he called to her softly from the stillness that those long buried there demanded.

"Julia, I am here, by Rabbi Loew."

"I know," Julia responded firmly, slowly inching her way through the mass of gravestones to where he was standing. The dark shadows cast across the graveyard by the night lights of the synagogue played on his face like small moving stage lights, adding an eerie dimension to the unfolding scene.

When she drew near, Julia stopped. And though Erich reached out to her, she would come no closer to him. All she could see was his face, but that was enough. With age, everyone's face becomes their story, their history, and it was no different with Erich. All that he had done and all that he became fifty years ago was there to be seen. Frail and wrinkled beyond belief, with eyes no longer alive, Erich stood before Julia more than a broken man because he had no soul. Julia searched his face for one tiny trace of the noble spirit that had captured her own soul, but there was none. Only a thousand rivers of sadness could be seen that once were wrinkles of joy. Though her heart was crying at what he had become, she would not let him know.

"You are still beautiful, Julia. Age has been kind to you. You seem quite well," he said, wanting to move closer to her.

"I am dying, Erich, slowly, but with certainty from congestive heart failure. Two years, perhaps less, is my time. It has been a good life, though, and I am ready when God is. But tell me about all that has happened in your life. Have you married?" Julia asked deliberately, hoping Erich would begin to talk about his dark past.

"No, I never married. And you?"

"The same. I was unable to find you after the war. Where have you been living?"

Erich thought a minute before answering Julia's question, then responded slowly as if he had rehearsed his words. "I sort of holed up in Triberg to get away from everything and everybody. The war left too many scars, especially in my family. A lot of veterans would come there to soak their crippled bodies in the springs. I figured it was a good place to set up my psychiatry practice. It never did get big, though."

"Did you try and find me?"

"Yes, many times, but I got nowhere. I went back to Prague several times looking for you, but thought—"

"That I had died with the rest of the Jews? That's what you were going to say, wasn't it?" Julia said curtly, interrupting Erich.

"No, but what you say will do."

"You have a beautiful daughter, you know, with your ocean blue eyes and sharp nose." Julia blurted out, frustrated at Erich's guarded manner.

Then Julia told him of Anna and Scotland and Hiram's death over Dresden and all she had done during the war, including the killing of Martin Drossen. But when she mentioned the photograph and Maria's name, Erich became restless, clenching his hands tightly, as if the first of many stories carefully wrapped and long hidden in the past was about to be opened. Julia could not help but see the sudden agitation in him.

"Did you know a Maria Drossen? She was from Mainz."

Erich paused for a second before answering her question, carefully selecting his words.

"Perhaps. There was a Maria Drossen with me at Görden Hospital." Erich hesitated, then stopped talking, realizing what he might have revealed.

Julia knew of Görden and the euthanizing of handicapped children and mental patients there, and the black horror of Erich's sudden confession quickly cleared her mind of any compassion she still felt for his pitiful humanity. The love for the Erich she once knew was still there, but she hated the man standing before her.

"You killed babies at Görden, and people who were mentally ill. How could you, Erich?" Julia demanded.

"Things just changed, got all mixed up. I was a good doctor who began treating people by putting them out of their miserable existence. Isn't that what you and I were trained to do as doctors, to ease suffering?"

Julia remained utterly stupefied and silent, looking at Erich, a man she no longer knew. What he had done so long ago was lost somewhere deep down inside of him, playing games with his mind, keeping him believing that what had happened never did. To him, what he and others had done was so totally unbelievable that he was incapable of believing it ever took place.

"I know you were at Auschwitz, Erich. And I know you murdered my mother and father. That is why I hoped you would come, so that you could hear these words."

At first, Erich looked puzzled by Julia's strong words and accusations for several seconds, but then began to cry. He had come looking for his soul in the only place it might be found, with Julia. And she had shut the door, leaving only God to open it.

"I was only a doctor, Julia, nothing more. My hands killed no one there."

"They loved you and took you into their home and broke bread with you, Erich, and yet you denied them their last shred of humanity by refusing to speak to them, to even say their names before they died. How could you be so cruel?"

"I had no choice, Julia, with the children at Görden, or with your mother and father. They would have died anyway," Erich said, sobbing loudly.

"No, I won't accept that. There were many choices for you."

"Not when one is afraid of dying, as I was. It's a terrible thing to live with fear, and surviving was all that mattered to me then, to live and see you again."

"An either/or always exists. God has seen to that. You should know that as a good Lutheran. You could have at least fought as a soldier for your country. I could have accepted that."

"You don't understand. All I want is forgiveness from you," Erich cried, sinking to his knees.

"I understand very well," Julia said, her voice trembling. "I can forgive you for what you are and have become, but only those that are dead can forgive you for what you have done. And that is between you and God to work out."

With Julia denying him forgiveness, Erich struggled to his feet, leaning on Rabbi Loew's gravestone, and shouted out in anger, "What about Dresden? Shouldn't you and the world and even Hiram ask forgiveness for that terrible night of hell? My mother and father were burned alive, too, with thousands of others, all for nothing."

Erich's words hit Julia hard. He had become the accuser, and she had no ready reply. Whether or not the bombing of Dresden, as it was done, was wrong, she didn't know. She had killed Germans, too, but they were soldiers, and in war that should lift the mantle of guilt a little, even though it never does for some. All that she did know now in listening to Erich was that there was nothing left of who he once was as a man.

"I am sorry about your parents. Perhaps their deaths were wrong, I don't know, but a thousand Dresdens would never excuse what you and all the other doctors did, hiding behind the mask of Hippocrates. They were only Jews, Erich, nothing more, trying to live their lives out as God intended for them," Julia said, almost in a whisper, as if trying to calm the soul of Rabbi Loew, whose grave they were standing on.

His anger stilled, Erich looked around at the shadows bouncing off the gravestones by passing lights, as if those buried had suddenly come alive to play for a while. He had watched them many times before when he and Julia would secretly huddle here, unafraid of what any tomorrow might bring. But for fifty years he had been afraid, and that was his life. Looking back at Julia as the shadows crossed her face, too, for one brief moment he remembered how innocently beautiful she was when he looked at her the very first time. And it was still there, unmarred by her aging wrinkles. Speaking now in a soft voice, tinged with a strange finality, he said, "Those moments of forever that we shared so long ago really did exist, didn't they?"

"Perhaps, I don't know. Memory can make a thing seem more than it was or ever could be. I must go now, Erich," Julia responded coldly, turning to leave the cemetery. Pausing at the small gate, she looked back one last time at the man she still loved.

"To me they did exist," she said, then left.

When Julia finished with the story, the last she would ever tell Anna, or anyone else, she took Anna's hands and placed them over her dying heart. Fighting for each breath, her voice barely audible to Anna, she whispered, "Erich was your father, Anna. I loved him more than life itself, but he betrayed me. And, like Papa, I will never know why. We were only Jews."

It was the only time Julia ever acknowledged that Erich was Anna's father, though Anna had always believed it to be true. But the words from Julia made her love her mother that much more. Taking Julia in her arms, Anna held her close, just as her mother had done with Eva, until she passed from this world, speaking Erich's name with her last breath. Perhaps, Anna thought, looking at the gentle, still face of her mother, one can love completely without a complete understanding. And Julia knew enough to know that for her it was enough to have loved him.

It was night now, and the throngs of visitors to the Holocaust Memorial at the Pinkas Synagogue and cemetery would be gone, leaving those buried there once more alone. Anna left the hotel with the box holding Julia's ashes and walked the six blocks to the cemetery. Her long journey home was nearing an end. Unlatching the small gate, she stepped gingerly into the graveyard, immediately feeling the soft and lumpy sod beneath her feet. With each step she stood on a grave, quickly becoming lost among the thousands of stones rising before her like ghosts from the darkness. Standing still, Anna tried to recall where Rabbi Loew's grave was located and began making her way slowly through the maze of graves surrounding her until she finally came upon the sacred plot.

Kneeling down, she took a silver tablespoon from her purse and lifted a small square of the soft sod next to Rabbi Loew's grave and cleared away several inches of the rich, black soil beneath it. For a few seconds she held the box of ashes close to her breast, caressing it softly before sprinkling the contents into the shallow grave. After covering the ashes with the plug of sod, Anna leaned forward and kissed the tiny grave and whispered, "There really was a golem when you were young, I know."

She left, feeling good about all that had happened today in satisfying the promise to her mother. The heavy spring rains would come soon to Prague, and Julia's ashes would sink deeper, nourishing and bringing new life to the soil around her, as she had done so often to all who knew her.

As her final story, Julia had come to rest at last among a hundred thousand Jews who knew her not and her dear childhood friends, the golem and Rabbi Loew. She would remain here for eternity, Anna believed, in her most sacred place.

OTHER BOOKS BY FRANK MARSH

Fiction

Rebekka's Children

Nonfiction

Biology, Crime and Ethics

Medicine and Money

In Defense of Political Trials

Punishment and Restitution

Children in Treatment for Mental and Physical Catastrophic Diseases

CPSIA information can be obtained at www.ICGtesting.com
Printed in the USA
BVOW041629241012

303800BV00005B/315/P